MacD
McDonough, Yona Zeldis.
The four temperaments
$ 23.95
1st ed.   ocm48241404

P9-ARB-680

THE FOUR

TEMPERAMENTS

Also by Yona Zeldis McDonough

The Barbie Chronicles: A Living Doll Turns Forty

All the Available Light: A Marilyn Monroe Reader

Doubleday

New York   London   Toronto   Sydney   Auckland

THE

FOUR

TEMPERAMENTS

Yona Zeldis McDonough

PUBLISHED BY DOUBLEDAY
a division of Random House, Inc.
1540 Broadway, New York, New York 10036

DOUBLEDAY and the portrayal of an anchor with a dolphin
are trademarks of Doubleday, a division of Random House, Inc.

This novel is a work of fiction. Although it is set against the backdrop of the New York
City Ballet, none of the characters are based on real individuals, and none of the events
actually occurred. Names, characters, businesses, organizations, places, events, and
incidents either are the product of the author's imagination or are used fictitiously. Any
resemblance to actual persons, living or dead, events, or locales is entirely coincidental.

Library of Congress Cataloging-in-Publication Data
McDonough, Yona Zeldis.
The four temperaments : a novel / by Yona McDonough—1st ed.
p.   cm.
1. Upper West Side (New York, N.Y.)—Fiction.   2. Fathers and sons—Fiction.
3. Grandmothers—Fiction.   4. Violinists—Fiction.   5. Ballerinas—Fiction.
6. Adultery—Fiction.   7. Ballet—Fiction.   I. Title.

PS3613.C39 F68 2002
813'.54—dc21   2001054777

ISBN 0-385-50361-X

Book design by Nicola Ferguson

Title page photograph by Nan Melville, Regina Larkin/
Joyce Trisler Danscompany archives

Copyright © 2002 by Yona Zeldis McDonough
All Rights Reserved

PRINTED IN THE UNITED STATES OF AMERICA
September 2002

FIRST EDITION

1 3 5 7 9 10 8 6 4 2

For Paul

Acknowledgments

As *this* story made its incremental way from idea to manuscript to finished book, I was lucky enough to have many talented and devoted friends who read, encouraged and advised on various aspects of it. These are: Hilton Als, Jules Azzi, Pamela Brandt, Caroline Leavitt, Ed LaMance, Eric Marcus, Leonard Marcus, Albert Mobilio, Kelly Parliman, Yvonne Poley, Sally Schloss, Susan Shapiro, Kenneth Silver and Evan Zimroth. My mother, Malcah Zeldis, listened patiently to my ongoing progress reports. Kate Elton shared her comments from across the ocean. Additionally, I owe a great debt to Sally Arteseros and to Olivia Blumer, for introducing me to her.

Minda Vollen, my first dance teacher, imbued me with her love of classical ballet, a love I have sustained these many years. Wendy Singer Jones shared so many of those crucial years with me. Toni Bentley's *Winter Season: A Dancer's Journal* and Evan Zimroth's *Collusion* added greatly to my understanding of the professional dancer's life and world. Kelly

Acknowledgments

Ryan in the press office of the New York City Ballet was exceptionally generous with both her time and her resources.

Finally, I wish to thank Constance Marks, Suzanne Gluck and Deborah Futter, a trio of benevolent graces it has been my extreme good fortune to know.

The Four

Temperaments

OSCAR

Oscar *Kornblatt* was in love. Never mind that he was gray-haired, soft around the middle and, despite his wife Ruth's patient ironing, always wearing a rumpled shirt. Forget all that. In his mind's eye, Oscar was Prince Siegfried, young, limber and lithe, as he waltzed Ginny Valentine, his exquisite swan, across the vast stage of his imagination.

Oscar's *Swan Lake* image of himself and Ginny was not as far-fetched as it may have seemed, for he was a violinist with the New York City Ballet and Ginny Valentine was a dancer in the corps. From the shadowed nether world of the orchestra pit, he could sense her moving across the floorboards of the stage above. And, sometimes, if the angle was just right, he could even see her, just the merest glimpse. Ginny never stayed in one place for long, and Oscar did have to pay attention to the score, after all. But those moments when she came skittering into his field of vision were blessed, and late at night, lying in bed as Ruth dreamed peacefully beside him, he thought about them and he smiled.

Ginny had been dancing with the company for a little more than a year. Oscar had been playing with the orchestra for nearly twenty-five. He had thought that by this time, he would be indifferent to the surge of eager young things who washed up on the gritty sands of the corps de ballet every year, each as bright and as innocuous as a bit of colored sea glass.

His reaction to these girls had nonetheless undergone a transformation over the years. In the beginning, he had despised them. He was in his early thirties then, old enough to realize that the flame of youthful brilliance would not be his, young enough still to feel embittered by that fact. He hadn't wanted the job with the ballet orchestra anyway, but by then he and his wife had two sons to support. The struggle of trying to assemble one ill-fated string quartet after another was wearing him down. And then there was Ruth. Ruth, who had patiently endured their first apartment, a dark basement on East Sixth Street, and, later, the burned-out buildings that lined the block of their apartment building on West 122nd Street. But when she became pregnant for the third—and Oscar prayed final—time, even he could see that enough was enough. The job was offered and he grudgingly took it.

Ruth, Oscar and the boys moved into a large, comfortable apartment on West End Avenue, an affordable option in the days before the Manhattan real estate boom. It had neither the grandeur of Riverside Drive—vistas that opened seamlessly onto an expanse of the rippling, dark waters of the Hudson River—nor the romance of Central Park West, with its lacy backdrop of flowering trees and shrubs, but it was nevertheless a big step up in the world. At least materially. The family was delighted: the boys went racing in their socks across the smooth, sun-checkered floors and spent hot, happy afternoons in Riverside Park. Ruth joined the local synagogue and befriended the owners of the small neighborhood shops. But Oscar, although outwardly cheerful, seethed within. He had become a breadwinner, not an artist. Secretly, he was mortified, pushed into the narrow world of conventional respectability. A world in which the hot star of genius, and all its urgent, unpredictable heat, was forever snuffed out.

He took out his resentment not on his family, or at least not much, but on the dancers, the skinny, silly girls for whom the audiences sat mesmer-ized, applauded and threw armloads of expensive, useless flowers. For these Philistines—and Oscar also lumped the dancers into this cate-gory—the music was just so much backdrop, part of the decor. Oh, he had heard the dancers talk about the music, how it inspired them, moved them, whatever. But he could see that it was all a sham, a poor cover for their own monumental narcissism that pranced onstage shouting, "Look at me! Look at me!" though of course they never actually said a word. He observed, more than once, the way they upstaged each other, intruding on one another's musical cues, anticipating a rival's exit from the stage and starting just a beat too soon. They gloated when another dancer was in-jured or ill. All this would have been comical in Oscar's eyes had it not been so naked.

Generally, there was very little personal contact between the dancers and the musicians. But, once in a while, the score called for a difficult mu-sical solo and the musician who performed it would be called onto the stage during the applause. Oscar had watched this happen—though for-tunately not to him—and found something both heartbreaking and pa-thetic about seeing the two performers up there together. There was the ballerina—arms filled with roses, resplendent in the scanty costume that revealed her sweat-soaked limbs—holding the musician by the hand. The musician would shuffle toward the front of the stage, a shaggy trained bear, a portent of death in his ill-fitting, dark suit, while she—all light and silver and air—held out the unspoken promise of immortality to the fatu-ous, cheering audience.

For years, Oscar had made it a point of honor to ignore the dancers, not bothering to learn their names or pretending not to know them if he somehow did; refusing to acknowledge them if he saw them in the halls or elevators of the theater. But, little by little, his sense of injury began to subside. His third son, Benjamin, was born; the two older boys, Gabriel and William, thrived. Ruth seemed happy, happier than he had seen her in a long time. She began singing again; true, it was only in the shower, but the rich, ripe sound of her powerful contralto filled him with wistful and sweet memories of their courtship in the mosquito-filled, lilac dusks at Tanglewood. He received professional recognition, such as it was, and the attention acted as balm to his touchy ego. He stopped hating the dancers. He no longer needed to.

It was during these years that he discovered that he was even occasionally attracted to one of them, though his interest never lighted upon the green girls of the corps. Instead, he was drawn to the older dancer, the established star whose hunger for fame had peaked into a gracious and perhaps even complacent acceptance of her exalted stature. Clarissa Castille was such a dancer: beautiful, poised and intelligent as far as her limited education permitted. She had studied piano for some years and could actually talk about music apart from how it related to her dancing. She was happily married, as was Oscar, so an affair was not a real option for either of them. Anyway, Oscar didn't want to have an affair. He loved Ruth, loved the life he had with her. But he couldn't deny that he also enjoyed, immensely, the hint of flirtation that laced the postperformance dinners he shared with Clarissa. He derived great pleasure from gazing at her expressive brown eyes, the intricately coiffed black hair that revealed her long, elegant neck, and the way she shifted and twisted the rings—of amber, garnet, opal, turquoise—around her lovely fingers. When she left the company to have a child, he was genuinely sorry.

There were two others like her over the years, women with whom he formed congenial though never constraining bonds of friendship. Then this phase too began to pass. His sons grew up, he and Ruth grew older. He watched as the two elder boys married. He moved up through the ranks of the orchestra. Though outwardly pleased, he remained fundamentally detached from the change in status. His youthful dreams had mercifully faded; he was no longer consumed by the desire to shine. Instead, he was grateful for the ongoing good fortune of his life—the joy of playing, and being transported by, his music. The love of his wife and sons. He relished the palpable, reassuring pleasures of the flesh: good food, good wine, a comfortable home, vacations in New England and, every so often, Europe. He took no more notice of the young dancers who buzzed around the theater than a gardener did of the bees.

It was into this bucolic landscape that Ginny Valentine burst, sudden and shocking as a sharp silver tack that lodged without warning in his naked foot.

One day after rehearsal was over, he was carefully putting his instrument back in its case when he heard behind him a high, clear voice that sounded faintly southern, though he couldn't have said whether its cadences emerged from Georgia or Texas. "Mr. Kornblatt," it said as he turned around, "do you think I could speak to you for a minute?" There was Ginny, in a red V-necked leotard and red tights. Even Oscar, who generally took little notice of such things, was surprised by this costume. Weren't they all supposed to wear black and pink?

"Why, of course, Miss . . . ?" he said.

"Valentine. But just call me Ginny."

"Ginny, then," he said. "What can I do for you?" He knew he sounded insincere, even patronizing, but, really, it was hard to take any of them, particularly a very young one outfitted like this, too seriously.

"It's about the music," she said.

"The music?"

"Yes, the Stravinsky. I think you're playing it too slowly."

"Do you, Miss Valentine?" he said, the patronizing tone now laced with the metallic edge of annoyance.

"Ginny," she said, flashing a smile filled with large, white, slightly protruding teeth. If she was aware of how she had offended him, she gave no sign. "I think it lags. Especially in the second movement."

"I've been playing that piece for more years than—" he began.

"That's just the point," she interrupted. "Maybe you need to think about it in a new way. It seems to me just a little bit stale."

Oscar looked at her, hardly able to believe his ears. To walk up to a seasoned musician, a well-respected violinist, and blithely tell him that you thought his playing lagged and had grown stale! She was either brazen or monumentally stupid. He could have her fired for saying such a thing. In fact, he would do that, he would speak to Erik Holtz, Ballet Master in Chief, and he would have her fired tomorrow. No, today, in fact. But before he could tell her as much, he heard her saying, "Look, are you busy now? Maybe we could have a cup of coffee or something. So I could tell you what I mean?"

It was only then that he really saw her: glossy, light brown hair parted in the center of a pale, smooth forehead beneath which were closely set, gray-green eyes. Ears as intricate and fine as nautilus shells revealed by her tightly bound bun. Luminous white teeth. Her arms were the merest ribbons; her legs, steel. She pinned him with a look at once so hopeful and warm, so eager and intense, that he found himself saying, "You go change. I'll wait here."

They went to one of the Upper West Side's once-ubiquitous and now disappearing coffee shops: Formica tables, leatherette seats, tiny boxes of cereal lining the upper shelves and plastic-coated menus that went on for pages. Ginny still wore the red leotard, only she had added a pair of jeans and a black crocheted shawl. Her pointe shoes peeped out like an improbable pair of rabbit ears from the large, ungainly bag that she—like the rest of them—hoisted over her delicate shoulder. At the base of her throat was a small, curved scar. Oscar found his eyes drawn to it; it seemed to wink with the movements of her throat as she spoke or swallowed. He wished he could reach over and put his finger—gently, so gently—upon it.

The waitress appeared. Oscar ordered black coffee, and despite Ruth's nagging concern over his weight, a glazed doughnut. Ginny's lips moved slightly as she scanned the menu. She settled finally on waffles with strawberries and whipped cream and a side order of bacon.

"Tell me about the music," he said when their orders arrived. He took a small bite of the doughnut, conscious of wanting to make it last, at least most of the way through her meal. But he needn't have worried; she fairly inhaled her food, consuming it with quick, eager bites that she washed down with large gulps of milk.

"It gets bogged down when you play it too slowly," she said. "I think he meant it to sound more energetic, more excited, you know?"

"He?" asked Oscar. The ordinary doughnut was suddenly rendered light, sweet, delicious; even the ersatz black coffee was a wonderful counterpoint to its sweetness.

"Stravinsky," she said, matter-of-factly. Her glazed lips shone with maple syrup. Oscar wasn't even surprised that she presumed to know the composer's thoughts.

They spent over an hour in the coffee shop, talking not only about the Stravinsky score, but also about Ravel, Bach, Tchaikovsky and Hindemith. She knew nothing about theory or terminology, but she had a bright, quirky way of looking at things that Oscar found appealing. And her appetite! He had never seen a dancer—nor anyone else—eat with such abandon. She licked her fingers, the back of her spoon, the end of her straw. Oscar wondered what such a girl would be like in bed and then hoped she couldn't tell what he was thinking. Fortunately, she just kept right on talking, about her dancing, now. Her eyes shone the way Joan of Arc's must have. Even Clarissa had never looked so possessed and it made Oscar uneasy. To change the subject, he asked about her accent, which seemed to grow increasingly southern as she spoke. She told him about the small Louisiana town where she had grown up and the ballet lessons she had taken in New Orleans. And what about that name; surely Valentine was something she had invented, like so many of them, for the stage? But it turned out he was wrong.

"My mother met my father at a Valentine's Day dance in Atlanta. She'd gone there with her church group for the weekend. He told her he was the son of the minister at the First Baptist Church. That his daddy was a big deal in the community. Guess that won her over."

"But it wasn't true?"

"Not a word. She went back home with a phony name and address on a piece of memo paper. Oh, and with me too—though she didn't know it yet." There was a noisy pause as Ginny drained her glass through her straw.

"So you never knew him?" Oscar asked.

"Only what Mama told me. She said he seemed so sincere. Genuine. And handsome too. She picked Valentine as a way of remembering him. For a long time, she really did think he'd come back."

"She must have been devastated when he didn't," Oscar said, not really knowing how she would have felt.

"My mama was class valedictorian and had a full scholarship to Randolph-Macon. She gave it up to stay home and have me. I don't think 'devastated' would have been the way she would have described it."

Oscar felt foolish.

"And Ginny is from . . . ?" he asked, looking for a diversion.

"Virginia," she said, looking suddenly shy. "For my grandmother. Though everyone thought it was kind of an odd choice, considering I was a bastard and all."

"No one really thinks that way anymore, do they?" Oscar said gently.

"Where I grew up, they did," she said.

By the time they rose to leave, the spring afternoon had deepened to a soft violet evening and Oscar was in love. He walked home feeling buoyant and terrified. He thought of Clarissa for the first time in years. Ginny was nothing like the elegant, cultivated sort of woman he usually liked, which was precisely what made her company so compelling and so unsettling. You're headed for trouble, Oscar, he thought as he let himself into the apartment. Ruth was not yet home and there was something poignant about the way darkness filled the rooms. He sat for a long while on the sofa, looking but not seeing out of the living room window. He was frightened, yes, but not so frightened that he wouldn't follow whatever he was feeling—this urge— a little farther along the path. Wherever it might take him.

"Oscar, you startled me!" Ruth said when she walked in some time later. "Why are you sitting here in the dark?"

After that first meeting, things followed a fairly predictable course: more meetings in coffee shops, dinners after the performance. But even in that insulated world of the ballet company, where gossip, and especially romantic gossip, was as necessary as air, Oscar and Ginny provoked no talk, no speculation of any kind. Oscar was of course glad, but also disappointed to realize that he was past the age of creating scandal.

He began to appear at rehearsals he was not required to attend, just to see more of her. From the unfamiliar vantage point of the back of the darkened theater, he watched raptly as Ginny moved through the intricate patterns of the ballet. While she never danced alone, she always seemed to stand out. There was an expansiveness to her movements, a breadth of arms and legs that he didn't see in the others. Her arabesques were clearer and sharper, her ports de bras filled with longing. He saw something ferocious in the way she danced, something fearless and even dangerous that knew no boundaries. Unlike many of the dancers, she didn't mark the steps during the rehearsals, but executed them full out. Though Oscar still had little regard for ballet, he had to admit that Ginny had something special, something that would, if she knew how to cultivate it, lift her out of the ranks and into the burning isolation and resplendent joy of the limelight.

She told Oscar how when she first had started dancing to live music, she kept anticipating her cues and charging out onstage ahead of time because she was so exhilarated. "Erik wasn't even angry about it," she said, laughing a little at the memory. "He said that he liked how eager I was."

"Have you ever had stage fright?" Oscar asked.

"Never," she said, and Oscar believed it.

———

He even had the audacity to bring her home to dinner. Ruth was her lovely, welcoming self, making sure Ginny's plate was filled with pot roast, buttered noodles and challah bread; for dessert, she had baked a glazed apple tart. Ginny ate and Ruth beamed. It was a successful evening, or so Oscar had thought. But lying in bed that night with his wife, Oscar was aware of Ruth's wakeful, fixed concentration on some unseen point on the ceiling.

"What's wrong?" he asked.

"Ben," she said.

"What's the matter with Ben? Did he call?" Their youngest son was a wanderer, a pilgrim whose feet had touched the streets of Paris, Bangkok, Moscow, Glasgow, Buenos Aires, Nairobi. He had barely finished college and ever since had taken whatever work was available—taxi driver, waiter, bartender—until he earned enough to set off again.

"No, he didn't," she said. "But I was thinking: we should introduce him to Ginny."

"Ben and Ginny?" said Oscar, trying to keep the incredulity—and anger—out of his voice. When he thought of the girls his peripatetic son had brought home, like the daughter of an impoverished Italian nobleman whose thick sheaf of pale hair, black sunglasses and wetly painted red mouth vied with the cool, chiseled beauties on the silver screens that illuminated Oscar's own youth, he knew that Ben would find nothing appealing in Ginny. Besides, he wanted this one for himself.

Not that she thought of him in that way. No, it was clear that she relied on Oscar the way she might have a father, or an indulgent, older uncle. He was always ready with a willing ear, a solid shoulder, a nugget of sound advice. When she had roommate troubles, he extricated her from her lease and found her an affordable studio apartment on West Seventy-first Street, only blocks from the theater. He helped her get a checking account and credit card (when they had met, she kept her crumpled bills in her pockets, where they were frequently lost or stolen); showed her the best wine shop, supermarket, drugstore in the neighborhood. Except for her dancing, where she was as focused and bright as the steady beam of a Tensor lamp, the ordinary business of living left her mostly baffled. "I don't know what I'd do without you, Oscar," she said more than once, touching her head to his chest, "I'd be lost."

Oscar was grateful for being needed by her, in any way at all, and encouraged her to confide in him, which she did easily and lavishly. But the confidences never seemed to be of the romantic sort, which is what Oscar sought. He couldn't help but want to know what sort of men attracted her.

"Who's got time for any of that?" she said one Sunday afternoon in September as they strolled through Central Park together. She was responding to his question about Boyd Michaels, a handsome young corps de ballet member. Oscar had observed how Michaels, who was short but had a compactly built body, smooth, hairless chest—maybe he shaved it?—and strong, well-defined features, seemed to hang around Ginny a lot. Was he a suitor? Ginny laughed. "You sound like my mama," she said, dismissing the notion. No, she was more interested in a small, solo role in an upcoming performance; company gossip said she was being considered for it.

The afternoon was hot. He held Ginny delicately by the elbow and steered her through the steady stream of cyclists, roller bladers, joggers, mothers with strollers and couples with their arms locked around each other's waists. Silver razor scooters, bright and quick as minnows, darted their way through the throng. Ruth was in California with their son Gabriel, his wife, Penelope, and their baby daughter, so Oscar did not have to feel overly guilty about spending time with Ginny. Not that his guilt was much of an impediment.

When Oscar and Ginny reached the boat pond, he bought her an ice cream that the vendor dipped in hot, liquid chocolate. It dried to a brittle shell that she cracked with her big, lovely front teeth. They sat down on a bench and watched the tiny sailboats slip by.

"Do you really think he'll give it to me?" she asked. Oscar knew by now that the "he" in question was Erik Holtz, the ballet master.

"You certainly deserve it," said Oscar.

"I heard that he was thinking about Mia McQuaid too. I can't believe he'd even consider giving her that part," Ginny fumed. "Have you seen her feet? No arch at all; they're as flat as Kansas." Mia had been Ginny's roommate, and there had been plenty of friction between the two young women when they lived together.

"Who told you that he was considering her?" asked Oscar.

"Boyd," she said. Oscar studied her carefully, but she seemed entirely focused on the part. "He says she's awful to partner. That it's like lifting a side of beef."

"Well, surely Erik won't give the part to a side of beef, will he?"
Ginny smiled.

But as it turned out, that was just what Erik did. Ginny was livid. She brooded and seemed to be dragging herself to rehearsals and classes. Above her garishly colored practice clothes—red, royal blue, plum, emerald—her face looked gray. On the third day after their conversation by the boat pond, she didn't show up for rehearsal at all. This had never happened as far as Oscar knew and it worried him. He went to her apartment, where he found her sitting listlessly amid the huge piles of soiled clothing that she was sorting.

"Washday," she said when she saw his gaze. "Want to help?"

"Where have you been?" Oscar asked, knowing he had no right to sound so demanding, but unable to help himself.

"You don't want to know," she said, depositing a purple garment, crunched beyond recognition, into one of the piles.

"Yes, I do," he said, looking straight into her eyes.

"All right, then, I'll tell you," she said, kicking her way past the clothes. "But not here."

She refused to go to any of the restaurants near Lincoln Center where the dancers from the company usually congregated. Oscar hailed a taxi that took them to the East Side, and he ushered her into a dark, noisy place on Third Avenue where neither of them had ever been before.

"I'm not eating," Ginny announced to the waiter when he came to take their order. "I'll have a banana daiquiri."

"Ginny, you should eat something," Oscar said in his best avuncular voice.

"Why?"

"What about a nice piece of broiled chicken?" He sounded like Ruth, personifying the food she tried to coax one of the boys to eat. Oscar could just imagine what the waiter was thinking.

"No, actually I'll have a steak," she said, snapping the menu shut suddenly. "Very rare. Bloody, in fact." She turned her gaze to the waiter. He looked down, pen poised over his pad. "And a baked potato, no, make that potato skins, and a salad. Oh, and what's the soup today?" He told her and she said, "I'll have that too."

When the waiter finally, mercifully, left, Ginny busied herself shredding her napkin and opening several packets of sugar, the contents of which she emptied onto the table. By the time the waiter reappeared with their drinks—Oscar's only a ginger ale, he thought someone had better stay sober tonight—she had created around herself a small white island of debris.

"I went to Mia's," she said abruptly. "I still have the key, you know."

"But you didn't stay," prompted Oscar, knowing that this was not what he was going to hear.

"I didn't mean for anything to happen, Oscar, I swear I didn't. I've just been feeling so upset. I mean, how could he give her that part over me? So I went there to see what it was."

"What it was?" he repeated, confused.

"Her secret," said Ginny, as if this were the most natural thing in the world. "What it was she had that I didn't. Because I know I can dance circles around her."

"Then what?" asked Oscar.

"I saw this dress of hers. I remembered it because I was still living there when she bought it and she made such a big deal of it. Some designer or other. I can't remember the name."

"You did something to the dress?" Oscar asked, getting worried. But she shook her head.

"I wanted to, though," she said. "I even had my scissors with me," she added. "See?" She held up a small, bright pair of scissors, no bigger than her hand. They glinted in the light. "I keep them in my bag. For sewing ribbons on my pointe shoes," she explained, as if this were somehow important.

"That's very practical," Oscar soothed. "But you left after you looked at the dress, right?"

"Not exactly." Her head went down.

"Ginny," Oscar said firmly, "what did you do in that apartment? I want you to tell me." There, now, that was better. The authoritative, parental approach usually worked. It did this time too.

"Not much, not really. I found a squeeze bottle of mustard in the fridge." She stopped.

"And?" Oscar prompted.

"I squirted some in her shoes. Not on the dress, though." As if that mattered. Still, it wasn't as bad as it could have been. Oscar almost wanted to smile; her gesture of revenge seemed so childish. The sort of thing the boys would have done to each other when they were young. But of course she really was a child.

"And then you left."

"Not exactly. I went into the bathroom and found her toothbrush. Dipped it in the toilet. *Then* I left."

"Thank God," said Oscar, exhaling now. It could have been much worse. He'd have to help her control herself, this wayward girl sitting there amidst the remains of the napkin. Because clearly those impulses could get her into real trouble someday. Even now, if Mia McQuaid were to figure out that Ginny had been in the apartment, and if she were to complain to someone in the company ... Oscar's mind raced ahead. Ginny would be suspended from dancing or fired, and he would never get to see her or be near her again.

"Y... 're never to go there again, do you understand?" he said, feeling ... d slipped back a decade and was lecturing one of his sons.

... ght," she said quietly. "I won't. I promise. But right now, I'm so thirsty. Could I have another drink? Please?" He saw then that her glass was empty.

By the time they left the restaurant an hour and a half later, Ginny was drunk. Oscar felt responsible; she had ordered a third drink before the meal came and another while she was eating it. But when he tried to suggest that she slow down, she argued, saying that she was old enough to do what she wanted. In the end, he didn't insist.

As he propelled her out into the street, she waved cheerfully at their waiter, at the hostess and several people who were just coming in. Then she began humming; Oscar thought he recognized the score from Stravinsky's *Firebird*. He was trying to hail a cab when she broke loose from his grasp and darted out into the middle of the street. A large dark car screeched to a halt and an angry face appeared at the window. "What the hell do you think you're doing, lady?" the driver hollered.

"Grands jetés?" Ginny replied in a small voice, her high spirits instantly evaporating. She looked frightened and near tears. Oscar put his arm firmly around her shoulders and led her back to the curb, where he was successful in his quest for a taxi. He gave the driver his address. He wasn't going to leave her alone. Not in her condition.

The apartment was dark when they arrived. Oscar was sorry that Ruth was still away. She would have been better at handling a drunk and weepy girl; Ginny had cried most of the way uptown in the cab. As it was, he took Ginny to the guest room, where he took off her shoes, wiped her face with a washcloth and watched solicitously as she downed a big glass of water and the two Tylenol he insisted she take. Then he gently helped her to lie down on one of the narrow beds where the boys had slept—a scruffy teddy bear still snuggled against the pillows. He went on into his own room, the room he and Ruth had shared for so many years. He left the door open, so he would hear her if she called out or needed anything. She must have passed out immediately, for by the time he had undressed, he could hear the raucous sounds of her snoring.

Later—*he* had been sleeping soundly under a cool, pale sheet—he was aware of something on his forehead. Was it Ruth returning early?

"Oscar," said a voice it took him a few seconds to identify. "Oscar, get up," Ginny whispered urgently.

He opened his eyes. Though the room was dark, he could see that she was naked; her white skin seemed to glow. Without hesitation, he reached for her, and at long last, she was in his arms. He kissed her frantically, as if she were a dangerously ill child whose raging fever had just broken. The scar, the tiny scar on her neck. He could feel it in the dark, and he kissed it over and over again. Oscar was surprised—but also deeply and humbly grateful—for the ardent way in which she responded to his fumbling. Under his hands, she seemed as delicate and easy to wield as his violin.

Oscar woke again at dawn and lay for a long while without moving as he watched the silver light brighten into the flat white glare of day. Ginny was sprawled out next to him, extended limbs as wide and flagrant as those of a starfish. Even in sleep, she was immoderate, expansive and enticing. Very carefully, Oscar raised himself from his prone position. But she opened her eyes, instantly alert.

"Good morning," she said, holding out her arms. Afterward, he drifted off to sleep, and when he woke again, she was gone. There was a note on the pillow: "See you at the theater. Love & XXX G."

Oscar reached for his robe and, when he had put it on, took the note into the kitchen, where he read it one last time before setting it on fire in the sink. He longed to save it—love, she had written *love*—but he knew his own carelessness all too well. One day, Ruth would find it and then what? Better to let it remain in memory's private, sanctified eye. The note burned quickly and the ashes washed easily down the drain. Then he went into the bathroom for a long, hot shower. As he lathered himself, he marveled at how her impossibly young touch had made his old bones feel quite new.

But euphoria evaporated quickly, to be replaced by a crushing sense of guilt and anxiety. How could he have betrayed Ruth? What would she do if she found out? Oscar gloomily predicted that she would find out, that the stink of guilt and deceit would rise up from his person and Ruth would wonder, wonder and recoil, at its rank smell. She would denounce him to his sons, leave him, and he would deserve it all. And, yet, he was sick with longing for the girl, scheming already about how he could meet her, touch her again.

He called his lawyer and asked some discreet questions, for he still had some lingering worry about what Ginny had done in Mia McQuaid's apartment the night before. Warren Greenberg, his attorney of some twenty years, was not terribly helpful and Oscar felt no better as he put down the receiver.

He was even more unsettled when he went back into the bedroom and saw his violin sitting precariously on top of the bureau, with the neck end jutting way over the edge. Although still in its case, Oscar knew how easily it could have been knocked over and damaged, perhaps even beyond repair. He quickly put it on the top shelf of the closet, in the spot where he always kept it when not in use. He had never forgotten to put it away before. But he must have been so addled last night, when he brought Ginny home, that he had, for the first time in memory, imperiled his instrument.

This was no small matter. Oscar had owned this violin for longer than he had been married. It had been crafted by a Milanese maker in the middle of the nineteenth century, and its graceful, symmetrical curves, stained with an amber brown varnish, had become—when he played—a part of his own body. It had cost several thousand dollars at the time, the kind of money Oscar didn't have but had paid out slowly, as if it had been a mortgage. Musicians talked of "dating" an instrument when they were considering its purchase; Oscar could still remember others—a French twentieth-century instrument made by Delanoy; another by the German maker Ernst Heinrich Roth—that he dated before settling on the Milanese. Now that he was more established and financially well off, he sometimes fantasized about an instrument crafted by a legendary maker. How he would love the light, bright and open tones of a Stradivarius or the darker, more somber sounds of a Guarneri. But, no, he was wed as surely to this instrument as he was to Ruth.

Ruth. She returned home from San Francisco later that day, filled with stories about Gabriel, Penelope and the baby. The trip had done her good, he could see that. Was it simply the pleasure of seeing her son and his family, or was it being away from Oscar? He had never had such a thought before; he had always relied on Ruth's unswerving devotion. But then he had never been unfaithful to her before and that astounding act seemed to throw all of his former assumptions into an unfamiliar and frightening configuration. He realized that he had cherished his dreams of Ginny far more than the complicated reality she presented. What had he done? he thought over and over.

"Oscar," Ruth said gently when she saw that he was barely listening to her, "Oscar, dear, are you all right?"

"I'm fine," he lied, wishing suddenly that he could just close his eyes and bury his face in her lap. "I'm perfectly fine."

GINNY

Ginny *Valentine* hated New York. She hated its horrible up and down shapes. To her, they looked like a million shoe boxes standing on end in a tacky factory outlet. She hated everyone packed in so tightly, no room to breathe. She hated the hundred and one kinds of dirt in New York—smog, soot, grime, grease, grit and of course dog excrement—everywhere she stepped. She couldn't understand why anyone would actually want to live here, and when she saw those T-shirts and bumper stickers with that idiotic slogan saying "I ♥ NY," she wanted to yell, "NOT ME!" There were only two things that redeemed the city in her eyes: George Balanchine and the New York City Ballet. Balanchine had been dead for years, but the New York City Ballet, the company he started and ran, was alive and kicking. And so here she was.

Back in New Orleans, before she came here, Wes had promised that in New York City, it wouldn't matter who her parents were. "New York never looks back," is what he said. "No one there gives a hoot about your past because they're too busy thinking about the future. And the future, my darling child, is you." He had smoothed the hair off her face in a gesture that was one-quarter father, three-quarters lover. "Think of it: VIRGINIA VALENTINE. They'll call you 'Queen of Hearts.' "

She would sit curled up on Wes's sky-blue sofa, the one with all the tasseled pillows and the ornate French legs, drinking in every damn word and dying for one of the cigarettes he waved around his handsome face as he talked. He refused to let her smoke. "Virgin lungs," he kept telling her, "virgin lungs. If you want to be a star, you'll keep them that way. The rest of you is open for corruption, of course. And I'm just the man to see to that." He leaned over to kiss her neck and her arms went around him. Sweet Wes! She did love him. Or she guessed she did. She certainly did need him. And what was love anyway, but need in a fancy dress?

Still, she knew that going into Oscar's room last night was a dumb thing to do. Dumb because it made things more complicated. Oscar was already crazy about her. He helped her ditch Mia and find her own apartment, bought her dinners and even loaned her money. All of this without sex. She never meant to get involved with him that way. But as her mama would surely have said, good intentions were shining brightly all along that hot and dusty road that led to hell.

She couldn't even blame it on the liquor, though she was certainly drunk enough when he brought her back to his apartment. But when she woke up—in the narrow bed with the one-eyed, nearly bald teddy bear staring at her—the effects of the alcohol had worn off and she was left with her own miserable self again. Mia. Erik chose Mia over her. By now, she had stopped feeling angry and was scared instead. Maybe she wasn't as talented as she thought. Maybe she was fooling herself, and was going to stay in the corps de ballet forever, while the Mias of the world danced right over her.

She thought about going into Mia's apartment: another dumb thing. But she had been so angry. Ginny remembered, with some distaste, the tantrums she used to have when she was little. Once she had stretched out on the floor of the church sobbing and pounding her fists against the worn oak planks, all because her mother had said no, she couldn't play with June Bell Taylor after the service that afternoon; she had to come home instead. Everyone had stood around her, even her mother, baffled about what to do, until finally the minister himself had appeared, with his dark pants and brilliantly shined shoes, to lift her from the floor and deliver her, sobbing, into her mother's arms. Later she was sorry she'd made such a scene and embarrassed her mother; she didn't even like June Bell all that much.

In Oscar's apartment, Ginny sat up and pushed the hair away from her face. Sweet Jesus, it was hot! She wriggled her toes and looked down to see that they were bare. Being the gentleman that he was, Oscar had removed her shoes but nothing else and she was sweating. "Don't say 'sweat,' Virginia," her mother would have scolded, "a lady never sweats, she just glows." But she was not and would never be a lady. Too bad for Mama; she tried so hard.

Stripping down was the logical thing to do, so she did it. Then she went looking for a bathroom. When she found it, she turned on the shower. Just as Ginny was about to step inside, under the spray of warm water, she knew that the contents of her stomach were about to come up and she leaned over the toilet bowl to vomit. Actually, it did not feel at all bad: the dark night, the cool, reassuring feel of her bare feet against the tile, and the lemony smell that wafted up from the bowl—Oscar's wife certainly kept things spick-and-span—all made it seem that Mia had been no more than a bad meal she had eaten.

She stepped under the shower and stayed there a long time, rinsing her mouth with streams of water and lathering herself with the bar of scented soap—magnolia! home!—from a ceramic dish. Thoughts of Mia were like the bubbles that slid from her chest to her waist to her legs, and then rushed effortlessly down the drain. This was only one part, and a small one too. Her turn would come soon. She knew it. In the meantime, she would have to work harder, and she would have to be patient. Maybe apologizing to Mia wouldn't be a bad idea either, though she wasn't sure how Mia would take it. Maybe Oscar could help with that. Oscar. Where was he now, anyway?

When Ginny got out of the shower, she wrapped herself up in one of Ruth's—she remembered her name now—big, fresh-smelling, pale blue towels. She felt better than she had in days. She was fully intending to walk back to the room where she had come from and get some sleep. But it was easy to get confused in the dark, what with the strange apartment and all, and she found herself walking right by the room where Oscar was sleeping. The door was wide open and his belly was moving up and down in the most peaceful way, and because of the light from the streetlights outside (another thing Ginny hated about New York was how it was never really, truly dark, which she knew must have accounted for a lot of the weird behavior of the people there), she could see his face, looking all screwed up and tense, as if he were trying to figure something out in his sleep. It was that look that drew her into the room. Oscar had been so good to her, and now that she was feeling good herself, she didn't want him to feel bad. She only meant to put her hand on his forehead, just to smooth the frown away, and she did. But then he opened his eyes and somehow the towel was on the floor and she was saying his name. His arms wound around her and pulled her gently down, toward the bed.

Afterward, Ginny realized that he talked to her as if she had been a virgin, the big, sweet fool. He should only have known. She had been having sex since she was fifteen, and she didn't think of it as a big deal. At least if she was careful not to get pregnant, the way her mother had. Mama hadn't been careful and she hadn't been smart, but Ginny was determined to be both. By the time she was fourteen, she had already been to a clinic downtown and after lying about her age—Lord knows that was easy enough—got herself a prescription for birth control pills and enough condoms for the next decade. There was a whole phone book's worth of sexually transmitted diseases that she didn't want any part of.

Her first lover was her ballet teacher, Wesley Landham. Wes had danced to standing ovations in Europe before he tore up every single one of the ligaments in his left knee and had to retire from the stage. Since he was a local boy who'd made good, he was something of a celebrity in New Orleans, and the studio he ran—upstairs from a perfume shop in the French Quarter—was filled with the daughters of the city's oldest and proudest families. Ginny was a better dancer than any of them, she knew that, just as she knew that she was not beautiful or smart in school. But she took to dancing right away, even though for the longest time Mama maintained that she had only sent her there so she could improve her posture and meet the right kind of girls.

Not that the right kind of girls would have anything to do with her. There she was, Rita Darcy's little bastard. This was somehow common knowledge and it didn't make Ginny too popular with the other girls who came to Wes's studio, girls like Deanna May Dixon and Violet Morgan, who were brought to class by black maids who hung up their pleated skirts and matching cardigans on hangers, and rolled their socks neatly into balls, while the girls changed into their fresh-from-the-package pink tights and black leotards.

Ginny came to class by herself because Rita worked afternoons at the mall and since she had to take two buses, she was always late. Her shucked clothes were left in a heap on the dressing room floor while she ran to find her place at the barre, still putting the last pins in her hair as the pliés began. But once class had started, she was happy: she knew she could dance circles around those snotty brats. They disliked her as much for that as for anything. She had a real gift for turning, Wes said so, and he always made her demonstrate first. While the others were still fumbling with double pirouettes, Wes had her doing fouettés, first two, then four, and soon enough eight in perfect, spin-like-a-top succession. At the Christmas recital, she brought down the house with that particular little trick.

She knew they made fun of her. They called her "fire engine" because of the bright colors she wore to class. She hated that pink-and-black look ballet dancers were supposed to wear. When she tried on her very first pair of pointe shoes, she looked down at the pink satin and frowned. Pink was such a sissy, spineless color. She wanted red, like Moira Shearer in *The Red Shoes*, or, at the very least, indigo blue.

"No one has ever, ever complained about the color before, miss," the salesman said coldly.

"Well, someone is complaining now," Ginny said, ignoring Mama's not-so-subtle fingers pressing on her shoulder. "Don't you have anything else?" With a disgusted sigh, he disappeared into the stockroom. Ginny could feel how the two other girls in the store looked down at the carpeting to avoid staring. The salesman returned with a dusty box that he laid on the floor.

"Black," he said, gesturing to the dark satin shoes in their nest of white tissue. "Take them or leave them."

She tried them on and rose up on her toes. They weren't red, but they weren't bad either. Once she sewed the ribbons on, they would be better. Like a Spanish dancer. She began to imagine flouncy skirts; the shoes improved as she mentally added a fringed silk shawl, castanets and a real rosebud pinned to the front of her V-neck leotard. "We'll take them," Ginny said. Mama sighed loudly, as if she had been holding her breath.

Whatever the other girls said, it made no difference to Wes, who recognized that she had something special and did his best to nurture it. Extra classes, special coaching, partnering lessons; Wes saw to all of it. "Your talent is the redemption for your mama's sins," he told her often enough, though he was always smiling when he did. After a while, he refused to let her pay for her classes. "Every serious school needs a scholarship student," he told her. "Virginia Valentine is mine." When it became too hard for Rita to pick Ginny up after class (she didn't want her riding the buses alone after dark), Wes started driving her home. She liked the rides because she liked him. He was as good-looking as his name promised, with thick, prematurely white hair, blue eyes and white, white teeth that he confessed to having had capped.

"When you're onstage, your smile has to count. Mine never did before I had my teeth done," he told her.

She nodded, self-conscious about her own teeth. Rita didn't have the money for braces. Wes saw her discomfort and said, "Now don't go worrying about your teeth. Those big white beauties will look just wonderful under the lights. Rub a little Vaseline on them before you go on. Makes 'em look even shinier." That's the way Wes talked to her—as if her success were a sure thing. But Ginny didn't entirely share his confidence. Not because she wasn't good enough, because she really thought she was. But New Orleans wasn't exactly the place for a girl to make a name for herself as a ballerina; the city didn't even have a resident company. How in the world was she going to succeed while living there? And how was she going to get out?

It was Wes who showed her the way.

He told her that every couple of years, the School of American Ballet held a regional audition in Atlanta and there was one scheduled for the next month. Ginny knew that the school was the godchild of the New York City Ballet, the company she'd wanted to dance in ever since Rita had taken her to a performance on her tenth birthday. They danced *Serenade* that night, and when she saw that girl who lets down her hair and dies for her dancing, she was stunned. She pored through the program notes to see who the choreographer was and saw the name George Balanchine. Well, obviously he was someone who understood the way she felt about dancing and she knew that she would have to find a way to audition for him. It turned out he was dead, but he'd choreographed dozens of ballets and, along with someone called Lincoln Kirstein, started the company besides. She swore to herself that she would find her way to New York City to dance in it.

For the next four weeks, Ginny practiced constantly for the audition. Mama even let her miss school so Wes could give her special coaching during the day, before her regular lessons. He offered to drive her to the audition because it was so hard for Rita to take off from work. Wes and Ginny would have to stay overnight in a motel, but Rita wasn't worried; she had this idea that Wes liked boys, not girls, and Ginny saw no reason to tell her otherwise. So it was in a room at the Peach Tree Palace that Wesley Landham carefully and cordially deflowered her. She let him do this because she understood that Wes was a gentleman. Once he had become her lover, he would feel more than interested in her career. He would feel obligated.

Afterward, she felt a little shaky, but it was more because the reality of the next day's audition had set in—what if she didn't do well? then what?—than the shock of losing her virginity. But Wes was very tender and sweet; he filled the motel's peach bathtub and carried her, still naked, to the bathroom. He left her soaking while he went out to buy a cold six-pack. Cigarettes were forbidden but Wes thought that the beers might take the edge off her nerves.

He was right. The next morning, Ginny got up feeling calm, centered and ready to dance as she had never danced in her life. She did, too. She could hear the whispers of the other girls at the barre as her feet beat their way through a tricky entrechat quatre combination; by the time she got to the fouettés, the girls were silent. Though the official word didn't come for several days, it was clear to everyone that Virginia Valentine was on her way to New York, on her way to the big time.

But she had told Oscar none of this. It was easier to let him think that she was still pretty innocent. Mama had always preached discretion, and in this case, she was right. And Ginny couldn't say she didn't enjoy being with Oscar. Lord knew he wasn't handsome like Wes, but he was so grateful, so humble, so adoring. She didn't know that Oscar had never been with anyone else besides Ruth—not ever, not even before he was married. And Ginny didn't know that he would fall in love so hard and so deep.

Oscar was still sleeping when she let herself out of his apartment. In the daylight, she could really appreciate how nice his place was. Not that the stuff in it looked expensive. But you could see the careful, loving way things were arranged: the apples in a blue-and-white bowl; the sheer white curtains that softened the light from the windows; the rugs placed just so and the wooden floors gleaming beneath them. She thought of Ruth—tall, big-boned, with a blond pageboy that was just turning to white at the sides and at the crown of her head—and she suddenly felt the sharp poke of conscience. Ruth had been so nice that time Oscar brought her home for dinner. This was how she repaid her.

Back in her own apartment, Ginny began cleaning for the first time in months. It was pretty funky in there, with dust bunnies grown to the size of warthogs under the bed, empty, greasy cartons all over the kitchen (from the Chinese restaurant on Seventy-seventh Street that Oscar recommended) and heaps of dirty clothes—most of them practice clothes— everywhere. The shower curtain had some unfamiliar pinkish-brown gunk growing on it—and she thought that as a southern girl she knew everything there was to know about mold. It was too disgusting to mess with, so she threw it away. She filled two big bags with garbage and two more with laundry, to be done later that night, after the performance. She actually liked going down to the laundry room around midnight, when she wouldn't have to wait for the dryers. When she told Oscar this once, he was horrified. You could be mugged. Or worse, he had said, and made her promise not to do it again. He was probably right. Her money had been stolen three times since she arrived in New York, the last time by a teenaged boy with mean eyes and the worst acne she'd ever seen. She actually saw him slip his hand into her bag while they were on a bus, but the look he gave her was filled with such menace that she hadn't dared to say a thing.

She was lucky to find some clean practice clothes hidden in the back of a drawer—stuck there for emergencies like this—and after shoving them into her bag, she splurged on a taxi to the theater. She had already missed company class—another dumb move—but she knew that there was at least one rehearsal where she belonged and she wasn't going to miss that. She checked the big bulletin board where the schedule was posted. Sure enough, there was her name, listed with a dozen or so others, for a rehearsal in Studio C. Also listed was Mia McQuaid. Ginny hesitated for a minute but realized she would not be able to avoid Mia forever. It was bad enough that she had missed class, she couldn't miss rehearsal too. And maybe it would be better to face Mia in the studio than onstage. Ginny changed quickly and took the stairs two at a time up to Studio C.

Rehearsal had just started, so she wasn't really late. The ballet was a new one, choreographed by a guest choreographer from Norway and everyone in the company seemed to think it was great. Ginny thought it was a piece of garbage. She couldn't understand why Erik was interested in commissioning this new stuff when there were so many perfectly good Balanchine ballets in the repertory, just waiting to be danced again. She knew this because she used to look through the old programs in the dance library near Lincoln Center; when she first got to New York, she had spent a lot of time there between rehearsals and classes. The library was clean and quiet and the librarian liked her.

The choreographer for the new ballet stood at the front of the room, a red bandanna tied tightly around his impossibly blond hair. She was willing to bet he bleached it, but since his eyelashes and brows were practically white, she had to give in and assume it was the real thing. First off, he had the corps members stand in a straight line, doing endless bourrées while their outstretched arms tipped in one direction and then the other, so that altogether they resembled a plane about to make a crash landing. Ginny could see their reflections in the big mirror up front, and couldn't believe how stupid they looked. Then she caught sight of Boyd Michaels, way at the other end of the studio. His eyes met hers in the mirror briefly and he smiled.

The rehearsal dragged on. They jumped around on pointe, arms held in stylized zigzags before and behind their torsos. After twenty minutes or so of this, she felt one blister pop and another start to ooze.

Finally, they were given a break and Ginny shot out of there to the vending machine, where she bought a Coke and a Mars bar. When she went back inside, she realized that Mia McQuaid was not in the studio. That was strange, because her name was there on the schedule. Ginny had seen it not an hour ago. She walked over to Boyd, who was stretching at the barre.

"Where's Mia?" she asked, gulping down her Coke. The candy bar was already gone; she wished she'd bought another.

"Mia McQuaid? Don't you know?" Boyd stopped stretching and turned to face her.

"Know what?"

"How she hurt herself. In class this morning."

"I wasn't in class this morning," Ginny said. The Coke can suddenly felt much too cold in her hand and she put it on the floor. "What happened? Is she okay?"

"If you call ripping the ligament in your knee okay, then I guess she is. But it looks like she'll be out for a while. Maybe even the rest of the season."

"That's terrible," said Ginny. Wes had hurt the ligaments in his knee and it had effectively ended his career. She remembered his telling her how ligaments weren't elastic, like muscles; once you tore one, it never healed right. Then she thought of being in Mia's apartment last night. The mustard. Her face burned at the memory, but Boyd didn't seem to notice.

"The part's already gone to the understudy," he was saying.

"The solo," murmured Ginny, looking past Boyd to the window on the far side of the studio. "The one I wanted so much." Abruptly, she turned back to him. "Has anyone started the collection yet?" Whenever a dancer was hurt or injured, all the others took up a collection; no one gave much, just a token, ten dollars, twenty at the most. It was the gesture that counted, the fact that despite their many rivalries and feuds, they would nonetheless rally around one of their own.

"I'm not sure," said Boyd. "Why? Do you want to give something? I know you were pretty steamed when she got that part instead of you." He put his other leg over the barre now. The break was almost over.

"That doesn't matter," said Ginny. "Will you take my money? Here." She handed Boyd five bills—all tens—that she extracted from somewhere inside her dance clothes.

"Fifty dollars!" said Boyd, smoothing the bills flat in his hand. "That's a lot of money."

"Just make sure she gets it, okay?" Ginny answered.

At the front of the room, Olaf, the choreographer, retied his red bandanna, called all the dancers to join him in the center and then they were at it, oh Lord, again.

RUTH

R*uth knew* that Oscar was aching to sleep with that girl. That was, if he hadn't done it already. Poor Oscar. Infidelity, or even the thought of it, sat so badly on him. He walked around all hangdog, wringing his hands and looking wretched. This behavior was accompanied by an air of great and unshakable distraction: she had to repeat herself three or four times just to get his attention. No sooner did she do this than he drifted off again, into that private little hell he had furnished, carpeted and made his own. Two weeks ago, she came back from visiting Gabriel, Penelope and the baby in California and found him sitting in the dark by himself in the living room. When she turned on the light, he looked startled, as if she were the last person he expected to see.

He actually brought her home once, this Ginny Valentine, for dinner. Ruth's first thought was, The poor thing! With those searching eyes and that wide, mobile mouth, her face had an intense, eager and above all needy look. And the clothes: a tight, off-the-shoulder gold lamé top, a floor-length flowered skirt and gold sandals that showed her maimed-looking, somewhat dirty feet. But Ginny had been sweet. She showed up with two bunches of asters from the Korean grocery stand on the corner, smiled her way all through the meal and ate third helpings of everything, although where she put it on that tiny, wiry frame was a mystery to Ruth. She helped clear the table and wanted to wash the dishes, though Ruth drew the line at that. By the end of the evening, Ruth had really warmed to her and even found her somewhat pretty, though she never could have imagined that Oscar would develop such a yen for her. His taste had always run to the refined. Or so she had thought.

In their many years together, Ruth had had ample opportunity to observe Oscar's little infatuations with the dancers in the company, and the women he selected all seemed to have something in common. There was the blonde who wore tiny diamond earrings and beautiful clothing in subdued shades of ivory, gray and brown; another who had studied music and spoke of it with great intelligence; and still another, a Brazilian woman who wore silk scarves from Hermès and a lush, sensual perfume whose name Ruth never learned. Despite the difference in their looks, they all shared some worldly quality that this child, this waif, seemed light-years away from possessing.

Yet Ruth was no longer furious with Oscar or jealous of these women. In fact, she had moved through both fury and jealousy and now had achieved something like acceptance. For one thing, with the exception of Ginny Valentine, she didn't believe Oscar ever consummated any of these infatuations; they were loves of the mind rather than of the body. And then there were the children to consider. It was one thing to leave a husband. It was quite another to separate three boys from their father, especially when he had been a good, loving father, as Oscar mostly had been all these years.

Ruth remembered the night before she and Oscar got married, when she tried on her wedding dress—heavy white satin without a ruffle or stitch of lace on it—for her two grandmothers, Pip and Lilli. Pip was tall and what was called statuesque in those days: she had a full, strong body and elaborately curled hair rinsed in a pale shade of blue. She wore vivid makeup and showy, dramatic clothes, like a pink taffeta dress with a rhinestone-studded bodice or a Persian lamb coat with a faux leopard collar and muff to match. Viennese-born Lilli, who privately thought Pip a bit vulgar, wore white blouses that she boiled on the stove with bleach before starching and ironing them. She never wore lipstick, pants, high heels or any adornment other than her gold wedding ring and the strand of coral beads that came from her mother. Her white hair was worn in thick braids on top of her head, which added a fraction of height to her diminutive frame. Yet despite their differences, these two women converged upon Ruth the night before the wedding ceremony, for a ritual viewing of the dress and to deliver what turned out to be surprisingly similar advice on marriage. Ruth's mother was in the next room, yelling at the caterer or the florist, and so the three of them were alone.

"Here, take my pin," urged Pip, unfastening the brooch from her dress. Ruth shook her head no, but Pip persisted. "A pearl necklace, then. Or some earrings. You look naked like that!" Lilli and Ruth exchanged glances but said nothing. Pip caught their looks and misinterpreted them. "Oh, you're thinking she'll be really naked soon enough?" she said, smiling. "That is, if she hasn't already ... Girls these days don't wait, do they, Lilli? Not like in our day." Pip shook her head; whether for today's girls or the ones of yesteryear wasn't clear.

"Not like in our day," Lilli agreed. She was sitting on a chair in the corner, hands folded over the polished handle of the cane she had only recently started using. "Girls were different then. It's not just that they waited. They made the men wait," she explained. "They had that power." Ruth fingered the heavy material of the dress and looked at the floor, not wanting either of them to try to figure out just what Oscar and she had done up in the Berkshires the summer before. "And power in a marriage, that's a good thing, *tochter*," Lilli continued. Ruth could feel her grandmother's eyes on her face.

"A good thing," echoed Pip. "You have to work at it. Keep it in your hands. Because you think the way you feel tonight and tomorrow and next month will be the way you feel forever, but it isn't."

"Once you have children, you'll never love him again in the same way," Lilli said solemnly. Ruth looked at her then. Pip was nodding vehemently, and the two of them looked at each other, as if she, Ruth, had left the room. What did they know that she didn't? Ruth didn't want to find out.

But the comment stayed with her all these years, and though Pip and Lilli were both long gone, she had found them to be right, at least about this. Once your children came, you never did feel the same way about your husband. Oh, it's not that you loved him less; on the contrary, it was easy to feel even more infatuated with this potent god who had bestowed upon you these treasures, these living miracles. It was rather that your focus, once so narrow and intense, widened and grew diffuse. Instead of being just the two of you, in your own private bubble of happiness (or anger, or disappointment), the bubble expanded to include three, then four and then five. And after a while, it burst altogether. There was no thinking about yourselves as just a couple anymore. You would forever and always be a couple with children. So while before she had the boys Ruth might have been crushed by Oscar's infidelities, real or imagined, by this point in their lives, she did not think she could have shattered the vessel that had been their marriage just because he had fantasized about sleeping with some other woman. Or even because he had slept with her.

Ruth also knew how these small infatuations helped take the sting out of his failed ambition and allowed him to forget that he was not on a level with Pinchas Zukerman or Yehudi Menuhin and not likely to be either. Though when Oscar and Ruth met, all those years ago, anything seemed possible for him. And she truly thought that back then, anything was.

They had met in the Berkshires, during an eight-week music workshop at Tanglewood. Ruth knew who Oscar was before he was aware of her; he was something of a star that summer, and very handsome besides. He was tall, even taller than she was, which mattered to her then, and although there was something graceless and boxy about his body, his face was arresting: thick, dark hair without a hint of shine, heavy, dark brows and, under them, eyes of an uncommon greenish-blue. Their first son, Gabriel, had those eyes and that hair. But he hadn't inherited the fierceness Oscar had had when he was young, nor the resolute set of lips and the nostrils that flared—wide and alarmed as those of a startled horse—with the least provocation.

Ruth had no reason to believe that Oscar would even notice her then. She was not having a good time, not at all. Though she knew she should have considered herself lucky—Lilli had insisted on paying Ruth's bill for the voice lessons and her mother had managed to get her a job that paid for room and board—she didn't like Tanglewood, or Massachusetts, or the fabled Berkshire mountains. "You're so lucky to get out of the heat," chorused her mother, her two grandmothers, her sister, Molly, her aunts Ida and Yetta and Cookie and Pessie, as they sweltered in Brooklyn.

But Ruth liked the summers in Brooklyn. Her room, the one she had slept in since she was nine, with its pink-and-white-striped wallpaper and white dotted-Swiss curtains, was a haven to her, even on the hottest nights. Her mother routinely ironed the sheets, so they were always sleek and cool to the touch. She left a pitcher of ice water on a nightstand by the bed, and although all the ice cubes would have melted by morning, the water would still be cold. A big rotating fan sat on the dresser and she became accustomed to the pleasant whirring of its massive old blades. No, Ruth had no desire to exchange all that for a room shared with three other girls, for mosquitoes the size of flies, flies the size of bees and bees the size of hummingbirds. But a summer in the country, said her mother. The country, echoed her grandmothers and aunts. She was unable to resist their collective pressure.

Once at Tanglewood, Ruth tried to make the best of it. She was given a job in the kitchen, helping to prepare the breakfast, which she didn't mind at all. Mornings were filled with classes and coaching; afternoons with re-hearsals—the students were giving a small concert at the end of the summer—and swimming at a nearby lake. It was at the lake that she had met Oscar. Late in the afternoon, Ruth had sat on the pebbled shore, watching him. Everyone else had already filtered back to their cabins to change and get ready for dinner. Oscar was a surprisingly graceful swimmer, his arms easily breaking the otherwise placid surface of the water. He seemed oblivious to her. After a while, he stopped and stood waist-deep, staring in her direction. When he started moving in toward the shore, Ruth impulsively decided to go for a swim and stood up. She wore an unadorned one-piece black bathing suit that she had purchased in town when a couple of her roommates had driven in and asked her along. The flowered suit with the flouncy skirt her mother had packed was stuffed at the bottom of the suitcase with the price tag still intact. Oscar was close enough to see her now. Ruth felt—and it was an odd feeling for her—totally comfortable with her body, and with his unwavering attention to it. He stood there, dripping water and breathing heavily in the late afternoon sun.

"You need a towel," Ruth said, and held hers out to him. He reached for it and grabbed her hand too.

"Oscar Kornblatt," he said, and he actually bowed.

"I know," Ruth said.

"And you are ...?"

"Ruth Fass."

"Ruth," he said softly, as if reciting a poem or a prayer. "Ruth Fass." She never got to the water.

And so the summer became much more interesting. Oscar was such a welcome change from the young men Ruth had been meeting, almost weekly, at her parents' insistence. The accountants, the clerks from her father's clothing store, the earnest would-be professionals at Temple Beth Elohim's Thursday-night singles' socials. And because Oscar was considered so talented, her being with him conferred upon her an immediate status that she had previously lacked. It was as if everyone could tell just how serious you were about your professional life as a musician. Oscar was known to be both passionate and gifted, whereas Ruth, despite her lovely voice, lacked the essential commitment that formed the core of every serious musician.

She had never even wanted to sing opera; that was her mother's idea. When her mother heard Ruth singing for the pure love of it, she decided to harness that love to something she could understand, and be proud of. She found a voice teacher, a plump, rounded woman who lived in Brighton Beach but who had performed at the Opéra in Paris and spoke enough German—with the right pronunciation—to please Lilli, so she was deemed acceptable. Then, when it was felt Ruth had outgrown her, there were lessons in Manhattan, in a studio on West Fifty-seventh Street, just across from Carnegie Hall. And it wasn't as if Ruth didn't enjoy what she learned; when she opened her mouth to sing, the music just welled up pure and strong, pouring out as if she were merely the conduit. But, inside, Ruth had another dream, one that she never shared with her family, her teachers, the other girls at Tanglewood that summer or even with Oscar.

In this dream, Ruth was singing, but something low and sultry; more Billie Holliday than Joan Sutherland. The musical accompaniment was minimal: a piano and perhaps a saxophone or clarinet. There was a clear pool of light around her and she stood in its center, wearing a simple black dress—maybe satin, maybe velvet—that was scooped out low in front and just kind of skimmed over the rest of her body. Her hair was pinned up and in it, she wore a few roses; she could smell them when she closed her eyes, which she did from time to time. When she opened her mouth to sing, all the sweet, sad and beautiful things she had ever known and felt, the audience was rapt with pleasure and with sorrow, but not for her; no, it was because she was singing all their secrets too, the ones they never dared to tell and were now so exhilarated to have finally revealed. This fantasy had no place at Tanglewood, or anywhere else in Ruth's life, for that matter. Once she started seeing Oscar, it was easy to let his dreams take over for both of them. She never minded; in fact, she was grateful. By the end of the summer, they were in love; by the winter, he had asked her to marry him.

Ruth's family was ecstatic: Oscar had bowed to her mother; he had gone so far as to kiss the hands of both Lilli and Pip when they were introduced. "A prince!" declared Pip. Even Ruth's father, coarsened by a Depression-era childhood and years in the garment trade, succumbed to Oscar's charm. "That boy is going somewhere" was his comment. And it seemed as if Ruth was meant to go with him.

Her parents insisted on a big wedding and neither Oscar nor Ruth tried to dissuade them. It would have been useless anyway. Oscar might as well really have been a prince and she his princess for all the effort and expense lavished on the single day. There was a four-course dinner, the famed Viennese table and a wedding cake the size of a small washing machine. Several of Oscar's cronies played classical selections throughout the meal and then still others played the waltz in which he spun her, not too adroitly but with much feeling, around the polished wooden dance floor. There were scads of white roses, an expensive dress and veil that came as a favor to Ruth's father from someone in the business, and wedding gifts of more china, crystal, linen and silver than they would ever need or want. It was only later, when the babies came and they were living in that basement on East Sixth Street, that the reality of their situation became clear to her.

Still, Ruth and Oscar had a good life together, and those early, lean years had made the years of plenty seem all the sweeter. Their boys were now men, good men, and Oscar seemed contented with his lot at the ballet. She still took care of him, of course, but with the children gone, her days were pretty much her own.

Two days a week, Ruth did volunteer work. On Mondays, she traveled up the West Side to a Jewish nursing home where the floors were cleaned and buffed only in the center; the sides—the hallways, the residents' rooms, the public areas—were always cloudy with dirt and dust. She always brought things: issues of the *New Yorker* that Oscar had finished with, a bottle or two of nail polish, the latest pictures of her baby grand-daughter, Isobel.

This was how her most recent morning at the home went: Ruth painted Mrs. Fishbein's nails with three coats of Revlon's Cherries in the Snow and then they watched a cooking show. Ruth brought the magazines to Mr. Blustain, who took them with hands afflicted by a permanent trembling. She visited with Tillie Dienstag, whose blue-rinsed hair and loud laugh reminded her a little of Pip. It was a good day until she reached Mrs. Goldenfarb's room and found it not only empty but also stripped of her things: the tiny framed pictures of her grandchildren and great-grandchildren, the papier-mâché bride and groom that had sat on her wedding cake sixty years ago, the porcelain bell she bought on a trip to Ireland with her late husband.

"She's gone," said the orderly who was pulling sheets off the rubber-encased mattress.

"Gone?" Ruth knew what he meant but was, as her children might have said, in denial.

"Last night. She went peacefully. In her sleep. Did you know her well?"

"Not very," Ruth said, thinking of the hands of gin rummy they would not play that day and of the baby pictures over which they would not ex-claim.

On Wednesdays, Ruth took the bus to the East Side of Manhattan, where she spent the morning playing with babies. These were not sick babies, al-though most were a little more frail than normal, given their difficult pas-sage into the world. She was not sure she would have been up to dealing with the ones who had AIDS or cancer, so she didn't try. But these were babies whose mothers were sick, or addicted to crack cocaine, and needed some sort of medical supervision. Often, there were no parents—they were in jail, or in detox—to hold and snuggle them, and the nurses, God bless these hardworking, wonderful girls, didn't have the time. But Ruth did. When she arrived, she went straight to see Blossom, one of her favorites. Blossom weighed barely three pounds when she was born and three months later, she weighed only seven. After putting on the gown, cap and mask—Blossom's immune system was still compromised—Ruth scooped her up and brought her to the window, which looked out over Fifth Avenue. "See the trees?" Ruth cooed. "See how the leaves are turning colors?" Blossom's eyes seemed to follow her gaze. Although small, she was very alert, which was part of what Ruth loved about her. Also her tiny dark curls, and beautifully shaped mouth.

When Ruth ordered something for her granddaughter, Isobel, she always ordered a few extra onesies and knitted caps and brought them with her to the hospital. Ruth let the nurses distribute them the way they thought best, but she did ask that Blossom get a cap. Recently, the stories here had been good: Blossom had been gaining weight; Michel's aunt and uncle were given custody and would be taking him home; Kyra's lung infection finally cleared up.

Sometimes Ruth thought about adding another day to her volunteering, but Oscar was against it. He thought she spent too much time with strangers as it was. "They're not strangers to me," Ruth tried to tell him. He thought she should spend more time with her family. God knew Ruth would have loved to. But Gabriel and Penelope were far away in California, and, besides, Penelope was what Ruth's mother would have called "highstrung." Ruth didn't really think Penelope would want her around that often, given the way she was so particular about every aspect of Isobel's life. Only breast milk and organically grown cereal and produce—which Penelope cooked and ground herself—to eat; only clothing from organically grown cotton to wear. Good thing Ruth found one of those environmentally friendly catalogs to order from, because Penelope wouldn't allow anything else to touch that child's skin. Ruth knew because she had sent a big batch of perfectly adorable things from Macy's when Isobel was born and Penelope sent them all back, with a lengthy note explaining her philosophy on the chemical toxins present in commercially made clothing and their potentially devastating effect on newborns. Ruth was disappointed, but instead of taking the things back to Macy's, she took them to the hospital, where it cheered her up to see the babies wearing them.

Ruth's second son, William, and his wife, Betsy, were closer—they lived in New Jersey—but Betsy had been trying unsuccessfully to get pregnant for more than two years and Ruth frankly thought her daughter-in-law avoided her. She was not sure why; maybe Betsy thought Ruth wanted grandchildren so badly (and, yes, that much was true) that seeing her felt like a kind of a reproach. And they were both so busy with their work—he was a cardiologist; she was in banking—that they didn't find much time to socialize. Then there was Ben, who was gone for so many months of the year. It was virtually impossible to pin him down, though his last postcard—the one with the picture of a beach in the Indian Ocean—said he would be home in November, in time for Thanksgiving.

"Isn't he a little old for all this wandering?" Oscar said when he inspected the card.

"Maybe," Ruth said, "but he's also too old for us to ground him."

Tuesdays and Thursdays Ruth swam in the pool at the YMCA on West Sixty-third Street, not far from Lincoln Center, where Oscar worked. Oscar was always after her to join the expensive gym on Eighty-sixth Street. "We can afford it now," he told her. But she preferred the more relaxed and democratic atmosphere at the YMCA. No women with diamond bracelets and expensive face-lifts there. It was right in front of the Y's big double doors, on a crisp Thursday in October, that Ruth ran into the girl Oscar had brought home, Ginny Valentine.

"Mrs. Kornblatt!" Ginny called out, waving her hand eagerly in greeting. The bag she carried over her shoulder looked as if it might have contained bricks. Ruth hadn't seen her actually, as she was intent on getting to the pool before three o'clock, which was when the free swim began. She knew from experience that there was no way to do laps when that happened. But before Ruth could pull open the heavy doors, Ginny strode quickly toward her.

"How are you? It's so nice to see you. I had the most wonderful time at your house; you are the best cook, really you are." Ruth paused, touched by the girl's effusive compliments. She found herself asking if Ginny had plans for Thanksgiving and when Ruth learned she didn't, inviting her to their apartment—Ruth had been making Thanksgiving dinner since the boys were little—the following month. "I would love to come!" Ginny said, "Can I bring something? Not home cooked, because I just don't, I mean I can't cook, but something I could buy?"

"No, no, I can take care of it," Ruth said to her. "Just bring your appetite."

"Don't worry about that." Ginny laughed as she continued down the street, toward the theater. As Ruth watched her go, she wondered whether she should have asked Oscar first, but it was, of course, too late.

Ruth's swim was refreshing if uneventful. Afterward, no longer in a hurry, she strolled slowly up Broadway, which had been the main street of her life for more than twenty years. She had watched it change and grow, and though there are those who preferred its older incarnation ("Too gentrified, too many big-box stores," people said), Ruth would always love Broadway, whatever form it took. She loved its four busy lanes of traffic, interrupted only by the small urban islands that were still home to wooden benches, pigeons and the occasional squirrel, its familiar and dense mosaic of shops and services that had sustained her over all these years. She had befriended many of the shopkeepers: Mr. Weiss, who owned the shop where she brought shoes for repair and resoling, knew Lilli's relatives in Vienna. Mr. Lee, who owned the Chinese laundry, had children Ruth watched grow up: his son was now at Fordham University and his daughter, who turned out to have a real talent for the violin, was at Juilliard; Oscar helped arrange that.

These events were the cornerstones of Ruth's weeks. In the evenings, she still sometimes cooked, although often she and Oscar went out for dinner. Friday nights, she tried to make a *Shabbas* dinner, with Lilli's brass candlesticks (though she now had someone come to clean once a week, they were polished by no other hand than hers) and a linen cloth on the table. Oscar was not a religious man, but he still enjoyed the ritual. When the ballet was in season, and he liked to eat out late after the performance (sometimes with another musician but usually with one of the dancers—yes, she knew all about it), she would get together with a friend, or with her sister, Molly, or attend the book club that had been running on and off for the last fifteen years. Every so often, she took a cooking class; not that she wasn't already an accomplished cook, but she enjoyed learning the techniques and skills required of some new cuisine. Fluted madeleines, Basque paella, ravioli hand-filled with pureed beets or pumpkin—all had been sampled and amply praised in her West End Avenue dining room. Though of late, given her concerns about health and weight—both Oscar's and her own—she had veered toward courses in lighter Asian fare. To find the ingredients required to prepare these foods, she made trips to Kalustyan on Lexington Avenue for earth-colored spices and curry powder; to Canal Street in Chinatown for slick baby eggplants and seasoned oils.

But soon it would be Thanksgiving, and Ruth would need to alter her routine somewhat to get ready. She loved these big holidays when she could count on seeing her family, and since Ben had said he was coming this year, she was especially excited. She wondered if he would like Ginny. Although now that she understood the extent of Oscar's feelings for Ginny, this seemed less like a good idea than she had initially thought. What if Ben and Ginny became a couple, or actually got married, and the bride had been the lover—real or imaginary—of the father-in-law? As tolerant as she was, Ruth didn't think she could tolerate a situation like *that*.

She therefore invited another young woman as a distraction. Molly had said something about her daughter's roommate not having anyplace to go for the day, so Ruth decided she should come along.

This was how she was before a holiday—planning, scheming, dreaming the event. She wrote out a menu in a big, spiral-bound notebook and started her shopping early, before the lines at Zabar's got too long. Once there, she bought things that would keep, like the special balsamic vinegar she used in the stuffing, and the imported crackers she served with cheese and sliced fruit as a snack hours after the meal. She ordered the turkey from a local butcher where she had shopped for years and the flowers from the florist nearby; from a company listed in the Yellow Pages, she rented folding chairs and a small card table. Just in case. The wine came from the store on Seventy-second Street, the one that had been supplying her family with spirits since Gabriel's bar mitzvah. Who said New York City wasn't a village?

Penelope called to tell Ruth when their flight was scheduled to arrive on Wednesday. They would be spending the night with her mother in Connecticut and then all of them would drive down on Thanksgiving. "How's Isobel?" Ruth asked. "Can you put her on the phone?" Not that at seven months she could speak, but Ruth delighted in the indescribable music of her babbling.

"I think it will scare her," said Penelope. "You'll be seeing her soon."

"The room is all ready," Ruth said, pushing her disappointment away. Penelope was right. She'd be seeing the baby soon enough. "Will you need a crib or can she just sleep with you?"

"No crib, no crib," said Penelope. "And, Ruth, did I mention that we have to leave a couple of days early?"

"No, you didn't," Ruth said. Now that really was a disappointment. Usually, they stayed four or five days; two days early would make it two or three.

"... and he can't miss that conference ..." Penelope was explaining. But Ruth couldn't help wondering if that was the real reason. She knew how unsafe and toxic a place Penelope considered New York City to be. Well, Ruth thought, she would just have to plan another trip out to San Francisco to see them.

William and Betsy were driving in from New Jersey for the day; they would bring Oscar's cousin Henry, his wife and their two children. Ruth's sister, Molly, her daughter Gwen and Gwen's roommate would be coming from various points in Manhattan. Who knew when Ben would arrive, but he did say he'd come, and Ben was not one to break his word. Oh, and

Ginny. As it turned out, Oscar was so pleased Ruth had invited her. A little too pleased, in fact.

"I think she's lonely, you know," he had said. "No family and no friends either."

"The family part I understand," Ruth said. "But why no friends? Doesn't she have friends in the company?"

"Not really," said Oscar, looking uncomfortable. "She hasn't had an easy time of it. Anyway, you've done a good deed."

"A *mitzvah?*" Ruth smiled.

"Yes, a *mitzvah,*" Oscar agreed, and he smiled too.

The morning of Thanksgiving Day was unseasonably mild and bright. Ruth opened the windows in the dining room and refrigerated the flowers, so they wouldn't wilt too soon. The turkey had been in the oven since dawn; she still had to make the salad, the rolls and the gravy but almost everything else—vegetables, pies, chocolate torte that came from the recipe book Lilli had received when she got married—had been done in advance. She set the table the night before, using her wedding silver, china and crystal. She even bought a new dress—navy crepe, with a V-neck and kick pleats along the bottom. Wearing a big white apron to protect it, she headed for the kitchen. It seemed that in no time at all, the doorbell was ringing and her guests—her family—had arrived.

Ruth's sister, Molly, came in first, dumping her mink coat on the living room sofa. "God, am I hot!" she complained.

"Who wears a fur coat when it's almost sixty degrees out?" said Oscar jovially.

"Who knew? I always wear my fur on Thanksgiving." Oscar hung the offending garment in the hall closet; Ruth kissed Molly and her niece Gwen; she shook hands with Gwen's roommate.

"Come in, come in!" Oscar loved playing master of ceremonies. The bell rang again, and it was William and Betsy and the cousins Oscar hadn't seen for at least five years. Ginny followed soon after, clutching two bottles of wine that she pressed into Ruth's hands. Even in her distraction, Ruth had to notice how Oscar beamed when he looked at her.

The apartment quickly filled up with voices and laughter and music—Oscar put on a Mozart CD—and the bell rang again. Here, finally, were Gabriel, Penelope and Isobel. "Let me hold her!" Ruth said as soon as she had kissed them all.

"Not now," said Penelope, arms tight around the baby. "She's overwhelmed by all these people." Ruth looked into Isobel's clear blue eyes and saw nothing that looked like alarm or confusion. Still, Penelope was her mother, and Ruth knew better than to interfere. So instead of cradling her granddaughter in her arms, she turned to greet Penelope's mother, Caroline, a tall, elegant woman with cheekbones that could have carved the turkey.

It was only when they had all moved inside and were somewhat settled that William said loudly, "So where's Ben?"

"He'll be here," Ruth said, as she moved briskly around the room, making sure there was a small bowl next to the olives for the pits, arranging the hard candy into a pleasing little mound in its glass dish. "He said he was coming home for Thanksgiving."

"Yeah, but did he say this Thanksgiving or next year?" William said. Everyone laughed, William and Gabriel loudest of all. Ruth didn't know why Ben had such a bad reputation with his brothers, but then, as if on cue, the bell rang again, and this time, it was Ben. Ruth rushed to the door to hug him. Could it be that he was taller? Look how tanned he was; there were even streaks of blond in his brown hair. She was so busy gazing up at him that it took her a moment to realize he was not alone. There was a woman with him.

"And this is ..." Oscar, ever the gentleman, said kindly as he came to embrace his boy.

"The newest Mrs. Kornblatt," Ben announced proudly. "Mom, Dad, I'd like you to meet my wife, Laura."

Oscar and Ruth looked at each other in astonishment. But there was Ben, holding the hand of this small woman with reddish, curly hair and a constellation of freckles across her face. William started to clap first. Then everyone else in the room joined in.

The story unfolded over the course of the meal. It seemed that they had met in Delhi, though in fact Laura was from London. She had been visiting the family of an Indian schoolmate during a break when she met Ben.... Yes, it was all very sudden; yes, they had surprised the family totally, bowled them over would have been more like it; no, they hadn't told anyone they were getting married. They had just gone and done it, in London, one Monday morning just two weeks ago. But as she watched her youngest boy hold the hand of this girl, now his wife, Ruth felt a sense of maternal completion and fulfillment. She knew how her own mother must have felt when she and Molly were both married: the job was done and now there was someone—husband, wife, the children you hoped would follow—to take your place. Amen.

Between Ben's wonderful news and the delirious pleasure of finally getting to hold Isobel in her arms, Ruth was fairly distracted most of the day. She didn't pay much attention to Oscar or Ginny or any of the other guests either. Instead, she settled on the sofa while Betsy and Penelope cleared the table; her three sons had not been in one room together for at least two years and they had plenty to say. Only at some point it seemed that Gabriel had disappeared and Ben, in the midst of some complicated story he was telling about a night he spent in Calcutta, noticed his absence. "Where did he go?" he asked, looking around. "I want him to hear this."

"You sit," Ruth instructed. "I'll find him." She stood up. Isobel still seemed content to be in her arms and Ruth could hear the voices of Penelope and Betsy in the kitchen. "Come," she said to Isobel, "let's go see where Daddy is."

Gabriel wasn't in the dining room or the bedroom. Had he been in the kitchen, Ruth would have heard him. He must have gone to the bathroom. Then she noticed that the door to the guest room was closed and she knew how stuffy that room could get, especially on such a mild day. Without thinking, she reached for the knob and opened the door.

There, wrapped in each other's arms, Gabriel and Ginny stood kissing. And what a kiss: their eyes were closed, their bodies welded together. Because she was so much shorter, Ginny had to rise up on her toes and tilt her head back. So intent were they that they didn't even notice Ruth, who was too shocked to move or to say anything, in the doorway. It was only when Isobel uttered, in her lilting, baby way, some gurgling sound in response to having seen her father that Gabriel finally lifted his face from Ginny's and returned Ruth's horrified stare.

GABRIEL

The first time Gabriel saw Penelope, she was sitting in front of the
Avery Library at Columbia University, eating an apple. She had
been wearing a rose-colored dress of a lightweight material (in those days,
she still wore colors) that left her shoulders and throat bare. As Gabriel
approached, he found himself mesmerized by her skin, so pale and beautiful, as if cream swirled through her veins, lending both texture and color
to its pigment. Her hair—dark, thick and shining—seemed to gleam
against her pallor. Her large, dark eyes appraised him coolly. Gabriel
stood there, transfixed. The red, interwoven bricks of the walkway seemed
to glow with an unnatural incandescence; the sky grew brighter and more
brilliantly blue; the green leaves of the shrubs were animate and electric.

"I have another one," she said finally.

"Another what?" he said, confused but willing to be drawn in.

"Apple. It's right here." She reached into her canvas carryall, and
handed him the fruit. When he bit into it, he thought he had never tasted

anything so delectable. And later, much later, when he had brought her to his apartment on Amsterdam Avenue, removed her clothing and pressed his lips—gently, reverently—to her face, her throat, her soft, smooth belly, he thought the same thing.

Gabriel was studying architecture at Columbia. He knew that he was a disappointment to his father, Oscar, who hoped he would become a musician. "You have the talent," Oscar had said, many times, when Gabriel was growing up, "I know you do, I can feel it in you." The talent, maybe, thought Gabriel, but the drive, never. Oscar had been Gabriel's first music teacher, just as he was William's and Ben's. He actually bought Gabriel a half-sized violin—most people rented rather than purchased these tiny instruments—when he was so young that he still sucked his thumb. "Do you really think he's ready?" Ruth had said, stroking Gabriel's hair.

"Do you know how it's held?" Oscar asked, handing Gabriel the violin. Gabriel had seen his father do this hundreds of times; he had heard the sounds that the instrument made. He wanted to please Oscar, so he reached out his arms and held it in the way he had observed.

"He's a natural," beamed Oscar, and the matter was settled. Every afternoon that he was available, Oscar gave Gabriel a music lesson. On the days when there was no lesson, he was to practice: Ruth saw to that. And at first it seemed to work fine. Gabriel was a shy, serious child who sought to please; pleasing meant holding the violin, and manipulating the bow in just the right way, so that the sounds emitting from it were ones that made Oscar smile rather than frown. It wasn't so hard; he could do it.

It was later that all the battles came. Gabriel resented the practicing, time when he could have been riding his bicycle, or drawing or hanging out in Riverside Park with a joint and his friends. Then William and Ben had to have lessons too. First violin lessons, with Oscar, although later, William settled on the piano—"A lowbrow instrument, but better than nothing," observed their father—and Ben, the flute. The apartment was filled with music; between the various lessons and practice times of the boys, and Oscar's own practicing, there was scarcely a quiet moment. When there was, Oscar would play one of his records—he had a collection of nearly one thousand albums—on the stereo system that dominated the living room. And if Oscar wasn't practicing or listening to music, he was talking about the superiority of the stringed instruments in general and the violin in particular; his reverence for Bach and his ambivalence about Beethoven. His dissection of some piece of music that he had heard when he was—mercifully—somewhere else. Gabriel longed for silence, silence that he could see and feel as well as hear.

He began to avoid his practicing, not so hard to do when his father wasn't there, as his mother didn't goad him in the same way. "You didn't practice today, did you?" she would say, knowing the answer but feeling obligated to ask, to try.

"Not yet," he'd tell her. "I'll do it after."

"But don't you have homework?"

"I did it in study hall," Gabriel would lie. He could see that she was wavering.

"Oh, all right," she would say. Gabriel was relieved and grateful in his escape. "See you later," he would tell her. He could hear Ben's flute from down the hallway; his playing wasn't bad, but Gabriel couldn't stand the sound. He had to get out of there. He found his silences in different places throughout the city: in the Metropolitan Museum of Art, where he liked to visit the galleries that housed early Renaissance paintings or archaic Greek sculpture. In Central Park, all the way uptown, where his parents distinctly forbade him to go. As time went on, he sought the eloquent silence of buildings, from the great to the ordinary. The Cathedral of Saint John the Divine. The New York Public Library. A row of brownstone houses in Brooklyn, the symmetry of their façades as gratifying and alive as faces. These edifices seemed to soothe and console him, in a way that music, mere sound, could not. By the time he was ready for college, all the subterfuge was gone, and he openly defied Oscar. He had made it clear that he would not attend Juilliard, no matter how Oscar tried to bribe him, no matter how many phone calls were made on his behalf. He wanted to go to Columbia, and eventually to study architecture. It was the only way he was going to get any peace.

"You're throwing away your gift," said Oscar sadly, defeated but still kicking.

"He has other gifts." This from Ruth, the mediator, the peacemaker.

"That's the most important one, though," said Oscar.

"Come on, Dad," said Gabriel. "There's still Willie and Ben. You might make musicians out of them."

"Your brother William thinks the highest form of musical expression is the Broadway show tune," said Oscar gloomily. It was true; William's natural facility with the piano turned to popular forms that everyone could sing to. Whenever there was a family gathering, he would inevitably find his way to the polished upright piano in the den and start improvising, letting his fingers roam the keyboard easily.

"Well, what about Ben?" asked Gabriel, not too sympathetic.

"You mean the Pied Piper of Hamelin?" Oscar said. But Gabriel didn't care if his father was disappointed in him, or in his brothers, or in the way that his own career had worked out. He had his own life to live, and it was not going to be such a goddamned noisy one. The handcrafted violin of spruce and flame maple Oscar had purchased and presented to him with such a flourish remained mute, locked in its unassuming black case. After a while, he didn't see it anymore, though he never asked what had become of it.

Once playing the violin was behind him, Gabriel attended Columbia, living first at home, and then finally in a dark but otherwise pleasant apartment on the ground floor of a building on Amsterdam Avenue and 118th Street, the very apartment where he first made love to Penelope.

Although he imagined that he would have some competition when it came to winning Penelope, he was wrong. Despite her astonishing beauty, Penelope was not at all confident or poised; she had little idea of what to do with herself. While a student at Barnard, she changed her major three times: first it was art history, then classics and then, in an abrupt turn away from the Occident, Asian studies. Eventually, she gave up everything, failing to get her degree at all, and was content to orbit around the quiet, steady star of Gabriel's ascension. For ascend he did.

Though he was neither talkative nor charismatic like his father, he nevertheless excelled in his chosen field, impressing first his teachers and later his clients, with the finely trained beam of his vision. He was not radical or iconoclastic in this; rather there was something conservative and even classical about his approach to buildings and the spaces within them. But he seemed to have a way of digesting and reinterpreting the past that was, as a senior architect in the firm where he first went to work put it, harmonious. "Gabriel designs a suite of rooms like he's composing a concerto," the man said of him, "everything is rhythmic." Oscar would have liked to hear that, Gabriel thought; then his father could imagine that Gabriel was the musician he had always dreamed of his being, a composer of space and light, dimension and form.

During those years, Penelope moved in with Gabriel, and spent her time cleaning and organizing the apartment. He had always been neat, but Penelope was obsessively, compulsively neat, from the very smallest aspect of household management—spices and foods must be arranged alphabetically in the cupboards, socks lined up evenly in the drawers—to the largest, like the ritual cleaning of windows, walls, rugs and even ceilings. He probably should have realized then that there was something slightly amiss in her focus, that her desire for external order sprang from a deep dread of the chaos that lived inside her. But, at the time, he was dazzled by her loveliness, and her apparent devotion to him. And it was nice to live in a place where the floors were always mopped and waxed, the bedsheets pressed, the windows, for what little light they admitted, sparkling. She placed fresh flowers in the rooms twice a week—never mind that they were always white, this thing about color was starting even then—arranging the blossoms, the petals, the stems, just so. She made their life hers, and it seemed to satisfy her. She accompanied him to the firm's Christmas party, a slim-fitting, scoop-necked velour dress accentuating the impossible whiteness of her neck, the swell of her breasts, and he knew the other men in the firm were envious of the beautiful, attentive woman at his side.

"You'd better marry her," one of the firm's partners said jokingly. "Or I may beat you to it." Gabriel just smiled, but something inside him clicked.

He and Penelope had lived together for three years; it was time to make a more formal arrangement.

His parents were, of course, delighted. Oscar kissed Penelope on both cheeks, grabbing her hands tightly in his. Ruth wept openly. "I'm so happy for both of you," she said, wiping her wet eyes with her fingers. "So very happy." They had little to do with planning the wedding; Penelope's mother, Caroline, handled everything and they were married in the back-yard of her big house in Greenwich, Connecticut. Penelope wore a long Victorian dress of a fine, fine cotton she told him was called "lawn" and a crown of gardenias in her upswept hair. Their heavy, sweet scent, as he leaned to kiss her before the rabbi and the minister who jointly officiated, actually made him feel a little light-headed, even nauseated, but he chalked that up to natural wedding-day jitters. The bride was radiant, the families and friends enthralled; the weather spectacular. Everything was perfect; wasn't it?

And for a time after the wedding, he continued to think so. Penelope returned to her cleaning and organizing with a new vigor. She scraped, plastered, sanded and painted—by herself, with no help from him or any-one—the walls of the 118th Street apartment where they still lived. She bought new sheets, pillows, a comforter and towels, mostly in pale shades of ivory, wheat or celadon. She dabbled with ideas for renovations—using river stones to re-cover the bathroom floor, or refacing the kitchen cabi-nets with hammered aluminum, while her mother urged that they move somewhere else entirely. And then the offer came from the firm in San Francisco. So leaving most of their furniture and other household posses-sions behind, they headed out west.

Gabriel had never been to San Francisco before, but when he got there, he was immediately captivated by the lyrical way the streets careened and ascended, the views of the Bay and the Golden Gate Bridge cropping up at odd moments, when he least expected them. He and Penelope moved into a large apartment on the top floor of an elegant, expensive 1930s apartment house in Pacific Heights, thanks to the sizable inheritance she had received when they married.

The building was made of limestone, with intricate metal Art Deco detailing at the top and base. There were steel casement windows that swung out, into the open, unfettered sky. The only thing he didn't like was the persistent rush of traffic from the street below; after living in New York, and on the ground floor besides, he wouldn't have guessed that it would have bothered him so much. Still, he considered the apartment an enviable piece of good fortune and, for a while, it seemed that Penelope felt the same way.

She resumed her decorating schemes, this time on an even grander scale: the walls were hung with textured Japanese rice paper; the floors sanded and bleached a color as pale as the moon. Furniture arrived, ordered from decorator showrooms, and was arranged, rearranged and then shrouded in linen slipcovers of a dozen shades of white. After a while, all the pale tones began to irritate Gabriel.

"I'm tired of all this white. Can't we have some other colors in here?" he asked her peevishly one night, after she had brought home a bunch of ivory silk brocade pillows and arranged them, with careful artlessness, on the couches and chairs. The discarded paper and shopping bags littered the floor until she scooped them up in her arms.

"White *is* a color," Penelope explained patiently, as if to a child. "Why does it bother you so much?" Gabriel had to stop to consider that.

"It's not that I don't like white," he said, trying to be tactful. "I think we need some contrasts, that's all. Some stronger visual interest. Instead of all this uniformity." He felt as if he were talking to a resistant, short-sighted client.

"I don't like contrasts," Penelope said. "They make me, I don't know, nervous." Gabriel looked at her clutching the wrappings to her chest, the intensity of her expression a little unsettling.

"Well, I certainly don't want you to feel nervous," he said, backing down. A few times lately, he had seen Penelope dissolve into pools of luxuriant and sorrowful tears when she felt something he said had wounded her. He had no desire to experience another of these episodes at that moment.

And so it continued. Sheer white drapes that lined the windows; thin, white bone china plates and saucers and cups to fill the cabinets in the kitchen. Gabriel began to feel the need to wear sunglasses inside the apartment, but said nothing. Instead, he went off to work in the cool, damp mornings, and without mentioning it to Penelope, ordered a crimson rug and several tall, faceted blue glass vases for his office.

Then, all at once, the decorating stopped, replaced by the kind of listlessness he had never seen in her before. This, as it turned out, was even more worrisome than her obsessive activity. "Do you think we should buy some furniture for the terrace? If you can wait until Saturday, I'll go with you," said Gabriel in an attempt to rekindle her enthusiasm for something, for anything.

"More furniture?" she said, sounding tired. "Don't we have enough?" It was early evening when they were having this conversation, but she was already undressed and in her bathrobe. It occurred to Gabriel that she might never have taken it off. He wanted to ask her what she did today, but felt it would sound as if he were interrogating her. Which he was. So he tried something else.

"Let's go out to dinner. We haven't been out in a long time." And he realized this was true. Penelope loved to cook and spent a great deal of time and energy on their meals, so they hadn't really wanted to. But now he wondered when she last went out. Or got dressed. It seemed as if she had been in that robe for days. And the apartment had become so dirty. Thick, velvety layers of dust on the windowsills, crumbs on the kitchen counters, newspapers littering the sofa, the table and the floor.

"Can't we order in?" Her eyes looked so big and sad that Gabriel was truly frightened for her.

"Nel," he said, sitting beside her on the whiter-than-white couch. "What's wrong? Can I help?" All at once she was sobbing, wetting the front of his shirt with her tears. Gabriel was mystified, but sat stroking her hair and back, hoping to calm her. Eventually, her crying subsided.

"I want a baby," she declared suddenly, raising her still-wet face from his shirt and staring directly into his eyes. "Let's have a baby. Please, Gabriel." He was a bit surprised, but not totally. They had talked about it before, and laughed together at Ruth's not-so-subtle hints on the subject. But they had been waiting: for Gabriel to finish school, for his career to take off, for the move to be completed. And, secretly, Gabriel knew he had been waiting too for some indefinable thing in Penelope to take shape, take root, take anchor. But maybe she was right, maybe they should have a baby. She seemed to think so.

"If that's what you want . . ." he said hesitantly.

"I do." She stood up, and untied her robe. It fell away easily, and there she was, white, white, white and as desirable as ever.

"What are you doing?" he said with a smile, as he caught her hand and pressed it to his face.

"Getting started, of course."

Pregnancy seemed to give Penelope a sense of purpose again; it had a galvanizing effect, and as Gabriel watched her make lists, buy and read books, attend prenatal exercise and labor and delivery classes, he remembered, as if in a bad dream, the stupefied languor of only weeks before. Now, she was up early and had herself on a strict schedule. She started cooking again, but with a new and sterner eye toward nutrition, and, of course, she shopped both for the baby and the room it would inhabit. Gabriel decided not to worry that everything she bought was white or cream or ivory; so what if she didn't like colors—"They jar my senses" was what she said—as long as she was happy.

And she seemed happy with him again too, happy that he had given her this unborn baby that stretched and distended the formerly slender outlines of her stomach, thighs and hips. She reveled in her new shape, preening naked before the mirror, rubbing her hands over her swollen belly like Aladdin with the magic lamp. "You did this," she said, fairly purring with contentment. "And this too," she added, offering him her breasts, now full and swollen. Everything, thought Gabriel as he reached for her, was going to be just fine.

There was one night, though, when the other part of Penelope, the dark side, as he privately thought of it, emerged again. They were sitting in bed, each propped up by several pillows. Gabriel was reading a magazine; Penelope pored over a book of baby names. They had had all the tests and although they told no one else in the family, they knew that she was carrying a girl. He had seen Penelope's little lists scattered about the apartment, along with her editorializing comments:

Grace—Right idea, but too Christian
Amber—Golden, but overdone these days
Jade—Does this mean a loose woman?
Allegra—Lovely, but now an allergy medicine. Think mucus & sneezing

All at once, she snapped the book shut and dropped it on the floor.

"Is something wrong?" Gabriel asked.

"Useless! That book is useless," she said. "I don't want her to have an ordinary name." Penelope said "ordinary" as if she were saying "loathsome" or "disgusting." "I want her name to be special."

"We'll find something you like," he soothed, preparing to go back to an article that he had been meaning to finish for days. Two people at work had asked what he thought of it; he wanted to be able to tell them.

"But I'll have the final say, right?" There was an edge to her voice that made Gabriel put down the magazine.

"You already have the name, don't you?" She nodded. "But you're worried I won't like it?"

"You have to let me pick it!" she said, sounding more shrill than she had since she became pregnant.

"Why don't you start by telling me what it is?"

"Isis." There was a long pause, while Gabriel tried to absorb the idea of raising a little girl in San Francisco, a little girl with Penelope's white skin and dark hair and eyes who when asked would say, on the playground, at nursery school, in day camp, that her name was Isis. Gabriel didn't think he could stand this, so he closed his eyes, and thought instead of what he could say that wouldn't make his wife burst into tears.

"It's different," he said finally.

"You hate it, don't you?"

"It's very different," he said.

"I know. That's part of what I love about it. No one else will have her name. And of course I love all the associations."

"Associations?"

"To the goddess," she said. "And all the things she stands for: water, the bounty of the earth. Life. I want her to be all that. Have all that." As if a name, that name or any other, would insure anything, thought Gabriel, but he did not say it. Instead, he put the magazine on the nightstand and retrieved the book of baby names from the floor.

"Can I look at this with you?" he asked. "I'm kind of curious."

Several months later, Penelope gave birth to a six-pound, six-ounce baby girl. Gabriel was there during the delivery—"Not like the old days, with the men pacing in the waiting room," Ruth had commented. Of course, Oscar didn't pace, not any of the three times. When Gabriel was being born, he sat up at the nurses' station, raptly listening to the Brahms string sextet that happened to be on the radio; the other two times he was home tending their other child, or children, while the baby was making its way into the world. Not that Ruth minded; there was, after all, something superfluous about husbands during a birth anyway.

But Gabriel was there, with all Penelope's instructions neatly written out in a series of lists that he kept in different pockets. There was the list of breathing patterns, another of baby names, still a third list of people to call as soon as the baby was born. There was also the cool washcloth, the bag of lollipops, the cup of chipped ice on which she could suck, the snapshot of her childhood cocker spaniel, Candy, that was meant to soothe and focus her throughout the birthing process. Gabriel was so worried about

Penelope—what she was going through—that the birth of the child was almost an afterthought. It is only when they handed him the swaddled bundle—the baby felt as warm and reassuring as a loaf of just-baked bread in his arms—that the point of all this strenuous exertion became real. He looked down into her face, which was puffy and rather yellow, and tried to peer into her eyes, which were still swollen and so not fully open. She had a soft coating of dark hair and the most delicately arched eyebrows he had ever seen.

"Hello, Isobel," he said softly.

"You've just named her," said Penelope, capitulating in an instant. "I guess we can't change it now." Isis became her middle name, a compromise that Gabriel at least felt was viable. A middle name was easily dropped or called into service, depending on the mood of its owner. Baby Isobel would have plenty of time to decide what to do.

Ruth flew out to San Francisco almost immediately. Although she and Caroline were quite different in style and substance, they became united in the presence of the baby, the princess, the angel, that was Isobel. Isobel herself seemed quite unaware of all the stir she was causing, and Gabriel supposed that was normal for a baby, though what did he know about it? The women kept him at arm's length; they were utterly focused on the baby and always attending to something she needed: diapering, dressing, cleaning, bathing. They did not want his help; they did not seem to need it. He turned to Penelope, but she too was otherwise occupied. Ruth and Caroline hovered around her, waving her back into a chair or bed when she tried to get up—the obstetrician had been required to sew several stitches, the sight of which made Gabriel avert his eyes—and she was still in some pain. Gabriel felt banished and hurt, which was not what he expected, but was what had happened. He went back to work after a couple of days, and he distinctly felt their relief: he had performed his function and he was not wanted there anymore. He imagined it would be different when his mother and mother-in-law returned to their respective homes.

Then he would get to know his infant daughter. Then he would become reacquainted with his wife.

But the mothers left, and still Penelope kept him away. For one thing, she was nursing Isobel, and that was something Gabriel admittedly could not do. When she held the baby to her taut and abundant breasts, a drugged, peaceful look settled on her face, as if she and the child had entered some kind of private trance that excluded him entirely. She would not let him hold the baby for more than a minute before she demanded her back and she insisted on attending to all of Isobel's incessant physical needs herself—the soiled diapers, spit-up cloths that needed replacements, tiny ears and nostrils that required irrigating. She asked him only to do the more peripheral chores: shop for food, tidy the apartment or fold the organic cotton diapers, for she would not allow the disposable kind next to Isobel's skin. Eventually, they hired someone to clean the apartment, since Penelope no longer had the inclination or the time; after that, Gabriel felt he had nothing at all to do in his own home. His sense of exclusion continued to grow, though no one else seemed to notice.

Still, the baby appeared to thrive. From his second-class position, Gabriel could see her fill out, losing the yellow and puffy look that followed her birth. Her eyes remained a clear, true blue, and her skin was as creamy and fine as Penelope's. She gurgled, she kicked, she reached, she grabbed. But Gabriel watched all of this as if from a distance, as if Penelope and Isobel were someone else's wife and child; lovely, but not his. And before she had turned a year old, she was taken aboard the airplane to New York City, where she spent her first Thanksgiving with her grandparents, Ruth and Oscar, and where her father fell head over heels in love with a skinny young ballet dancer by the name of Ginny Valentine.

OSCAR

scar was aware that something terrible happened during the Thanksgiving dinner that Ruth had so painstakingly prepared, and to which they had both looked forward—in different ways, for different reasons—for weeks. He didn't know what the something was, only that Ruth's face, which just moments ago was so animated, now looked entirely different. Drained of color, contracted into a worried, tense scowl, it seemed a different face entirely, one that was older, and more desolate than he would have believed possible.

No one else seemed to have noticed this change when she came back into the room, still holding Isobel. The others were talking, arguing about something. Well, at least William was not playing the piano, not yet anyway, and Oscar didn't have to listen to Rodgers and Hammerstein or, worse, Stephen Sondheim. Penelope immediately reached for the baby and Ruth handed her over with a quick, perfunctory gesture that by itself would have made Oscar suspect something. But that face. How was it that no one else saw it?

He stared hard, trying to catch her eye, but she seemed determined not to let this happen and busied herself with plates and cups of coffee. Oscar kept watching, though, and when she headed for the kitchen, he found it easy enough to follow her without anyone noticing anything. "Ruth," he said quietly when they were alone. "What's the matter?"

"I can't tell you now," she said in an urgent whisper, and her face looked as if it were in danger of breaking apart entirely. "Oscar, please, go back to the other room." So he did, rather sheepishly, carrying out a fistful of spoons that he dropped to the table with a clatter. No one paid attention.

"I'm ready for some music," said Ruth's sister, Molly, loudly. Good old Molly, thought Oscar. Depend on her to get those ivories tinkling. For the first time he could remember, he was actually grateful for the way they all clustered around William, calling out the names of songs, and singing them—cheerful, off-key and with the wrong words, no doubt—as he played. Oscar sat down heavily on a chair, wondering how this day got ruined—for ruined it surely was—and how he would get through the rest of it. His eyes roamed around the room, looking for solace in the faces of his family. William, bent over the piano, happy to be the center of attention; Betsy, anxiously biting her lip as she watched him; Ben with his new bride; the baby Isobel held by her beautiful mother. His cousin Henry, whom he had always liked, and whom he hadn't seen in years. Molly, now a widow, and her daughter, the one who caused her mother so much grief when she shaved her head that summer they all took the house together on Cape Cod. The daughter's roommate, though Oscar could not remember her name. Suddenly, he was aware that something was missing from this picture. Gabriel was not in the room. And neither was Ginny. But before he could add the two and two that inevitably made four, Ruth returned.

"Who wants dessert?" she called out. She had reclaimed herself in some way, Oscar could see that as she set out the apple and pecan pies, the bowl of whipped cream. There was fresh lipstick coating her mouth and some pinkish tint in her cheeks. Only her eyes—steely, ever so slightly crazed, and much too bright, as if unshed tears were making them glitter—gave her away.

"Oh, I do," said Molly, who was out of her seat and moving toward the table.

"Who said dessert?" Oscar glanced over and saw his beloved Ginny walk back into the room, followed by an abashed-looking Gabriel. Ginny and Gabriel? It wasn't possible. Oscar felt sick even thinking about it.

Since that ecstatic, guilt-provoking night in her arms, Oscar had made love to Ginny only one other time. This took place in her laundry-littered apartment—had she never heard of a hamper?—on sheets that probably hadn't been changed in a month. He had insisted on seeing her home after a performance, and she had, rather halfheartedly, he could tell, invited him up. As soon as they were alone and the door was locked, he grabbed her in an insistent, clumsy embrace that seemed to embarrass more than arouse either of them.

"Oh, Oscar!" She laughed, but she hardly looked pleased. Oscar knew he was making an ass of himself, but he couldn't help it, and he began to kiss her face and neck until finally she said, "All right, all right. Let's at least go lie down somewhere we can be comfortable." So they did, and it was all over in minutes, and she seemed glad of that and much more interested in talking about *The Nutcracker,* which was standard winter fare for the company, and which they would start performing very soon.

"I think I may be getting a new part," she confided. "Even though the season has started." She was still naked as she said this, knees drawn to her chest and slender arms wrapped around them. *The Nutcracker,* for God's sake. Oscar had been playing that saccharine score for so many years, the thought of it made his teeth ache. But he said nothing, just watched and drank in the scent, the sound, the sight of her. She talked on, cheerful and confident, apparently oblivious to his distress. She seemed ready for him to leave and it was only when he got to the door that something seemed to open in her and she reached out to squeeze his shoulder.

"Good night, Oscar," she said. "I love you." Then the door gently closed. Love you! Oscar was astonished. What could she mean by this?

Why then had she fairly pushed him out of the apartment? He stood there for a long while, staring at the closed door.

Though he knew it was hopeless, Oscar began to behave like a besotted suitor—he sent pale yellow roses on long stems to the dressing room after a performance, bought her expensive imported chocolates (he was certain she would like these) and a pair of garnet and pearl earrings (these he was less sure of, but wanted to buy them anyway)—trying to win an elusive lover. Ginny never seemed to take any of his offerings seriously, and after a while, he stopped. He felt wounded and foolish, but her lack of interest was all too clear and Oscar wouldn't bring himself to beg, though he was tempted to, many times.

Soon, they reverted to their former relationship, the one that seemed to resemble that of a kindly, generous uncle with his fond and grateful niece. Once they were no longer lovers, Ginny was indeed again grateful for all his help: she seemed more genuinely pleased by his gift of a huge shrink-wrapped package of individual cartons of iced tea that he had seen in the window of D'Agostino's and which reminded him of her ("Oh, you remembered that I really am a southern girl at heart! I love iced tea!") than by the chocolates or the earrings. For days after that, she kept one or two of the little cartons in her ballet bag, and when she pulled out the straw and stuck it in, she raised it toward him, as if in a toast. Still, Oscar would make do with whatever crumbs she offered: he was that hungry for her.

The rest of the day passed at an infuriatingly slow pace. Fortunately, William's singing and dessert wine brought by Ben and his wife made the assembled group merry and not all that discerning. Oscar kept looking at his son and at Ginny, searching for evidence. And he found it. Just a slight, subtle thing that he wouldn't have noticed had he not been looking so hard. But there it was, a glance that was at once shy and bold, that passed between them, and suddenly Oscar understood what it was that Ruth had seen.

Gabriel and Ginny. So that *was* it. Oscar was consumed by a feeling of jealousy and humiliation unlike any he had ever felt before. Not only had Gabriel married a beautiful and rich woman, now he had somehow managed to steal the one girl in all those years for whom Oscar had actually risked his own marriage. Goddamn him.

The wretched day finally drew to a close. Coats were fetched from the bedroom, hugs and kisses were exchanged at the apartment's door, parcels of food pressed into willing hands. William's wife offered to stay late and help clean up, but Ruth shooed them out. Oscar knew this too was a sign: ordinarily, Ruth would have leaped at the chance to spend more time with one of her daughters-in-law. He knew that she felt hurt that neither of these young women, for whatever reasons, had become close to her. Maybe Ben's new bride would be different. Just then, Oscar didn't feel too hopeful about anything. He tugged at the belt that encircled his expanding waistline, and braced himself for the storm that he knew would break as soon as he was alone with his wife.

But when the last guest was gone, and the door clicked shut for the final time, Ruth was suddenly nowhere to be found. Oscar looked around the dining room. The plates were still on the table; the cups filled with the dregs of cold coffee hadn't been touched. He moved to the kitchen, calling her name. He saw the large white ironstone platter with its turkey carcass still sat on the counter; pots of various sizes covered all the burners of the stove. There was a large sticky patch on the floor—gravy? wine?—that no one had wiped. And still no Ruth. He backed out of the kitchen and headed toward their bedroom, the very one he had defiled with Ginny's presence, but that too was empty. He was about to really worry, to panic even, when, all at once, he heard her voice—low and dull—calling out, "Oscar. I'm in here."

Oscar hurried to the back bedroom, now the guest room. Ruth was lying stretched out on the twin bed, one of the boys' old and battered teddy bears cradled in her arms. She stared up at the ceiling, and the expression on her face made Oscar pause. He did not feel wanted in this room, and he remained on the threshold until there was a sign from her that he was welcome.

"I saw them kissing. Right in here. Not on the bed, thank God—standing up." Oscar did not have to ask who she was talking about. He wanted to say he was sorry. But then he would have to tell Ruth all about Ginny, and he was not ready to do that. "Oscar, she frightens me. It's as if she was born without something—a heart, a conscience, I don't know. But I do know she's going to ruin Gabriel's life. And when she does, Penelope isn't going to be as understanding as I am." Oscar stood very still as an ugly flush that started somewhere on his neck slowly rose to his face. Ruth shook her head, and the tears she had struggled to hold back seeped from the corners of her eyes. "Did you really think," she said, her voice breaking only slightly, "that I didn't know you were sleeping with her?"

"Only twice!" he asserted, feeling dumb and ashamed. "And if you knew how sorry I was, how sorry I am—"

"Not as sorry as you're going to be," said Ruth. "Not as sorry as we're all going to be. Because I hope you understand that this is happening to *all* of us." She pulled herself up and looked at him steadily. "You'd better come in and sit down. There are some things we ought to talk about. If Penelope finds out . . ." She didn't need to finish the sentence. Even without knowing all the details, Oscar could guess at the fragility of his son's wife. He knew the story about his granddaughter's name—thank God Gabriel had prevailed on that—and the rejected baby clothes. Today he had seen how oblivious to everyone Penelope seemed, everyone except Isobel, of course. And then there was the eating. Penelope was a vegetarian, and Ruth was happy to prepare a soy casserole and to make sure there were lots of vegetable dishes for her. But today she refused cooked food altogether. "It's too greasy or something," she explained to Ruth. "I don't know. It seems fermented or rotten to me. Do you have any raw vegetables?" Oscar, who watched all this, knew that Ruth was hurt, but she graciously tried to hide it.

"I could grate you some carrots," Ruth said. "And some cabbage. Oh, I also have some plain lettuce left from the salad."

"Cabbage! No cabbage, please. But the lettuce and raw carrots would be perfect," said Penelope.

"What about the baby?" Ruth had asked. "Can she have some of the rice pilaf? Or the cooked carrots? She loved how I made them when I came out to visit you."

"No, no, that's all right," said Penelope. "I brought food for her. She'll just eat what Mommy brings," she said, and nuzzled Isobel's nose with her own.

"*What can* we do?" Oscar asked Ruth, feeling helpless. He was ashamed of asking Ruth this; he realized that he was the one who had brought Ginny into their lives. Why should his wife help him now?

"I'm not really sure," Ruth said slowly. "But we ought to do something."

"How much longer are they going to be on the East Coast?" Oscar asked.

"Only a couple of days. They're making it short this year."

"Thank God for small blessings," he murmured.

"We should see them before they go. I told Penelope we'd go up to Greenwich for the day. They're staying with Caroline."

"When?"

"Tomorrow. I think you should find a way to be alone with Gabriel. Tell him to stay away from Ginny."

"Why should he listen to me?" Oscar said. "He never has before."

That night, Oscar lay stiffly next to Ruth, not daring to touch her, even in the most casual way. Still, he was keenly aware of her presence next to him in the dark. He was sure that she was awake too. He wanted to talk to her—about Gabriel, about Penelope and, most of all, about Ginny. But how to begin? Then there was a loud, long sigh from Ruth. Oscar opened his mouth and said her name very softly.

"I'm here," she said. "What is it?"

"I wanted to talk to you—"

"About her? Ginny?"

"Yes, yes, about Ginny," said Oscar, relieved that she would listen, that she hadn't stopped her ears or thrown him out or barred the doors.

"You will," she said calmly. "You'll tell me everything. But not now. For one thing, I don't think I can hear it yet. And we have to think about Gabriel and Penelope. That's the most important thing. More important than you and me. Because we've done our job. Our children are grown. But Isobel . . ." Oscar reached over to take her hand. She didn't return the pressure, but she didn't withdraw her hand either. "Promise me you'll talk to him tomorrow," said Ruth. "Promise you'll do everything you can."

The next day was cold and clear. Oscar and Ruth took a taxi to Grand Central Terminal and from there the train to Greenwich, Connecticut. Oscar looked out the window at the bare trees, the bright sky, the landscape that was patched and brown. He liked the brief glimpses of the passing houses and liked to imagine the lives they might contain. It took his mind off his own life, and the mess he had made of it. He thought of Ginny too, and although he would be ashamed to have admitted it, he knew that he still wanted her.

Caroline met them at the train station; Penelope and Gabriel had slept late and were still at the house with Isobel. "Penelope seems a little tired to me," said Caroline. "I don't think she's getting enough rest."

"Well, she's still nursing," Ruth said sympathetically.

"I know," said Caroline. "That's the problem. Time to wean that baby if you ask me. But of course Penelope doesn't want my advice. She never did."

Penelope's mother lived in a big old house right on the shore of Long

Island Sound. The windows all along one side overlooked the water. It was the house in which Penelope had grown up, and the one in which her father had died. She and Caroline were somewhat indifferent to its grandeur. Inside, it had the kind of shabby, genteel elegance Oscar associated with old WASPs who had plenty of money but didn't care to advertise it. The rooms needed painting and the chintz slipcovers were faded by the sun. Caroline kept several cats, and bits of their shed fur could be seen in the corners and under the Chippendale furniture. In fact, Oscar saw one cat snoozing on a sofa, and discovered another sleeping on the dining room chair where Caroline had just told him to sit.

"Go on now," said Caroline, shaking the chair a bit and waking the cat, who blinked at her several times before jumping to the floor and walking off with an indignant twitch of its tail. Then they all sat down to lunch, where Oscar had the chance to observe his son and daughter-in-law. Gabriel was more relaxed today. He tilted his chair back from the table—how many times had Ruth chided him for this in the past?—or draped his arm protectively around the back of Penelope's seat. Penelope and Ruth were absorbed with Isobel, who was seated in her high chair, so Gabriel advised Caroline about some work she was considering doing on the house, though privately Oscar suspected that she would never embark upon this or any other renovation project, and was just finding a way to be polite to her son-in-law. After the meal, when Penelope had gone upstairs to nurse Isobel and put her down for a nap, Oscar rose from the table and trying to sound casual said, "Gabriel. I'm stuffed. Let's go take a walk on the beach."

"All right," Gabriel agreed, and went to get their coats. Oscar felt Ruth looking at him, but he didn't trust himself to look back.

The beach on which they walked was deserted on this November day and the wind stronger than it was in the city. The sand down by the water was packed hard and damp from the receding tide and it was along this sand that Gabriel strode quickly and Oscar—older, heavier—was forced to struggle to keep up.

Oscar remembered the beach in another, more benign season: he and Gabriel walked here on the day of Gabriel's wedding. The party was winding down; still wearing their formal clothes, father and son ducked out for a short stroll along the rippled and fragrant shoreline. Oscar recalled how happy Gabriel seemed that day, with the breeze blowing his tie back and ruffling his hair. What had happened since then to bring Gabriel to this moment?

"You'll have to slow down just a bit," Oscar finally said, panting slightly.

"Sorry, Dad," said Gabriel, immediately slowing his pace. "I wasn't thinking. Or I mean I was thinking. But not about walking."

"What were you thinking, then?" Oscar asked. His heart was beating very quickly in his chest. Was it the exertion, or was he that nervous about what was to take place?

"You know." He stopped and looked at Oscar then. "I'm sure Mom told you about yesterday."

"She did." Oscar started moving again and Gabriel followed along.

"Look, it's nothing I planned or intended. I mean, why would I even look at anyone else with Penelope around, right? But that girl. There's something about that girl."

"I know," said Oscar, and without meaning to, he sighed deeply. There was an uncomfortable pause in which Gabriel tried to assimilate the significance of that sigh.

"Are you saying that you and Ginny . . . ?"

"Yes" was the only thing Oscar could say. This had to be the worst, most painful conversation he had ever had with his son, and it had scarcely even begun. There was a momentary silence in which they came to a group of rocks that stretched out into the Sound; far out at the tip the rocks were wet and black, but here near the shore they were gray and dry enough for sitting. Oscar eased himself onto one of them and waited.

"Jesus Christ!" said Gabriel. He did not sit, but continued to stand, glaring down at Oscar. "How could you?"

"How could I? Well, let me ask you the same question. How could you?" said Oscar, feeling the need to reassert himself; even at this late and wholly compromised juncture, he was still the father, the authority, the one in charge. He stood up.

"What about Mom? Does she know about this?"

"Not that it's any of your business but, yes, she does."

"Jesus Christ," Gabriel repeated, but this time more softly, almost like an entreaty.

"Look, Gabriel, you're a grown man now. It's not my place to tell you what to do. But I promised your mother I would talk to you. Warn you. Think about what you're doing. About what it will mean to Penelope if she finds out."

"You haven't told her, have you?"

"No, of course not. But someone always finds out, don't they?"

"You should know," Gabriel said bitterly. Oscar said nothing, for he knew he deserved this. "Poor Mom," he added.

"Your mother is special," Oscar said. "She takes a broader view of things than most people." He took a deep breath to steel himself. "Penelope isn't like her."

"And I'm not like you!" Gabriel shot back, and then he was gone, striding once more down the shoreline at his angry, young man's pace. Oscar sat back down on the rock; only after he was seated did he realize that the rock was now wet, drenched by a cold, foamy wave that had splashed over it. He stared out at the wide expanse of water, wondering what in the world he would tell Ruth when she asked how this conversation had gone.

GINNY

In December, the ballet company would start dancing *The Nutcracker*
again. Ginny couldn't wait. They did it last year, of course—the company danced it every year in time for Christmas—and she had been so
excited that during her first performance, she anticipated her cue and
came onstage a full sixteen beats early. The group of dancers already
there had to try very hard not to laugh out loud. Ginny knew she must
have looked ridiculous prancing around the outside of the stage, but she
had tried to make the best of the situation. Later, Erik didn't even yell at
her. He seemed to understand how thrilling it was to perform to live music when all you were used to was the canned stuff.

But it wasn't just the music. Ginny believed *The Nutcracker* was part of
her destiny. Rita used to take her to see it when she was very small. She remembered how they sold souvenir books and other trinkets in the lobby
of the theater, and, after some pestering, Rita had bought her a tiny silver
pin shaped like a pair of pointe shoes. Ginny wore that pin for years, dur-

ing ballet classes and the performances of the one-act *Nutcracker* that Wes staged for the winter recital. One year, Ginny was the little girl, Marie. Another time she was a snowflake and the best of all was when she danced Dewdrop. Rita sewed the costume herself. The skirt was net and over it were layers of filmy, silver material that lifted and floated like petals. The top was an iridescent silver and pink fabric, and the whole neckline was studded with rhinestones. Ginny was dazzled—her mama had outdone herself. Most of the other girls, even the rich ones, went to the costume shop over in the strip mall just outside of town. Rita and Ginny tried going there too, but Rita fingered the crudely made satin and rickrack numbers with disdain. "Pretty ugly and pretty apt to stay that way," was her verdict, and instead they went to a sewing shop where the fabric came from France and Italy. Rita bought everything she needed—trim, material, silver thread and bobbins—and when they went home, she pulled out her portable Singer sewing machine from the bedroom closet and set it out on the pink-and-white-checked plastic tablecloth that covered the kitchen table. "You'd better strip," she told Ginny, a mouth full of pins muffling her speech, "I'm going to have to fit you."

When Rita had finished, Ginny thought the result looked terrific. And it did: she had the pictures to prove it. The best one showed her in an arabesque, arms raised high in front, and her leg even higher in the back. You'd never guess that she was an amateur from looking at that picture. Even then, she looked like the real thing. She wore the little pin right at the place where the neckline of the costume dipped low. Although you couldn't see it what with all those glittery stones, Ginny knew it was there. Funny how she managed to lose it somehow; she couldn't say where it had gone to, but from time to time, she wished she had it back. It was a kind of charm, she thought, a reminder of the promises you made to yourself, the ones that were the hardest and the most important of all to keep.

The Nutcracker was also the first ballet Ginny learned when she joined the company. The production here was the best she had ever seen. There was a part in which the Christmas tree in Marie's parlor started growing out of the floor until it finally took up the whole height of the stage. The parlor window grew large too, and so did the doll bed where the wounded Nutcracker slept. The children in the audience always cheered and whooped when that happened. It was the only time Ginny didn't mind the noise because she knew that it was impossible to be quiet during a performance of *Nutcracker*. Then there were those iridescent white squares— they shimmered pink, blue, lilac and gold under the brightness of the stage lights—that were used as snowflakes at the end of act one. Later, they turned up everywhere: in her hair, in the bodice of her costume, at the bottom of her pointe shoes. And there were stray ones that appeared in the dressing room or on the stage for months afterward. Ginny kept them all in an envelope somewhere in her apartment. She wanted to find that envelope soon because she was going to add some more this year. And these snowflakes would be extra-special, because this was the first year that she was going to dance a solo. A solo in *The Nutcracker*. She knew it for a fact—Erik told her so himself.

He called her into his office to give her the news. Erik Holtz was compact and tightly muscled, with extremely dark eyes, a beak of a nose and a few lines around his mouth that looked as if they had been etched with a blade. He wore the black outfit that day—black sweatshirt, tight black jeans, black leather sneakers—as opposed to the faded blue jeans and Knicks jersey he wore during rehearsals. On one wrist was a complicated, expensive-looking watch; on the other, a large turquoise cuff. Ginny knew that lots of girls in the company—and not just the ones in the corps de ballet, either—had a crush on him. But not her.

"I'm going to try you out in a solo," he said, getting right to the point. "Coffee. The Arabian dance. Think you can handle it?" Did she think she could handle it? Was he kidding? But Ginny tried to remember what Mama might have wanted her to say and she answered him as nicely as she could. Coffee was one of the variations that came near the end of the ballet, when Marie and the Prince were being offered treats from all over the world. Seated on a pair of golden thrones, they watched the dances, each of which represented some tasty thing or other. The whole stage looked like a sweet shop gone wild—giant dishes of ice cream studded with gumdrops; pillars made of peppermint canes; enormous cakes and fruit tarts everywhere. The stage was backlit with a deep pink light, and, for once, Ginny didn't object to the color.

There was a Chinese dance that represented Tea; a Spanish dance that represented Hot Chocolate. Her dance—and Ginny thought of it that way already—was Coffee, and it was inspired by traditional Middle Eastern forms, like belly dancing. She was so giddy at the thought that she scarcely heard the rest of what Erik was saying, though she caught some bits of it like "... check the bulletin board for the rehearsal schedule. And you'll have to visit the costume shop for a fitting ..." But mostly the refrain running through her head sang, "Coffee, coffee, coffee."

After that, Ginny was wrapped up in learning the new part. Not that it was long—she would be on the stage for a matter of minutes—but she would be dancing alone on the stage of the New York State Theater for the very first time. She went to the dance library and got video tapes of past performances. She wanted to see how the variation had been danced before, but, in her heart, she knew how she wanted it to look. Aromatic and sensual, with a slightly bitter undertone that was the true taste of the coffee bean itself.

She had so many things to think about. There was a new rehearsal schedule, private coaching from one of the soloists, plus the costume fittings that had to be squeezed in somehow. All of the ballet company's costumes were still cut and sewn by hand. Ginny thought of Mama, and how hard she had worked just making that one. It reminded her not to annoy Madame Dubrovska, the costume mistress, who was always chastising the dancers for tearing, sweating in and otherwise destroying the exquisitely wrought creations that were her life. Lord help you if you dumped a tutu on the floor during a particularly quick change. Madame would go on about it for weeks, bringing it up whenever she saw you in the elevators or hallways.

Ginny had looked forward to Thanksgiving, anticipating how she could safely spend a day with Oscar then. She had tried to discourage him without actually telling him that the sexual thing between them was over. It wasn't that she didn't feel affection for him. But sex upset things too much.

It made her the one with all the power, and she didn't like it. She liked things the way they had been. Oscar had been like a father, the father she never knew but used to invent sometimes: in control, solid, wise, like Robert Young in the old reruns of *Father Knows Best*. She missed that. So she tried to bring them back to where they had been before, even though she could see it wasn't working. At least not for him.

Instead, he had begun courting her again, and how embarrassing was *that*. He sent expensive flowers to a communal dressing room where everyone knew your business, right down to the brand of tampons and deodorant you used. All the other dancers wanted to know who her secret admirer was; she couldn't get them to stop bothering her, so she finally said it was one of those guys—and there was always a little cluster of them at the stage door—who hung around hoping to talk to or maybe even arrange a date with a dancer. Someone once told her that one of the principals had met her husband this way. Anyway, the story seemed to work. But when the chocolates arrived and, after that, the earrings, the questions started all over again. The iced tea was a much better present; everyone thought it came from her mother, and in fact it was just the sort of thing that Rita would have sent. Ginny made sure to let him know just how much she appreciated the tea.

But Thanksgiving would be different. Since there was absolutely no chance of their being alone, she wouldn't have to worry about things getting out of hand. But, oh, how wrong she turned out to be. Things certainly did get out of hand. Only the problem wasn't Oscar. It was his son Gabriel, incredible, beautiful, she-wanted-him-like-she'd-never-wanted-anyone-in-her-life Gabriel.

This was a shock to Ginny, because even though she could certainly appreciate good looks from an aesthetic point of view—she was a dancer, after all, and dancers lived for beauty—her appreciation never translated into her wanting to kiss, hug, fondle or get naked with a person just because they were good-looking. Now Wes was quite handsome, but he was the one who pursued her—she could have taken the sex or left it. Of course her being with Oscar had nothing to do with lust. At least not with hers. And when she heard the girls go on about Erik, she could only wonder, because though she admired him as a teacher and choreographer, the thought of having sex with him left her cold as a corpse.

Ginny had always thought of herself as being immune to that sort of thing. Not to sex, because sex felt good. But so did taking a long, hot shower after a grueling rehearsal or eating dinner when you were starving. Romance—all that starry-eyed stuff—seemed beside the point to her. Like the song said, What's love got to do with it? She was too busy being in love with dancing to be in love with anyone else. But that was before she met Gabriel.

When she first saw him, he was standing in the middle of Oscar's living room next to his wife. Ginny couldn't stop staring, even though she could hear her mother's voice saying, "Virginia, if you leave your mouth open for long enough, you may find a fly sunbathing on your tongue."

Finally, Ginny had the presence of mind to shut her mouth, though she kept staring. She stared while they took off their coats—Penelope's was smooth and white, how in the Lord's name did she keep it clean?— and handed them to Ruth. Stared while they hugged and kissed their relatives and in-laws. Stared while Penelope sat down on the sofa, hauled out one of her ample breasts—you could certainly tell she wasn't a ballet dancer—and the baby, she couldn't think of her name, began to nurse. Ginny was made uncomfortable by that, so she turned back to Gabriel.

He was tall, like Oscar, with Oscar's unusual blue-green eyes, only his were much clearer and brighter-looking. His hair was black and curled up a little around his ears and collar; Ginny saw that it was threaded ever so slightly with gray, but to her, the gray glinted like silver. She watched his body carefully; dancers always looked at bodies, and Gabriel's was lean and fit. Maybe he jogged or lifted weights. He had a full bottom lip and a slight space between his two front teeth and she began imagining, to her own surprise, how delicious it would be to touch her tongue against that opening, when there he was, pressing his hand into hers.

"I'm Gabriel. Oscar's son," he said. Ginny liked his voice. It was low, but somehow smooth too.

"Virginia," she said, demure as you please. "Virginia Valentine."

"From City Ballet? Mom told me you were coming. Is this your first winter in New York?"

And so it started innocently enough, party chatter that moved from the hallway to the living room to the dining room and back again. No one else seemed to bother about them. Penelope was totally absorbed by the baby, as were the older women. The cousins and the other brothers had each other. Gabriel and Ginny were free to talk, and all the while, she kept looking at his mouth, his hands, his shoulders. Though she couldn't help her response, she was nonetheless shamed by it. He was married after all. Then he asked if she had ever been to the apartment before.

"Only once," she lied. "Your father invited me for dinner."

"Then you've never seen the rest of it?"

"Never."

"Come on, then. I'll show you where I slept. I grew up here, you know."

"You did?" she asked, hardly caring about that, but instead thinking, We're going to be alone together. They walked down the hallway toward a bedroom—actually, she remembered it quite well, because it was where Oscar had put her to sleep on that other night she had been there, the night nobody knew about—and Gabriel opened the door. Here was the narrow bed, here was the teddy bear. And, yes, here was Gabriel—thank you, sweet Jesus!—pulling her into his arms and kissing her as if he would never stop. They stood like that, arms around each other, kissing, until the door must have opened—neither of them heard it—and there was Ruth and the baby gesturing toward Gabriel.

Of course, the rest of the afternoon was ruined. Ginny didn't trust herself to look at Gabriel and she could only glance—for a few embarrassed seconds—at Ruth. Ginny felt awful when she saw the older woman's glittering eyes, her pained mouth. But he kissed me, she wanted to tell her, to tell all of them.

When she was finally able to leave, she forced herself to say a cheery good-bye to everyone in the room. Then she turned to Ruth.

"Thank you so much for inviting me," she said. On impulse, Ginny hugged her. Though she knew Ruth wouldn't believe it, Ginny was sorry for what she had seen, sorry for having hurt her. The older woman went rigid in Ginny's arms but was too stunned to push her away.

"Thank you for coming," Ruth managed to get out. Ginny left. From the hallway where she waited for the elevator, she could hear more good-byes; she must have started the exodus. She didn't want to have to talk to any of the other guests in the elevator, so she found her way to the stairwell and hurried down.

Ginny walked back to her apartment slowly, trying to make sense of the strangest afternoon of her life. Could this really be her, Virginia Louise Valentine, consumed by desire for a man she had just met? A man who was the son of the man she had just stopped sleeping with? Before, whatever passion there was in her had been reserved for her dancing; she burned to execute entrechats quatre as sharp as knives in the air, arabesques that grazed the sky. She understood that being a classical ballet dancer was rigorous and awful enough that in order to even hope to succeed, she had to want it more than anything else under the sun. And she had. Now she wanted Gabriel with what felt like an equal intensity. It scared her.

Soon she reached her street, but instead of heading into the building, she kept walking. West End Avenue was quiet on this holiday afternoon, with the dark just starting to settle in. The warmth had seeped from the air when the sun set, and her hands felt cold, so she shoved them down deep into her pockets. That's when she felt it: the smooth, folded bit of paper. She pulled it out and found a small white square that hadn't been there when she had left her apartment. She opened the note quickly, and read the words again and again:

I'm leaving New York in a couple of days but will be back soon. Will you see me?
Gabriel

Did he need to ask? It all slipped away then: Ruth's face, Oscar's gloom, Penelope, the baby. She knew it was wrong, but she also knew she couldn't help it. Gabriel wanted to see her again and Lord she wanted to see him.

Ginny looked left and right; only a handful of other people were in the street. Although she hadn't had class that morning, hadn't warmed up at all, she did a leap—a large, joy-filled, I'm-in-love kind of leap—across the empty pavement. It felt so good she did another and another until the few pedestrians who were out began to stare and only then could she bring herself to stop.

RUTH

B*oys were* a stretch: to understand, to raise, to love. Ruth knew, because she had raised three. Of course they weren't so difficult at first. In the beginning, they were just generic babies, pressing their faces into your collarbone, beating their tiny feet gleefully in the air when you leaned over to diaper them. It was only later, like on that morning when your scarcely three-year-old son said, "Mommy, look at that big truck!" and you marveled, knowing with utter certainty that you had never pointed out a truck, big or otherwise, to him or anyone else. That's when it started.

Ruth remembered taking the boys to visit the Botanic Garden in Brooklyn, where her father so often had taken her and Molly. She was in her maternal element, gesturing eagerly to the flowers, the gracefully arching trees, the family of ducks that walked sedately around the pond scavenging for scraps of bread left behind by visitors. Did her sons listen? Not at all. Instead, all three, even Gabriel, the most sensitive, were mesmerized by the sight of a flannel-shirted construction worker—the area around the pond was being repaved—with his loud, pounding jackhammer. That's all they remembered of the day. Ruth knew because she asked them all on the long subway ride home what they liked best about what they had seen. "The cool guy with the jackhammer," William said immediately.

"What else besides that?" she prompted. William looked at his brothers and then said, "What else was there?"

Gabriel was the easiest. He spent a lot of time practicing the violin, and when he didn't do that, he would paint or draw for long stretches of time. Ruth still had a large box of his artwork: careful, linear renditions of himself, his family, their apartment, the small violin with which he sought to please his father. But William was something else again. Baseball was like a fever that overtook him when he was about seven. Ruth and Oscar were mystified, because they knew he hadn't caught it from them. No, it seemed to happen all of a sudden. He'd come in from playing in Riverside Park with the Wycoffs—Lenny and Marc, who lived two floors below—and announced that he wanted to join one of the local Little League teams.

"You do?" asked Oscar, unable to keep the amazement out of his voice. "Why?"

"Because it's fun, Dad," said William, patronizing even at four feet high. Oscar looked at Ruth. She shrugged. Certainly this wasn't going to be her area of expertise. But it didn't seem that it would be Oscar's either. Oscar had never joined bat to ball in his life—not only did he lack the interest, he had always worried about injuring his hands or arms—and he had turned out all right. So why should it be any different for his sons? Particularly when they had the advantage of having him—a talented classical musician—for their father. In the end, Ruth asked Lenny and Marc's father where they played baseball; arrangements were made, and soon William was on the team. He spent long hours on the park's baseball diamonds, wielding the leather mitt that she eventually bought him and yelling, "Put 'er there, put 'er RIGHT there!" Where had he learned to talk like that?

Baseball was followed by soccer, basketball and later—it scared her still to think of it—football. Of course whatever William did, Ben had to do as well, and so all their closets and the spaces beneath the boys' beds became repositories for the bats—wooden and aluminum—the leather gloves of brown and black, the helmets, balls, mouth guards, shin guards, pucks, sticks and whatever else they had cajoled Ruth into buying.

Gabriel stood apart from all this activity. Team sports held little appeal for him, though, oddly enough, he liked the baseball cards William and Ben brought home. Gabriel was the one who sorted and organized them into neat, clearly labeled albums, albums that were probably still in the closet of that back bedroom that was once his. He did like jogging in Central Park, and he very much enjoyed playing tennis. Ruth had loved watching him sweep across the court with his particular, loping gait, the racquet an extension of his easy, fluid gesture. He looked as poised as, well as a ballet dancer, though she was careful never to make this comparison in front of Oscar. Those were the bitter ballet years, as she called them, when she knew that Oscar hated the dancing, the performances, the very professional life he had chosen. The idea that his son was likened to one of *them* would not have appealed to him.

So many of the things Ruth's sons loved as boys still remained a mystery to her. Not that she didn't love her boys deeply, but it was a love that she learned, not one that came naturally. Their interests, their pursuits, their very ways of being confused, even maddened her. The wet towel snapping, the marathon burping contests, the way everything— stuffed animals, house slippers, forks—became projectile objects in their hands.

Then there were their friends, the procession of boys that traipsed into Ruth's apartment with their big feet. They talked, laughed, argued, punched each other on the arms or messed up each other's hair. Soon enough they made themselves right at home, putting their sneakers up on the furniture, helping themselves from the refrigerator. At times, Ruth missed having her sons at home with her, but she never missed their friends.

Her sister, Molly, had girls. Gwen and Robin, roughly the same ages as

Gabriel and William. Ruth envied her those girls. Never mind about the summer that Gwen shaved her head or the fact that she currently had both eyebrows, a nostril and her navel pierced, or that Robin, who majored in film, now made the most graphically explicit documentaries about people's sexual habits and proclivities that she insisted on inviting members of the family over to preview. "You just think the grass is greener," Molly used to say. "You should only know."

Still, when Molly's daughters were little and she brought them over at Hanukkah or Pesach in their matching velvet dresses, white tights and black patent leather Mary Janes, Ruth couldn't help but wish that they were hers. One afternoon, she let them play with the miniature Limoges tea service that had belonged to her grandmother Lilli. Ruth knelt down on the floor to fill the tiny, hand-painted cups with real tea, the creamer with cream and the sugar bowl with crystals she had ground down with a rolling pin and two sheets of waxed paper.

"It's so much fun here!" said Gwen, drinking the now-cold tea. "Our mommy never plays with us like this."

"That's because she's your mother," Ruth said, glad her sister was not hearing this. "Mommies are so busy they don't always have time to play. But aunts do."

"Our mom never has time to play." This from Robin, who was draping a dish towel over a hat box—another memento from Lilli—to form a table. "Aunt Ruth, next time can we bring over our Barbie dolls? Please?"

Of course Ruth got over this in time. Her sons were wonderful boys. And as they grew up and became interested in girls, she began to envision a different scenario, one in which she would shop for sheets and table linens with a daughter-in-law. There would be cozy lunches before the shopping and later maybe a cup of coffee, with a pastry to pick them up from all that walking. When this fantasy didn't work out, Ruth began to hope—yes, even to pray, because she was getting older and how much time was left to her anyway?—for a granddaughter. Now there was Isobel, a dark-haired, blue-eyed little baby girl who had completely undone her.

When Gabriel called to tell his parents that Isobel had been born,

Ruth clutched the receiver to her chest, closed her eyes and said her silent but profoundly grateful thanks to God for granting her wish. "Ruth, are you all right?" Oscar had asked. "Is it the baby? Is something wrong?"

"No, nothing's wrong. Everything is right. They had a girl, a little girl!" She hung up the telephone. Oscar looked perplexed.

"Why did you do that? I didn't have a chance to talk to him."

"I have to call the airline to make a reservation. I want to go out there right away." She looked at Oscar's disappointed face. "We'll call right back," she reassured him. "I promise."

Ruth flew out to San Francisco as soon as she could and got to see and hold Isobel, child of her child, baby of her heart. Caroline came too, and the three women were united in their devotion to Isobel. Ruth was so very happy. Penelope had never been much disposed toward her before, but perhaps Isobel would be the bridge that connected them at last. Ruth could remember feeling this way through much of the visit, and all during the flight home too. It was only later, when Penelope began returning the gifts she sent and responding so coldly to any advice Ruth offered, that she realized nothing had changed. She also remembered sensing that Gabriel was somehow left out of the equation. He rattled around on the periphery of Penelope's world, offering to make lunch or shop and for the most part being ignored. Ruth thought all this would settle itself later, when the two grandmas had packed their tents and gone their separate ways. But it seemed she was wrong about that too.

Those weeks after Thanksgiving were some of the worst in Ruth's long and mostly happy marriage. Oscar wore his guilt so badly that Ruth felt as if he were the one who had to be comforted and consoled, though by any objective standard, she was certainly the injured party. The conversation in which he actually described the particulars of his affair with her, the girl called Ginny, whom Ruth now thought of as some horrible, abstract force that had come into their lives—took place in the living room of the apartment where Oscar and Ruth had lived for more than twenty years.

This was intentional on her part. Although she and Oscar enjoyed travel-ing, Ruth had an abiding love that at times felt almost sacred for the place they called home. Three big windows looked out onto West End Avenue, and filled the room with a pleasant, almost constant light that was diffused by the sheer, light curtains that spanned them. The floors—which they had sanded themselves when they moved in and later had done by profes-sionals when they could afford it—were a honey-colored parquet, with darker borders around their perimeters. There were bookshelves crafted by the carpenter who exchanged his labor for his daughter's violin lessons; Ruth painted those herself, with layer after layer of ivory enamel paint. The furniture was simple and comfortable. The rugs were handsome Ori-entals with muted yet oddly brilliant colors, and designs that seemed to hold intricate and mysterious significance. She and Oscar had purchased them during a trip they made to Turkey.

Once the rugs had become a part of her life, Ruth liked to imagine that their creators were proud of their efforts, that they were woven not only with exceptional skill, but also with love. When she said as much to Ben, he said, "Nice fantasy, Mom, but what planet have you been living on?"

"What do you mean?" she had asked.

"Don't you realize who made those things? Kids from poor families whose parents sold them into bondage. Kids are good because their hands are so small—all those tiny knots, you know? They used to blind them to make their fingers more sensitive."

"I didn't know," Ruth said, feeling sickened at the thought. "I never would have bought them if I did."

"Guess you're stuck with them now, though, right?" Ben had said, with that casual cruelty of a child toward a parent. Ruth sighed. She recalled wanting to wound her own mother in much the same offhand way. Ruth supposed they could have sold the rugs, but Oscar never would have agreed. "Would you boycott the Louvre because so much of the art there was stolen—the spoils of war?" he replied when she repeated what Ben had said. "It has to end somewhere, Ruth. You're not accountable for everything." So the rugs were still here, reminding her of how so much of what was lovely had such quiet sorrow hidden beneath its surface.

It was the patterns of these beautiful rugs—tightly wrought and complex in their meanderings of line and color—that Ruth stared at while Oscar told her, at long last, about Ginny. The way he never intended to act on his feelings for her. The night she got so drunk and he brought her back here to this apartment she loved so much. How he wished Ruth had been home. How Ginny came into the room and it never would have happened if not for that, never, and it only happened one other time since and he was so unbelievably, deeply sorry.

"She put an end to it, didn't she?" Ruth said, knowing this only as it came out of her mouth. The rug she was staring at had a deep blue ground, the color of the night sky over the ocean, with flowers and tear-drop-shaped medallions—in garnet, russet, gold and green—scattered all over it. Looking at the soothing design, she felt as if she were drawing strength from its buried pain.

"Why do you say that?" Oscar asked, and from his voice she knew she was right.

"She didn't need to have sex with you anymore. She already had what she wanted from you."

"And what was that?" Oscar asked, as if he were afraid to hear the answer. Everything that mattered to you, you big damn fool, Ruth wanted to say. But she didn't. She didn't because as she sat there looking at the rug, she was remembering the trip on which they bought it, the way he took her hand in the shop and waltzed her around its glowing, flower-covered surface as the shopkeeper, sensing an imminent sale, rocked back and forth on his heels and smiled. She raised her eyes and looked at Oscar, sitting morosely across from her with his fingers tensely knotted in his lap, his hair in need of cutting. Ruth saw her first and only lover, her husband and the father of her children, and knew that despite every stupid, heedless thing he had done, he was hers and she loved him still.

———

That night, Oscar made love to her, which was a surprise to both of them. The pleasure they took in this act was genuine and deep. There may have been few surprises in married love, but there was great tenderness, one of the rewards of long intimacy. Did Ginny ever rub that place in his lower back that so often ached at the end of the day? Had she ever trimmed the tiny hairs that grew from his ears and nostrils, while he patiently sat, wrapped in a towel, on the closed seat of the toilet? Did Oscar ever pluck a splinter from Ginny's foot as deftly as he extracted one from Ruth's? She doubted it. That kind of intimacy paled before the urgency, the insistence of sex. Ruth knew, she remembered how it was.

The first time they were together was in Oscar's cabin at Tanglewood. All the students had at least two roommates, but one of his left before the summer ended; the other one Oscar bribed to stay away. Still, there was always the possibility of someone seeing you walk in—or out—of someone else's cabin in the middle of the night. Or disturbing you while you were there. And Ruth and Oscar wanted to be discreet.

On the chosen night, she waited in her room until her own roommates had fallen asleep and then she quietly left the cabin, using the tiny flashlight her mother had so thoughtfully packed, to find her way on the dark path. Oscar was waiting at the door; he pulled her inside and locked it. They didn't even get undressed, but hurriedly pulled up or down the strategic articles of each other's clothing. He gripped her shoulders so hard it hurt; she accidentally poked his eye with her elbow. There was no intimacy that night, there were only the sovereign commands of the flesh. That must have been what Oscar had with Ginny. But not the other thing; there simply hadn't been the time for it to develop, and to grow.

After the conversation in the living room, they came to some uneasy truce, Ruth and Oscar, united in their desire to avert what they perceived as impending disaster for their son. They both knew Penelope and were both aware that her view of Gabriel's infidelity would be neither tolerant nor forgiving. And then there was Ginny herself. She scared Ruth even more than Penelope did, and for the opposite reason. If Penelope's grip on herself was tenuous, Ginny's was like steel. That girl would hold on to whatever she wanted and never let go, no matter what the outcome. The day Ruth saw them kissing in the bedroom, Ginny actually had the gall to hug her when she said good-bye. Ruth never wanted to smack someone as much as she had wanted to smack Ginny then, but she could do no such thing. And Ginny knew it too—that was why she was brazen enough to dare.

Of course what Ruth and Oscar were to do was unclear. Oscar told Ruth about the walk he and Gabriel took the day they went up to Connecticut. Now Gabriel would not talk to Oscar. The answering machine picked up all the time at home and clearly Gabriel's assistant at the office had been given instructions not to take Oscar's calls either.

"Why don't *you* try?" Oscar suggested to Ruth late one Sunday morning when they were seated in the dining room, eating the bagels and lox he had brought from the place on Amsterdam Avenue they liked so much. "All right," Ruth agreed, and when the food was finished and the plates cleared away, she did.

The machine picked up at first—it was early out in San Francisco; maybe they were still sleeping. But when Ruth started to leave a message, she heard Gabriel's voice.

"Mom. Hello," he said, pausing distinctly between each word.

"How are you, honey?" Ruth said. "How's Penelope? How's the baby?" There were a few minutes during which he told her about something that Isobel had done; in the background, she heard Penelope adding her bit to the story. Finally, Ruth said, "Gabriel. I know you're not free to talk now but we should talk soon. Your father and I are both very upset—"

"That's all right, we miss you too," he was saying, for Penelope's ears, no doubt. "But we'll fly out again soon, I promise. Everything is fine here, though. Don't worry about anything." He sounded very reassuring and in control. She stared into the receiver, as if she could see his face dissolving in the small square of black dots that made up the mouthpiece. He said good-bye before she could hand the phone over to Oscar. When she had hung up, they both looked at each other dumbly. Now what? Ruth wondered, and she could see that Oscar was thinking the same thing.

Christmas was coming. The ward of the hospital Ruth visited was decorated with green-and-red metallic fringe and cardboard cutouts of Santa and his reindeer. At the nurses' station, there was a small artificial tree. Someone had decorated it with baby paraphernalia: pacifiers, large diaper pins, booties, teething rings and rattles. There was a new baby on the ward now: Kristopher, whose fifteen-year-old mother had been sniffing God-knows-what inhalants during her troubled and undesired pregnancy. Kris was born two months early, weighing less than four pounds. Still, he was thriving and scrappy, his hair beginning to grow in shiny and thick, his laugh a deep, throaty gurgle when Ruth bounced him on her knee or shook her head wildly from side to side.

At the nursing home, there were no Christmas decorations. Instead, the halls were lined with blue-and-silver "Happy Hanukkah" signs and large pairs of blue plastic dreidels that looked like oversized dashboard decorations. Someone had set up a plastic menorah with electric lights in the large meeting room downstairs. Several of the residents asked to be taken to see it daily, and they put small wrapped parcels around its base, gifts for staff and friends. Ruth had a brass menorah tucked away somewhere in the apartment. It had belonged to Lilli. She reminded herself to take it out and polish it when she got home. In the past, she used to make a little Hanukkah gathering every year. It was nothing elaborate, but when the boys and Molly's girls were young, they looked forward to the lighting of the candles, the songs and the small wooden dreidels Ruth handed out.

Ruth hadn't made one of these parties in a long while, but it occurred to her that she should start doing it again soon. For the grandchildren, though the only one she had was on the West Coast, and the likelihood of Penelope bringing Isobel to New York for such an event was slim. In the meantime, Ruth contented herself with buying a few gifts, small things for her family, the women in her reading group, the babies at the hospital, the residents of the nursing home. She allowed herself to be taken up with the getting and spending, the wrapping and delivering.

Then Gabriel called. Oscar was at the theater and Ruth was spending a quiet evening at home. Since it was only five o'clock in San Francisco, she assumed that he was still at his office.

"Look, Ma, I know what you saw, and I know what you think. But it isn't like that." He had reverted to the childish epithet, "Ma," as if he were trying to wheedle his way out of bad behavior.

"It isn't like what?" Ruth prompted. She needed him to say everything, spell out every little word.

"Like we're going to have an affair or something," he said with a huge sigh, as if all of this were some vast annoyance she had dreamed up for him.

"Thank God," Ruth said, and her own mother's voice, her intonation, echoed in Ruth's ears.

"Not that it's any of your business, Mother." Now they had moved on to "Mother." A rung up the evolutionary ladder. He seldom called her that, except when exasperated.

"No, it isn't," she agreed. "So next time you decide to kiss a woman who isn't your wife, make sure you do it somewhere other than in my home." He was silent, chastened, Ruth supposed, by her tone.

"I didn't mean anything by it," he said, more open and pleading now. He was back to being the child, seeking forgiveness. "Things with Penelope have just been so strained since the baby. You know how she is." Ruth knew but found herself wanting to defend her daughter-in-law.

"What I know is that you like the life the two of you lead together. The life you couldn't afford on your salary."

"Well, *she* kissed me. Not the other way around." Ruth hadn't noticed him resisting. But why say this? She changed her tactic.

"Gabriel, I wish to God I hadn't seen the two of you that day. But I did. I'm just worried about you, that's all. You and Penelope, and especially the baby." She stopped, because she felt the tears coming and she did not want to be crying as she had this conversation with her son.

"I know you are, Mom," he said gently. Mom. That was friendly, grown-up and neutral, wasn't it? "And I want you to know there's nothing to worry about."

"Well, I'm certainly glad of that," Ruth said. In the end, she acted as if she believed him because, really, what else could she do?

Hanukkah came and went without a party. None of the children were in town, and Molly had gone to Florida for several weeks. Ruth didn't have the heart for a celebration and was just as glad to have had the excuse not to make one. But on the first night—she knew this because she saw the menorahs in the windows of other people's houses—she never did find or polish the one she owned—Oscar surprised her with a gift. This was odd because they had never exchanged Hanukkah gifts; it was always something they did for the children. And it was an expensive gift besides, a ring made of diamonds that circled its entire circumference. She slipped it on her finger, and held it up to the light to see it shine.

"It's lovely," Ruth made herself say, though inside she was thinking how frightened Oscar must be of losing her, and how frightened his fear made her feel.

"The jeweler called it an eternity band," said Oscar, looking right into her eyes. "I told him that I liked the name."

On Christmas Day, Ruth and Oscar were invited to a party at the home of one of the orchestra members. Ruth wore a decade-old brown wool dress with a lace collar and the new diamond ring. Oscar told her she was looking better than she had in a while. They spent the afternoon pleasantly enough, chatting with other musicians and their spouses in a large East Side apartment whose living room was dominated by an imposing Christmas tree decorated entirely in white—white silk ribbons, white paper snowflakes, a large white angel, made of ceramic or glass, perched at the top. Penelope would have approved, Ruth thought. Then she remembered how much Penelope disliked the "senseless annual slaughter of so many trees." Still, Oscar's fellow musicians were a congenial bunch and Ruth enjoyed herself more than she had expected to.

The following day she began to think about New Year's Eve. She knew that Oscar would be playing in the orchestra that night—there was always a special New Year's performance of the ballet—and they had been invited to some parties afterward. But Ruth had no desire to attend another party so soon after Christmas, and instead thought she would make reservations at a French restaurant they liked. Just a quiet evening together. Maybe they would drink a toast to the coming year—and hope that it had something better in store for all of them. Ruth was just about to pick up the telephone to make a reservation when it rang.

"Ruth. This is Penelope." There was no warmth in her voice, only a kind of urgency that immediately made Ruth's stomach tighten with apprehension.

"Well, hello, darling, how is everything—"

"I just want to talk to him. That's all. Would you please put him on?"

"Put who on?" Ruth said. She had no idea what Penelope was talking about.

"Gabriel."

"But he's not here."

"Of course he's there," Penelope said calmly. Now Ruth was really worried: she had always known that Penelope was fragile, but she had never realized that her daughter-in-law was delusional. Ruth gestured frantically toward Oscar, who was on the other side of the room, reading. When he finally looked up, she conveyed to him by a series of hand movements and silent mouthing of words that she wanted him to go in the other room and quietly pick up the receiver. Which he did, but apparently not quietly enough, for Penelope said, "Gabriel? Is that you? Talk to me!"

"It's just me, Penelope," Oscar said soothingly. "Can you tell us what's wrong?"

"Gabriel is gone." Her voice sounded more agitated now.

"Gone?"

"This morning. He said he was going on a business trip. To see some clients in Santa Barbara. He's working on a house there."

"Well, he'll be back then," Ruth said, trying to calm both herself and Penelope. "That's nothing to get alarmed about, is it?"

"But those clients called here today wanting to talk to him. He hasn't been in touch in a while. He didn't go to Santa Barbara."

"He didn't?" Ruth said.

"Then where did he go?" Oscar added.

"To New York."

Ruth's stomach started jumping.

"How do you know that?" Oscar asked.

"I found the reservation on the computer. He thinks I don't know how to use it, but he's wrong. He's wrong about a lot of things. Anyway, he's in New York right now. And I want to talk to him."

"Look, Penelope, even if he is in New York, he's not here with us. I swear to you, we haven't heard from him." There was a silence on the other end of the line.

"Then what is he doing in New York that he doesn't want to tell me about?" Ruth couldn't say anything to that and neither could Oscar, though they could both guess. Their failure to say anything was clearly damning to Penelope, for she repeated her question, only with a glinting edge of hysteria in her voice. "Is there someone there that he's seeing? Some woman?"

"I can't imagine that's true," said Oscar, and Ruth marveled at his ability to stay so calm.

"Neither can I," Penelope said. "But he told me he was going to Santa Barbara, and I find out he's in New York. What would you think?"

"Just what you're thinking, dear, but I'm sure there is some reasonable explanation for all this—" began Oscar.

"Don't call me 'dear' and *please* don't patronize me. Do you think I don't know how you feel about me—'Poor, crazy Penelope,' that's what you think, you and Ruth both. I can't stand the pair of you."

Ruth felt her cheeks and neck burn during this outburst and could only imagine how Oscar was feeling. Then, all at once, Penelope was calm again. This abrupt switch in her mood frightened Ruth as much as anything she had said.

"Maybe it's true. Maybe he isn't at your apartment. But if you happen to see him, you had better tell him to come home in a hurry. Tell him his *wife* wants to talk to him." Then she hung up. Oscar and Ruth were left holding the receivers in their separate rooms and listening to the sounds of one another's breathing.

GABRIEL

Gabriel sat in the first tier of the New York State Theater, trying to shield himself with the *Stagebill*. Not that he really thought anyone would see him and wonder what he was doing there. He knew, of course, that his father was there, buried somewhere deep in the orchestra pit, though Oscar would not be able to see Gabriel so high above him, even if he were looking. Which he surely was not. But still. So holding the little booklet in both hands, he positioned it at eye level and tried to bury his face in its pages. Soon, the theater's lights—which looked like outsized, imitation gems—would dim, and he could relax. At least a little. If a man who had intentionally lied to his wife and flown to another city for the express purpose of making love to someone else can be said to relax. It wasn't as if he didn't know that he was betraying Penelope. And it wasn't as if he didn't care. But that kiss had been his undoing.

Gabriel was no stranger to this theater, the place where his father had made music for so many years. His mother used to bring them all here when they were little. William and Ben liked *Stars and Stripes*, with its big Sousa marches and even bigger American flag emblazoned across the backdrop of the stage. Also *Western Symphony*, which they called the Cowboy Ballet. This made Ruth smile and ruffle their hair with her fingers. Gabriel, though he didn't like to admit it, preferred the more overtly romantic ballets, the ones where the dancers wore flowing, diaphanous costumes, or short, starchy-looking tutus which gave them an endearingly comic appearance. He liked the way the dancers looked altogether, their supple, slender arms moving in time to the music his father made, their delicate necks held so erect and yet so mobile. For a time, he would develop a crush on this or that particular ballerina, and he had even stood at the stage door a few times waiting to get his program autographed. Of course Oscar could easily have done this for him, but Gabriel didn't want to tell Oscar—or anyone else—about his secret loves. The programs were then stored in a fireproof metal box under his bed to which only he had the key. But the phase passed, and eventually he and his brothers stopped going to the ballet.

Having finished reading the *Stagebill* from start to finish—program notes, where he first turned just to find Ginny's name listed for her small solo, restaurant reviews, advertisements for estate jewelry and custom furriers—Gabriel ventured a look around at the theater itself. The architect in him found something uninspired about the place, with its gaudy round lights and cheesy gold curtain. Like the inside of a candy box, he thought, remembering theaters he had seen in Europe—the Maryinsky in Saint Petersburg, the fantastic blue-and-gold marvel in the Châtelet in Paris. Theaters where there was a sense of majesty—this place was just too damn democratic for Gabriel's taste. Much pomp but no splendor here. No romance either. Though Ginny said it was a wonderful place to dance, with a specially engineered floor and all sorts of other dancer-friendly innovations. "Some places have you dancing on concrete," she told him that day in his parents' apartment. "Can you imagine what that does to your knees?" He could imagine what he would like to do to her knees, her thighs and any other parts of herself that she offered. He could not re-member feeling so excited by a woman in his entire life.

Ginny was the reason he was here after all, the reason he had left his wife and child, lied to them too, with that story about the clients in Santa Barbara. Penelope scarcely seemed to care when he told her he was going. And despite the long plane ride, he planned to stay only a single night, so as not to arouse her suspicions. He would call her later, after the perfor-mance, but before he met with Ginny. Ginny who was coming to the East Side hotel where he had booked a room, a room where he would finally get to hold her, pull off whatever ridiculous clothes she was wearing and devour her fierce, vibrant and anything but pliant body.

Finally, the lights dimmed and the curtain rose. There on the stage be-fore him were the Victorian parlor and shining snowflakes of *The Nut-cracker,* and Gabriel was lost again in memory, reliving something he hadn't thought of for years. This time, he was quite small and he and Ruth were here alone—William was a baby and Ben not even born. In fact, Oscar had not started playing in the orchestra yet. But Ruth had this idea about *The Nutcracker* being something all New York children should see, and she took him to it by herself, on the subway, one winter afternoon. She had a coat of some camel-colored wool, which made Gabriel think of caramels and butterscotch, and because he still felt chilly when they got to the the-ater, Ruth draped it around his shoulders and knees as he watched. It had her scent, whatever light, floral cologne she wore, and some other indefin-able but infinitely reassuring quality too. Sitting in the dark, Gabriel was dazzled by the performance, the toys and candy that came to life, the Christmas tree that grew—like an ogre or a giant—to dominate the stage. He drank it all in as he dreamily sucked his thumb and nestled in the warmth of Ruth's arm, which she had placed around him.

And now he was back again, back with the snowflakes and the flowers that danced and, finally, there was Ginny, dancing the Coffee variation. She wore something that could have belonged to an odalisque, at least one painted by a voyeuristic nineteenth-century Frenchman like Ingres or

Delacroix. The abbreviated top left her midriff bare, scarlet fabric fringed in gold was wrapped around her slim hips. Nude colored tights and pointe shoes gave the illusion that her legs and feet were bare. The costume must have been trimmed with bells or metal coins; there was a musical tinkling when she moved. Her hair was pulled back tightly, the way they all wore it, and he was more aware than ever of her long, pale neck, her eloquent shoulders. She moved with an electricity and a precision that to Gabriel seemed astonishing. He did not know the names of the steps, though he knew he would ask her about them later. But he could appreciate the sense of attack in her movements, the bright, crisp way her body silently moved through space to command and dominate it. All this happened in mere minutes; her appearance on the stage seemed achingly brief and he felt abandoned when it was over. Only the sound of the applause after she had stopped let him know that his vision of her was one that other people shared and not entirely colored by his desire.

The rest of the ballet was pleasant if anticlimactic. His mind wandered over the program again, and back to San Francisco and Penelope. It would be after five o'clock there now, which meant that she would be feeding Isobel one of her organic concoctions.

"Can't she start eating some real food soon?" Gabriel asked one day as he watched her spoon some rather unappetizing-looking greenish-brown mixture into Isobel's small, open mouth. He had a sudden desire to take the child on his lap and feed her chocolate chip ice cream, a bagel whose cream cheese she would use to decorate her face and hair, tiny bites of pizza and buttered toast. But Penelope would have none of that. "Do you want to start poisoning her already?" she demanded when he suggested this. "Do you have any idea how fragile her immune system still is? There are toxins that exist today that hadn't been dreamed of when we were babies. It scares me even to think about it." So Gabriel backed off, as he always did, retreating to his world of work, the lines on paper and the shapes in space that he patiently conceived and designed. At first, after

Isobel's birth, the world of work was infinitely soothing and appealing to him. Here was a place where he still had some effect. But as the months wore on, and Penelope remained as preoccupied as ever, he grew restless. How could she so completely have lost interest in him? Wasn't he the father of this miraculous life that held her so in thrall? Didn't he count?

There was, of course, no sex during these months. In the beginning, he was tender and solicitous; he had seen her labor through childbirth and knew how her body had been stretched and torn. But surely, all these months later, she must have healed? He wanted to ask her, but the whole subject seemed to leave her cold. "You want to put what where?" she had said, half-mocking, a couple of months ago when he had nuzzled up to her on one of the rare nights that Isobel was not in their bed. That was another thing: the baby slept with them nearly all the time, and the pale dye-and-resin-free natural hardwood crib his parents had bought, at her specifications, remained mostly unused. "She's so tiny," Penelope would murmur when Gabriel tried to suggest that maybe Isobel could start sleeping in her own room. Or she would say, "It's so much easier to nurse when she's right there next to me." Which of course was true. But Isobel was a restless, noisy sleeper; her small body and limbs rotating, like the hands of a clock, in the bed so that Gabriel would wake with her heel wedged between his neck and shoulder or her fist in his eye. And the sounds she made! She didn't so much snore as hoot and wheeze through the night. Then she woke wailing, and only Penelope's breasts—ripe with hormones and milk and denied to him—would quiet her. Often, Gabriel would just take his pillow and curl up on the sofa. Soon, he stopped even trying to sleep with his wife. Penelope didn't seem to mind.

He spoke, tentatively at first, and then with greater candor, to some of the other men in his office who also had young children at home. Most treated the subject with patient resignation or mildly hostile humor. All of them agreed that a new baby had turned their once lovely and loving wives into unrecognizable mommy-pods. But none of the wives Gabriel described seemed quite so exclusive, even obsessive in their focus, as Penelope.

Not that this was justification for what he was about to do, he knew that. His present situation was merely the jumping-off point for some leap he may have been destined to take, no matter what was happening in his marriage. He only knew that the force of his feelings for Ginny—the pull, the draw she exerted—was something he couldn't resist.

The performance was over, the curtain coming down on the enchanted winter world below him. There was more applause, many curtain calls, and flowers were delivered to the stage. Ginny curtsied and Gabriel clapped so hard his palms stung. Sometimes, Gabriel knew, if there had been a particularly beautiful or complex musical solo, one of the musicians might be invited onto the stage for a bow. Tonight was not one of those nights and Gabriel was glad. Oscar was already too present in this situation; Gabriel had no desire to see him.

In fact, it was Oscar's sickening connection to Ginny that kept Gabriel from racing back to New York right after he first met her, which is what he had wanted to do. But that day on the beach with his father offered him a new and frightening glimpse into his parents' marriage. Oscar unfaithful to Ruth. It was a vision he had done everything to obliterate from his mind ever since. Still, he replayed the conversation over and over: the salt-tanged air, Oscar's doleful look, the way he said "I know" and sighed, the angry, accusing words that came after, then stalking down the beach by himself alone, soles of his shoes smacking against the hard, wet sand, ocean spray wetting his cheeks and his hair. He began to run, past the house until he came to a flight of wooden stairs leading up from the beach. He climbed them, no longer running now, but still out of breath, and kept walking, toward town, until he found someplace open that would serve him a cup of coffee.

When he finally returned to Caroline's house, he found his parents and Caroline chatting amiably in front of a fire. Several cats slept in various corners of the room; one cat's tongue was always sticking out, as if perpetually mocking the other felines and humans whom she was forced to endure. Caroline had explained that her two front teeth were missing, and the tongue just slipped through the open cavity it created, but Gabriel still wondered. Penelope and Isobel were nowhere to be seen.

"Nursing again," Caroline said in response to his query, and she pouted dramatically. "Penelope says that Isobel gets distracted by the cats, but we know she's just keeping that baby to herself!" His parents just nodded and smiled. Gabriel could not look at either of them, and abruptly went upstairs.

Later, when he spoke to his mother, he would not permit himself to allude to the sense of betrayal she must have been feeling. He didn't want to face those dark places in his parents' marriage. Bad enough that he was facing them in his own.

After the performance was over, Gabriel hurried out of the theater. He had planned to catch a cab to the hotel on Madison Avenue, but he had forgotten about the crush of people lining Columbus Avenue and Broadway who were also hailing cabs. So instead he started walking east. It was not a bitter evening and he inhaled the refreshing night air as he walked quickly along the street. In the end, whatever had gone on between his father and Ginny was not enough to stop him from coming here. Thinking about it, as he did endlessly in the weeks between that day on the beach and the moment he boarded the plane, he accepted that whatever had happened between them was over. That much was clear from Oscar's mournful expression. And if Gabriel had learned of Ginny's connection to his father before he had kissed her, maybe things would have been different. Maybe he wouldn't be striding across the city in the dark on his way toward her.

It had been easy to get her telephone number from Directory Assistance, and he took care not to call from home. The first few tries didn't find her in, and the phone rang and rang in the empty apartment. No answering machine or cell phone for her. Then one morning he was in his office by six o'clock to reach her at nine, and there she was, groggily saying, "What is it?" on the other end of the wire.

"It's me, Gabriel," he said, feeling foolish but elated to have reached her at last.

"Gabriel," she said, quickly sounding wide awake. "Where are you? Are you in New York?"

"Not yet," he said. "But I will be."

That had been several days ago. As he now neared Central Park, he was stopped by the large display of flowers in front of a Korean fruit and vegetable market. Flowers. He wished he had thought to have ordered some for the hotel room, and then realized he could buy a bunch and have someone there arrange them in a vase. The selection was not great, but once inside the market, he bought two bunches of dark red roses and a couple of Toblerone chocolate bars, the ones shaped like prisms with bits of honey and nougat inside. He had watched Ginny eat, and he guessed that she would like them. He planned to feed them to her, actually, bite by bite, the melted chocolate from his fingers coating her lips. Then he stepped back outside and continued his journey.

When he actually reached Central Park, he stopped again. He didn't think it was a good idea to walk across the park alone at this hour, so he tried again to get a cab. Several passed by with passengers already inside. He saw an empty one, but the off-duty light was turned on, and the driver did not stop. Finally, after about fifteen minutes, he was successful, and found himself hurtling through the darkness of the park, on his way to the hotel.

He arrived in the lobby later than he expected—he had checked in earlier in the day, so at least he was not worried about losing the room— and realized that there would be no time to call Penelope. Damn. Then a movement—it was a woman, getting to her feet—caught his attention and he saw that Ginny was here already, waiting for him. He almost wanted to drop the flowers he was holding—the chocolate bars were nestled safely in his coat pocket—to crush her in his arms, but he was too aware of the hotel staff who stood by idly, watching them. Instead, he moved very close, so their conversation would not be audible.

"You came" was all she said, but Gabriel knew that the delight painted on her face must have mirrored his own. She was wearing a very peculiar black coat that looked as if it had been new forty years ago. It had huge black buttons down the front and an enormous fuzzy collar. He could see that she had not taken off her stage makeup. No wonder the bellboys had been giving her the once-over. But Gabriel was dazzled by the dramatic blue and green shading around her eyes, the vivid lines of her painted eyebrows, the hectic stain of her cheeks, the wet look of her dark red lips. He was standing close enough to touch her now, and he shifted the flowers awkwardly under one arm before he reached for her hands, which were small and cold.

"Let's go upstairs," he murmured and she nodded. Her eyes gleamed in the low light and the pressure of her hands was strong. Together, they moved toward the elevator, which carried them swiftly and without pause up to the room.

PENELOPE

Penelope *loved* her mother, but it was her father she worshiped. With his fine, sand-colored hair, sparse brows and quiet voice, he had a gentle and at times ethereal quality that always soothed her. She could almost believe that he put his head into the clouds to talk to God. When she asked him about this once, he laughed.

Penelope was a little hurt; she hadn't meant to amuse him, she really was curious. Most of the time, though, he didn't laugh at her, but listened carefully to whatever she had to say. He talked to her too. Of course her mother also talked to her, though what she said was much more predictable: don't bite your nails, brush your hair, make your bed, stop procrastinating and go to sleep. Whereas her father's conversations tended to surprise her. Did she dream in color? he wanted to know. Would she rather be an ocelot or a raccoon? Did she know that it was possible to crush rose petals, make them into jam and eat them?

There was ample time for them to have these conversations. Penelope's father was a professor who taught in the English department of a small, private Connecticut college; his classes met only two days a week. There were occasional faculty meetings and meetings with students, but he spent a lot of time at home writing or with Penelope: driving her to school and horseback-riding lessons, reading her stories, putting her to bed. None of her friends' fathers spent so much time with their daughters. Mostly, they took the train into the city every day, where they went to offices. They came home at night tired and irritable, looking for a drink and the newspaper, not their children. Penelope knew she was privileged, but she never took it for granted.

"He certainly doesn't have to work very hard" was the comment Penelope overheard one of her aunts make. "He must have tenure."

"Better than that," the other aunt said. "He married money. A different kind of tenure." They both laughed.

Penelope was puzzled. How could her father be married to money when he was married to her mother? And, besides, a person couldn't marry money anyway. It made no sense. She asked her father about it, hoping that she would cause him to burst out laughing, uttering that irrepressible yelp of glee that she sometimes elicited. But this time he did not laugh. He looked unhappy and frowned.

"Who said that?" he asked.

"I don't remember," Penelope lied, wishing she hadn't brought it up.

"People are jealous," he said, as if that explained anything. When he saw she didn't understand, he continued: "Your mother comes from a family with a lot of money. I don't. Some people think that I married her so I could have that money. But you know that isn't true. You know how much I love your mother, sweet pea. And how much I love you."

This reassured Penelope. He did love her mother, she could tell by the way the two of them held hands and gave each other those grown-up glances when they thought she wasn't looking. Still, Penelope didn't mind because her father loved her too, and she loved him back.

Then her father got sick. Penelope didn't understand at first why he was so tired, why he couldn't play, read to her or put her to bed anymore.

"Daddy's resting," said her mother. "I'll read to you tonight." Penelope shook her head no and pressed her face into the pillow, which was uncomfortably warm and creased. Her father always knew to turn it over, so that the smooth, cool side touched her heated cheek. But her mother didn't know that Penelope wanted her to do this. Instead she said, "All right then. Be selfish and spoiled," and she got up from the bed, leaving Penelope alone in the dark room.

It seemed her father needed an operation for which he had to go to the hospital. Penelope was sad that he had to leave. She made him a special picture of a deep pink heart bordered by a white, scalloped ruffle. Inside the heart she wrote "I LOV YOU," which looked wrong to her, but he was the one she always asked about spelling and she wanted this to be a surprise. Penelope gave the heart to her mother, who looked at it for a moment before tucking it into the bag she was packing for the hospital visit. "It's a beautiful picture," said Penelope's mother. Penelope was shocked to see tears in her mother's eyes.

After the operation, her father came home, but he was still not better. "No, Daddy can't read to you tonight," said Penelope's mother. Penelope took the book back to her own room, where she carefully and quietly ripped out all the pages, one by one. Not only couldn't he read to her, her father couldn't do much of anything else either. He stopped teaching his classes at the college, stopped taking bicycle rides and going out for dinner with Penelope's mother. Instead, Caroline had to drive him to the doctor's office every week, for something called chemotherapy. Penelope was not allowed to go along; left with a baby-sitter, she sat by the window downstairs, waiting for the car to pull up. When it did, she raced out to greet her parents, but when she saw her father—gaunt, pale, knitted cap cover-ing his now-bald head—she stopped. It was the hair loss that frightened her most. She knew that losing your hair meant you were getting ready to die, and she so desperately did not want her father to die.

But he did anyway. Penelope was not in the house when it happened, and by the time she got home from school, the body had already been taken away. There was only the empty hospital bed, blankets still turned back, sheets still bearing the imprint of his wasted form. Penelope's mother gathered her in her arms, weeping, but Penelope did not cry. Nor did she cry at the funeral, which took place a few days later.

She wore a new dress that was much too warm for the mild spring day, but her mother explained that she had had a hard time finding a black dress in Penelope's size. Many people attended the funeral. Some of them Penelope recognized, like the aunt who said her father had married money, while others—students and faculty members from the college— she did not. The casket was closed, so she could not actually see her fa-ther's body lying in it and she almost believed that he was not inside at all, but had disappeared, back into the clouds, where Penelope was convinced he belonged. At the cemetery, there was a big, gaping hole in the ground. Strangely enough, the sight of the raw, open space gave her some kind of comfort; it looked like the hole that was now in her heart.

Things seemed to go back to normal after that. There was still school and riding lessons, though now it was her mother and not her father who drove her back and forth. There were visits with friends, trips to the den-tist, birthday parties and Christmas celebrations. The year Penelope turned eleven, her mother bought her a horse. It did not come to live with them in their large backyard, as Penelope imagined it might, but re-mained at the stable where Penelope went for her riding lessons.

"There, darling, isn't he beautiful?" said her mother as she circled slowly around the enormous brown animal. Penelope said nothing. She had never said she wanted a horse. The horse swished his thick, coarse tail and blinked his large brown eyes. "Let's give him a treat, shall we?" her mother continued, and pulled a carrot from her bag, which she handed to Penelope. Penelope placed the carrot on her open palm and extended it, as she had been taught. The horse moved first his lips and then his huge, stained teeth around the proffered food. Penelope's hand was wet with saliva, which she vigorously dried on her riding jacket.

"Don't do that," her mother chided. "Where is your handkerchief?" She shook her head and turned from Penelope to the owner of the stable. "It will be good for her," Caroline told the other woman. "Give her something to hold on to. A sense of responsibility. An outlet for her feelings."

As it turned out, the horse, whom Penelope refused to name, did none of these things. She had no interest in feeding, washing or grooming him, though she could see how the other girls who boarded horses at the same stable reverently performed all these tasks. She continued to ride him, because she had been riding horses for a while now and saw no reason to stop. But the horse was not hers in any real way, nor would he ever be. It was her mother who finally named him. "We'll call him Touchstone," she told Penelope. "After the fool in *As You Like It*. Daddy would have loved that." Penelope didn't care. In fact, she found it galling, even obscene, that this stupid animal, with his big haunches and rank smell, should be alive at all, while her father was dead.

The lessons continued, and Penelope developed into an able rider. Though she still had no feeling for the horse (in the privacy of her own thoughts, she did not deign to use the silly name her mother had thought up), she liked the feelings he permitted her to experience: speed, control, mastery, power. She liked taking the crop to him and reining him in tightly, to show him who was in charge. When Kelly, the riding teacher, told Penelope that they were going to start jumping, Penelope was excited. She wanted to feel the speed burning under her, smoldering and igniting like a flame, until the horse reached the hurdle and in a single flash cleared it. Caroline was pleased that Penelope was taking an interest in the sport; the lessons increased to twice and then three times a week. "Best thing I could have done for her," she told Kelly as together they watched Penelope and Touchstone canter around the ring.

The only thing that annoyed Caroline was that Penelope still refused to clean and care for the horse. Nothing Caroline said had any effect. Penelope was disgusted by the fine cloud of barn-smelling dust that always emanated from his coat, the large and odoriferous droppings he left behind, the wet look of his eyes. At first, Caroline tried to make her take an interest. "After all, he's yours, darling," she would admonish. "You need to take some responsibility for him. Like any pet." When this failed to work, she switched her tactics. "I'll sell him, Penelope, honestly I will."

"Fine," Penelope answered sullenly. "See if I care."

This stymied Caroline, who really did think the horse was doing her daughter good. Though it had been several years now, Penelope never seemed to have gotten over her father's death: though intelligent, she was an indifferent student, prone to doodling and staring out the classroom windows, and she had few friends. No, the horse had to stay, Caroline decided, and she eventually hired another young girl from a nearby town to take care of him. Although she said nothing, Penelope reveled in her victory. She would be the one to choose what she would and wouldn't do. Let her mother get used to it.

Penelope had been jumping for about a year when Kelly suggested that she enter one of the local horse shows. "I think you're ready," she said. "Do you want to try?" Penelope nodded. Yes, she wanted to try. Not only because she wanted to win but because she wanted the audience. She wanted to be watched as she commanded the horse to jump high, then higher and higher still, an obedient servant to her will. Caroline worried a bit about the jumping competition, thinking it would put too much pressure on Penelope—"I don't want you to get hurt" was what she told her daughter—but eventually she came round to see the event as the natural and appropriate consequence of all Penelope's hard work. "She can do this.

She's thirteen," Kelly assured Caroline more than once. Caroline had only to look at her daughter on Touchstone's back—poised, erect, serious as a soldier—to be convinced.

The morning of the competition arrived. Penelope wore a cable-knit Shetland sweater under her tweed riding jacket and fine silk long johns under her jodhpurs. Her boots were polished and her long dark hair plaited into a thick braid. She didn't have any appetite for breakfast, though she wished that Caroline would have let her drink a cup of strong, black coffee. As a compromise, Caroline gave her a cup of tea with only a trace of milk.

The other girls who were competing seemed to know each other; Penelope saw them talking with great animation, gesturing to their horses, adjusting one another's hard velvet hats. No one said anything to her, but she didn't care. She looked at the horse, whose huge head was turned away from her. His ears were erect with concentration.

When it was her turn, she gave the horse the signal to start. He responded immediately and they took the first two jumps easily. There was a smattering of applause from the audience and Penelope felt her face and indeed her whole body warm with pride. The horse trotted briskly around the ring, preparing for the next jump when it happened. Penelope never knew just what made him twist his head around and shy away from the jump. She tightened her grasp on the reins and tried to yank him back into position but he was strong, stronger than she was. Even as she tugged and pulled, he was moving back, back and away.

Penelope was angry now, angry at the horse for disobeying her, angry at herself for being too weak. She was angry enough to want to hurt him, and she tried to, pulling on the bit with all her strength and using the crop, hard, against his hindquarters. But the horse would not submit: he reared back suddenly, eliciting gasps of dismay from the audience, and then he took off, galloping around the ring. The horses on the other side whinnied in distress as Touchstone moved faster and faster, oblivious to Penelope's commands. The gate at the far end of the ring was open; Penelope hoped that someone would be quick enough to bolt it shut, but the horse was galloping at full speed toward the opening.

Once out of the ring, he crossed the open, grassy field outside and headed straight toward the small patch of woods. Penelope was furious. She would not let this animal take her through the tight net of trees, not at this pace. Instead, she would let go of the reins and slide off and away from him. But before this could happen, his hoof caught something on the ground and she was pitched forward into the air, braid flying out behind her like a comet. She managed to curl her body into an almost fetal position and tuck her head down before she hit the ground. The packed earth seemed to fly up and smack her hard in the face and she remained where she was, momentarily stunned.

"Penelope! Penelope!" It was Kelly's voice now, Kelly who came rushing out after them. "Are you all right?" She knelt in front of Penelope, moving the dark braid away from her cheek, where it lay coiled.

"I think so," Penelope said, struggling to sit up. In the distance, she saw her mother and several other people approaching. A strange, strangled noise diverted her attention and she turned to see the horse, Touchstone, lying on the ground a few feet away.

"He went down," Penelope said, not quite able to believe it.

"He went down," repeated Kelly.

Everyone converged on Penelope then: her mother, the judges, the paramedic who was always present at these events. Penelope was examined and, when it seemed she was all right, helped to her feet. Her left cheek was abraded and bloody and her ribs ached, but apart from that, she was without injury.

Touchstone was less fortunate. Penelope hobbled over to where the horse was still lying on the ground, thrashing his head and making the pained sound she had heard earlier. White foam coated his lips.

A woman Penelope had not met but knew by sight knelt before him: the veterinarian who was another staple figure at the competitions.

"How is he?" she asked. The woman didn't turn around immediately, but searched hurriedly through her large nylon bag for something. Kelly and Caroline came over to join them.

"He'll be all right, won't he?" Penelope tried again.

The woman turned to face her. "No," she said. "He won't."

"Why not? What's wrong with him?"

"That leg," the vet gestured. Penelope saw how it was bent and twisted into some absurd angle. "And there's been some internal injury from the fall. He's bleeding inside. I'm going to have to put him down." She called out to the stable hands. "Rob, Johnny. Could you boys start digging a hole?"

"You're going to shoot him?" Penelope asked in a voice that she didn't quite recognize as belonging to her. "And then bury him?" The veterinarian stared at her before turning back to the horse.

"They use injections now," said Kelly. "You shouldn't watch."

"But I want to," Penelope said.

"Really, Penelope," said Caroline, putting a hand on her daughter's shoulder. "This is all very traumatic and I don't think—"

"He's my horse!" said Penelope, her voice growing louder and wilder. "I'm going to watch and you won't stop me!" She shook off her mother's hand. Touchstone's eyes were closed, and he was breathing heavily. The foam that painted his lips was tinged pink with blood.

"I want to be here," she told the woman.

"All right," said the vet tersely. "Don't make it worse, though. He's in a lot of pain." Kelly and Caroline exchanged looks. Caroline moved forward as if to restrain Penelope, but Kelly stopped her.

"Let her," she said softly.

The veterinarian filled the hypodermic needle, all the while soothing the horse with her words, her gestures. Penelope watched, transfixed, as the needle was raised, positioned and then plunged into the horse's flesh. His body shuddered gently and his nostrils dilated. The two stable hands were busy digging, and their shovels sent clods of earth flying up and around Penelope's legs.

"Is that it?" she asked.

"That's just the sedative," the vet explained. "I'm going to give him the barbiturate now." She prepared another injection and administered it quickly. Touchstone shook his mane once, as if trying to dislodge a fly.

Then his great head slumped forward. Penelope was flooded with a feeling so intense she could barely contain it. Finally, she had seen it, that mysterious, shrouded passage from life to death, the one she had been cheated of when her father was taking his final breaths.

There was no new horse to replace Touchstone, and the riding lessons were abandoned. Caroline worried less about this than she might have a few years earlier because finally Penelope seemed to have found some friends. In her freshman year of high school, she joined the Drama Society and the French Club. By junior year, the good looks she had as a child metamorphosed into an astonishing and uncommon beauty. Boys called day and night; girls were respectful and awed. Although her grades were no more than mediocre, she surprised everyone with her high-ranking test scores. She was placed on the waiting list at Barnard College in New York City and at the last minute she was admitted to the freshman class. Caroline was somewhat apprehensive about letting her go, but ultimately gave in. Driving her daughter down from Greenwich and into the heart of the city, Caroline knew there was something in Penelope that resisted all probing or parental concern; she would have to find her own way.

And it seemed that she did, although there were detours along the way. She switched majors, made and dropped friends, couldn't really settle down and focus on anything. Though she tried to apply herself to her studies, the hours spent in Butler Library's dark stacks or reading rooms left her apathetic and uninspired.

She was as lonely at Barnard as she had been everywhere else. Sitting outside the Avery Library at Columbia one spring afternoon during her senior year, she thought of the listless day she had spent, and the one that faced her tomorrow. Her stomach gently growled; she was hungry and reached into her bag for an apple, which she began to eat slowly and carefully, with a clear and focused appreciation for its sweet-tart taste, its crisp texture in her mouth as she bit, chewed and swallowed. It was only after several minutes that she even saw him, the tall, dark-haired young man who was staring—no, gawking—openly at her. As she continued to eat the apple, he moved closer but didn't say anything. Finally, Penelope broke the silence between them. "I have another one," she said and looked down into the bag to find an apple. He took it from her hand. His eyes never left her face as he began to eat.

O S C A R

*O*scar *could* not forget the conversation with his daughter-in-law earlier this evening. The way her voice had moved from impatience to anger to something like hysteria, and back to calm again. The hurtful things she had said. After Penelope had hung up, he really couldn't bear to face Ruth, because he had no idea what they were going to do. Then, the phone rang again, startling him from his momentary torpor. Maybe it was Gabriel. Or Penelope. But instead it was Molly, and since Ruth had picked up the phone as well, he gently set down the receiver and began to get ready for the theater. The company would be performing *The Nutcracker* again tonight.

Oscar readied himself for the performance as he had readied himself hundreds, even thousands, of times before. As the winter sky quickly darkened, he stepped into a hot shower and washed himself with brisk, automatic movements. Out of habit, he still filled his palm with a generous squirt of shampoo, though he no longer had the luxuriant hair he once did. There was a large pale blue towel waiting to dry him—Ruth made sure it was an oversized one—and when he had used it, he put on fresh powder blue boxer shorts and a sleeveless white undershirt. He shaved carefully, using a shaving brush and cake of shaving soap that resided in a small, cedar wood bowl with a lid—a gift from Ruth.

In the bedroom, Oscar put on black silk socks that had decorations called clocks above the ankle. No one would see these, of course, but Oscar liked to know that they were there. Then came the black trousers with the shiny black stripe down the outside of each leg and a long-sleeved white shirt. Buttons were buttoned and zippers zipped. He fastened a pair of black suspenders onto the waistband of the pants and snapped the suspenders over his shoulders. Since the shirt had no buttons at the wrist, Oscar put on a pair of simple gold cuff links, the ones his father used to own. He tied a black bow tie at the collar, not bothering with the mirror, though he would use the mirror later to make sure it was straight. He slipped on the black tuxedo jacket whose shining black lapels matched the seam that ran up the pants. Over this, he wore his black overcoat, a gray scarf of soft wool and a tweed hat. Although Oscar was frequently rumpled in his everyday incarnation, he was always meticulously groomed when he performed.

He felt around inside his pockets for his gloves because he didn't like his hands to be chilled before a performance—it took too long for them to warm up. Also in his pocket were two fresh handkerchiefs—one for the ordinary purpose of blowing his nose, the other to place under his chin while he played. He quickly unsnapped the three brass hinges on his violin case, and performed the routine check of his instrument that he had performed hundreds of times before. Strings in proper position and not frayed, bridge perfectly perpendicular, chin rest securely in place. Satisfied that everything was in order, he checked the bow as well, making sure that it was still properly loosened. He snapped the case shut, walked into the other room and kissed Ruth good-bye. He nodded at his sister-in-law, Molly, who had somehow appeared and was now seated in the living room with Ruth. Then he headed down in the elevator and out into the street.

The walk to the theater was a short one, and Oscar didn't notice a thing along the way. Displays of sweaters on sale at the Gap, card shops with half-priced Christmas wrap and cards, supermarkets with dozens of bottles of soda and cases of beer lined up in the windows, newsstands, bookstores, watch and shoe repair shops, all went unheeded.

At the theater, he went downstairs to the locker room and left his belongings in the same dark green metal locker he had used for years: number 632. Carrying his violin and bow, he walked down the short hall, made a left turn and proceeded down a longer hall, until he reached the door that led to the orchestra pit. Several of his colleagues were already there, looking at their scores and warming up. Oscar heard the sound but didn't listen to it. He nodded to the cellist he had played with for two decades, to the French horn and several of the woodwinds. He took his seat and glanced at the music. The violin was picked up and placed under his chin, just so. The handkerchief came out of his pocket and was placed between his skin and his instrument. Then the conductor moved to the podium, the baton light and graceful as a wand in his agile fingers. The curtain went up and the performance was about to begin.

In all the years Oscar had been doing this, he had never felt so deadened to these rituals as he did tonight, so completely unmoved by the humble but sacred preparations in service of his music. Even when he had been furious, depressed or exhausted, the simple movements that led him from the domestic world of family to this place had always calmed and centered him, always readied him for the task.

Tonight, he found he was capable of playing the music and even of hearing it, but it did not resonate inside him; he was a somnambulist. The performance took on an abstract quality: there was sound, which he knew to be music, then more sound, which was applause, then silence, before it started all over again. Then there was the intermission, which had a different set of sounds, and more light. After the intermission, the sequence began again, and soon the performance was over, and he moved back, through the series of movements that had brought him here, only in reverse, like a videotape rewinding. Back down one hall and then the other, violin (whose residual rosin he wiped clean with a soft cloth) in the case instead of out, handkerchief—no longer fresh but damp with his exertion—back in the pocket, coat on again, walk uptown not down. On the way home, he slowed a bit when he came to Seventy-first Street, which was where Ginny lived. Oscar wondered whether she was there, or on her way home, and whether his son was with her. What would happen if he were to wait there, and confront them?

He stood on the corner of Broadway and Seventy-first Street, staring down the avenue as if the force of his concentration would summon Ginny and Gabriel into view. But of course they did not appear. The street was bustling with people coming from Lincoln Center or from movie theaters, on their way to a late supper or a round of drinks with friends. He continued to stand there, his hands, now gloveless, growing cold and stiff, his feet beginning to hurt. This was foolish, he realized. Why would she bring him to that indifferently furnished, untidy place she called home? There was scarcely anything in it: a bed consisting of a box spring and mattress on the floor, a chest of drawers, a television on top of that. A couple of those fold-up canvas director's chairs, and a small table in the corner. Nothing hanging on the walls or at the windows, the soiled shades belonging to the last tenant. All the surfaces, and much of the floor, covered with clothes, some clean, some dirty, and a kitchen littered with take-out cartons and empty soda cans. "I can help you organize this a bit better," Oscar had said months ago, when he was first getting to know her.

"What for?" was her reply. "I don't spend much time here."

Oscar looked at his watch. Ginny could still be at the theater, changing her clothes and taking off her makeup. Or on her way to a hotel, where Gabriel would fuck her. Oscar regretted his own part in all of this, and felt ashamed that despite everything, he still wanted to fuck her himself. He ached not only with remorse for his culpability, but also with jealousy. He could admit it now: he was jealous of his own son. Really, he was a pathetic old man.

Back at home, he barely said hello to Ruth and to Molly, who was still there. He went into the bedroom, changed his clothes, which he hung up carefully, put on his pajamas and got into bed. Sleep came easily, which was no surprise to him, since he felt as though he had already been asleep for hours.

When he woke in the morning, Ruth was not there. A note on the table said that she had gone shopping. Oscar wondered whether this was true, or whether she too had been seized with some impulse to find the offending pair. But even if he and Ruth did find them, what good would it do? Was it really any of their business if Gabriel fucked Ginny and wrecked his marriage? He stood brooding for a moment, and then took out the butter, the orange juice and the milk from the refrigerator. It was only nine o'clock and he didn't have to be at the theater for hours. He glanced out the window and down at the newspaper, which Ruth had left neatly folded by his place at the table, as she always did. Was it mere chance that had caused her to leave it open to the dance review? Oscar picked up the paper and began to read.

GINNY

ancers knew all about pain. It was like an old friend or a member of the family. There were different kinds of pain. Pain in muscles, pain in tendons, pain in joints. Some kinds of pain stabbed, others throbbed. Then there was pain in your feet, which seemed to encompass everything, a kind of lightning rod for all the other pain. And those first weeks and months dancing on pointe revealed a special kind of pain, maybe because it was so unfamiliar.

After the jumps Wes told Ginny and several other girls in her class to take off the soft leather ballet slippers they all wore and exchange them for the hard, satin-covered pointe shoes. Since they had been thinking about this, waiting for this, talking about this, for months, they were primed. The satin shoes—theirs were pink; Ginny's, black—came out of the narrow cardboard boxes and were examined, exclaimed over, compared. Some of the other girls had fancy little rabbitskin pouches to line the insides of the shoes. Ginny had a box of Red Cross lamb's wool, purchased at the drugstore by her mother. She wrapped a bit of it carefully around her toes, and slipped on the shoes, which were hard and ugly, at least while she was standing, and not dancing, in them. Tying the ribbons around the ankles improved things somewhat. Then Wes sent the girls back to the barre, where they did their first relevés onto pointe. What a sensation. Ginny felt she was being lifted up to a place she had never been before, her whole body, legs, arms, everything, impossibly balanced on two small earthbound spots. The contact with the floor was so slight that she could fool herself into thinking she didn't need it at all, that she would rise right up into the air itself. "Good work, Ginny," she heard Wes murmur as he passed her.

That first day, Wes didn't push too hard. They did relevés, some échappés and then some bourrées, while still holding on to the barre. Ginny heard the other girls complain about the pain, but she didn't feel it at all, at least not then. Even after the lesson, she stayed at the barre by herself, going over the simple movements, unable to believe the way she felt when she was just a few more inches off the ground. It was only later, when she removed the shoes and the lamb's wool, that she saw her tights were plastered to her toes with blood: she had danced them raw.

At home, Rita studied Ginny's toes, with their flayed, peeled-off skin. She had Ginny immerse her feet in all different sorts of solutions, and fed her aspirin and ibuprofen tablets as if they were candy. Ginny's toes still burned and stung, keeping her awake most of the night. And they hurt the next day too, but she went to class anyway, and when Wes said it was time for pointe work again, Ginny was the first one to have her shoes on. That day, the relevés and échappés hurt so much that she really did see stars, but she didn't care, she kept doing them anyway. If pain was what it took to leave the ground and be up there like that, then pain was what she'd have to accept.

Of course, it didn't always hurt so much. Ginny learned that pain, at least physical pain, was something she got used to, something she could control. But the kind of pain that starts inside, where it can't be seen or found, that was another thing entirely. And that was the sort of pain Ginny felt in those days and weeks after Thanksgiving, when Gabriel first kissed her.

She kept the note he had given her tucked inside her dance bag so she could take it out and reread it whenever she wanted, which was often. At first, she was expectant and giddy, waiting for this phone call, this message to arrive. But, after a while, when it didn't, she felt deflated, like a bicycle tire that had just gone over a piece of a broken beer bottle. She called the telephone company to make sure her phone was working. Still nothing. She began to feel sick from all the waiting and wondering. But Ginny couldn't call him, though she supposed finding him would have been easy enough. She didn't want to risk talking to his wife and she didn't know the name of the place where he worked. She considered writing to him, but what if Penelope was the sort to steam open a letter and read it? Better not take any chances.

It used to be that Ginny would listen to the other girls talk about men when they were all in the dressing room, getting ready for class or rehearsal. How she had looked down on them. As if any of that mattered when you were a dancer. And now here she was, in the same boat, only she had no one to tell about it, since she had no friends here in New York. The person Ginny really wanted to talk to was Oscar, and that was clearly not going to be possible. They both took great care to avoid each other during this period. If they met in one of the backstage elevators or hallways, he quickly looked down at the floor, or turned his head away. But not so quickly that she couldn't see that hurt look in his eyes. She even felt sorry for him. But what could she do? Gabriel was looming between them, making it impossible for them even to say hello, let alone have one of those long, soulful talks she had come to like so much. So she went to class and rehearsals, and performed onstage all the while thinking of Gabriel, willing him to call her. And then he did.

He told her when he would be in New York and where she was to meet him. When they hung up, she kissed the receiver. He was coming to see her. Soon.

Now the pain vanished, as if by magic, and in its place was the most wonderful kind of anticipation. Gabriel was coming, and Ginny was getting ready for a solo in *The Nutcracker*. She danced especially well during that time; when Erik taught company class, as he did sometimes, he would pay her compliments, the sort that made the others, even the principals and soloists, look at her again. After all, when the artistic director of the company told a member of the corps de ballet that the line of her arabesque was perfect, everyone else in the room took a second look.

Christmas came and went. Mama called her in the morning, to see if she had opened the packages she sent. Ginny thanked her profusely for everything: the cans of chicory roast coffee from the Café du Monde in New Orleans. The two pairs of leg warmers and the black lamb's wool cardigan to wear to class on winter mornings. And the Barbie doll; she couldn't forget to say thank you for that.

Every year, since Ginny was about eight, Rita had given her an elaborate Barbie at Christmas. Though Ginny despised most dolls—babies with fat cheeks, toddlers with dimpled knees—she did have a weakness for Barbie. More than the body, Ginny was in love with the doll's face. She loved the serene expression, the angelic smile. No matter what you did to her—turned her upside down, attempted to deflate her protruding breasts with a hammer and nail—she retained her beatific and imperturbable calm. Although Ginny probed the secret of that calm, she was never able to uncover it. Nor was she, despite her ardent prayers at church on Sunday mornings, able to emulate it.

Even though Ginny had long ago stopped playing with the dolls, she still liked to own them and Rita was happy to comply. In her room back at home in Louisiana, Ginny had a blond Barbie dressed as Sleeping Beauty and an auburn-haired Barbie dressed as Glinda, the Good Witch from *The Wizard of Oz*. She also owned Barbie as a cheerleader, bobby-soxer, mermaid and, of course, ballerina.

This year, Rita sent a trio consisting of Barbie and her two younger sisters, Stacie and Kelly. All three dolls were dressed in coordinating silver-and-green metallic dresses; all wore silver shoes. They came equipped with a black plastic stairway on which they could be posed; a button on its side played a syrupy version of "Deck the Halls" meant to suggest the dolls themselves were singing. Ginny loved it. She carefully took the dolls out of the box (which she saved) and arranged them next to the potted ten-dollar tree she bought at the fruit stand.

Ginny lied and told her mother that she was spending Christmas with Oscar's family, the way she had on Thanksgiving. "Why, what friendly people," Rita said, evidently not realizing that they were Jewish. "I really should write and thank them for taking you under their wing. What's their address?"

"Oh, that's all right, Mama," Ginny said. "Just send a note to me and I'll pass it along."

After they hung up, she spent the rest of the day doing laundry—the machines in the basement were all empty, which was like a gift all by itself—and later watched *It's a Wonderful Life* and *Miracle on Thirty-fourth Street* on television. The second one made her kind of weepy, as it was about a little girl without a father and she and Rita had always watched it together. But Barbie and her sisters smiled consolingly from their plastic perch and Ginny took solace from their benign expressions. Later, she took herself out to a restaurant and ordered Christmas dinner—roast goose, candied yams and all the trimmings—and felt much better. She went to bed early and slept for what felt like days.

The next night, she was going to dance her solo in *The Nutcracker* and meet Gabriel after the performance. Ginny thought that the coupling of those two events was significant, as if each would cast an auspicious light on the other. There it was, her name on the schedule and in the *Stagebill*. Gabriel wasn't sure if he was going to see her dance or not; he said that he felt uncomfortable about being in the theater when Oscar would be there. Ginny told him to make up his own mind. She would understand either way.

Getting ready for the performance actually forced him from her thoughts for a while anyway: applying the makeup a bit more dramatically than usual, adjusting the new costume. Tonight she wasn't going to dance in the corps at all. She had the Coffee solo and that was all. She saw the other corps members putting on their makeup and getting into their costumes. Ginny was all ready, the wardrobe mistress having brought the costume up some time earlier. It was gorgeous, all slinky red and gold, and Ginny was sorry she hadn't thought to bring a camera. If she had, she would have asked someone to snap her picture so she could have sent it home to Rita.

Ginny sat very still while the noise and buzz went on around her. People were making last-minute repairs to pointe shoe ribbons that had popped, putting on antiperspirant, slicking back their hair with a tiny daub of gel or a mist of hair spray. She had the feeling that tonight was a turning point; if it went well, she might not be in this shared dressing room much longer. She might instead have one of her own.

Then the dancers took their places backstage, the curtain went up and the ballet began. As the artificial snowflakes fluttered down onstage, one settled very near where Ginny was standing. She quickly reached to get it, and slipped it down the front of her costume. When the cue came, she imagined she could feel it there, warm, glowing and white, sending her the energy and the poise to dazzle the hushed, expectant audience. And she did. The variation went by so quickly, so very quickly. That sensation of space and expanse, of dancing alone, without all those other bodies around her, now *that* was intoxicating. She could feel the audience like a single live creature, a creature with one heart, and one mind, but a thousand eyes and hands. They were there with her, every second of the way, and then it was over. Applause showered her and she could have soaked it up forever. During the curtain call, she glanced at the orchestra for a second, and there was the top of Oscar's head. He wasn't looking in her direction, though. Instead, he was staring straight off, into space. There was no way she could have reached him, even if she had wanted to.

Afterward, people congratulated her, including a principal dancer whom Ginny admired a lot. She took off the costume carefully; in her mind, she could hear Madame Dubrovska's voice: "Not on the floor, don't let it touch the floor!" She hung it up carefully so that it could be brought back to wardrobe. She didn't bother with the makeup, though; she was that eager to see Gabriel. So she got dressed quickly and was lucky enough to get a cab right away. When she reached the hotel and asked for Gabriel's room, the clerk at the desk looked at her, struggling to hide his disdain.

"He's not here, miss," he replied to her inquiry.

"He will be," Ginny told him. "I'll wait." She pulled a *Stagebill* out of her bag, and opened it to the page where the cast was listed. She handed it to the clerk, pointing out her name. "By the way, that's me. I danced at New York State Theater tonight," Ginny said before she sat down.

"Charming, I'm sure," he said and looked back at his computer screen.

Who cared what he thought, anyway? Especially when a few minutes later, Gabriel appeared in the hotel lobby. She stood up and walked toward him. When he took her hands in his, Ginny felt as if she had come home at last.

The next morning, Gabriel ordered breakfast brought up to the room. Never having stayed in the sort of hotel where they had room service, Ginny was unprepared for how quickly the food appeared. Since she had neither robe nor nightgown, she wrapped herself in a sheet when she heard the knock, and stood there while Gabriel thanked the man and tipped him. It was only after he left that Gabriel went into the bathroom and brought out another white terry cloth robe identical to the one he was wearing. Ginny looked at the robe, and at him, and then burst out laughing. "Did you see his face?" she said, hardly able to talk. Gabriel laughed too. Then he stopped and reached for the sheet, gently tugging it away. She let it drop and moved toward him. Later, he fed her breakfast— berries, one at a time, bits of croissant with jam—while they were nestled together in bed.

"You know we won't be able to see each other very often," he said, face pressed against her neck. "I have a wife. And a daughter."

"I don't care about them. I just care about you."

He pulled his face away, then, and turned her around so they were looking at each other. He was quiet for what seemed like a long time.

"You're such a strange girl," he said finally.

"How am I strange?"

"I thought women couldn't stand the idea of sharing. Another woman would want me to get a divorce. Get married to her. Give her a baby."

"I don't want to be married," Ginny said. "And I certainly don't want to have a baby." Then she told Gabriel about her own mother, the scholarship she had, and how it all went down the drain. How instead of college, a degree and awards, she got eighteen years of raising Ginny, by herself, with no help from anyone. He was quiet again. Ginny wanted to tell him that there had never been anyone like him for her, that she had no convenient slot into which he could fit. She knew he was not going to be a boyfriend or a lover in the usual sense and she didn't care—she just wanted what they had last night and this morning to go on and on. But she didn't know how to say that. So instead she said, "What about your mother? When she saw us that day?"

"That's okay now," he said. "I told her that I wouldn't see you again. That there was nothing to worry about."

"Does she believe you?"

"People believe what they want to believe." He shrugged. "What they can stand to believe."

"How about your father? What does he believe?" Ginny was not sure if Gabriel knew about what happened with Oscar before she met him.

"We haven't spoken since Thanksgiving." Gabriel looked down and fiddled with the blanket binding as if it were the most interesting thing he had ever seen.

"You know about us, then? About Oscar and me?"

"Not really. He didn't tell me anything. I put it together." He lifted his eyes.

"Does it bother you?"

"It did."

"And now?"

"What do you think?" he asked, kissing her. "I'll give you my cell phone number and my number at work. You can call me there, only not too often. And I'll call you. Whenever I can."

"The company will be in California," Ginny says.

"When?"

"After we go to Saratoga—that's in July. So some time in August, I guess."

"You let me know where and when. I'll be there."

Ginny took a shower. Last night's stage makeup felt as if it were embedded into her skin; it took her a long time to get it off. Then there was her hair, which was stiff and matted with styling gel and spray. When she finally emerged, she put on the terry robe, and then started hunting for her clothes, which had been tossed Lord knows where last night. It was only when Gabriel moved the breakfast cart out of the way that she noticed the rolled-up newspaper on the breakfast tray.

"Is that today's *New York Times?*" Ginny asked.

"I guess so. They must send one up with room service. Why?"

"There may be a review in there. Of the performance." She reached over, and quickly started looking through the paper.

"I saw you dance, you know," Gabriel said quietly.

"You did?" She stopped pawing the pages. "You didn't tell me."

"I know. But I had other things on my mind last night." He smiled with such charm that Ginny wished they could get right back into bed. "Still, I was going to mention it." He put his hand under her chin, tilting it up ever so slightly. "I'm hardly a connoisseur, but I thought you were extraordinary."

"You did?" Ginny knew her voice was squeaky, the way it got when she was happy or embarrassed, both of which she was right then.

"I did. And other people did too. I heard the applause when you finished. I could tell."

She stood there, foolishly beaming at him.

"Go ahead," he said, gesturing to the newspaper. "Find the review. You can read it to me if you like." After a few seconds, she found it. There were some remarks about the staging of the performance, which she skimmed, and some things about the principals who danced last night. Then she saw her own name and read silently, though she could feel her lips moving, sounding out the words, seeing how they would feel when she read them aloud.

Newcomer Virginia Valentine dazzled the audience in her all too brief role as Coffee, a variation she imbued with her own grace and sensuality. Ms. Valentine, who has been with the corps de ballet for just over a year, danced like a demon child. Her extensions were lofty, her pointe work both crisp and cutting. She performed the short variation with such passion, such grace, such attack, that one would swear her pointe shoes were on fire as she danced. This reviewer knows she is not alone when she says she hopes to see more of her in the not too distant future.

"Well?" said Gabriel. "Aren't you going to read it to me?" But Ginny found that she couldn't. Instead, she handed him the paper and let him read it for himself. He did and then put it down to stare at her again, in a kind of wonder this time.

"Congratulations," he said tenderly. "It seems that you have arrived."

When Ginny kissed Gabriel good-bye, she cried, but only a little. She felt as if she were in mild shock, what with the lack of sleep last night, and what she and Gabriel had done while they weren't sleeping. Then waking up to all those glorious things written about her in the *New York Times* of all places. Wait until Mama and Wes saw that. She took a taxi home to her apartment. Once there, she went straight to bed and, even though she was all keyed up, still managed to sleep, at least for a little while.

When she woke, Ginny found fresh practice clothes and headed for the theater. She had missed company class this morning and hoped she wouldn't hear too much about that. But when she got there, no one said anything about class, and instead she was treated like a minor movie star. Almost everyone had something to say about the performance, the review or both. Even Erik made a point of congratulating her.

Ginny felt no pressure from the review at all. She did feel a bit stiff from missing class, but she gave herself a short, brisk barre and felt fine after that. Of course she had to shower all over again before she got back into the glamorous costume and the makeup that changed her ordinary-looking face into one that held mystery, fire and romance. She heard the orchestra warming up, and took her place backstage. When the time came to dance again, she was ready, sweet Jesus, was she ready.

It went even better than the night before. After all the applause and the curtain calls, there was still the steady hum of excitement she could feel from the other dancers in the company. The one that said, "Now here's someone to reckon with." Ginny was even asked out to dinner with a group of dancers for the first time since she joined the New York City Ballet, and for the first time she went. She even had fun. So much fun, in fact, that she didn't get back to her apartment building until late, and when she entered the lobby and saw the time, she cursed because she had missed company class once this week already and she couldn't afford to miss it again.

"I'll just go straight to bed," Ginny decided. She cursed again when the elevator didn't come immediately and, instead of waiting, she hurried up the stairs. The key was already in her hand when she jumped back, as if she had stepped on a wasp. There was a big, dark shape hovering by her apartment door. Ginny didn't know whether to be relieved or more frightened still when she realized that the shape was Oscar.

RUTH

"You *mean* he's schtuping *her*? That scrawny, toothy one who was here on Thanksgiving?" Molly shook her head in disbelief. "When he's married to that goddess? Men."

"I guess it isn't about her looks," Ruth said weakly.

"And she's a *shiksa* besides!" added Molly.

"So is Penelope," Ruth pointed out. "If you want to get technical about it."

"But Penelope is a classy *shiksa*. The other one is straight out of a trailer park. It's a matter of style, Ruth. You know what I mean."

"Yes," Ruth said, "I suppose I do."

Oscar was at the theater tonight and Molly had dropped by unannounced, which was good because Ruth wanted to see her, though she wouldn't have summoned her here. To do that would have made it seem like an emergency, and it felt essential to her, if she was to keep soul and body together, to pretend that it was not.

"If it's not about her looks, then what is it? Her brains?" Molly reached for one of the rugalach she had brought with her in a white, string-tied bakery box.

"I don't know. I don't understand her appeal." Ruth regretted this as soon as she said it; she hadn't told Molly about Ginny and Oscar yet. She would, because eventually she told Molly almost everything. She just wasn't ready to discuss this particular hurt; she needed to nurse it by herself for a while, like a sore tooth that you run your tongue over again and again before finally breaking down and phoning the dentist.

"So you saw them kissing that day she was here. So what. Maybe they both had too much to drink and got a little frisky. I remember in the old days, when Bernie and I used to have those big parties. There was always someone kissing someone else's husband in the kitchen. It never amounted to anything." She munched noisily on the pastry and Ruth heard their mother's words, repeated often and with exasperation, "Molly, stop chomping like a *chazzer* and eat like a lady!"

"Well, that's what I thought too. But then he told Penelope that he was going to Santa Barbara to visit clients and it turned out that he was here. In New York."

"How do you know?"

"Penelope called here. She was very upset."

"So you think he's seeing her? This what's her name, Gina—"

"Ginny," Ruth corrected. "I'm sure he's seeing her. Why would he lie, unless he was doing something he didn't want Penelope to know about. And what would that be, other than—"

"Schtuping that girl." Molly sighed. "You're probably right, though it makes no sense. Still, he might get over it quickly. Penelope just has to sit tight and wait for him to get tired of her."

"Molly," Ruth said, feeling a little annoyed at how obtuse her sister was being. "Molly, we both know that Penelope is not the type to sit tight and wait for anything like that. You should have heard her on the phone."

"All right, then. So she's angry. Can you blame her? But she'll calm down. She has the baby to think of. Look at it this way—" she paused to pop another piece of pastry, whole, into her mouth—"even if she did leave him, she'd have to reconsider. After all, how many men are going to want the trouble of a baby that isn't even theirs?"

"She might go home to her mother's in Connecticut," Ruth said. "I'm sure Caroline would have her back."

"Well, and if she did? Would it be so terrible? Everybody gets divorced now. Gabriel would get married again. She might too. You would get to see Isobel, I'm sure. Divorce isn't such a dirty word anymore. We're just behind the times, you and I."

"And I intend to remain that way," Ruth said firmly. "Divorce is fine for the two people who are doing it. But it's not fine for the children." Ruth remembered the phrase "broken home" from her own childhood, and remembered too the sense of shame and sorrow it conveyed. "You have to forgive her," Ruth's mother would say of a playmate who had, in her opinion, behaved badly. "She's from a broken home." Somehow, even all these years later, the words seemed apt. From the child's point of view, divorce—that abstract, impersonal word—meant something broken, shattered, beyond repair. Ruth had no intention of sitting by and watching it happen to Isobel.

"I don't see what you can do about it," said Molly. "You can't send Gabriel to his room anymore. Or take away his allowance."

"Maybe I can't do anything," Ruth conceded, "but I am certainly going to try."

"You're meddling," Molly warned.

"Molly, you don't know her!" Ruth burst out. "If they get divorced, Penelope will never let us see Isobel! We'll lose her, don't you understand?" Molly looked at Ruth wordlessly, then reached out to hug her.

When Molly left, a short while later, there were only two pieces of rugalach left. Ruth decided to save them for Oscar and she retied the string on the box. She called two of her friends from the reading group, but neither one was home.

Then she found herself looking around, as a stranger might, at the apartment, the place she had called home all these years. She could still feel calmed by the cleanliness and order: the floors that were washed weekly with Murphy Oil Soap, the surfaced dusted, cushions on the sofa and chairs freshly plumped, beds made and folded towels neatly stacked in the linen closet. When her sons were little, she used to despair of the clutter they created in their wake: dirty socks and underwear, Popsicle sticks, cookie crumbs, wet towels, treasured rocks, toys and candy wrappers they left behind. She asked them to pick up after themselves, of course, and when asking failed, she nagged, scolded, threatened, cajoled and at times shouted. None of it did any lasting good. Now they were all married, and their mess was someone else's to contend with. Ruth's own little corner of the world was tidy and within her control. Or so she would have liked to think.

Glancing up at the clock, Ruth saw that it was still early; Oscar wouldn't be home for nearly two hours. She brewed a pot of herbal tea, and brought it over to the low table by the couch. *All About Eve* was on, and it suited her mood exactly. She slipped off her shoes, and drew her feet up as she clicked the remote control. Even though she had seen the film many times before, she still laughed when Thelma Ritter compared the pile of fur coats in the bedroom to a dead animal act and when Marilyn Monroe pointed out that somebody's name might be Butler. Sipping the fragrant tea, Ruth watched the screen and waited patiently for her husband to return.

OSCAR

Oscar sat on the terrazzo floor, carefully studying its flecked surface. There was something solid, well made and, yes, even elegant about it, despite the fact the apartment building—a modest one on Seventy-first Street—had been never intended as a luxury dwelling. He reached out to press his fingers against the heavy metal door of the apartment; he inspected the thick molding that separated the floor from the walls. Everything he touched had that same well-made feeling. Oscar felt as if he knew this building, and so many of the buildings like it, that lined the streets and the avenues of the Upper West Side. They were good, substantial and dependable structures, places where a person could comfortably lead a life. All the sweet and humble domestic pleasures—making dinner, making love, raising children—could be contained in spaces like this. Oscar loved them all.

Of course, since the real estate market had shot up beyond imagining, this building had become expensive, much too expensive for the sort of modest life he was conjuring up, the life he and Ruth had led when they moved here all those years ago. These apartments had become high-priced cooperatives or condominiums, affordable only to wealthy couples who worked on Wall Street or in Park Avenue law firms. This very build-ing was a condo; Oscar knew the owner of Apartment 6B, in front of whose door he now sat. The clarinet player from the orchestra used to live here until she retired and moved to Scottsdale. She had bought the apart-ment years ago, and now rented it out. Oscar was able to secure its lease for Ginny, and it was Ginny for whom he now waited, seated and patient on the chilly terrazzo. He could have waited in the lobby, he knew that, but he had no desire to endure the speculative glances of everyone who entered or left the building tonight. Ginny had given him the keys to the apartment; he used one to let himself in downstairs, though somehow he couldn't bring himself to actually go into the apartment without her. So instead he sat here by the door, looking only occasionally at his watch, and waited.

The performance had been over for quite some time, but since she had that solo role, he suspected that she was enjoying a newfound bit of celebrity with her fellow dancers. He thought of the review in which the critic had raved about her dancing. Oscar had read it silently and offered no comment. What could he say? That he agreed with what the critic had written? That he believed in this girl's talent, and was awed by her furious cultivation of it? That this was one of the things he had loved about her? That despite everything, he loved her still?

But Oscar was not a cruel man, nor a stupid one. There was no life for him with Ginny, no future other than the one painted in such vivid hues by his imagination. His place was with Ruth, and he was grateful, more grateful than he could express to her, that she had forgiven him. He knew that preserving Gabriel's marriage to Penelope was the most important thing in the world to her right now, so here he was, his immediate plans unclear but motivation firm and unwavering. He must talk to Ginny about Gabriel and, if at all possible, he must extract from her a promise that she would not see him again. He listened carefully to the sounds made by the elevator as it rose and descended. So intent was he on trying to determine if the elevator would stop at the sixth floor that he hardly noticed the light tapping of footsteps on the stairs. But then he intuitively knew who it was, and when he looked up, there, standing over him, was Ginny.

"Oscar," was all she said when she saw him. In the soft light from the fixture above them, her hair—loose and spread out now over her shoulders and back—gleamed pale, almost blond. She was wearing a nubby black coat with a fluffy black collar. It was absurd, of course, the way all of her sartorial choices were, but endearing too: it made her look like some small animal, a rabbit, perhaps, or a kitten. Oscar got to his feet with difficulty, as he had been sitting for a while and the cold floor had made his legs stiff.

"Here," she said matter-of-factly, giving him her arm. "You might as well come in."

The apartment was as cluttered and disheveled as he remembered; as he took off his coat, he gingerly tried to avoid stepping on a large mound of towels. Ginny, meanwhile, dropped her own coat on the table. Oscar kept his in his arms.

"I needed to see you," he said. "I suppose you know why."

"It's about Gabriel." Oscar nodded, looking around in vain for somewhere to sit. Ginny watched him. "We can go in the bedroom," she said. So Oscar followed her dutifully, still clutching his coat. He noticed a small, potted Christmas tree in a corner. Next to it were three gaudily dressed dolls posed on what appeared to be a staircase. Oscar couldn't place the dolls, though he felt he had seen them before. Hadn't Molly's daughters played with such things, years ago?

Once in the other room, he sat down carefully on the bare mattress. He could see that the dirty sheets—were they the ones that were on the bed when he was last here?—had been dumped on the floor but he did not see any clean replacements. Maybe there were none, and she would have to sleep wrapped in her soft, dark coat all night long. Ginny bounced more than sat down, and the bed springs bent slightly beneath her weight. "Look," she told him earnestly, "I know how awkward all this is. I mean, because of what happened between us. And because he's married. But what I have or want with your son—" she stopped for a deep breath— "has nothing to do with you."

"That's not true," said Oscar slowly. He was having trouble concentrating on the task at hand. Under the coat, she was wearing a very tight black Angora sweater. Beneath its deeply scooped neck, he could see the outline of her tiny breasts; above, the long, eloquent line of her neck. Her scar seemed to smile at him. Suddenly, Oscar felt he had nothing to say, nothing to demand. All he wanted was to reach out, grab her slender arm and pull her down under him on the quilted blue surface of the mattress.

"Oscar," Ginny said gently. "Oscar, wake up." She smiled and Oscar felt an overwhelming urge to weep. "I know how you feel about me."

"You do?" he said. But then his wanting her was so obvious, of course she saw it.

"Because it's just how I feel about Gabriel." She wrapped her arms around herself, as if she were cold. "But you don't have to worry. No one will find out."

"Ruth and I already have," Oscar pointed out.

"I'm sorry about that. Really I am. Can't you pretend that you haven't? It would be so much easier." Oscar stared at her, remembering the girl who criticized his playing that first night. Could she really be in earnest? Or was she mocking him?

"No," he said finally. "I can't pretend."

"All right, then. It's up to you. Look, I know what a bad idea it is to get involved with him—"

"Then don't," Oscar said.

"I can't help it," Ginny said. "And neither can he."

"There's nothing I can say that will make you stop? That will make you leave him alone?"

She shook her head, still holding herself tightly.

"Can you leave me alone? Didn't you come here tonight knowing what a bad idea it was? Aren't you sitting here on my bed right now"—she uncoiled one arm and patted the mattress—"wishing you could get me in it?"

"I came because of Gabriel," Oscar said, but he felt as if he were sinking, drowning in his desire for her.

"Really, Oscar? Just because of Gabriel?" Her arms moved down to her sides now, and she splayed her small hands against the mattress. This caused her back to arch, just a bit, and the subtle movement pushed her breasts—her maddening, lovely little breasts—up and out. Oscar could contain himself no longer. He reached across the quilted expanse that separated them, pulled her into his arms and kissed her. Surprisingly, she neither pushed him away nor resisted; instead, she kissed him back. Oscar's mind was reeling, but he didn't let go. Tentatively, he moved his fingers up the furred front of her torso until—finally—they cupped her breasts. Only then did she move back, place both her hands on his heaving chest and disengage herself.

"You see?" she said, almost sweetly. "No matter how wrong, how crazy it is, you still want me. And if I hadn't stopped you . . ." She didn't have to finish. Oscar knew she was right. Despite Ruth, despite Gabriel, Penelope and Isobel, he would have let himself fall, all over again, right into her arms. He didn't look at her because he couldn't.

"Maybe you'd better go now," she said. Oscar said nothing, but started to look for his coat, which he had let drop when he embraced her. Ginny walked him to the door.

"You have no clean sheets," he said stupidly, for want of anything else to say. "How will you sleep tonight?"

"Don't worry about me," she said as the door closed. "I'll find something."

Once in the street, Oscar saw many vacant cabs heading uptown but he didn't stop to hail any of them. He was not sure how he would face Ruth, and he needed some time to compose himself before he did. Instead of going toward West End Avenue, where he lived, he turned the other way, toward Central Park West, and walked along its edge, the side that actually bordered the park. This was inviting trouble, he knew, as it would have been all too easy for a mugger to demand his wallet and disappear into the dark sanctuary of trees. Still, Oscar continued on, soothed somehow by the bare, delicate branches, almost indistinguishable from the night sky, and the throb of life—unseen and mysterious—that lay beyond the park's low stone walls. Birds and rodents lived there; also stray cats and maybe some stray dogs too. Snakes. Frogs. Once, years ago, he saw a group of parrots squawking companionably in a pine tree. A whole world that neither included nor excluded him, but existed on its own plane, parallel to the one that was his. Why this made him feel better, he didn't know, but it did, and by the time he reached his own apartment door, he had regained some sense of equanimity.

He understood that he had been spared, though he could take no credit for it. Had Ginny been willing, he would have done anything she wanted. But she had said no, and in so doing, she had set him free. Oscar realized just how lucky he was. He could face Ruth with a clear conscience, because in fact nothing had happened. His desire remained just that; there was no action, no consequence that he need feel ashamed of. He would not seek Ginny out again, because he knew just how frail his resolve really was. But if he could avoid the transgression by avoiding the temptation, well, that was something. Something he could hold on to.

"Oscar?" Ruth called out as he slipped his key quietly into the lock. "Oscar, is that you?"

"Yes," he was able to say with some real assurance. "Yes, it's me."

GABRIEL

I t *was* only as Gabriel guided his car into the parking space that adjoined the back of his apartment building that he remembered he had
not called Penelope. The trip across town had taken so long; there hadn't
been time. And he hadn't wanted to do it when he was actually with
Ginny. Later, it had seemed wiser to just come home and not call too
much attention to his whereabouts.

The car, which was dark green, new and imported from Europe, glided
smoothly into place, stopping precisely and immediately within the painted
lines. He had never owned such a car before, and were it not for Penelope's
largesse, he would not have owned it now. Why did this make him angry?
She hadn't offered any objection to his buying it. But he was nonetheless always aware that his own salary could not provide him with this kind of luxury. For that, he depended on Nel. And while he could truly say that money
was not the reason he had married her, he also had to admit that he didn't

like the prospect of giving it up should their marriage end. Not that he wanted it to end.

He still loved Penelope, although her sickness—there, he had said it—made that love a burden rather than a joy. Couldn't Ginny be his antidote? Maybe the affair would actually help keep his marriage together rather than pull it apart. Gabriel knew that this was an indefensible rationalization. But he couldn't help making it all the same.

Pulling the key from the ignition, he checked his appearance in the rearview mirror for any telltale sign of betrayal. There was none—he looked the same as always. Penelope would have scarcely noticed that he was gone. She was so wrapped up in the baby, she wouldn't even have missed him.

Once the car was parked, he picked up the small bag he brought with him and walked to the elevator. The ascent was slow—this was an older building, after all—but steady and quiet. He took this as a good omen as he set down his bag.

"Nel?" he called out tentatively, trying to open the door. "Nel, I'm home." Why wouldn't the door open? He manipulated the key around in the lock and then realized the lock was fine, its brass tumbler smooth and fluid. There was something blocking the door, that was all, though he wondered what it could be.

"Penelope," he called again, beginning to feel annoyed. "Let me in." He kept pushing, first with his hands and then harder, with his shoulder. There. The door finally gave way, at least a bit, so he could peer inside to see what in fact was obstructing his entry. At first, he couldn't see anything, but as he looked down, he noticed it. The pile of straw? Fabric? No—paper. There were mounds and mounds of shredded paper wedged under and around the doorjamb—that was why it wouldn't open.

"Shit," he said softly as he dropped to his knees. He slipped an arm through the door's small aperture and began digging, like a rodent, through the mess. He thought he could recognize some of the fragments. Wasn't that a page from this week's *New Yorker*? Who had done this? And why?

He began to feel frightened. Was there someone here, a burglar, a rapist, a killer? Could someone have broken in, hurt Penelope and Isobel, and then left this pile of debris as a cryptic message for whoever found them?

Gabriel could feel his heart beating heavy and hard in his chest. He kept digging, clawing really, and found more glossy magazine pages that had all been neatly and methodically shredded. "Penelope!" he called, louder now, an urgent note rising in his voice. "Penelope, are you all right?" Stupid question, but he could think of no other. There was no response. Gabriel kept working, grabbing bits of paper, pulling them through so that they littered the clean, polished floor of the hallway, or stuffing them back into the apartment, far enough away from the door to prevent its remaining stuck. He was sweating with exertion now, for he worked quickly, and with mounting panic. Finally, there was enough space cleared so that he could push the door open to get inside.

"PENELOPE!" he shouted and went tearing through the hall, scraps of paper like mounds of snow gathered around his ankles, impeding his motion. Gabriel could see that the paper filled the entire hallway, and much of the living room. He kicked at it clumsily as he made his way toward the bedroom, in search of his wife and child. He saw more pictures from architectural magazines, the ones that were usually stacked neatly on a nightstand by their bed, but then he saw something else too: smaller pages from what appeared to be books. He reached down to pick up a crumpled sheet from the floor and smoothed it out. It was a page from a now out-of-print volume by the architectural historian Vincent Scully, one that Scully autographed and gave to Gabriel when he guest-taught a course at Yale. Gabriel put a hand up to his eyes, feeling momentarily sick. When he took the hand away, there was Penelope.

"Welcome home," she said.

"Penelope! What happened? Where's Isobel?" he demanded.

"She's asleep. Unless your yelling woke her up."

"What happened here?" he asked, but as he looked at her calm face, it was suddenly clear. "You did this," he said, in a voice filled with amazement.

"I did it," she repeated in a flat, dead tone. The sound of her voice scared him. He looked around at this sea of paper, paper that she had carefully ripped, crumpled and left, like a sacrificial offering at his feet. He didn't ask her why because he already knew. Silently, he sunk down to the floor, where the paper covered his feet and knees.

"I didn't go to Santa Barbara," he began.

"I know that," she said, still in the same dead voice.

"I went to New York. To see a woman," he said. "I made love to her," he continued, eyes lifted to her face now, "but it was you I thought of the entire time." Gabriel was amazed at how easily this lie slipped out of him, and how easily Penelope seemed to accept it. Her eyes suddenly lost that opaque flatness and he could see something register in her face.

"You did?" she asked, and her voice was no longer dead, but small and childlike now, infused with something like hope. He nodded, and reached out his hand to her. She waded across the paper that separated them and took his outstretched palm in hers. The paper rustled as she dropped down beside him. "Why?"

"I missed you," he said simply. "You're never here for me anymore. Everything is the baby, always the baby. This woman that I met—"

"Who is she?" Penelope asked quickly, ready to pounce.

"Her name is Solange. Solange Roussel."

"She's French?"

"Canadian. From Quebec."

"You met her when you went there for that conference?" Gabriel nodded, and it all came together in his mind, this imaginary woman he had never met, her imaginary problems with her imaginary husband, their imaginary plans to meet in New York for a very real tryst. During the recitation of all this, he was both grave and humble, the very model of a repentant husband asking his forebearing wife for another chance. He kept her hand tightly clasped in his, hypnotically caressing the space above her wrist over and over again as he talked.

"It was a huge mistake," he told her. "I never should have lied to you, never should have gone there."

"Maybe I drove you to it," said Penelope, leaning her head against his chest.

"Do you think you can forgive me?" he asked. Her mouth quivered but she nodded. Gabriel tilted her face toward his and kissed her. "Isobel is . . . ?" he murmured.

"Sleeping," she said. "Really." They made love there on the floor, with the torn paper beneath them as a mattress.

"It's been too long . . ." he said softly, but although he could still be aroused by Penelope's dairy-fresh skin and abundant dark hair, these things no longer bound him. His senses had been altered—tainted, even—by Ginny's heated and intoxicating touch, and it was her image that burned in his mind, even as he gripped Penelope's lovely shoulders. Later on, they found scraps of paper stuck to Penelope's back and legs, and as he helped her peel it off, they actually managed to laugh. Then Isobel awoke and Penelope went in to nurse her, so Gabriel was left with the job of cleaning up.

He found a box of large plastic garbage bags and began, slowly, to fill them full of paper. Magazines, books, many of them out-of-print and hard to come by, had been destroyed, but still their loss caused little pain compared to his sense of relief, of elation, at not having really been found out. The fictive Solange had served her purpose and could be deposited, like the shredded paper he now handled, in the trash. His true secret was safe and he intended to keep it that way. He had been sloppy, thinking Penelope was too absorbed by Isobel to notice. Next time—and Gabriel had no doubt there would be a next time—he would be more careful.

After he had filled all the available garbage bags with paper, the floor was still covered with it, so Gabriel decided to go out and get another box. Or two. On his way out, he hauled some of the paper-filled bags with him, because there were too many to leave in the incinerator room. He ran into the superintendent of the building, who eyed his massive load with a smile.

"Spring cleaning?" he asked.

"Something like that," said Gabriel, returning the smile.

———

After this, Gabriel experienced a halcyon period of calm with his wife and daughter. Penelope was, of course, overwhelmingly involved with Isobel, but she now sometimes allowed Gabriel to enter the charmed circle as well. There were family baths in the scooped-out melon of a Jacuzzi tub Gabriel had installed for her when they first moved into the apartment; there were shared outings to the playground, where he stood behind Isobel in the black, hard rubber baby swing and Penelope stood in front, and together they pushed her back and forth, back and forth, while she opened her baby mouth in a wide O of delight. And if Isobel was sleeping soundly enough, there were moments when Penelope shimmied out of the soft white cotton nightgown she wore and turned to him in the night.

Gabriel was grateful for all of this, basking in the newly restored attention of his wife, but all the while he knew it was too late: something had changed in him that was beyond mending, and the something was Ginny. The memory of their night together was like a bright secret hidden deep in his pocket: the way she laughed out loud when he repeated a dirty joke he'd heard (he would not even have tried it on Penelope), the way she listened so avidly to everything he said, the way she touched him, held him, the glorious way that she ate. She couldn't have been more different from Penelope, whose various and ever-multiplying anxieties had slowly permeated their life together. Penelope was the moon—remote, distant, beautiful—while Ginny was a star—a supernova, exploding again and again with a white, fiery heat.

Gabriel knew she would be in San Francisco that summer; she told him that when they were together. That was months away, he realized, but he could wait. Wait and plan. It would be easy enough to get a schedule for the ballet; perhaps he would suggest to Penelope that they get tickets, or even a subscription. He had told her how much he loved going to the ballet when he was young. She might remember that, and like the idea.

Carefully, slowly, he made his preparations. He phoned his mother again, managing to make her believe that he told Penelope about his indiscretion. He didn't mention that Penelope believed he came to New York to see a French-Canadian woman named Solange Roussel, not the ballet dancer Virginia Valentine. There was no reason to. Ruth was very relieved to hear this, though she had trouble believing Penelope had really and truly forgiven him.

He hung up the phone and fairly panted with relief. He had been so stupid, such a fucking self-centered teenager about all this—kissing Ginny in his parents' apartment, flying off to see her with such a pathetic alibi—and look what pain it caused. Penelope, his parents—each of them had been hurt by his behavior, although Gabriel had no desire to hurt anyone. This feeling he had for Ginny was his alone. If he could keep it that way, no one need be hurt again.

Lying in bed with Penelope beside him, he stared at the mute, white curve of her shoulder. Was she dreaming? He remembered a recurring nightmare she used to have, one that always made her wake in tears. He couldn't recall the substance really, only that she seemed so grateful for his comfort. She never told him about her dreams anymore. Maybe she no longer believed he could comfort her. Maybe she was right.

PENELOPE

Penelope had obsessive-compulsive disorder—OCD for short. She knew this because she had been reading about it on the Internet. When Gabriel was at work and Isobel slept, she logged on and clicked her way to the chat rooms that had become a major sustaining force in her life. Once there, she traded stories and advice with other people like her, people whose need to control the way they lived overshadowed the substance of the lives themselves. She didn't tell Gabriel, or anyone else in the family, about what she had learned.

Just discovering that what she had was a known syndrome, with recognizable features and traits, was reassuring to her. OCD was like a box into which Penelope could put so many of the things that had troubled her since childhood. She remembered the many rituals required to soothe herself: tapping three times on the headboard before she got into bed, and another three times before she left it. There were a certain number of taps on the door when she wanted to leave her room, and another number when she wanted to enter it. Different foods on her plate couldn't touch each other. She worried, even then, about the germs she might catch from holding her partner's hand as the class filed out to recess.

The rituals seemed to get worse after her father died, but her mother didn't give them much credence. "It's just a phase" was Caroline's assessment.

By the time Penelope reached Barnard, the rituals governed much of her life. She couldn't go out when it rained because umbrellas upset her. She couldn't wear a scarf around her neck for fear of being choked. Certain small, sharp objects like tweezers and manicure scissors filled her with an ugly and palpable terror. She suffered from what she called "contamination attacks," when she was convinced that something she loved had been dirtied or poisoned. The need to tap before leaving and entering a room intensified, though to avoid being detected, she was able to quiet herself by tapping on the square wooden block she carried—in a pocket or a handbag—with her everywhere.

Then she met Gabriel, and some of the fears seemed to subside, at least for a while. When they returned, it was in a new guise: she became obsessively neat and devoted much of her energy to cleaning and organizing their apartment. Funneling all that anxiety into the apartment was a good thing, Penelope decided. It made her seem less odd, less troubled. Lots of people dreamed of having their homes be picture-perfect; look at all the magazines devoted to just that goal.

Moving to San Francisco gave her an even grander outlet for her obsessions. And having an architect for a husband didn't hurt. He cared about the way things looked, and so did many of the people he knew, people who came to visit and exclaimed about what a restful oasis the apartment was.

"Look at what you've done with the place," said the wife of the senior partner in Gabriel's office. "It's fabulous."

"Thank you," murmured Penelope, glancing at Gabriel. "White is such a restful color. It helps me stay focused, you know?"

"Absolutely," agreed the other woman. "Gabriel," she said, turning to him, "why have you been hiding Penelope from us all this time? I think she has a lot to offer. Maybe she could come over to our apartment some time. Give me some ideas."

"I'd love to," Penelope said, trying to read Gabriel's face as if it were a book. She knew how he felt about all the white; she had seen his office after all, seen it and been personally affronted by the hideous colors of the rug and the vases he had chosen. But Gabriel just smiled at her as if he had never found fault with Penelope's craving for the solace of white.

After the company had left, Penelope turned to Gabriel. "Other people like it here," she said, gesturing around the white room. "They think it feels peaceful. You're the only one who objects."

"Who said I object?"

"You've complained about it often enough."

"Once. I complained once. That hardly qualifies as often."

"Still, I know how much it irritates you. I can tell." Penelope flipped her sleek, dark hair away from her face in an impatient gesture.

"Look, Nel, do you really want to start a fight?" asked Gabriel. He sat down on the sofa, his shoulders slumped. In his arms, he clutched one of the white pillows.

"No, I guess not," Penelope said, not at all sure of what she wanted. But the answer came to her soon enough. She wanted a baby.

Penelope got pregnant almost at once. Being pregnant made her feel happier than she had at any time in her whole life. Although she quickly gained ten pounds, her body felt buoyant, and weightless. Suddenly she had the kind of energy she never had before: for the apartment, yes, but also for the baby. Everything now was directed toward the baby. Gabriel didn't seem to mind. In fact, he seemed pleased by her renewed interest in things, by her zeal.

The only clash came over the issue of the baby's name. Once Isobel was born, though, Penelope felt so bonded to her that the name ceased to matter. Their two souls were inextricably intertwined; what difference did it make what she was called?

"Baby girl," she crooned over and over again to the newborn in her arms. "Baby love." Her mother and Gabriel's both came to help out in the beginning. Penelope felt she could manage perfectly well on her own; still, she wasn't all that unhappy to have them there. Later on, Penelope's bad feelings resurfaced again, when her mother-in-law insisted on remaining clueless about how Penelope wished to care for Isobel. The awful, tacky clothes the older woman sent. And the things she would have fed Isobel if she had the chance. Penelope could feel the start of a contamination attack when she thought about it.

Through all this, Gabriel seemed superfluous. Not that this would always be the case, because Penelope knew that once Isobel grew a little older, she would want another child, and another one after that. For now, though, he ought to understand how engrossed she had become. Understand and approve. When he told her he was going to Santa Barbara, she was actually grateful. She didn't have to pretend to include him. She and the baby could exist, a perfect unit, all by themselves.

Which they would have done, had it not been for that phone call. The call that came from Austin and Janice Levy, the couple whose house Gabriel was supposedly on his way to see. After that conversation, Penelope went to Gabriel's desk and turned on the computer. Without fully knowing why, she didn't log on to the familiar OCD sites; not yet. Instead, she scrolled through the recent history and found the airline booking to New York. New York. Why was he going there without telling her? Even without knowing the reason, Penelope was already furious.

GINNY

Ginny *had* known for a long time that the mirror was everything: her friend, her enemy; her partner, her audience. The walls of every ballet studio in the world were lined with mirrors, and it was those mirrors that told her everything she ever needed to know. She first understood the mirror's power years ago, when she started taking Wes's ballet class in New Orleans. That was where she learned to love the mirror or, more accurately, her reflection in it. The mirror showed her a girl different from the one she knew everywhere else: in the mirror, she could do anything. Her extensions were higher than anyone else's, her jumps bouncier, her feet more quick; the mirror told her all that and more.

Everywhere else, Ginny couldn't do anything right: she failed math tests, couldn't memorize a thing in history or geography. She wore the wrong clothes, said the wrong things, was nobody's friend, and the principal's special mission. But there in the mirror, everything was reversed: she was the best, the most talented, and all the rest of the girls were pushed to the background.

Wes started putting her in the front line of the class early on, so Ginny had a chance to see herself in the mirror without so many other bodies in the way. After a while, she danced for that mirror as if it were the president of the United States. Wes didn't approve of this, so he made the girls all turn away from the mirror and dance with their backs to it. It was so strange dancing without the mirror—like being lost in a fog with no map or compass. No one liked that, and of course it was all Ginny's fault—another reason for them to resent her. Which they did already. Eventually, though, he let the girls turn around, and this time Ginny was more careful. She still loved that magic mirror, but she wasn't letting it show.

So by the time she came to New York, she was very good about concealing her love affair with the mirror. During the barre exercises, she had developed a trick of keeping her eyes down, which allowed her to look in the mirror without making it obvious. In the center it was easier, of course. There she didn't have to pretend so much, especially since she was hardly ever in the front row. But after her success in the *Nutcracker* solo, Ginny began to find herself up front a lot more. Now she could drink in that mirrored image of herself without distraction. To her surprise, no one seemed to mind. When she and Rita went to church years ago, there used to be a hymn about how loving Jesus was like water to a parched soul. That was what those moments in front of the mirror felt like to Ginny. Water to a parched soul.

Falling in love—the way she had with Gabriel—was like finding another kind of mirror. There you were, reflected in someone else's eyes, only the reflection was better than the real thing. Gabriel thought she was beautiful. Wrong. He thought she was captivating, self-possessed, powerful. Wrong, wrong, wrong. But in the mirror of his love, she was all those things and more. What did she reflect back to him? That, to her, was a mystery.

After that solo, a lot of things changed. The way the other dancers looked at her, for one thing. And the teachers too. Then she was picked to be the understudy of the Sugarplum Fairy, which was one of the best roles in the ballet. Usually understudies didn't get to dance because most principal dancers would walk barefoot on smoldering coals before they would miss dancing during a scheduled performance. But right at the end of the season, the ballerina who was dancing the role turned her ankle stepping off the curb and crumpled down in the street, just like that. So as Ginny was coming into the theater, she was practically assaulted by one of Erik's assistants. He hurried her downstairs to Madame Dubrovska, who was waiting with a threaded needle in one hand and a pair of scissors in the other, ready to alter the costume.

The one for the pas de deux was exceptional. It had a tight-fitting pale green satin bodice and a short net tutu of the same color. Petals of slightly darker green brocade fanned out from the waist. Twinkling bits of green rhinestone framed the neckline and were scattered on the skirt. The straps were made of braided gold trim. "Hurry up and put it on," Madame Dubrovska said. It felt a little loose because the dancer Ginny was replacing was taller than she was, so Madame had to shorten the straps and take in the waist. All the while, Ginny stood there in front of her friend the mirror and watched as her transformation from corps member to ballerina took place. "There," said Madame Dubrovska triumphantly. "Someone get her the crown."

Ginny was not nervous about dancing that solo—the longest and hardest one of her career. Once the crown was on, and her makeup complete, she couldn't wait to get out and face the biggest mirror of all: the audience.

The role of the Sugarplum Fairy couldn't be more different from that of Coffee. Coffee burned and spat; Sugarplum was cool and poised, a queen looking out over her subjects. Near the end of the ballet, she danced a pas de deux with her cavalier. Ginny knew how real life was supposed to interfere with art: she saw *The Red Shoes* about six times as a child and believed that dancers had no place for love in their lives. She didn't cry at all when Victoria lay dying on the train tracks; Ginny thought she deserved it. But when Ginny danced Sugarplum that night, everything she ever thought about that particular subject flew right out the stage door. She understood the pas de deux in a whole new way, as an outpouring, a river of love, from the ballerina to her partner. She danced the whole thing thinking of Gabriel: how it felt when he touched her. And it brought down the house. Later, the reviewer for the newspaper said she danced with "brilliantly articulated passion" and "magisterial authority." Evidently, Erik liked the sound of that, because he told her that when the new season began in the spring, she was being moved up to the rank of soloist. From corps de ballet member to soloist in less than two years; that was a quick rise. So many dancers spent years—sometimes seven or eight—in the corps before moving up. Most never moved up at all.

After the winter season was over, there was a short break before the spring season began. Ginny went to bed early, ate plenty, attended class every day. Sometimes she took a jazz dance class at a studio on Seventy-seventh Street, just for a change. Then it got cold for a spell, a bitter, punishing cold that she couldn't stand, so she stopped doing even that. She began to feel stir-crazy, sitting in her apartment, watching TV and ordering in from the Chinese take-out place on Amsterdam Avenue. It got so that she started thinking of going down to Louisiana to see her mother, when all at once, the cold was over and spring had come to New York.

Spring in the city was an amazing thing. The dirty, pee-stained snow and ice melted all at once and there were piles of slush everywhere. No one seemed to mind, though, they were just that elated, dazed even, by the mild air, the buds on the bushes and trees, the mounds of flowers that sat in buckets outside the Korean greengrocers on every other street corner. Ginny received a huge bouquet of lilies and freesia from Gabriel. Naturally, she had no place to put all those flowers so she had to go out and buy a great big glass vase, though really an umbrella stand would have been a better choice.

Seeing those pretty flowers inspired her to clean up her apartment, which she hadn't done since fall. Barbie and her sisters were slipped back into their box, and stored in the closet. Ginny might have had the dolls on permanent view in Louisiana. But this was New York.

She took a cab over to Bloomingdale's and bought wineglasses, sheets, a whole box of long, white candles with some fancy pewter candleholders, potpourri with a big bowl to put it in, a pair of striped canvas covers that slipped over the folding chairs she already had and some lipstick-red towels for the bathroom. She could afford these things now; her new position meant a raise, though that was hardly what mattered. She found a little black love seat on sale, and a standing lamp, and she bought those things too.

The lamp was delivered right away and the love seat a few days later. The candles went into the candlesticks, the candlesticks went on the table, the bowl of potpourri between them. Ginny sat on the couch, sipping iced tea from one of the new wineglasses and surveying the effect. All in all, it was pretty good. Though she wasn't sure what she intended to do in this spiffy, fixed-up apartment: the only visitor she had ever had was Oscar, and that couldn't happen again.

Ginny hadn't seen him since that night she had found him waiting outside her door, and she supposed that was a good thing. She'd see him enough during the spring season, though she knew that the orchestra wouldn't travel with the company to Saratoga Springs. Or to San Francisco.

San Francisco. Just thinking those words gave her an excited buzz, because that's when she would see Gabriel again. Apart from the flowers, they hadn't been in touch very often during these last months. It made sense, what with his wife and his parents breathing down their necks. But in San Francisco, they would both be in the same city at the same time. And if they were careful, everything would be just fine.

Once the spring season began, she was busy all the time. So many new roles to learn, and good ones too, like one of the leads in the "Emeralds" section of *Jewels* and a solo in *Ballo della Regina*. There were other roles too, in ballets not choreographed by Balanchine, but it was the roles in those Balanchine ballets that she lived for. Wes used to say that Balanchine was unrivaled in the twentieth century; no one else even came close to doing what he did. Ginny was in total agreement.

She was up early every day, and was often the first one there for the ten o'clock company class. Sometimes Erik taught, though class was usually conducted by the ballet mistress, Althea Johnson. Ginny liked Althea, who was a former dancer of around forty, which seemed to Ginny very old. She was also one of the few black people Ginny had seen in or around the company. Althea had been one of Balanchine's special protégées, but that was a long time ago, before a hip injury ruined her career. That must have been hard, because from watching her teach class, Ginny could see just how good she must have been. Ginny thought she looked like a black swan, and after she came to know her a bit better, she learned that Althea did in fact dance the Black Swan pas de deux from *Swan Lake* in the regional company of Birmingham, her hometown. In class, Althea was always immaculate, with her hair neatly bound and adorned with a chiffon scarf the same color as the leotard and chiffon ballet skirts she wore. Though she favored light colors—mint green, robin's-egg blue, rose, peach and lavender—against her dark skin they read rich and interesting, not bland and pasty.

Ginny and Althea had "talked Balanchine" after class; Ginny was always asking her what Mr. B. thought about such-and-such or how did he see this or that particular role. Apart from Wes, who didn't exactly count, Ginny had never had a dancer as a friend before, and she liked it. Althea was flattered by Ginny's interest—most of the dancers were too busy trying to court Erik's favor to bother with Althea—and always paid attention to Ginny in class. When Ginny told her that she was promoted to soloist, the older woman's pleasure seemed genuine. "We have to celebrate," she had said, hugging her. "My treat." But Ginny wanted someone to see her born-again apartment, so she convinced Althea to come over, though Althea insisted on bringing all the food.

Althea came to dinner on a Monday, when the theater was dark, so they were able to sit down and eat by seven, which was early compared to most nights, when the dancers didn't eat until the performance was over and the audience had all gone home. Ginny had actually gone over to Pottery Barn on Broadway and bought plates, place mats and real cloth napkins. Mama would have been proud.

Althea brought several shopping bags full of food from an Indian restaurant and the two women set the food out on the table.

"*Mmm*, this is very good," said Althea, biting into a piece of tandoori chicken. "Do you want some?" Ginny nodded and Althea put a piece on her plate with her own fork. Ginny hadn't remembered to buy serving utensils. Next time. They ate their chicken for a while in silence, until Althea set down the naked bone and patted her stomach. She waited until Ginny was finished too and then said, "Are you going into the bathroom now?"

"Excuse me?" Ginny said, confused. Was this some kind of New York code for drug use that she didn't know about?

"To throw up," Althea said, matter-of-factly.

"Jesus, no!" Ginny understood. Everyone in the company was so worried about their weight that lots of dancers had become habitual vomiters, running into the bathroom after a meal to send it all back up again.

"Me neither," she said, smiling. "Another reason why I like you." Ginny smiled back. "There's dessert too," Althea said. "It's that delicious pudding they make. With the almonds and the rose water." While they ate the pudding—spooned into the wineglasses because Ginny had no small bowls—Althea told her things about Balanchine.

"He used to give perfume to each of his principal dancers. Really good perfume. You know, the expensive stuff. Worth. Dior. Balenciaga. He spent a lot of time shopping for it."

"He did?" Ginny tried to summon a picture of George Balanchine at the perfume counter of a department store. Macy's, was her first thought. No, tonier than that. Saks. Bergdorf Goodman. "But whatever for?"

"He wanted them each to have a signature fragrance. So he was always looking for new ones. No two dancers ever got the same scent."

"Why not?"

"He said it helped him keep track of the dancers while he was in the theater. He would walk through the halls sniffing, and his nose could tell him just who had been in what studio, or elevator or wherever."

"Imagine having Mr. B. pick out your perfume," Ginny said reverently. "Did he ever pick out one for you?"

"Chanel Number Nineteen," Althea said. "I still wear it." Ginny stared, trying to imagine the moment when Mr. B. presented it to her for the first time.

The two women eventually moved from the table to the love seat, still talking, until Althea stood up and stretched. "I'd better get to bed," she said. "You too. Company class is at nine tomorrow."

"Why so early?" Ginny stood too, picking up some of the dishes and dirty napkins. She didn't want the apartment to become that familiar old pigsty. At least not right away.

"Extra rehearsals," said Althea. "We're learning some new things for San Francisco."

"San Francisco," Ginny said, thinking not of the roles she would be dancing, but of Gabriel watching her. The mirror again.

"Do you want to room with me?" Althea said, not noticing how Ginny's attention had drifted.

"Room with you?"

"Ginny, quit repeating everything I say or I'll tell Erik you're going a little soft in the head. No more solos," she teased.

"I'd love to room with you," Ginny said, snapping back to the present. "It'll be a blast." But then she was far away again. A blast. Blast of a whistle, blast of a rocket. She was thinking of the town where she had grown up, the way the night sky was lit with fireworks every Fourth of July. She and Mama would walk, along with just about everyone else in town, to the big field by the high school. Lying there on a blanket in the matted grass, Ginny would stare up at the sky, watching how burst after burst of color would explode, bloom and melt away. At the time, she thought she had never seen anything so beautiful. She now knew that those bits of light were like ballerinas, bursting onto the stage with their color and fire, then fading away again, into black. She was that light-filled sky, Ginny thought as Althea prattled on cheerfully at the door, and soon Gabriel would be there in the dark, watching her.

RUTH

There *was* someone new in Mrs. Goldenfarb's room. Ruth saw her just briefly the last time she visited the home because the new woman was on her way to Physical Therapy when Ruth got to the eleventh floor. Only the back of her small, bent form was visible, culminating in the crown of white braids that reminded Ruth of Lilli. But today, when Ruth began her visits—pushing a heavy metal trolley filled with slightly outdated magazines and dog-eared paperback novels—she stopped at her room first. Her name was printed on a white index card taped outside the door: "Esther Vogel." Ruth repeated the name a few times, a little trick she used to help her keep the many different names straight. Esther Vogel was seated in bed when Ruth entered, and her concentration was absorbed by the contents of the metal bed tray placed before her. Very carefully and deliberately, she cut her food into small pieces that she then moved to one side of her plate. She didn't actually seem to be eating.

"Hello, Mrs. Vogel," Ruth said. "Enjoying your lunch?"

"What's to enjoy?" the older woman replied without looking up. "Everything smells like shit. Tastes like it too."

Ruth sighed. So many of the new residents were angry about being here, and who could blame them? They grew up in a world where their own aging grandparents lived and died at home, cared for by other family members. What sense could they make of this place, with its linoleum hallways, its mural-like bulletin board on the ground floor announcing news of the residents?

"Maybe you'd like something else. You can always have a sandwich if you don't care for the hot lunch. Would you like me to see about getting you one? I think it's tuna today."

"What for?" Mrs. Vogel said, still cutting and arranging. "It will only taste the same. All the food here tastes like shit."

"What about something to read then?" asked Ruth. "Here's a new Stephen King novel. And I have the *New Yorker, Cosmopolitan, Vogue* and *Ladies' Home Journal.*"

"Who are you?" said Mrs. Vogel, finally looking up. Her eyes were a pale watery hazel, but her gaze was focused and her expression alert.

"Ruth Kornblatt," Ruth said, touching the name tag pinned to the pink smock all the volunteers wore. "I come once a week to visit."

"Why?" Mrs. Vogel asked.

"Because I like to," Ruth said. In fact, her question took Ruth by surprise and she had trouble framing a reply.

"You *like* to?" Mrs. Vogel seized on the word. "What is there to like about this place? Or about anyone here?" Ruth didn't respond and the older woman continued: "Well, maybe it's better than some place else you could be, right? Maybe it's like an escape. You come here so you won't feel so bad about your own *tsouris.* You get to see someone who's a lot worse off than you." She leaned back against the pillows and abruptly pushed the tray away. A plastic cup was jarred by the motion and tipped over, spilling apple juice all over the bed.

"I'll just go and get some paper towels," Ruth said, glad for an excuse to leave. Mrs. Vogel closed her eyes and said nothing.

The rest of Ruth's visit was soured by the encounter with Mrs. Vogel, despite the warmth with which she was met elsewhere on the floor. Mr. Blustain was happy to get the *New Yorkers*—Ruth had three issues today—and she played several hands of gin with Mrs. Dienstag, who beat her every time. "You're not paying attention, Ruthie," Mrs. Dienstag scolded as she took the deck from Ruth's hands to shuffle. Mrs. Fishbein was so eager to see Ruth that she actually came to find her in Mrs. Dienstag's room. They played a hand together, and then Ruth walked Mrs. Fishbein back to her own room, where she showed Ruth the package she had received from her granddaughter in Los Angeles: several bottles of nail polish tucked into a small wicker basket and tied with a gold ribbon. "Did you ever see such colors?" she exclaimed, holding the little bottles up to the light. "Sky blue? Lime green? Black?"

"That's what the girls are wearing these days," Ruth said, remembering that William's wife, Betsy, was sporting those light blue nails the last time Ruth saw her. When was that? Thanksgiving? What an awful day. Maybe Mrs. Vogel was right, Ruth thought. She came here to escape her own problems.

"Well, I could give it a try, couldn't I?" said Mrs. Fishbein. "What do you think, Ruthie? Green or blue? No black for me, though. Not yet. Time enough for that, right?"

"The blue suits you best," Ruth told her firmly. "I'll paint your nails and we'll take a picture. Send it to your granddaughter. We'll show her that East Coast ladies still have what it takes."

"She'll be so tickled!" said Mrs. Fishbein and she spread her fingers wide, imagining the effect.

But even after the quiet rewards the morning had to offer, Ruth still replayed the exchange with Mrs. Vogel in her mind on the way home. Why couldn't she have said something that would have broken the spell the woman seemed to cast on her; something kind and wise that would have helped her. Because if there was no point to making these visits to the home, why was she doing it? Maybe Oscar was right when he said that she should spend more time with her own family.

It was this thought that guided Ruth's hand to the telephone later that evening. Oscar and she had been so worried about Gabriel and Penelope that Ruth had scarcely spoken to either of the other boys since Thanksgiving. Of course, Ben hadn't been in New York; he and his new wife left for London before Christmas. But William and Betsy were close enough, in New Jersey, just across the river. It was their number that Ruth dialed.

"Oh, hello, Ruth," Betsy said, sounding not at all pleased. "Will's not here. He's going to be late tonight."

"I'm happy to talk to you," Ruth said, ignoring her tone. "We hardly had a chance on Thanksgiving." There was a pause, so she kept going. "Someone at the nursing home today had a bottle of sky blue nail polish and it made me think of you. I remembered how pretty yours looked." Ruth, she berated herself. Is this the best you can do? No wonder your daughters-in-law don't want to talk to you.

"Actually, Will and I have some news for you," said Betsy, not seeming to have heard this last inane remark. "Good news." But her voice didn't sound happy. "We're going to China. To adopt a baby girl. We just got the call from the agency and we have three weeks to get ready."

"Betsy, that's wonderful. We had no idea you were even thinking of adopting—"

"We've been trying for over two years," Betsy interrupted. "And we can't do it. I mean, Will can, but I can't. And so we're going to adopt."

"Honey, I'm so happy for you both. Oscar will be too. I can't wait to tell him." This was a lot of information to assimilate all at once, but it did make many things fall into place. The kind of discomfort she sensed in Betsy whenever the subject of children came up. The way she looked at Isobel. The way she avoided Ruth.

"Thank you." Why did she sound so sad? Ruth kept wondering. But she herself was not sad, not at all. This was the best news she had heard in a long time and she was thrilled.

"Betsy, let's celebrate. What about you and William meeting us somewhere for dinner? In Chinatown? Wouldn't that be just perfect?"

"All right," Betsy said, hesitating only slightly. "I'll tell Will you called."

Ruth realized that the conversation was over, and despite the fact that she was brimming with things to ask, she instead said good-bye and hung up the telephone.

They all agreed to meet for dinner at the Red Dragon Inn, on Mott Street, one night when the ballet company was between seasons. As Ruth and Oscar ascended from the subway station, the air felt warm and moist; even humid. Not truly spring weather, but not winter either. Ruth was glad for the change. They all needed one, she thought, as she walked through the crowded streets, holding on to Oscar's arm. There was going to be a new baby in the family; that would be something good to focus on. God knew she needed it. They picked their way through the shop vendors, whose wares spilled out onto the sidewalk, and the true itinerant merchants who set up with tiny folding tables and blankets just inches from the curb. Eels and skinned ducks, persimmons and embroidered slippers, lobsters, fans, key chains, watches, sweatshirts, suitcases. So many things in so small a space.

As always, when confronted by such an array, Ruth wanted to buy something for someone. Wouldn't Ben's new wife like a padded silk jacket with silken frogs in place of buttons? What about those painted hand fans? Surely some of the ladies at the nursing home would like those; they're always complaining that the rooms are overheated. But Oscar said there was no time to stop, so Ruth clutched her handbag tightly under her arm and hurried alongside him, until they reached the restaurant.

William and Betsy were already there and hugs and kisses were exchanged all around as they took their seats. Large, plastic-coated red menus were placed in their hands almost immediately, so all conversation centered around the food for a few minutes. It was only when the order was taken and the menus swiftly whisked away that Ruth could sit and look at, really focus on, her middle-born son. He was tall—all Ruth's boys were tall—with dark brown hair and eyes. His looks were neither astonishingly good nor displeasing, though she did notice that he had put on a few pounds. No matter. Seated next to his wife, holding her hand as he talked to his father, he looked happy.

William had always been the defiant one. Ruth was ashamed of herself for thinking this way, especially after so many years. She could remember how her mother did the same thing, sorting her children into neat categories, like the mail or the bills. In her eyes, Molly was the one with bad manners and a good head for math; Ruth was refined but reticent and retiring; a wallflower to Molly's showy blossom. She vowed she would never define her own children this way, like so many butterflies, fixed and immobile under the scientist's stark pin. Yet she'd done it anyway, despite her best intentions.

Gabriel, the eldest, was both clingy and remote, the sort of child whose kisses seemed rationed but who was apt to burst into tears even when she left him merely to go check the mailbox in the lobby. Ben was the cuddler, always climbing into Ruth's lap, or snuggling up beside her on the sofa. "Mommy, your skin is so soft," he would say; "Mommy, my toes are cold—will you rub them?" How Ruth loved that. But Willy was the one who said no before he said anything else, and it seemed to her that once he started, he didn't stop saying it for the next twenty years. Ruth heard no at bedtime, bath time, mealtime and everywhere in between. He said no to haircuts, to homework and to music lessons, and though she managed to prevail in all of these things, more or less, it was never without a struggle. Finally, when he got too old for his parents to tell him what to do, all the nos seemed to melt away, and he had been transformed into a successful and prosperous doctor. "Though how he got through medical school without telling his professors no to every exam, quiz, paper and report is a mystery to me," Oscar used to say.

"So *tell* me about China. About our new granddaughter," Oscar said now, while William smiled and Betsy looked anxious.

"She's seven months old. Black hair—of course. But her face, Dad, wait until you see her face." William pulled a picture out of his pocket. Ruth and Oscar peered down to look. Ruth saw an Asian baby in a knit cap and bulky, dark clothes. She had a full, round face, and a small, serious mouth. Ruth stared at the photograph and then touched the precious image captured within it. Her new granddaughter.

"We're going to call her Hannah," William added.

"Hannah," Ruth repeated. Hannah was her mother's name. Then she turned to Betsy. "She's beautiful." Instead of answering, though, Betsy burst into tears. Oscar and William looked alarmed and the waiter came hurrying over, but Betsy, her head still bent over her blouse, waved him away.

"What's wrong?" asked Oscar and William, nearly in unison. There was no immediate response, but when Ruth offered her a packet of tissues from her purse, Betsy took one and began to dab at her wet eyes and cheeks.

"I'm so sorry," she finally said.

"Sorry for what?" William said.

"I didn't mean to break down like that. It's just that we haven't told you"—she gestured toward Ruth and Oscar—"about what the last two years have been like. Wanting a baby, trying to have a baby, enduring every damn treatment under the sun and *still* not being able to have a baby. And then watching Penelope and Gabriel have Isobel just like that! It's been really hard."

"But now we are going to have a baby," said William with a quiet authority that made Ruth proud of him. "We're going to China. In two weeks. And we're bringing her home with us."

"I know. And I'm happy about it, I really am."

"Then why ...?" asked William. Oscar and Ruth were silent; they had nothing to say here, they were outsiders, intruders even.

"It's just that getting her, finally getting her, feels like I'm saying goodbye to the other thing." William looked confused. "I guess it's hard to accept that I'll never have one of my own."

"Oh, but she will be your own," Ruth couldn't help saying. "You don't know that yet, but she will be. She is already."

"How can you say that?" asked Betsy, staring intently into Ruth's face.

She seemed not hostile, but curious. "You've had children of your own. Three of them. How can you know what it feels like for me?" Her voice sounded as if she were ready to cry again.

"I don't," Ruth said, desperate not to offend but equally desperate to comfort her. "I just know that what makes them yours doesn't have that much to do with carrying them and giving birth to them. It has to do with the way it feels when they're in your arms. Holding them, feeding them, bathing them, loving them. That's what makes them yours." Ruth's face felt all red and flushed. She saw that Oscar and William were staring, not sure what to make of this. Just then, the waiter appeared with the appetizers—prawns, baby egg rolls, soup with curls of steam that rose from its golden surface—and they all looked down at their plates and chopsticks until he was gone.

"I never really thought of it that way," Betsy said slowly, looking at Ruth as if she were revising every single thing she had ever thought of her. "But now I will." She picked up a spoon and began to eat her soup. William casually draped an arm over her shoulders, managing to eat his food with surprising grace despite using only one hand to do it. The rest of the meal passed without incident. When they said good night, Betsy hugged Ruth tightly.

"Thank you," Betsy said into her ear, "so much. I'll call you before we go, all right?"

"Do that," Ruth said, returning the embrace. Then she turned to her son, who kissed her not once but twice, on either cheek, like a dapper European gentleman.

Later, as Ruth was lying next to Oscar in the peaceful oasis of their bed, he turned to her, hand propped under his head.

"You amaze me, you know," he said quietly.

"Amaze you? After all this time?" Ruth's tone was playful; surely he was teasing.

"Yes, you really do," he said, and she realized he was not mocking at all, but instead quite serious.

"In what way?" she asked, turning to face him so that their noses were almost touching. She had always thought Oscar had a fine, beautiful, even noble nose.

"It's your desire to mend things. Most people don't bother to fix what they've broken. But you're different."

"Well," Ruth said, not sure how to respond to this unexpected and lovely compliment. Was it true? She couldn't say. She only knew that she had to keep trying, as Oscar said, to put things together again.

They made love after that and when Oscar rolled away from her, back to his part of the bed, Ruth thought some more about what he had said. He seemed to have great faith in her power. But as she watched her husband's recumbent form relax and drift into sleep, Ruth herself felt strangely powerless. She wanted to physically shake the feeling off, as if it were an annoying insect hovering around her head. Still it persisted, buzzing steadily and quietly all through the night.

GABRIEL

Gabriel had always been a collector. As a boy, he gravitated toward the usual assortment of boyish things: bottle caps, seashells, polished rocks, mint-condition coins that winked brightly in their protective plastic cases, albums filled with page after page of lavishly colored, exotic stamps. He also collected ticket stubs and programs from the ballet performances he went to with his mother; he even saved a few pairs of signed point shoes—the dancers often gave them away to fans—but he quickly abandoned that. The shoes were bulky and hard to store, and he didn't want to hear his brothers' teasing about them anyway.

As he got older, his collections grew more arcane and specialized. There were the vintage game pieces: Bakelite dice, poker chips and faded wooden markers that began with the thirty-pound carton he bought on a whim at an auction in Massachusetts. Then there was the outmoded scientific equipment—hydrometers from the 1930s still in their crumbling, cardboard boxes, turn-of-the-century glass beakers and cork-topped test tubes—that he purchased from a dealer in Queens.

Most recently, he had started to collect old neon signs, a habit that Penelope would not abide, at least not in their apartment. "You mean you would bring those awful things in here?" she said when she saw the first one, a green sign that read HOT COFFEE on one line and ROLLS on the line below. In between was a stylized, green neon coffee cup with a vivid orange plume of steam emanating from its surface. "Isn't neon a poisonous gas?" When he assured her that it was contained, she didn't believe him. "What about seepage? Don't you read the newspapers? Don't you know anything?" She also objected to the colors, which she found garish, and the noise, a soft but raspy buzzing sound, rather like the intermittent humming of insects on a hot summer night.

Gabriel hadn't intended to collect the signs, but that was true of most of his collections—he didn't set out to do it, but somehow the object, whatever it was, found its way to him, like a signal, a portent whose meaning was only that which he conferred upon it later. The first time he became interested in neon, he had been visiting with clients up the coast and, on the drive home, had to stop because of construction in the road. At the same time, a group of men were dismantling an old, roadside diner. As Gabriel slowed his car to a halt, two of them were carrying the HOT COFFEE/ROLLS sign almost directly past his open window, to a large Dumpster nearby. "How much do you want for that?" Gabriel found himself saying. The men looked around, not sure what they had that could be of value. "The sign," Gabriel said, gesturing toward it. "The one you're carrying. How much?" The two looked at each other and then back to Gabriel. The shorter one said, "You mean you want this? What for?" Gabriel couldn't answer that, but got them to agree to put it in the trunk of his car. At first they didn't want any money, but eventually they accepted the pair of twenties that he pressed into their palms.

The rest of the way home, Gabriel was acutely conscious of the sign he was carrying. He felt warmed and reassured by its humble promise of food and drink; the steaming cup was an unexpected visual delight, a gift of sorts. He could hardly believe it was his. When Penelope vetoed it, he was not surprised or even bothered; he just took it to his office, where it seemed to fit right in.

After that, he began hunting for signs, tracking them down at out-of-the-way places: a family-run drugstore about to succumb to the might of a large, national chain (he loved the stout red cross surrounded by a red circle he found there) or a shoe repair shop (where he was drawn to the deep blue cat's face that was meant to advertise the once popular Cat's Paw brand of soles and heels) whose owner had recently died. These signs, and many others, came back with him, and joined the first on the large white wall of his office that he had cleared just for that purpose. There was a blue rectangle with the word OPEN inside it; a set of crimson block letters that spelled out BERKELEY MEAT MARKET; a sign in pink script that read LOLLY'S HOUSE OF BEAUTY and showed a woman's face in profile. Her features were not rendered, but her long hair was wonderfully articulated in delicate curls and waves of pink neon.

They began to attract notice, these signs Gabriel had been accumulating. First the other architects in his firm would stop and comment on the shape of one, the color of another. Then it was a client. "They're like poems that you just find in the urban landscape," said Austin Levy, the husband of the couple from Santa Barbara, the ones Gabriel had pretended to be visiting the time he flew to New York to see Ginny. Austin asked if Gabriel could get him a sign for his living room. So Gabriel came up with a pair of rakish green-and-yellow neon cocktail glasses that floated in a yellow oval of neon. The word BAR was written in green script above the oval. Austin was delighted, couldn't stop exclaiming about it. Soon other clients started requesting them too and Gabriel found himself tracking down the perfect vintage neon sign for a health clinic downtown, an upscale art gallery and a fancy house in Palo Alto. His boss, the senior partner in the firm, was pleased with the way Gabriel's idiosyncratic hobby had turned into a sought-after design element.

Gabriel thought the whole thing rather funny. Still, he kept looking for and buying signs, mainly because he continued to enjoy them himself. And as long as they did not enter their apartment, Penelope didn't mind them either. In fact, apart from this latest interest of his, she generally regarded Gabriel's collections with a kind of indulgent fondness. He had told her about all the things he collected as a boy, even the pointe shoes. Which turned out to be quite handy when she discovered—in the most unlikely way, since he was sure he had hidden them safely—the pair of battered salmon-colored pointe shoes that Ginny had given him.

As they were leaving the hotel room in New York, Gabriel noticed that Ginny was about to toss out the pair she had worn during the performance the night before.

"Why are you throwing them out?" he had asked.

"Oh, they never last more than one performance. I usually do it at the theater, but I was in such a hurry last night." She beamed at him. "No sense lugging them back across town, though. The bag's heavy enough as it is." And she tapped the large, rather soiled zebra-print tote that was slung over her shoulder.

"Let me have them," he said impulsively.

"Well, all right," she said, clearly pleased. "But I won't sign them, okay?" So the pointe shoes had flown back across the country with him, tucked way at the bottom of the small bag he carried. They remained there for quite a while; after the scene with the shredded paper and the reconciliation that followed, he had actually forgotten that he'd taken them. When he did remember, he thought he'd bring them to the office. Penelope almost never went there, and when she did, he was always with her. It was unlikely that she'd search his desk or file cabinets, so he felt reasonably comfortable with the thought of putting them there. Once they were there, he could consider at length the best place to keep them. So he slipped them into a bag and the bag into the glove compartment of his car. Penelope claimed not to trust Gabriel's natty little Audi, and unless there was some pressing reason, she never drove it. So how was he to know that during the brief few hours between the afternoon he tucked the shoes into the glove compartment and the morning he would have taken them to the office, Penelope would decide that she needed a flashlight in her car, look all over their apartment and, when she didn't find it, check that very glove compartment in search of one?

"What are these?" she asked, coming into the apartment, holding the shoes aloft.

"Those?" Gabriel willed himself not to look alarmed.

"Aren't they ballet shoes? Toe shoes?"

"They're called pointe shoes, actually," he said calmly enough.

"Oh, so *these* are what you used to collect?"

"That's right," he said, hardly daring to believe that she herself had supplied the alibi he so desperately needed. "Though I never had that many to begin with."

"I thought you got rid of them," she said.

"I did. But I found those tucked into a box somewhere. So I thought I'd keep them after all."

"A little bit of your youth?" she said, smiling now.

"A little bit of my youth," he agreed. She handed him the slippers, nestled toe to heel, their sweat-stained satin ribbons binding them neatly together. He could feel the relief coursing through him now as his hands closed around them. Goddamn it! Almost caught again! And he had sworn he would be so careful! She turned to leave the room.

"Whose were they, anyway?" she asked over her shoulder.

"I honestly don't remember anymore," he said, looking down at the book he had been reading when she first came in. The shoes were never mentioned again.

Spring came slowly to San Francisco. There was lots of rain and even when there wasn't, there seemed to be an uncommon number of damp, cold days. Penelope and Isobel remained indoors much of the time, Isobel toddling around their now fully baby-proofed apartment and Penelope trailing after her. Gabriel spent long hours at his office, working mostly, but also logging on to Web sites that he dared not log on to at home, like the one for the *New York Times,* which gave him access, albeit indirectly, to Ginny. In the Arts section, he could read reviews of her performances. One critic described her as "magisterial" and Gabriel knew precisely what the reviewer meant. There were other reviews too, equally stellar. He read them over and over again, imagining her dancing in ballets he remembered from childhood.

Finally, it got warm. Late in April, they had a birthday party for Isobel—her first. There were only the three of them in attendance, but Penelope bought paper hats and streamers and even produced a heart-shaped cake made by an organic baker. Gabriel thought it tasted like sand, but he didn't say so. There were no balloons; Penelope had read of too many cases where a baby ingested a scrap of popped balloon and died as a result. Still, Isobel seemed delighted, waving her fists in the air and pressing her thumb into the sliver of cake that Penelope offered her.

Gabriel's parents called earlier in the day and despite a certain anxiety he detected in Ruth's tone, there was no overt reference to Ginny. Instead, both his parents asked to speak to Isobel, and although usually Penelope insisted that Isobel was frightened by the telephone, today she relented enough to let the baby make a few babbling noises into the receiver. Both Ruth and Oscar seemed to be listening when she did this; Gabriel could visualize their heads close together, one almost on top of the other, as they strained to hear their grandchild. Then there was the news about William and Betsy's new baby, who had arrived a few weeks earlier. "She's just darling," Ruth told Gabriel when the phone was passed back to him. "I've never seen eyes quite like that—so big and so dark. I can't wait for her to meet Isobel. They're first cousins, after all." Gabriel thought about that for a few seconds: he could imagine Penelope's fears about strains of foreign viruses being transmitted between the babies. Probably best to delay this meeting for a while, though he didn't say so to his mother.

———

In July, the New York City Ballet went to Saratoga, in Upstate New York, for a month; Gabriel learned this from logging on to the NYCB Web site, which tracked their whereabouts. He was pleased to find short profiles of all the soloists and principal dancers, and since Ginny had recently been made a soloist, hers was among them.

Sitting in his office in the early evening, after everyone had left, he stared at her image on the screen. The light had just begun to fade outside, and a few minutes before, he had turned on, one at a time, all the neon signs on his wall. They filled the room with their noisy, convivial hum. Ginny wore a long sleeved black leotard, cut very low in front so that he could make out, even on the screen, the shallow division between her breasts. The tiny, crescent-shaped scar at the base of her neck—a freak childhood accident involving a dropped knife that ricocheted off a table—was hidden though, and this made Gabriel feel happy; a private bit of her to remember and savor that was not on view to the world. Over the leotard, she had on a long, diaphanous skirt, under which her legs, in their pale tights, were clearly visible.

He learned that she was born in Bakerstown, Louisiana, that she started studying ballet when she was eight, that *Serenade* was her favorite ballet. He studied her face for a long while. She was heavily made up in this picture, as she was the night he met her at the hotel. Still, he could see that she was not beautiful, at least not in the way that Penelope was. But even in this frozen, digital likeness, he could see the animation that sparked her face, her body. She was avid, rapacious, bold, eager; Gabriel wanted to inhale, ingest, consume her, incorporate those aspects of her being into his own. What a pair of contrasts they were, his wife and lover. One was rich, well educated, classy, beautiful. The other was low-class, poor and without even a decent high school education. But how alive she was, how completely, totally alive. Whereas it often felt as if something in Penelope had died. He hadn't realized just how exhausting his life with her was until he met Ginny; Penelope's fears and anxieties had led to so many small renunciations and denials. But Ginny renounced nothing; to be in her presence was to be embraced.

Yet Gabriel did not wish to leave Penelope. The thought of disrupting their life together and his home held no promise of relief. If he were to do that, what would happen to Isobel? Would Penelope even let him see her? Even though he often felt Isobel was something of a stranger to him—guarded so vigilantly by her mother—he didn't want to lose her.

And then of course there was Nel's money. Certainly, as Ruth was fond of pointing out, Gabriel enjoyed the material comforts that Penelope's wealth allowed him. But at the same time, he resented that wealth, because it usurped his own prerogative in earning it. How many architects at his stage of a career could afford their apartment with its expensive furniture or the car he drove?

No, rather than face the pain of upheaval, both psychological and material, he would rather accept Penelope just as she was. But he wanted Ginny too, and he had to find a way to have them both. It was an awful, selfish wish: Gabriel knew this. Yet Ginny didn't mind being part of this triangle, and if Penelope never found out, who, in the end, would be hurt? This was what he told himself in an effort to justify something for which he knew there was no justification. He thought then about his father. It still made him sick to contemplate Oscar and Ginny together. How had Oscar justified it? Though now that he knew Ginny better, he had the feeling that she was the one who decided—for what reason, Gabriel could not fathom—that she wanted Oscar. Because when Ginny wanted something, she got it.

Quite apart from his guilt over betraying her with Ginny, Gabriel was genuinely concerned about Penelope's increasing emotional turmoil, and he wanted to help her. Not that she would admit she needed help. But Gabriel was aware of the anxieties that held her, most days, tightly by the throat. The cupboards were filled with bottles of the antibacterial soap she ordered in bulk from an organic produce supplier; its vaguely spicy, geranium-like scent hovered over her skin at all times. She talked to her-self, quietly, not out loud, but her lips seemed to move in an ongoing, self-referential monologue. She was getting worse. A lot worse. He did a little research on some of her symptoms using the Internet; he questioned people—very casually, of course—at his office. He even called, with some misgivings, his brother Will, who was a cardiologist in New York.

"Hey, Gabe," William had said, answering the phone in that bluff and hearty way Gabriel remembered and hated. "What's the score?" Still the jock even all these years later, Gabriel thought. But he controlled himself for Penelope's sake. Once he explained what had been going on with his wife, William turned suddenly serious and concerned.

"I'm not really sure," he had said. "Sounds like she could be manic-depressive. With a little obsessive compulsive stuff happening on the side. There are a lot of new medications on the market now. But you really need an expert opinion. I know a couple of people you could call."

"I really appreciate it," Gabriel said sincerely, as he jotted down the names and telephone numbers.

"There's one more thing, Gabriel," William had said.

"What's that?" Gabriel sat, his pen poised midair.

"She has to want it," William said.

"Want what?"

"To get help. To get better."

"What if she doesn't?" There was a long pause during which Gabriel uncoiled a paper clip, stretching out the metal filament into a long, taut line.

"No magic bullets, Gabe. No magic bullets," William said finally.

Gabriel hung up the phone and stared at the names he had written down. By a crazy coincidence, one of them was named Dr. Giselle Klaubis. Giselle. In the story told by the ballet, Giselle went mad when she discov-ered her lover, Albrecht, had betrayed her. Went mad and died. Gabriel crumpled the piece of paper and threw it in the trash. Only later did he retrieve it, and tentatively mentioned one of the doctors to Penelope. But he did not mention Giselle Klaubis.

———

Now, as he sat, still staring at Ginny's picture, he wished he could download it and the little box of text beside it, but he didn't dare. Somehow Penelope would find it, just the way she found the pointe shoes, the ones he had since buried at the very back of his least-accessible file cabinet. So he regretfully clicked off the image and instead found the scheduled performance dates for the company's stay in San Francisco. He printed out the schedule and folded it into neat thirds, which he then slipped into the outermost flap of the leather case in which he carried his papers. He wanted it to be very visible—he had nothing to hide, after all—to Penelope should she choose to look through his things. And if she did, he could casually mention that the ballet was coming to town, and how much he would like to see it, for old time's sake. How he planned to see Ginny alone he hadn't yet figured out. But just being able to sit quietly in the theater and watch her dance—that thought was enough. The rest of it would come. He didn't know how yet, but it would. He toyed momentarily with the idea of clicking back to her image again, but he did not. Instead, he turned off the machine, and the dozen humming lights behind him, and went home, to his wife and child.

Later that evening, he mentioned the idea of going to the ballet.

"That would be nice," Penelope mused, looking down at Isobel, who was, as usual, at her breast. "But what about the baby?" The baby. Penelope would not go out for the evening and leave Isobel with anyone; how could he have forgotten? When Isobel was a newborn, they took her with them. Now she was too big and too lively to spend a whole evening in her mother's arms, so Penelope preferred to stay home. "Of course, if you really want to, you can go by yourself," Penelope was saying. She had shifted Isobel to her other breast and the nipple of the first one, glimpsed quickly by Gabriel before she covered herself, was still wet and shining. "I don't mind. Really I don't." She looked up at him and smiled.

"We'll see," said Gabriel neutrally, but inside he was throbbing with pure, unalloyed joy. Here he had been so worried about how he would manage this, and Penelope had made it so easy. He could watch Ginny alone. And afterward, well, he would think of something. Gabriel's gaze lifted up and over Penelope's dark head. Through the window he saw the lights of the city spread out below him. Their distant glow gave him hope, and he could feel a plan taking shape inside of him.

PENELOPE

Penelope still dreamed of the accident, even all these years later. In her dreams, she was driving down that road again, hands steady on the steering wheel, the August light dappling yellow through the canopy of trees above her. It was her last summer at home; in September, she would be starting her first term at college. Where had she been going that afternoon? She didn't remember. What she remembered and what she dreamed of were the car, the quiet swerve of the road, the light. And the blurred, brown shape that darted from its invisible place by the trees. The shape that materialized into a doe who chose that precise moment to cross the road. Penelope felt, more than remembered, the impact of the deer's body as it slammed against the hood of the car. At that point, she always woke up.

She hadn't been driving that fast, so the deer had not been killed. At least not immediately. She remembered hitting the brakes suddenly and getting out of the car. No sign of the doe, who had vanished into the woods. Looking down, Penelope saw that the hood was smeared with blood. She put her hand to the spot and found that coarse dark bits of the animal's fur were mixed in it. She wanted to atone, somehow, for hitting it, so she ran her bloodied fingers across her cheeks and forehead. Getting back into the car, she surveyed the result in the rearview mirror. Interesting. Like war paint.

"I hit a deer," Penelope said calmly as she headed for the bathroom to wash her hands, rather sticky now, and her face.

"But you're bleeding," said Caroline. "Let me see." Penelope walked past her mother without saying anything else. When she emerged from the bathroom, face and hands newly clean, hair brushed and gleaming, Caroline said nothing, but looked steadily at her, as if trying to assess the extent of the damage.

Penelope wondered why she had so many dreams of the accident. She didn't dream of her horse, whose death she actually witnessed. Or of her father. She didn't even know what happened to the doe. Maybe the wounds were minor and the animal recovered. Maybe she went on to live a long, long life in the forest, mothering fawn after fawn, delicate Bambi-like creatures who hovered by the side of the road, drawn by some mysterious force to cross it, only to be hit again and again. Sometimes, the dreams ended with Penelope waking in tears; other times, in a frantic sweat.

When she first met and fell in love with Gabriel, she used to tell him about these dreams. He was always so sweet with her then; he would have her lie resting her head in his lap as he stroked the long dark hair away from her forehead in an effort to soothe her. Sometimes she even woke him up in the middle of the night. He never seemed to mind; he always wanted to comfort her. But since Isobel's birth, she found herself confiding less and less in Gabriel. He had become more of an opponent than an ally. On one occasion, he even suggested that she see a therapist. He actually went so far as to get a referral from that brother of his, William, the one who was a doctor back east.

"It might be helpful," he suggested, as they sat on the soft white sofa, watching the news one evening. Penelope hated the news. Murders, catastrophes, encroaching poisons with which the world was being consumed. But Gabriel liked the news, and she watched to please him.

"Helpful in what way?" she asked.

"You know, Nel. With the washing, for instance. And the tapping."

"I don't have a problem with those things." So he had seen her, been spying on her, no doubt.

"You don't?" he asked, sounding surprised. There was a commercial on now, for the kind of industrial-strength detergent whose residue Penelope was sure would forever taint the waters, the soil, the very air they were required to breathe.

"No. You have a problem with them." She got up. News be damned. "I think I hear Isobel," she said, retreating to the baby's room. Isobel had not stirred, but remained peacefully asleep. See a therapist. As if Penelope actually *wanted* to stop washing. Or tapping.

Still, she realized after her conversation with Gabriel that she needed to be more careful. She didn't want him or anyone to know the full extent of her rituals. Or her preparations, which was how she liked to think of them. Preparations for the world, and all the terrifying cruelty it could contain. So she washed when he wasn't there, tapped only on the piece of wood that she kept in a pocket.

After Gabriel returned from that trip to New York, Penelope decided to buy a new car. She had never trusted the sleek green sports car Gabriel bought after he was selected to build the new extension of an important northern California museum, and so she had been driving their old Toyota. But the Toyota, in perpetual need of repair, was faltering. Penelope thought it was time for a change.

"What did you have in mind?" Gabriel asked when she told him her plan. But they both knew the money—and therefore the decision—was hers.

She began to research cars. Their safety and their fuel emissions. Their gas consumption and their maneuverability. She logged on to the Web site of *Consumer Reports*, downloaded and printed back issues. The Insurance Institute did crash tests that simulated cars hitting walls; she studied their reports as if committing them to memory. As Gabriel sat watching the evening news, Penelope spread the pages around her, forming a giant fan on the living room floor. She crouched in the center, marking and cross-referencing. Gabriel offered his comments and occasionally a suggestion, but mostly he seemed happy to let her select whatever she wanted.

Then there were the visits to showrooms, the protracted conversations with car salesmen, the numerous test-drives. Gabriel had offered to watch Isobel during this process, but Penelope insisted on taking the baby with her to each and every test-drive. Securely strapped into her car seat, Isobel enjoyed the activity. Her hands, clenched into small fists, beat the air around her; her feet in their white cotton socks kicked merrily.

Although Penelope told this to no one, she felt certain that Isobel could actually help her choose the right car. Not that the baby would be able to articulate her choice in words. But Penelope was convinced that when Isobel's energy was right, she would be able to feel it. They were that much in tune with each other.

Early on a cold, foggy Sunday morning, she dressed Isobel warmly in a knitted cotton sweater and cap, tucked a soft blanket around her legs. They had an appointment to test-drive a Volvo station wagon. Penelope was closing in on her target; it was either this or a Mercedes. She didn't really think she would buy a Mercedes, though. Too expensive, too ostentatious. But she hadn't fully settled on the Volvo yet either. She had read some good things about the Subaru Outback, a vehicle known for its modest gas consumption and overall reliability. But the Volvo had the side curtain air bags, to protect that tiny skull, in the backseat. She would have to see.

Gabriel drove them to the dealership. "Do you want me to go with you? Or to wait?" he asked.

"That's all right," she said. "The salesman promised to drive me home." She had talked to this particular salesman on the phone four times already; sometimes, she woke up in the middle of the night with a question that she wrote down so she could ask him as soon as it was morning. He was eager to make this sale, and the offer to drive her was part of that eagerness. But there was also something else that Penelope didn't want to tell Gabriel. If Gabriel was in the car with her, she was afraid that she wouldn't be able to sense Isobel's energy. The connection between mother and child might be somehow impeded or clouded. So she leaned down to the open window of the car, where his breath made soft, white puffs in the chilly air, and lightly kissed him. Then he was gone.

"Mrs. Kornblatt?" Penelope turned around, and there was the salesman, arm already outstretched, ready to wring her hand in greeting. They were all this way; they must have studied at the same school. "Be firm, yet friendly," she could imagine them being instructed. "Make the customer feel confident in your confidence." This one was a bit older than she was used to, with strands of thin, graying hair hopelessly combed and plastered over his mostly bald head. His glasses had thick, black frames. His nose was shiny.

"Car's right here," he told her. Penelope turned to see the car—white, of course, with a tan interior—that was waiting on the lot. As it happened, white turned out to be the safest color for a car. Statistically speaking, that is. Even Gabriel seemed impressed when she showed him the figures. "Are you and the little lady ready?" She looked down at Isobel and extended her finger for the baby to grasp.

Penelope liked the feeling the car had in her hands; solid, yet pliable. "Mind if I take it outside the city a little ways?" she asked the salesman, whose name was Burt.

"Anywhere you want," Burt said affably. "You're in the driver's seat."

He chuckled at his own wit. Penelope kept her eyes on the road. The traffic was light and she was able to leave the city behind quickly.

She liked how the car handled on the highway; the acceleration was smooth and quiet. Now she wanted to find a winding back road, so she could get a sense of the way it handled the curves and dips of a more circuitous route. Burt kept up a steady stream of patter; Penelope caught certain phrases like *sunroof* and *fully loaded*. He had obviously been schooled on what features appealed to the gals. Penelope gave him an occasional tight smile or nod, but mostly she concentrated on the car and the road as it ribboned out in front of her. The fog drifted down through the still-bare tree branches. At the side of the road, Penelope saw a large male deer and although she slowed down, her heart accelerated, as if she, or the animal, were in great danger. But the deer remained immobile until she passed.

Burt twisted his head around. "Smart buck," he said to himself as much as to her. "Just a few seconds earlier and he'd have been roadkill for sure."

"Why did you say that?" Penelope asked quickly. The deer startled her; his antlers looked like beseeching, bony arms.

"This baby is built like a truck. You don't want to get in its way."

Penelope checked the rearview mirror. She could just see the deer as he moved, slowly, sedately, into the group of naked shrubs at the far side of the road. Isobel's eyes caught hers in the small rectangle of reflective glass. The baby wrinkled her nose and let out a squeal of laughter when she saw her mother's face. The deer. The child. Yes. The signs she was waiting for—there they were. Everything was right with the world. The car, pure and gleaming white, was built as sturdily as a ship. It would glide through the swirling waters of their lives, keeping them safe.

"We'll take it," she said, turning her beautiful and radiant face to the salesman.

OSCAR

scar and Ruth had been coming here, to this isolated New Hampshire lakeside, for about five years. When their sons were young, they always rented places on Cape Cod. The boys had loved the ocean and they did too. But when the children no longer accompanied them and the Cape grew more and more crowded, they began to look for something else. The alternative they found pleased them both and the weeks they spent here were idyllic, even for a couple married as long as they had been. True, this past year had been harder than most. All the more reason, then, to look forward to the restorative powers the place had always had.

It was the water that had originally drawn Oscar to the spot; the cottage itself was modest, even cramped, and though the surrounding woods were pleasant enough, they lacked any real character. But outside the cottage was an ambling wraparound porch, punctuated with several large, heavy glass windows that extended nearly from its floor to its ceiling. No matter where he sat, he could see the open expanse of the lake, and there was always something to see. In the morning, he and Ruth brought their breakfast out to the porch to watch the water, which was sometimes smooth as glass and other times animated by small, noisy waves. Since the sun rose on the other side of the cottage, the morning light was cool and muted—shades of gray, silver, blue—on the water's surface. As the sun climbed higher in the sky, the light spilled down over the water, turning it first gold, then bronze and, as the daylight faded, silver again. Morning was a good time for birds too: there were loons, herons and ducks, and Oscar liked to watch them. Some nights when the moon was low and full, the water threw back its radiance, making everything around it seem impossibly bright.

All through the day, the lake was their beacon, their touchstone. They swam in it, of course, pushing back the water with their legs and arms, spraying it out of their mouths. They took their lunch down to its edge and late in the day, their cocktails, which they consumed while seated at the rusted little table and chairs that had sat there for years. The cottage came equipped with a canoe, so they frequently took rides across the lake before dinner, paddles dipping into the water as they moved peaceably along its surface.

When he was feeling lazy, Oscar skipped the swimming and boating and instead took a book or the local newspapers to read, positioning his chair on the narrow strip of a dock that extended outward into the lake, so that everywhere he looked he was embraced by water. And one afternoon, he took his music stand down to the dock, where he played the violin solo in Bach's Concerto in D Minor for Two Violins; this was the score for Balanchine's *Concerto Barocco*, which he knew the company would be dancing in the fall.

He hadn't played this music in a long while, and he needed the practice. There were two solo violin parts, and although Oscar knew that he would be playing the first, he decided to practice both. The relationship between the two was so quicksilver, so cunning; the first violin began a melody that the second might echo, in another pitch, only a split second later. If he were familiar with both parts, he would have better command of the intricate, even breathtaking pace of the timing.

Ruth came down from the cottage to listen. She sat in a chair, facing the lake rather than Oscar; still, when he finished, he saw that her face was wet with tears. He reached out his arms to her as she rose from the chair and they stood there together for a few minutes, looking out at the water, whose silent approval seemed to have blessed them both. He felt he had never loved her so much.

"*We should* invite the boys up here some year," Ruth said later that day. She always said this while they were at the lake. "I think William and Betsy would love it, don't you? And what about Ben and Laura?" Oscar nodded but knew she would not do anything about it, for which he was grateful. He thought she—they—were too immersed in their sons' lives, and he had come to enjoy this bit of forced separation. Did he really need to know about Gabriel and Ginny? Was anything in his life made better for the knowledge? Although Gabriel had done his best to reassure his parents that whatever happened with Ginny was totally and completely over, Oscar didn't believe him. Not that he would say this to Ruth—after all, what could he do about it and why worry her?—but he knew Ginny better than that. *She* never said that things were finished with Gabriel. Quite the opposite. Oscar remembered that night in her apartment, the stripped-down bed as naked as he had wanted her to be, and he shuddered—in disappointment and in shame.

Oscar tried his best not to think of Ginny. It was as if the water, and the mellow tenor of his days in its company, pushed all thoughts of New York and his life there to the periphery of his mind. Of course, when he started playing the Bach, that brought him back, mentally at least, to New York, for he was aware that it might occasion a moment when he and Ginny—as musical soloist and leading ballerina—were onstage together. He knew of her promotion within the company—that much hadn't escaped him. And she might be given that role. But even this thought didn't trouble him much. What could possibly happen if they were forced to take the stage together? The entire company, orchestra and audience would be watching. It was only when they were alone that his good intentions receded, overpowered by the perplexing, dismaying tide of feeling he still, despite everything, had for her. So pushing those thoughts away, he instead focused on the music—mournful, complex, beautiful—and tried to find his peace within it.

Oscar could remember the first time that he heard George Balanchine had actually choreographed a ballet to what had to be one of the most sublime pieces of music ever written. He couldn't believe the audacity, the arrogance of it. Forget about Bach rolling over in his grave—Oscar imagined the great man tearing out his hair and banging his head against the carved, wooden coffin in vexation. But then he calmed down and actually watched the ballet, and he had to admit the thing had a power commensurate with the music it so skillfully employed. The stage was bare, lit only by a deep blue light, a color that made Oscar think of the sky over the Mediterranean. As if to continue the classical mood inspired by the light, the dancers wore sleeveless white leotards with short white skirts; they might have been the figures on a Grecian urn, come suddenly and stunningly to life. Apart from that, no costumes, no scenery attempted to compete with the music, or the choreography that articulated it so fluidly. Oscar was transfixed. He had never understood the Bach score so deeply as when it was danced by Balanchine's dancers; he had been wrong and the knowledge humbled him. He would never complain about *Concerto Barocco* again.

Returning to it all these years later, he found that the feeling it inspired had not deserted him. He practiced the Bach to the exclusion of anything else. Around it, his days unfolded calmly and cleanly. He and Ruth took the canoe out the whole length of the lake early one morning; they stopped at one of the tiny islands that interrupted its surface and picked two pails of wild blueberries and added some of them to pancake batter for their breakfast. Another day, they reluctantly pulled themselves away from the lake and drove to Portsmouth. They spent the morning walking through its well-tended streets and playing a game from their early married life: they each picked their favorite house, the one they would like to live in, without telling the other which one it was. Only later, over a lunch of steamers and cold lobster salad eaten at Newick's (big picnic tables covered with torn red-and-white oilcloth, paper napkins and plastic bibs), did they discover that the house each had selected was the same one, a fine old Federal at the crest of a hill, its warm red bricks so well and seamlessly joined that they looked like cloth.

Near the end of their stay at the cottage, Oscar decided to look at some of the other music he had brought. Opening up the old leather case, he began to sift through the white sheets with their black notations; in his mind, he could hear the music while reading the score. But then another piece of paper fluttered loose from the pile, and this one was typed with words rather than notes. It was a schedule for the ballet company, something that must have been handed out before he left and which he had not looked at since. He saw that there was a break after the spring season, after which the company went upstate for its month-long stay at Saratoga. Oscar had never been to Saratoga. Its association with the ballet was too strong for him, and he never wanted to go. After Saratoga, the dancers were traveling to another city. And since the musicians never accompanied them, Oscar seldom paid much attention to where they went. He scanned the sheet quickly, and then stopped, reading over the destination San Francisco several times. The company would be in San Francisco in August.

Although he had not looked at a calendar in days, Oscar knew that it must be August already. Which meant that the 120-person ballet company—including Ginny Valentine—would be in San Francisco any day now. Why did this thought fill him with apprehension? Gabriel might not even have known the ballet was coming to town.

A sound distracted Oscar from these thoughts. Ruth had walked over, carrying a plate of blueberry muffins and a pitcher of iced tea on a tray. The ice cubes tinkled like bells. "Oscar, darling, what's wrong?" she said. Oscar looked at her tender and trusting expression and said nothing. Instead, he handed her the schedule. Ruth set down the tray. Then she herself sank heavily to the flowered wicker sofa, fists clenched tightly around the sheet of paper.

GINNY

Ginny *liked* Saratoga. She would take it over New York City any day. Saratoga reminded her, just a bit, of the town in Louisiana where she grew up. Old houses, old trees. Porches, lots of them, with rocking chairs, swings or wicker settees, and pots of flowers that someone watered every day. Clean sidewalks, without any dog shit.

Ginny had been in Saratoga with the company last year, and she liked it then too, but this year, she was sharing a room with Althea Johnson and that made it even better. Since they arrived in July, Althea had taken Ginny to all of her favorite spots, like the store that sold the secondhand clothes—Althea called them "vintage"—where they spent three solid hours.

Now these were the kinds of clothes Ginny had always liked, only she had never been able to put a name to them. She found a silk robe with great big orange poppies all over it; a tight red dress with bugle beads sewn up and down the front and a short, tight red bolero jacket to match;

black platform shoes that looked as if they were new when her Grandma Virginia was young, with more bugle beads, cut-out toes and a sexy strap that wound up and around her ankle. Ginny also bought a long, magenta silk scarf with marabou trim and a rhinestone necklace, star-burst earrings and bracelet that came in their original black velveteen box. Althea approved of everything and Althea was a person whose taste she could trust.

Another day they went to the spa, where they were dunked in Saratoga's famous mineral water and taciturn old ladies in sweat-stained uniforms gave them massages. Althea even convinced her to have a mud wrap, which consisted of being smeared all over with some very suspicious-looking brown stuff and then rubbed off with salt and a big, stiff brush. Afterward, though, Ginny's skin did seem positively dewy, so she went back to have her face done, which she hadn't agreed to the first time.

At night, after the performances, they went out to eat, just the two of them or occasionally with some of the other dancers. Sometimes Ginny thought she could detect a wistful look in Althea's eyes when the dancers were dissecting some aspect or other of that evening's performance. But mostly Althea maintained what Ginny privately thought of as a kind of regal detachment: poised, lovely and interested in the conversation, yet a little aloof from it as well. With her arms draped casually across the table and one of her signature chiffon scarves around her throat or shoulders, it seemed that she was beyond feeling, beyond pain, and Ginny admired her for it.

In the middle of the company's stay in Saratoga, the Federal Express truck that brought all the boxes of pointe shoes arrived. This was a big deal because the shipment—it usually came once a month—was late, and lots of the dancers thought they would have to scour the dance-supply stores around town to find shoes in a hurry. Finding ones that fit wasn't easy, and the local Capezio or Selva didn't have the best selection—or the necessary quantities. Dancers went through lots of shoes during a season, at least twelve pairs a week. The ballet company ordered them in bulk from England, where little old men (Ginny thought of Pinocchio's father,

Gepetto) sat at their workbenches. Each girl had a "maker" whose mark—
a tiny *x* or *y* or *p*—appeared on the bottom of the shoe, like a brand.
"Know thy maker" was a joke the dancers liked to repeat to each other
and, in fact, they all did know their makers, very well. Store-bought shoes
just couldn't compare.

When the custom-made shoes had finally arrived, praise and hosannas
poured out from all the dancers who worried that they wouldn't get there
in time. Althea had the job of sorting and distributing them. Ginny
grabbed hers. Time to break them in.

First she tested the toes: if they felt too soft, she brushed them with
shellac or clear nail polish to make them harder. But if they were too hard,
which did happen with certain batches, she soaked the toes in water or
rubbing alcohol; otherwise, they would make her bleed. Next, she had to
snip out the satin toe and roughen the leather on the bottom—she used
sandpaper—to make the soles of the shoes less slippery. She also needed
to yank out the cotton insole, which was as bulky as a sanitary napkin.
Then she sewed on the ribbons and elastic. Each girl had her own way of
doing this, a private ritual that she believed would bring her luck onstage;
Ginny used dental floss in place of thread for hers. But there was still
more: she had to step on the toes to flatten them, and bend the shank, to
make it flexible. Then she smacked the shoes against the wall a few times,
because otherwise they were just too damn noisy. No one wanted to hear
a ballerina clomping like a horse onstage—it killed the illusion of weightlessness and grace that she had spent her whole professional life trying to
perfect. After that, Ginny could finally put the shoes on, for all of fifteen
or twenty minutes, the time that it took to dance a single ballet. Then
they were finished and would be tossed out, unless there was some sentimental reason to keep them.

Ginny still had her first pair. The blood inside had seeped through and
turned the toes a dull shade of brown, but that was part of their appeal.
And before she left New York, Ginny gave Gabriel the pair she had worn
the night he watched her dance. Ginny was a little worried about his having them—that wife of his sounded positively cuckoo—but hopefully,

he'd be careful and put them somewhere out of harm's way. He had told Ginny about how she had cut up all the books and magazines. Poor Gabriel. She wondered—but only for a second—what sort of wife she herself would have been. Then the thought passed. Ginny knew that she didn't want to be a wife—not even Gabriel's wife—for a long time. Maybe never.

Since Ginny had started sharing a room with Althea, they became even more friendly. Over dinner in the one southern-style restaurant in town, Althea confided how hard it had been to be a black girl in the resolutely white world of ballet.

"No matter how high my arabesques were, I was never going to look right," she said. "There was this line of white bread girls with their white bread skin and white bread hair. And then there was me. I always stuck out."

"Or stood out," Ginny said. "Mr. B. must have thought that."

"He did," Althea said, and she smiled, remembering.

"But I know what you mean about sticking out. I did too."

"You? Weren't you a star even back in Louisiana?"

"In ballet class. Not anywhere else."

"So we were both misfits," Althea said. She had ordered coconut cake for dessert, though both she and Ginny agreed that it was a poor imitation of the cakes they were used to back home, in the South. "The kind my grandmother made had coconut flakes as long as your nail," Althea said, frowning at the tiny, minced bits topping the piece she was eating.

Althea also told Ginny how much she had hated New York when she first got there. Ginny could certainly relate to *that*. "I still hate New York," she said.

"Give it time," Althea advised. She ate the last bit of her cake and put down her fork.

"Do I have a choice?" Ginny asked.

———

One night, Althea didn't come back to the room at all. Ginny was curious, but since Althea didn't volunteer any information the next morning, it seemed nosy to ask. All she said was, "Everyone has a right to a private life. Even the ballet mistress." Ginny said "Amen," and Althea laughed.

"How about you?" Althea then asked, looking at Ginny carefully as if she had missed something. "What about your private life?"

"Let's just keep it private, okay?" Ginny answered. She was fixing her hair for class and Althea gave her ponytail a yank, but that was all.

After Saratoga, the ballet company returned to New York. They had a few days off before they were scheduled to fly to San Francisco, and some of the dancers went to the beach at East Hampton or Fire Island. Not Ginny. She had things to do. First there was the packing. All those clothes she had bought in Saratoga were coming with her. Instead of stuffing everything into the suitcase and sitting on it to make it close, Ginny folded things neatly, even pausing to put tissue paper in the sleeves of the jacket and the toes of the shoes. Rita would have liked that.

Once the packing was completed, Ginny took a walk down Broadway, where she decided, on impulse, to have her nails and toes done. Not that she usually paid attention to things like that, but Althea and her mud wraps had started her thinking. Ginny picked bright red polish for her toes and clear for her fingernails—she knew that Erik didn't allow red fingernails onstage. As the young, pretty Korean woman filed and painted, she watched the other women who were getting their hair cut and styled. Dancers always wore their hair long, so that they could put it up into a bun. But it did occur to her that she could have the ends trimmed with something other than the same pair of tiny scissors she used for sewing the ribbons on her pointe shoes.

The black-clad man with the crew cut and the earring who was blow-drying the hair of another customer must have read her mind because he asked, "How about a trim? If you wait until your nails dry, I'll have some time then."

"All right," Ginny said, and then surprised herself by adding, "What about the color? Can you do something about that?"

"Maybe some blond highlights? That would really bring out your eyes."

"Blond," Ginny repeated. "Sounds good to me." She waited until her nails were dry, and then moved over to the other chair, the one by the sink.

"Winter Wheat," the hairdresser was saying, looking at a row of bottles on a shelf. "Or maybe Golden Autumn." In the end, he trimmed about two inches off the bottom and didn't do the highlights after all. Instead, he dyed her whole head blond.

All this took quite a while; first her hair had to be washed, cut and combed out. There was a nasty-smelling shade of dye used on her entire head. This was followed by crimped foil packets applied to carefully selected strands of hair; the packets contained still another nasty-smelling shade, another permutation of blond. "So it will look natural," explained the stylist. "Not like you dipped your head into a vat of peroxide."

Ginny decided she liked him. While she waited for the various colors to take, the stylist offered her a batch of fashion magazines, but Ginny shook her head.

"How about a latte, then?" he asked. Ginny happily accepted the coffee and the hazelnut biscotti that he offered.

"So you're a ballerina," said the stylist, whose name turned out to be Craig, as he sat down next to her.

"Right." She blew on the coffee to cool it.

"Where do you dance?"

"Lincoln Center. New York City Ballet."

"Wow," he said. "City Ballet." A wistful look crossed his face. "I love the ballet."

"You do?"

"I even wanted to be a dancer," he confided.

"Did you ever take lessons?" Ginny asked, and not just out of politeness.

"My parents wouldn't let me. Thought it would make me a sissy. So I fooled them and became a hairdresser instead!" He laughed and Ginny joined in.

"You'll have to come see me dance," she offered. "I'll make sure you get comp tickets."

"Really?" Craig asked. "That would be great."

After the color had taken, someone else washed Ginny's hair and then Craig set to work combing and styling it. The color they had finally settled on was called Honey Kissed Blonde; the highlights, Midnight Sun.

"Are you dancing tonight?" Craig asked. His hands fluttered gracefully as small birds around her face. "Because when you do, you're going to knock 'em dead!" He called two other stylists over to see his handiwork and they exclaimed over her transformation. Ginny turned her head this way and that, to get a better view in the mirror. Her hair glowed like a sunset. Blond. Why had she never thought of it before? She and Craig exchanged phone numbers before she gave him a hug and a big tip. Then she ambled out onto Broadway again.

She could see how people—men—were suddenly checking her out as she passed. She stopped in front of a drugstore that had a mirror in the window, and rummaged through her bag for a red lipstick, the kind she usually saved for the stage. She couldn't believe the effect. Wait until Gabriel saw it.

She went inside the drugstore and bought a pair of dark sunglasses. Then she went back outside, checked the mirror again. She liked what she saw. Not even caring who might hear her, she addressed her reflection. "California, here I come!"

RUTH

When *Ruth* packed for the trip to New Hampshire, she brought along all the novels of Jane Austen, which she had not looked at since she was a girl. She no longer had the books from all those years ago—her mother was not a keeper—but she found almost all of them in trim Penguin paperback editions at the local Barnes & Noble. The only one she couldn't find, *Northanger Abbey,* was available at the library. When she arrived at the cottage, Ruth unpacked the books first thing and set them in a neat pile on a table right by the flowered wicker sofa on the wraparound porch. It was there that she sat every day with one book or another in her lap. Now and then, she looked up from the book to the lake, mostly to register the changes that light, air and clouds had wrought across its surface. She cooked some, but only casually, and listened to Oscar's practicing, which seemed to her more haunting, more nuanced than anything she had heard him play in recent memory. One day, they drove to Portsmouth; another, to Kittery. It seemed to Ruth that Oscar was more solicitous, more tender than usual. As if he were still trying to repent.

The mostly pleasant rhythm of their days was abruptly shattered shortly before they were scheduled to go back to New York, when Oscar put the piece of paper—the one about the ballet company traveling to San Francisco—into Ruth's hands.

"She'll be there. And he'll be there," he said.

"Maybe he doesn't even know the company is in town," Ruth said. "He told me he was finished with her."

"That's not what she told me," Oscar said. "And even if she had, I'd think she was lying."

"You talked to her?"

"I asked her to stay away from him."

"And . . . ?"

"And she told me she wouldn't. Or couldn't."

"Couldn't?" Ruth repeated. "Doesn't she understand the trouble she'll cause? Doesn't she care?" Ruth handed the paper back to Oscar. "Maybe we should go to San Francisco. Right away. Leave the cottage early, book a flight—"

"What for?" Oscar said. "Even if they're together in some motel room, what can we do about it? Storm in and tell Gabriel to put on his clothes and go home? Tell Penelope not to mind?" He put his head in his hands and was silent. Then he said, "It's out of our control now, Ruth."

So they didn't pack up and go anywhere, at least not until the end of the week. But the rest of the time felt ruined beyond repair. It rained heavily for two days; the weather turned cool and they stayed indoors, watching the needles of water that poured down onto the roiled surface of the lake. Oscar tried to make a fire, but the chimney was stopped up. The smoke that filled the rooms was so bad that they had to go outside and sit in the car, feeling cranky and exiled.

When the rain finally ended, Ruth and Oscar decided to drive north, toward Concord. On the way they stopped for lunch, but on the trip back,

Oscar felt sick and had to get out of the car to throw up. Ruth was grateful when it came time to pack up and leave New Hampshire.

Back in New York, the weather was steamy, but Ruth didn't mind. She took her time unpacking. At the hospital, she held the babies in her arms and thought of her granddaughters, Isobel and Hannah, both far away at the moment. The residents at the nursing home were, for the most part, glad to see her. Ruth noticed that Mrs. Vogel was no longer there; one of the nurses reported that she had died earlier in the month. The room's new resident, Mr. Plotkin, asked if Ruth could get him copies of *Playboy* or, better still, *Penthouse*. Old ones, new ones—he didn't care.

Through all of this, Ruth felt as though she were waiting for something to happen. And she was not wrong. Around 4:00 one morning, when Oscar was sound asleep and she had gotten up to go to the bathroom, the phone rang. She stared at it before answering, because she knew, she just knew, that she was about to hear something awful.

"Ruth? Is that the phone?" Oscar called sleepily. She picked up the receiver cautiously. At first, she heard what sounded like static. Then she realized that it was crying.

"Mom?" said Gabriel after a moment. "Mom, I think you and Dad should fly out here right away."

GABRIEL

At first, Gabriel didn't recognize Ginny. He looked from her name in the program to the stage and back again several times. Then he realized it was the hair, which at first he took to be a trick of the light or maybe a wig. But then he looked through the opera glasses he had recently purchased and saw that the hair was real, and that it had been dyed. He loved it. Not that he had any particular attraction to blondes; in fact, he had always been drawn to women with dark hair, like Penelope. But this was so in keeping with the electric nature of Ginny's soul that he couldn't believe she hadn't always been blond. Gabriel stared at the stage. When her variation ended and she skittered into the wings, he felt as though a light had been extinguished. He looked down at the program again, searching for her name again. He didn't recognize the ballet—it was something new, by a Scandinavian choreographer—and he didn't much like it. But when Ginny was dancing, there wasn't anything he wouldn't watch.

It hadn't been hard coming here at all. Penelope actually laid out his clothes for him, solicitously brushing lint from the shoulders of the jacket. The only vaguely unsettling note came when she was standing at the door with Isobel riding on her hip. "Maybe you'll find the dancer whose pointe shoes you have. Like Cinderella," she said lightly, but the remark made Gabriel's stomach clench with anxiety. What a shit he was. In a way, he hated himself for going to the ballet tonight, but he knew he was going anyway. Hating himself was part of the price for his connection to Ginny. He was willing to pay it.

"I doubt it. Whoever that was is long retired by now. She probably has three kids, an SUV and a house in the suburbs." She laughed. The tense moment passed and he gave her a quick kiss good-bye. Then he took the elevator down, got into his car and drove—easily, swiftly—to the San Francisco Opera House. He had actually bought Penelope a ticket, in case she changed her mind at the last minute. Not that she would. But Gabriel thought it would look better if he seemed to want her company. She took the ticket from him and put it in her desk, with the bills.

"Should I wait up?" Penelope asked.

"If you want. Though Jeff and his wife will be there. I told him we might have a drink afterward." Jeff worked in Gabriel's office and had said nothing about attending the ballet. But he wanted to buy himself a little time with Ginny. Penelope looked as if she wanted to wait up for him, though, so he added, "I'll call you and let you know, okay? You won't be able to call me. I'll have the cell phone turned off during the performance."

"Oh, right," she said. Then she turned to Isobel.

Gabriel parked his car in the underground lot beneath the theater, and then made the ascent to the opera house and to his seat. He had been here only once or twice before, but never with the excitement or the sense of expectation that he felt tonight. He sat down and placed his elbow on the armrest of the empty seat beside him; it was a tangible reminder of Penelope. He knew how careful he had to be; if she found out about

Ginny, she wouldn't forgive him again. Which was why he told Ginny that he couldn't spend much time with her tonight—going to a motel was out of the question. But he planned to see her after the performance, when he could at least be with her for a little while, hold her hands, put an arm around her thin, tensile shoulders. Then tomorrow he could find a way to meet her. He knew she had a ballet class in the morning, but maybe she could meet him back at her hotel around noon. Her roommate was the ballet mistress, and Ginny said that she would be gone all day. That would work for Gabriel too, because Penelope didn't call him often at the office, and, anyway, he could forestall it by calling her first and mentioning that he was on his way out to lunch. Lunch was not likely to arouse her suspicions, since she knew he went out nearly every day.

After the intermission, Ginny did not dance again, so Gabriel had a hard time concentrating on the performance. He fidgeted and tried to calm himself with thoughts of Ginny sitting in the dressing room, changing her clothes, perhaps, or combing out her long, newly blond hair. He was tempted to find his way down there now; if he gave the usher a note, she might be able to come out and meet him even earlier. Suddenly, this seemed like a very good idea and to the extreme annoyance of the other people in the row, he got up and pressed his way past them.

In the empty lobby, he took a paper schedule and wrote a hurried note to Ginny. Then he found an usher who was willing to deliver the note for the twenty-dollar bill that Gabriel gave him with it. A few minutes later, the usher returned and Gabriel followed him down two flights of stairs and through several wide, brightly lit corridors. Finally, they arrived at an unmarked door. Gabriel knocked gently. The door opened and there she was, all painted like the last time, only now her hair—still bound tightly in its austere bun—gleamed even brighter than her glowing face.

"I'm so glad you thought of coming early," she said. "I missed you." She wrapped her arms around him and he stood there feeling the heat from her small body. Then he pulled away, suddenly aware that they were standing in the hallway and someone might walk by. "Come in for a minute," she said, and pulled the door shut. "I don't think anyone will be down for a while."

Gabriel looked around the dressing room with costumes hanging upside down—Ginny told him that this was how they were stored—and its row of built-in dressing tables and lighted mirrors. The tables were densely covered—he could see tubes, jars, packages of cotton puffs, Q-Tips, hair spray, combs, brushes, bobby pins.

"Which one is yours?" Gabriel asked, and Ginny sat down on the small stool in front of one of the mirrors.

"Do you want to wait while I take my makeup off?"

"Leave it on," he said. "I like the way it looks. And your hair too."

"I'll take that down now," she said. He nodded, and watched while she deftly extracted the bobby pins and uncoiled the tightly wound bun until it was a shining ponytail, snaking down her back.

"Let me help," he said and moved behind her. He gently loosened the elastic band from her hair, and when it fanned out around her shoulders, he leaned his face down into it. He felt himself grow hard and wanted to push her forward, pull up her dress, right there, right then. But she was pressing something into his hand, a hairbrush, and he began instead to brush her hair, watching it become even more smooth and glossy under his even strokes.

"*Mmm,* that feels so good." Gabriel stopped brushing and leaned over to kiss her neck. He was reaching for her zipper when he heard a sound outside. Ginny must have heard it too because she got up quickly and reached the door before it opened. One of the other dancers moved past Ginny into the dressing room. She looked curiously at Gabriel but Ginny had him by the hand and out the door before they could even be introduced.

"What about your coat?" he asked. They stopped walking. Ginny was wearing a tight, beaded red dress with a matching jacket. Gabriel thought it looked really good on her, especially with her blond hair. But the jacket was cut so short and high it would do nothing to protect her against the damp, foggy air outside.

"I left it in the dressing room," she said and they both knew that she didn't want to go back.

"Here, take this," he said, shrugging off his jacket and handing it to her. Of course it was much too large, and its masculine boxy shape made her look unusually delicate. She put her hand in the pocket and pulled out a small gold box.

"For me?" she teased.

"Actually, it is."

"Oh," she said in a small voice.

"Go on, open it." She did, and lifted out a silver charm bracelet on which dangled two tiny silver charms. One was a pair of pointe shoes; the other was a crown. Gabriel had found the bracelet in a jewelry store near his office; he selected the charms there too. He knew they were tacky— he could imagine Penelope's disdain of such a thing—but somehow the silly sentimental gift seemed right for Ginny. Still, she hadn't said anything. Maybe he had miscalculated. "I hope you like it. The charms, well, they seemed to fit."

"Like it? I love it," she said softly. "How did you know about the silver slippers?"

"What about them?"

"Oh, I had a pair almost exactly like this, ages ago. It was a pin my mother bought me. Not nearly so nice as these slippers, but I loved it too."

"But you don't have it anymore?"

"I lost it. I don't know how. And now you've given them back to me, only better." She raised her face and he bent to kiss her.

"We should go," she said finally. "Maybe you could drive me back to my hotel. And when we get there we'll sit in the car and kiss good-night, like teenagers." Gabriel thought that she was not so far away from being a teenager, but didn't say it. They left the theater through the stage door, and walked back to the underground parking lot.

When they reached Gabriel's Audi, he looked at his watch. "You know, it's not that late," he said. "I have a little more time than I thought."

"Enough time to go to the hotel?"

He shook his head. The hotel was even farther from his apartment than the theater. "Isn't there someplace closer?"

"What about right here?"

"In the garage?" She wasn't serious.

"In the car. The performance isn't over for a while." Ginny got in the car and first shrugged off Gabriel's jacket and then her own. He watched while she reached around to unzip her dress and pull it over her head. She was serious, all right. He quickly opened the door and joined her in the cramped backseat. "Take your shirt off," she instructed and Gabriel began undoing the buttons. "We don't have a lot of time." He pulled her close then, her small, pink nipples cool and smooth against his bare skin.

PENELOPE

enelope hoped there would be a spot at the garage. She had decided to join Gabriel at the ballet after all, and she didn't want to have to waste any more time looking for parking. As it was, she was going to be late. But she still was determined to go. She knew that he was perpetually annoyed because she wouldn't leave the baby, wouldn't spend time alone with him. Penelope wasn't sympathetic; she thought he was selfish. Nonetheless, she would try to accommodate him, at least a little bit. Tonight, for instance. She wouldn't leave the baby—she couldn't bring herself to do that—but she would compromise by taking Isobel with her. That way she and Gabriel could watch part of the ballet together. And maybe after that they could take a drive somewhere, over to the Bay to look at the lights, the way they used to before Isobel was born.

Penelope had grudgingly come to appreciate San Francisco. At first, though, the sharp ascent and swerve of the streets gave her an intense sense of vertigo and she blamed Gabriel for bringing her here. That feeling gradually subsided, and there were times she even liked the city; she had felt herself grow taut and strong pushing Isobel's stroller up and down its hills.

The hills seemed to bear some analogy to her moods. The other OCD sufferers she chatted with on-line claimed to experience similar mood swings. It was frustrating because on the up days, Penelope felt she had some control of her life, but on the down days, she required new and more stringent preparations to keep it from disintegrating completely. She now had to disinfect her nipples before the baby nursed as well as wash her hands and dry them two separate times every time she changed Isobel's diaper. Exhausting, but Penelope rarely allowed herself to think that. These things were *necessary*. And it was the necessity that made her comply.

Ever since Gabriel had gone to New York to see that woman, the one with the sinister French name, a small alarm had been steadily bleating in Penelope's mind. Even though she was often impatient with her husband's mere presence, she didn't want to lose him. The life they had built together was better than any she could remember: the calm, white apartment was just a sign, the outward manifestation of that order she had finally brought to bear on things. Isobel was at the center of it all, and Isobel was part of Gabriel. Penelope couldn't bear the thought of Gabriel with anyone else, not because she felt so betrayed—she hadn't had a shred of interest in sex after Isobel came along—but because Gabriel was Isobel's father, and the idea that he could be intimate with someone outside their circle nearly choked her with anxiety. So she would have to start paying more attention to her husband if she wanted to keep him. And she did want to keep him—for Isobel's sake as well as her own.

Joining him at the ballet would be part of her campaign. She stood in front of the bedroom mirror brushing her hair. She wore a lightweight silk sweater in a pale shade of apricot along with a pair of white slacks. The sweater was something she had bought several years ago, and because the color was so pale and soft, she could tolerate it, especially since she knew Gabriel was exasperated by her refusal to wear anything but white. I'm trying, she told herself, I really am. She anointed her throat and earlobes with scented oil from a tiny bottle—not an actual perfume, which would be filled with potentially noxious chemicals and dyes—but a wholly natural, flower-based essence. Then she rapped three times on the doorjamb before leaving her room to fetch Isobel, who was already asleep for the night.

But the muted sound of the doorbell—she had made Gabriel replace the vicious-sounding buzzer that had been there when they moved in—stopped her and she went to open the door. There stood her downstairs neighbor, Mrs. Erikson.

"Hello," said Mrs. Erikson, whose sun-freckled hands held a large, leafy green mass. "I went to the farmers' market today and picked you up some of that organic kale you like." Although Mrs. Erikson had often asked Penelope to call her by her first name, Lissa, Penelope couldn't bring herself to do it. Something about the woman's manner seemed to demand a more formal address. Yet Penelope liked her. Mrs. Erikson was a radical vegan too, and the two often discussed how their refusal to eat meat and dairy foods was misunderstood by their respective families.

"Thank you," Penelope replied. "That was so thoughtful."

"Well, I know you're busy," Mrs. Erikson said. Her face was as tanned and spotted as her hands, and tiny lines spread from the corners of her eyes. "Isobel is a lucky little girl."

"I wish I could invite you in," Penelope said. Mrs. Erikson was the only person who really seemed to approve of Penelope as a mother. Everyone else was filled with criticism. "Only I'm on my way out now."

"That's all right," said the older woman. "I just wanted to give you the kale. In case you wanted to steam it for the baby."

"I will. Tomorrow. Tonight I'm going to the ballet."

"The ballet?"

"I'm meeting Gabriel there."

"Are you bringing Isobel?"

"Of course," Penelope said. Mrs. Erikson nodded in a satisfied way. "I wish my daughters-in-law were more like you." Mrs. Erikson had frequently complained about the wives of her two sons. One was a lawyer and the other a teacher. Both left their babies with sitters while they went to work. Penelope had sympathized with Mrs. Erikson's lament and wished, more than once, that she were her mother-in-law—or mother. She was well aware of how both Ruth and Caroline patronized and pitied her. As if all her careful rituals were going to harm Isobel in some way.

"Come by in the morning," Penelope said to Mrs. Erikson. "I'll tell you about the ballet."

"Can I give you a hand going downstairs?" Mrs. Erikson asked, looking at the heavy diaper bag Penelope had waiting by the door. Folded neatly on top of the bag was a white cotton blanket.

"That would be great." Penelope walked quickly into Isobel's room. The baby stirred a little as Penelope lifted her up but then settled peacefully against her mother as Penelope walked down the hallway. Mrs. Erikson walked slightly ahead and pushed the button for the elevator. She carried Penelope's bag over her shoulder and Isobel's blanket under her arm. In the lobby, she started toward the parking area out in back of the building, but Penelope stopped her.

"I'm parked out front," she told Mrs. Erikson. "There's a waiting list for a second parking spot. I should be getting one next month." Mrs. Erikson followed Penelope through the front doors. They nodded to the doorman, who smiled at both women but let his eyes linger on Penelope.

In the street, Penelope awkwardly moved Isobel from the baby sling into the car seat in back. Isobel opened her eyes briefly, but at the sound of Penelope's soothing voice, she closed them.

"Asleep?" Mrs. Erikson asked.

"We were out a lot today," Penelope explained. "She's really tired. I'm hoping she'll sleep through the ballet." Once the baby was settled again, Penelope tucked the blanket around her, picked up the diaper bag and got in the car. She had popped the trunk, intending to put the bag inside. But she then decided it would be easier to retrieve the bag from the front seat when they finally arrived at the theater. Only after she had said good night to Mrs. Erikson and strapped her seat belt did she remember that the trunk was still open.

She got out of the car, intending to pull the trunk shut. That's when she saw something marring the smooth, white finish. Was that a smear of dirt? Or, worse, a scratch? Penelope was very particular about the Volvo, which engendered its own set of rituals and preparations. Lead-free gasoline and regular tune-ups. Weekly trips to the eco-friendly car wash. And now something had spoiled the pristine surface she tried so hard to maintain and protect. Damn it.

Penelope marched around the other side of the car to inspect it better. It wasn't as bad as she thought; the repair shop could easily fix it. Penelope was now frustrated by all the delays. She wanted to be on her way. If she lost much more time, she would miss the ballet entirely and her whole plan would be ruined.

She didn't see the SUV as its driver hurriedly turned a corner and gunned the engine before the light changed again, but was aware of its hot air enveloping her. The large, dark vehicle swerved slightly. It was enough. The SUV slammed her shoulder; the impact then threw her up and into the path of an oncoming red hatchback. The hatchback's driver frantically put on his brakes, but the startled body flying through the air and toward his windshield came too suddenly, and with too much force. Penelope's last thought was of the deer by the side of the road. Don't hit her again, she pleaded. Don't.

GABRIEL

The first people had just begun to trickle down from the theater as Ginny was gathering her disheveled hair back into some kind of ponytail. Gabriel consulted his watch again. Just a little after eleven. If the traffic wasn't bad, he wouldn't even have to lie about Jeff and the drink. While Ginny was smoothing her dress, he tried calling Nel, but there was no answer. She had probably gone to sleep. He pulled out of the parking lot and out into the light stream of cars. They were at Ginny's hotel in minutes. He kissed her twice and watched while she disappeared through the revolving door.

As he turned the corner that led up to his street, he noticed the police car sitting at the curb in front of his apartment building. What was it doing there? The red light was off, though, and he didn't see anyone around, so it probably wasn't anything serious. Still, he pulled over to check before taking his car around to the parking area behind the building.

But before he could do that, the police officer who had been sitting at the wheel of the car now got out. His mustache, thick and dark brown, looked too big for his upper lip, which it nearly covered. He bent down to Gabriel's open window.

"Mr. Kornblatt?" he said quietly. "I'm Officer Carmichael. We've been trying to reach you." The cell phone. He had turned off the cell phone in the theater and never turned it on again. Looking past the officer's earnest face, his eyes were drawn to something he hadn't noticed before—a large, dark stain on the sidewalk. "I think you should get out of the car now, Mr. Kornblatt." Gabriel turned off the ignition and got out. The stain was wet. There was another officer in the car, and he joined Carmichael. This one was very thin and young. When he took off his hat and gripped it in his hands, Gabriel began to shake.

"Is it my daughter? Is she all right?" Gabriel asked the thin one, who said his name was Baxter.

"Your daughter is fine," Carmichael said.

"It's your wife," Baxter added. "There's been an accident. We'd like you to come with us. Please."

"What happened? Is she all right?"

"That's why we want you to come with us. To the hospital." Gabriel noticed that he didn't answer the question. The shaking intensified.

"Is that where Isobel is?"

"That's where she is, Mr. Kornblatt," Carmichael said.

"The hospital." Gabriel looked at the dark patch on the sidewalk once more before getting into his car. "I'll follow you, all right?" Baxter and Carmichael looked at each other.

"Why don't you come with us instead?" Baxter said.

Gabriel couldn't believe there was so much blood. Blood matted Penelope's hair, caked her eyelashes, clotted her nostrils; blood was smeared on her face, neck and arms. With her pale skin, who would have thought that so much bright red blood could have been hidden—seething, churning— inside, just waiting to find its way out? He nodded dumbly as the morgue attendant pulled the sheet back over her. Yes, the woman lying there was his wife. Or had been. Then he followed an orderly back upstairs, where he was brought into a small, windowless cubicle. He saw their neighbor, Mrs. Erikson, waiting for him. Tears pooled in her eyes and as soon as she saw him, she began crying again.

"I didn't see it happen," she said between sobs. "But I heard it." She stood up and pressed herself into his arms. Gabriel didn't think he had spoken more than ten words to this woman in his life; Penelope was the one who had known and liked her. Right now, though, he was grateful for her presence. Baxter said something about the two drivers—the one who had first hit her and the one who ultimately killed her. Gabriel knew he would need to hear all of this. Now was not the time, though. He lifted his face from Mrs. Erikson's head.

"And my daughter? You said she's all right?"

"Just fine," said Carmichael. "She's in Pediatrics, upstairs. The car never even touched her."

"I want to see her," Gabriel said. "Take me to her right now. Please."

"Of course, Mr. Kornblatt," said Carmichael, who nodded to the orderly. Gabriel leaned down to kiss Mrs. Erikson's browned, wet cheek. Then he followed the man through the halls and upstairs to the pediatric ward, where he saw Isobel from a distance, in the arms of a nurse. When he was close enough for her to see him, she began waving her arms in the air, conducting a silent concert of recognition and reunion.

"Dada!" he heard her say, as the nurse, observing her reaction, handed her over to him. As the policeman had told him, she was perfectly fine, her white skin, so like her mother's, unmarred by scratches or bruises of any kind. It was only when he looked down to touch her hands that he saw the tiny, confetti-like dots of blood—Penelope's blood—speckling her arms. It was then that he broke down, sobbing with the kind of despair and sorrow he had not felt since he was a child. He turned Isobel over to the alarmed-looking nurse, who whispered something to one of her coworkers about a sedative.

Gabriel cried for a few minutes before pulling out his handkerchief to mop his wet face. It was white, white as everything and anything Penelope had ever loved. He asked if he could make a telephone call, and a nurse led him to the phone. She punched in the number he gave her and she handed him the receiver. When he heard his mother's voice, the sobbing started again. But he gained control more quickly this time, and he begged her to fly out immediately to see him. Then he told her what had happened to Penelope.

OSCAR

A *s they* sat together in the American Airlines terminal at JFK, Oscar gripped Ruth's hand tightly. It was morning, and they were all cried out. They cried when Ruth got the call about Penelope; they cried while they hurriedly packed their bags, called the airline and hailed a taxi. They cried all the way out to the airport. Now they were waiting for their flight to take off, and for the moment, the crying had stopped. The airport was not very crowded. There were only two other passengers waiting for the flight. One was sleeping and the other reading the *Wall Street Journal;* neither had any interest in Oscar or Ruth.

"We should have gone out there sooner," Ruth said, breaking the silence. Oscar didn't answer. "It might have helped. At least we would have tried. Instead, we left it alone and now look. And I was worried about a divorce!" Her voice was low, but Oscar heard the tears that were in it. What could he say? That he was wrong, and they should have flown out to San Francisco as soon as they learned Ginny would be there with the company? But what good would that have done? Gabriel was an adult. He made his own choices. Just like me, Oscar thought. Because deep down, he felt he was responsible for all this. He was the one who had brought Ginny into their lives. He could remember that spring evening he sat with her in the coffee shop. He could still taste the doughnut, feel the black scald of the coffee in his mouth. By the time he had finished, he was thoroughly, completely in her thrall. And this was where that sensation of falling, headlong, had brought him. Had brought all of them.

"We'll call Caroline as soon as we get there," he said to change the subject. He and Ruth had argued over that. Oscar thought they should call her immediately. Ruth felt that they should wait until the morning. "Why deprive her of the last good night's sleep she'll be getting for a long time?" she had reasoned. "We'll call her from San Francisco. Then we can reassure her about Isobel." In the end, he went along with her, not because he agreed, but because he could not face calling Caroline himself.

"Maybe she'll want to fly out with us," Oscar had said in a last attempt to sway her.

"Is that what you want?" Ruth asked. "To spend five hours sitting next to Caroline when we know what Gabriel did to her daughter?"

"It's not like he killed her, Ruth. He wasn't even there when she was hit."

"No, he wasn't. He was with that girl. While his wife was lying dead on the pavement and his daughter was alone!" Oscar had no reply.

"Yes, we'll call her as soon as we get there," Ruth agreed now. She didn't bother to mask the exasperation in her voice. The flight attendant called for the passengers to board the flight and Oscar and Ruth were the first in line.

On the flight, Oscar slept. And while he slept, he dreamed, fretful, unhappy dreams, in which Gabriel was a child, crying for comfort. But Oscar was a child too, even younger and smaller than his son. There was no comfort he could give. He woke to see the attendant holding a shiny metal pitcher of coffee. Oscar shook his head and went back to sleep. This time, he was marrying Ruth all over again. Only instead of the temple on Ocean Parkway in Brooklyn, they were standing—hands joined, heads bowed—before the rabbi in what seemed to be a sewer or a well. Everything was dripping and sodden. The hem of Ruth's white dress was dark with filth. Oscar shook himself awake and looked around. Now Ruth was asleep. He fervently wished her better dreams than his own. He gestured to the attendant. No coffee—coffee was too brutal for his unsettled stomach—but he gratefully accepted the tea bag and plastic cup of not very hot water that she offered. With it there was a sticky, jelly-filled bun, wrapped in cellophane. Oscar opened the wrapper quietly and raised it to his mouth. A bit stale, but satisfyingly sweet nevertheless. He glanced out the window and saw nothing but clouds.

In San Francisco, they took a taxi to Gabriel's apartment. He met them at the door looking white and haggard. Oscar hugged his son tightly and realized he had not done so since Gabriel was a little boy. Why had he waited so long? "Thank you for coming," Gabriel said. His voice sounded strange and hoarse. He too had been crying. "Isobel is asleep," he said in answer to Ruth's anxious question. The three of them peered through the open door to her room. Isobel was stretched out in her crib. Her mouth was open and she was breathing peacefully. Against her pale skin, the inverted arcs of her dark lashes smiled. "I don't think she's ever slept in the crib before," Gabriel said quietly, so as not to wake her. "Before she always slept with us ..." He stopped, visibly trying to regain control of himself. "But she was so tired out by the time we got home, I don't think she cared where she was."

After they looked at the baby, Ruth went into the kitchen, where she attempted to prepare some sort of meal. However, the ingredients in Penelope's kitchen—rice milk, dried seaweed, a head of kale, soy powder and the like—were unfamiliar to her and she abandoned the idea. Instead, she boiled water for the herbal tea she found in the cabinet. When she brought the steaming cups to the table and set them down, Oscar took his and blew on the surface to cool it. "About Caroline," he began hesitantly. "Isn't it time she knew?"

"She does," Gabriel said, to Oscar's relief. From the look on Ruth's face, it was clear she shared his reaction. "I called her myself."

"Oh," said Oscar. He sipped the tea and made a face. What was in it that made it taste so bad? "How did she take it?"

"Not too well," Gabriel said quietly. "I'm sorry someone wasn't there to tell her in person." Oscar and Ruth said nothing. "I told her you were coming. And that we'd call her together. To talk about the funeral."

"The funeral," repeated Oscar. "I hadn't thought about the funeral."

"Caroline wants to have it in Connecticut. That's where Penelope's father is buried."

"That sounds reasonable," said Oscar, looking over at Ruth. She had been very quiet. Usually she had opinions about everything and was seldom afraid to express them. At least to the members of her family. Did she perhaps object to the idea of the funeral being held back east? But why?

"Actually," Gabriel was saying in a low voice, "I didn't say this to her on the phone, but Penelope always said she wanted to be cremated."

"Well, people do that and bury the ashes," Oscar said uneasily as he glanced again at his wife.

"No, she didn't want to be buried. The idea of being underground bothered her. She wanted the ashes to be scattered someplace that was wide open. Over the water. Or a huge field or something," he said, looking beseechingly at his parents.

"Oh, so she didn't want to be buried?" said Ruth, finally joining in. "She would deprive her daughter of a decent place to mourn? Well, fuck what Penelope wanted!" Her voice was so filled with fury that Oscar and Gabriel could only stare, bewildered and alarmed, at her angry face.

GINNY

Spotting was a way of focusing your eyes on the same fixed point—like the small crack in the wall above the mirror or that weird, oily smudge right next to it—every time you whipped your head around in the turn. Before you could learn to turn, you had to learn to spot. Ginny had known that for a long time. If you didn't spot, you got dizzy and wound up on the floor instead of on your feet. And if you were doing turns that traveled across the stage, like chaînés, you might even end up in the orchestra pit.

Ginny actually did start turning before she had really learned to spot. She was a natural, she could feel that, even as a child, and she spun around in a neat triple pirouette before she had a clue about what to do with her eyes. She liked turning so much that she did it a lot, in spite of that dizzy, sick-to-your-stomach sensation she had when her eyes couldn't focus and the room spun madly and out of control. Then Wes taught her how to spot and she never forgot it. Turning became pure pleasure: a perfect balance between abandon and control.

But the morning when Gabriel called her to tell her that his wife had been hit by a car and killed, she felt the way she did before she learned to spot. Her hotel room, with its chenille bedspread and braided rug, seemed to whirl; she thought she might throw up. She didn't, though. Althea appeared while Ginny was still holding the receiver in her hand. "Is anything wrong?" she asked, taking in Ginny's tight, drawn face.

"Even a soloist has a right to a private life, right?" Ginny reminded her. Althea didn't ask anything else. Ginny got dressed quickly and went to class, where everything was all right, though the turning-without-spotting sensation came and went throughout the entire hour and a half.

The next day, Ginny saw Gabriel for breakfast early, before her ballet class began. He looked terrible. His face was yellowish-gray and there were rings under his eyes. She could barely stand to look at him. But when he took her hand, it felt as warm and familiar as ever. He looked down and saw the bracelet on her wrist. "I'm glad you're wearing it," he said, and drawing Ginny's hand to his face, he kissed her palm.

"What will you do?"

"I'm not sure," he said, closing his eyes and rubbing his cheek against her hand. "The funeral will be in Connecticut. At her mother's. Then I'll fly back here to empty out the apartment."

"You're leaving San Francisco?"

He nodded.

"And going . . . ?"

"Back to New York. At least for a while. Though maybe I'll stay. It all depends." Depends on what? she wanted to say. But she kept her eyes focused on an open sack of coffee beans somewhere just beyond Gabriel's left shoulder. She was spotting, even while she was sitting still. The pressure of his hand felt good. Still, Ginny was not prepared for his next words. "I'd like to see you again before I go."

"You would?" He reached for her other hand then, and held both of them tightly in his.

"I know it's crazy, it's depraved, it's awful, but, yes, I would."

Well, what could she say to that? They met the next morning, after company class, in a motel room that Gabriel found all the way on the other side of town.

At first, it seemed strange, as if his wife were in the room with them. Did he feel it too? She couldn't bring herself to ask. Instead, she stared straight up at the ceiling as they lay on the bed with their clothes on, not kissing or touching. Then Ginny put her arms around him and he put his around her. That felt right, and so one thing led to another. It wasn't like it was before, but, then, what ever was? Afterward, they remained there for a while, still not saying anything. His eyes were closed, but at least he had some color in his face now; he didn't look so gray.

"You know how sorry I am," Ginny said. She hadn't intended to say anything, the thought just bubbled up and out.

"You have nothing to be sorry for," he said, opening his eyes. "I'm the one who should be sorry. She was my wife. I betrayed her. You didn't."

"Are you sorry?"

"Yes. No. I don't know. Of course I'm sorry that she's dead—God, am I sorry about that. But I'm not sorry about you."

"You'll be in New York soon. And so will I."

"I know. We can see each other there. If you want to, that is."

"Gabriel, of course I want to," Ginny said, but inside she was hardly so sure. She looked at the glowing red numbers on the digital clock by the side of the bed and jumped up. "I've got a rehearsal at two," she said. "I'd better go."

It was then that Ginny noticed the big, purple hickeys he had left all over her neck, where they would absolutely show in class and onstage. She would need a tube and a half of concealer to cover them. She dressed quickly. Good thing she had that long magenta scarf with her; she could wrap it around her neck for the time being.

Gabriel hadn't moved. He was still lying there in that extra-large-sized motel bed with the blanket pulled up around his chin. "I'll call you when

I'm in New York," he said as she slipped on her shoes and hoisted her bag up and onto her shoulder. All the while, his eyes never left her face.

After that, Ginny just couldn't settle down to do anything right. She screwed up in class several times and even once onstage in San Francisco, where she fell, flat on her face, in the middle of the grands jetés en tournant. There was nothing quite so humiliating as falling in front of an audience. There you were, willing them to believe in the illusion of your weightlessness, your perfect control, and all of a sudden, it was over, you were mortal again, lying there with your nose scrunched up against the floor and your backside in the air. Of course, you would be up in a flash, up and dancing again. Most times, the audience even applauded, but the applause was all wrong too, a paltry consolation prize when you were going after the gold ring.

Althea took Ginny aside after the matinee performance and asked again if anything was wrong. "I've never seen you fall onstage before. Are you okay?" She looked like she really wanted to know. Ginny wasn't ready to tell, though. Not yet, anyway.

"I'm all right," Ginny lied. But she wasn't. Back at the hotel, she found a phone booth in the lobby, so she could have some privacy. She didn't want Althea hearing the conversation she hoped to have with Wes. She didn't actually think he would be in, but even the sound of his voice on the answering machine would be comforting. To her surprise, he picked up right away.

"Virginia," he said. "Your mama sent me your reviews. I'm not surprised. Are you calling with some more good news?"

"I wish," Ginny said. He was the only one who called her Virginia. It suddenly made her want to cry. But she didn't. Instead, the whole ugly story came pouring out, about Oscar, Gabriel and most of all about Penelope. Wes was quiet while he listened, so quiet Ginny thought he might have gone away from the phone. "Wes?" she said. "Wes, are you there?"

"I'm here," he answered. "I'm just trying to think of something to say to you."

"Was it my fault?" Ginny asked.

"You think it was."

"At first I didn't think so. But now I don't know. He was with me when she was hit. No one could call to tell him because he'd turned off his phone." There was a long pause in which Wes didn't say anything. Ginny thought he might have hung up.

"I think you need a different kind of answer than the one I can give," he finally said.

"What are you talking about?"

"Pray."

"Pray?" Ginny couldn't believe he was telling her this. "Pray for what?"

"Forgiveness, understanding, guidance. It doesn't matter. Just pray."

"You mean in a church? What kind of church?" Wouldn't it be just like Wes to tell her that?

"Catholic, Protestant, Baptist. Pray in the street or in your hotel room. Anywhere you can. God is always listening."

"Wes!" she said in frustration. That was the kind of advice her mother always gave, and Ginny had been in no hurry to call *her*.

But once she got off the phone, she left the hotel and went wandering around the streets of San Francisco, looking for a church. It took a while, but she did manage to find one. And it was a Catholic church too, with a round, stained-glass window, a whitewashed tower and a very tarnished bell. Now wouldn't Wes take that as a sign?

The building was small and, at the moment, unoccupied. Ginny slipped into a pew and bowed her head. Wes's words came back to her: forgiveness, understanding, guidance. She tried to pray but instead found herself remembering the long, hot Sunday mornings in Bakerstown, her mother at her side. She had been required to pray then, though she often felt nothing at all, and simply pretended, so Rita would leave her alone. But now she was by herself, no one watching. Just God, she supposed. That's what Wes thought.

She looked up at the stained-glass window. The colors were pretty, though she couldn't figure out what it depicted. Ginny didn't know the stories of all those saints; Baptists didn't go in for that sort of thing. She stayed in the church until she started to get cold. As she left, she took a last look at the stained glass, but since the light had faded, even the colors had gone dark.

RUTH

R uth *Fass* Kornblatt was angry. She had never been so angry in her life. In fact, angry didn't even begin to describe it: she was enraged, furious, seething, boiling. She didn't know how to contain all her anger and she didn't care. That in and of itself was unsettling enough. Usually, when she was angry, she looked for ways to turn it around, to calm herself. Not this time.

Ruth's anger was not a sudden thing. It had needed time to gather and grow. At first, she was just sick at heart, for Penelope, for Caroline, for Gabriel, but most of all for Isobel, who wouldn't even remember the awful day her mother died. But once the plane took off, the questions had started, tumbling over each other in her mind, like clothes in the dryer. How could Gabriel have lied like that? How was it that while Penelope's life was ending in that hideous, violent way, he had been with Ginny? What had Isobel seen and heard?

It was the dream that gave Ruth the clue: she was in the kitchen of her apartment, opening cabinets and methodically removing stacks of dishes, which she then sent flying across the room, just to hear them break. When she woke up, the pilot was announcing that they were flying over the Great Salt Lake. Oscar was dozing, but she was awake and seething.

She was angry at Ginny, of course. That was a given. But Ruth was angry at Oscar too, for bringing Ginny into their lives, and at Gabriel, for making sure that she stayed there. Ruth was even angry at poor Penelope, for not having looked before stepping out into the street.

Finally, they arrived in San Francisco. Ruth's anger retreated a little when she saw him, her firstborn, looking gray and drawn in a way she had never seen before. Then they all looked in on the baby, and it was impossible to feel angry while peering over the railing of her crib.

When Gabriel started talking about Penelope's wanting to have her ashes scattered, Ruth's anger rose again. "Someplace wide open . . ." he was saying. Of all the ridiculous, thoughtless ideas! What would Gabriel tell Isobel when she asked, as she must someday, where her mother was? "She floated out to sea" hardly seemed like an answer a child could comprehend. At least if they buried her, there would be a spot, a marker, a tangible place for Isobel to go and mourn. So Ruth uttered a word that she was sure she had never said in front of her husband, let alone her son.

She was deeply gratified by the shock and horror they both registered. Good! Let them know how angry she was. Furious and proud of it. Then something in Gabriel's expression made Ruth turn away. She had to. She wouldn't apologize, not then. But she couldn't keep looking at his hurt, confused face.

"Your mother is very upset," Oscar said to Gabriel, his hand awkwardly on his son's shoulder. Ruth turned to leave the room. "She's upset," she heard him saying, "she'll be herself again soon." Don't count on it, Ruth thought. She went into the bathroom and closed the door. She splashed cold water on her hot face and looked at her reflection in the mirror. The attractive, middle-aged woman who looked back at her might seem, at least to her family and friends, the practical, sensible Ruth they had always known. But she knew differently. For one thing, she had just said "fuck" in front of her husband and son and wasn't the least bit sorry. Something had changed.

Isobel woke up a little while later and Ruth was busy taking care of her, so it was easy to avoid her husband and son. There were many phone calls to be made, and Ruth said a few halting, inadequate words to Caroline, who sobbed quietly into the phone. Oscar seemed to take Gabriel in hand, which was good, and the two of them drove off for a while, perhaps to Gabriel's office, where he needed to get some things, or perhaps just to get out, away from Ruth and her scalding, furious glances.

Oscar and Gabriel picked up some Japanese take-out food on the way back, which they all tried to eat for dinner, though no one was very hungry and most of it ended up in the garbage. Ruth was too occupied trying to feed Isobel to eat anyway. A few spoonfuls of yogurt, a bite of bread. She licked a banana but wouldn't actually eat it; the tiny sections of tangerine Ruth offered were squeezed delightedly in her hand and then thrown against the wall.

"Penelope didn't give her citrus," Gabriel said, sounding apologetic. "She probably doesn't know what it is."

"What about milk?" Ruth was worried that Isobel would want to nurse and that when she did, only milk would satisfy her.

"Just Penelope's," he said miserably. "She's never had cow's milk."

"Well, tonight will be a first." Ruth heated milk in a pot and poured it into the plastic baby bottle she had instructed Oscar to buy. She squeezed a few drops on her wrist, just as she had done when the boys were babies, to make sure it wasn't too hot. Then she handed the bottle to Isobel.

Isobel seemed intrigued, waving it around and lifting it up over her head. Some milk dripped on her hair and in her eye, which she didn't like and she threw the bottle down, her face clouding. Ruth quickly picked it up and tried to bring it to her lips. Maybe the smell would entice her to taste it. No such luck. She threw it down again. Her face screwed up and the tears were gathered in her eyes when Ruth handed her the milk once more, this time in a small white cup she had found high up in the cabinet. Isobel's eyes opened and she grasped it with both hands, staring down at its contents. Then without any help, she drank the milk. It ran down her chin and her upper lip was wet.

"She likes it!" said Gabriel, sounding better than he had since Ruth and Oscar arrived. "She wants more!" Anger set aside for the moment, Ruth looked at him and smiled too.

That night, Gabriel insisted that Ruth and Oscar sleep in his room; he would sleep on the living room couch. Ruth discovered that there was something strangely intimate and discomforting about sleeping in the bed that her grown son had shared with his wife. Oscar went to sleep almost instantly, but Ruth remained awake for a long while, keenly aware of the feel of the mattress, the softness of the pillows, the smooth sheen of the white cotton duvet cover. In most marriages, it was the wife who dressed and made the bed; her bed was a window onto her soul. And now Penelope's soul had left her ruined body and was flying untethered through the heavens. Ruth was still here on earth, touching Penelope's blankets and trying to imagine the life she had constructed here, between these sheets, with Gabriel. Had they made love often? Had she wanted to have another child? Was she a late sleeper or did she rise with the sun? There was a light over the bed; did she read at night and, if so, what? Magazines? A novel? Ruth used the sheet to wipe tears from her face. There was so much about Penelope that she would now never know, but Ruth could say with certainty that her daughter-in-law had selected these linen pillow shams with their discreet border of lace, this comforter, these pillows, the soft white mohair afghan at the foot of the bed to guide and soothe the passage of night into day.

In the morning, they were all a bit amazed to find that Isobel was still asleep. She did not awaken even once during the night, which Gabriel said was highly unusual. Ruth was actually hungry and Oscar said he was too. He volunteered to go to the supermarket while Ruth stayed with Isobel. Gabriel said he had an appointment and would eat later. He took a long shower and disappeared into the bedroom to find some clothes. He emerged looking significantly better: he had shaved and his hair was freshly washed and combed. He wore a shirt that brought out the color of his eyes and a wheat-colored jacket. "I'll be back early this afternoon," he told Ruth.

"Your father went shopping," Ruth said. "We'll have supper here. I'll fix a salad and some pasta." Tomorrow, they would all fly to New York. Penelope's body was being flown back this morning. The funeral director in Greenwich was taking care of everything. Ruth thought she heard stirring, and peeked into Isobel's room to check. Still asleep. When she came back, Gabriel was standing at the door. His aftershave left a fresh, citrus smell in the air.

"Bye, Mom," he said. His eyes didn't meet hers.

All at once Ruth understood that he was going to see Ginny. She was still in San Francisco and he was on his way to see her, kiss her, schtup her, for all Ruth knew. And Penelope not even buried yet. My God, was this the son she had raised? She was shocked, offended and most of all ashamed. Before she was able to tell him any of this, the door had closed quietly behind him. He was gone.

Ruth looked at the spot where he had stood. It was a good thing Oscar wasn't there, because she just might have taken out her anger on him. Then there was a sound again, and, this time, Isobel was awake and standing a little unsteadily, her hands grasping the slats of the crib.

"Mama," she called and Ruth felt stabbed hearing the word. "Mama!" She hurried in to pick Isobel up, hold her tightly. When she did, she was suddenly seized by the most outrageous desire she had ever felt in her life: to leave Oscar, to leave Gabriel, Ginny and Caroline. She knew how impractical and even insane such a desire was. Which made it all the more compelling. Everyone else had gone and done what they wanted without thinking about the result. Ruth thought about everything that had gone on in the past year—Oscar's infidelity, the gnawing worry about her son's marriage, the sorrow she had felt at Penelope's rejection, the knowledge that it was, of course, too late to ever make it right with her—and all these feelings rose up, with the force of a tidal wave. But instead of running for cover, a new and entirely unfamiliar Ruth just stood there and waited for it all to break.

She walked to the window and looked out at the street. She was pleased to see that people were walking along calmly, totally unaware of the seismic shift going on inside this apartment, inside *her*. Abandon her family. The thought, once formed, shone dangerous and alluring as a knife. Ruth did not let herself think about the consequences.

She would take Isobel. They would go somewhere else, somewhere far away, like Mexico. Ruth would raise Isobel alone. She had always wanted a daughter; maybe this whole awful sequence of events was God's way of granting her wish. Ruth realized she even had her passport. She always took it with her when she traveled. Of course Isobel didn't have a passport, but Ruth would find some way around that.

The improbable plan quickly took shape in her mind. She would need money, but that wouldn't be a problem as her wallet contained both cash and credit cards. This should get them through the first few days at least. After that, Ruth would contact Warren Greenberg, who had been their attorney forever, about getting more money. Surely after all these years of marriage, she should be entitled to something. The bag she brought from New York was still packed. Isobel would need a few things, but Ruth could buy the rest as they went along.

It was only when she was taking the remaining pairs of Oscar's underwear and his shirts—shirts that she herself had packed—out of the bag that she stopped. How long would it take him to realize she had left him? Would the worry about where she had gone break him in two? She found paper and wrote a quick note. It would be better than nothing.

The next step was renting a car. Ruth thought of the stroller parked by the door. Isobel could ride in it while they walked to a car rental office. Good thing she had brought along some really comfortable shoes. With all those hills, she was going to need them.

Ruth looked at Isobel, whose head was snuggled just under her collarbone. The baby's clenched fist was beating lightly on her chest. "You must be hungry," Ruth said as she carried her to the kitchen. "Well, we'd better hurry up and get you fed before Grandpa comes back." She seated Isobel in the high chair, where Isobel guzzled her milk and gummed her banana. Meanwhile, Ruth pulled out the telephone book and began to search for the number of a car-rental agency nearby.

As she made her plans, Ruth felt as if she were observing herself. The old Ruth watched the new one with disbelief and admiration. What daring this new Ruth possessed. What spirit. The new Ruth confidently held the receiver to her ear. She took it as a sign, another good sign, like having the passport, that someone picked up on the very first ring.

GABRIEL

Gabriel knew that he frightened Ginny. He didn't mean to, but when they were at that motel, he was desperate, he was wild. He wanted to blot out the image of Penelope lying on the morgue table. So he wound her newly blond hair tightly around his fists, sucked her skin hard enough to leave marks. And scared her. He could tell she was eager to get up, get out, leave him to go to her rehearsal. When he talked about seeing her in New York, she looked alarmed. Not that he could imagine any kind of life for them together. He couldn't see Ginny preparing a meal, changing a diaper, remembering to renew the subscription to the *New York Times*, all the things Penelope did that made his life harmonious and sweet, all the things he had taken for granted, and now had lost.

After Ginny left, Gabriel got up, dressed and drove home. He found his father in the apartment, clumsily making himself a roast beef sandwich, but both his mother and his daughter were gone.

"Where's Mom?" he asked, looking hungrily at the sandwich. He realized he hadn't eaten yet today and it was close to one o'clock.

"I don't know," said his father. "I went out for groceries and she was gone when I got back."

"Maybe she took Isobel for a walk. The stroller is missing."

"Maybe," said Oscar. "Anyway, I waited for a long time and finally decided to make myself something to eat." He looked at Gabriel eyeing his food. "Would you like a sandwich? I can make you one." Gabriel nodded and Oscar spent the next few minutes assembling the rye bread, the mayonnaise. Together, they took their plates into the dining room.

"Where do you think they could have gone?" Oscar asked between bites.

"There's a playground a couple of blocks away. Maybe they went there. Isobel really likes it. Maybe she's having such a good time Mom wanted to let her stay."

"Could we take a walk over there? See if we can find them?"

There were lots of children in the playground. But Isobel was not one of them. They stood there for a moment, watching other people's children run and slide, swing and climb. Gabriel remembered coming here with Penelope and Isobel, pushing her in the swing, guiding her down the baby slide.

"I wonder where she could be," said Oscar, more to himself than to Gabriel.

"Are you worried about her? She was pretty upset last night."

"She was," Oscar agreed. "Can we sit down?" The bench was clammy with condensation from rain the night before, but Gabriel still felt good to be sitting there with Oscar. He thought of the day at the beach last November, and how angry he had been. That anger was gone now, replaced by something else Gabriel was still trying to decipher.

"There's something I've been wanting to say to you," Oscar began.

"What's that, Dad?"

"I want you to know that what happened with Ginny happened only twice. But those were the only two times in my life I've been unfaithful to your mother."

Gabriel did not want to hear about Ginny and Oscar. But he didn't want to look at Penelope's body beneath the sheet either. If he could stand that, he could stand this. Especially since Oscar seemed to need to tell him. Gabriel stared straight ahead, at a little girl toddling toward a man who seemed to be her father, and suddenly he wanted to see Isobel.

"That's all right, Dad." He stood up. "Let's get going. Maybe Mom is back at the apartment." He waited for Oscar, who seemed to be having a hard time getting up. Gabriel felt a pang: Oscar was not old, but he was not in the best physical shape and this whole thing must have been pretty wearing on him. He gave his father his arm. Oscar took it, looking up and straight into his eyes. "Thank you," he said, and together they left the playground.

OSCAR

Ruth *was* gone. Try as he might, Oscar could not digest this information. If she hadn't left him when she first found out about Ginny, why had she left him now? And even more bewildering was the fact that she had taken Isobel with her. How could she have done that to Gabriel? Hadn't he lost enough already?

Earlier in the day, when he and Gabriel had returned to the empty apartment, Oscar was puzzled but not unduly alarmed. Maybe she had forgotten to ask him to buy a melon or a pint of cherry tomatoes, and she had stopped to get these things herself. But as the day wore on into evening, he finally had to accept the fact that Ruth was not shopping, not at the playground, not taking Isobel for a walk. Ruth was gone.

He heard Gabriel talking to Ben and to William, both of whom planned to be in Connecticut for Penelope's funeral. There were more calls from Caroline, calls from friends and from colleagues, and Gabriel dealt with those as well. Oscar just sat in the white armchair across from the white sofa, watching the sky from the windows of the apartment. Every time the phone rang, which it did with some frequency, he expected it to be Ruth, but every time he was disappointed. Finally, when the dark had settled all around the city and filled the windows with its blackness, Gabriel knelt before him and took his hand. "Are you okay, Dad?" he asked. "Can I get you something to drink?" Oscar just shook his head. Ruth is gone was the refrain that played over and over in his mind, gone, gone, Ruth is gone.

More time passed and Gabriel was at his elbow again, urging him to get up and go into the bedroom. "Why don't we both try to get some sleep?" he said.

"Do you think we should call the police?" The act of standing up had galvanized him into speech.

"No, not the police." Oscar could see the pain that contorted his handsome face. Even in his fog, he could understand that Gabriel had had enough of the police for the time being. And didn't a person have to be missing for at least twenty-four hours before the police would get involved?

Oscar shuffled into the bedroom, where he closed the door and took off his clothes. The suitcase was missing. The things that were in it were now stacked neatly on a chair. A piece of paper was wedged between his shirts. A note. He pulled it out and read it quickly.

Dear Oscar,

I know it will seem crazy to you but I felt I couldn't bear another minute of this. I can't believe the selfishness of our son. It fills me with despair. Though right now, everything fills me with despair. I took Isobel because I couldn't stand to leave her. I'm not sure where we're going. Or for how long. Please don't try to find us. I'll be in touch when I can.

Ruth

Oscar read this note over several times, as if it might have contained some clue he had missed on an earlier reading. He knew he must show it to Gabriel, but it would have to wait. He couldn't face his son now. Oscar climbed into the bed, pulled the white comforter up around his chin. He could not bear to extinguish the light above the bed, to feel the darkness without Ruth there next to him. So he left the light on, and after a while, marginally calmed by its steady, ambient glow, he drifted off into an uneasy sleep. He woke several times during the night, though, and when he did, he could hear Gabriel moving around in the apartment.

The next morning, Oscar remembered that he, Ruth, Gabriel and Isobel were scheduled to take an early flight back to New York. If they didn't start getting ready to leave, they would miss the plane.

"What are we going to do?" asked Oscar. "Are we going to leave without them?" He stared at his son's face, which revealed nothing.

"I'll call Caroline," Gabriel said finally. "Then I'm calling the police."

"Before you do that, you should read this." Oscar handed Gabriel the note, which was creased from having spent the night under Oscar's pillow. Gabriel's eyes scanned it quickly.

"So *I'm* selfish." He gave the note back to his father. "But it didn't give her the right to take Isobel. That's kidnapping."

"She wouldn't think of it that way."

"Why are you defending her? She left you. She took my daughter. Goddamn her!" He pressed his hands against his face and closed his eyes. When he opened them, he reached for the phone.

"What are you doing?" Oscar asked.

"I told you. I'm calling Caroline. To see if she'll postpone the funeral."

"And if she won't?"

"It will have to take place without me. I'm not going east until I find them."

"Your mother said not to do that."

"Dad," Gabriel said impatiently, "I don't have to take orders from her, remember? I'm a grown-up." Why didn't you think of that before you went off with Ginny that night? Oscar thought. But he didn't say it. After all, who was he to throw stones?

Oscar listened as Gabriel spent the next hour on the telephone. He talked to Caroline, who agreed to postpone the funeral until Ruth and Isobel had been found. How she reacted to this latest bit of grief Oscar didn't know and didn't have the strength to ask. He thought he would leave the room when Gabriel phoned the police; he didn't think he could stand to hear his wife described as a kidnapper. But Gabriel surprised him by calling the credit card company instead. He was finding out if Ruth had used her card and, if so, where. If he knew that, it wouldn't be so hard to follow her. At first, the person who took Gabriel's call wouldn't give out the information, so Oscar had to get on the phone. The card was in his name. Then they learned it would take at least twenty-four hours for the information to be posted. Maybe even forty-eight.

"Shit," Gabriel said when he heard that. "Shit, shit, shit!"

The next day, Oscar watched as his son hastily packed a bag. "Do you want to come with me?" he kept asking. "Are you sure you'll be all right here alone?" Oscar was very sure he didn't want to join Gabriel in going after Ruth; he felt he had no right to. But he was less sure about how he would manage on his own. "Maybe you want to go back to New York and wait there?" That alternative seemed even worse. Ruth's imprint, Oscar knew, would be everywhere, from the comfortable furniture—swathed in the beige-and-cream-checked slipcovers she put on every summer—to the simply framed botanical prints on the walls and the big blue-and-white bowl she had kept on their dining room table for as long as he could remember. He would feel her all around him, like a scent in the air or the muted hum of music from another room.

Gabriel was worried about leaving him even as he got ready to go. They had come to no clear resolution, when an answer of sorts presented itself in the soft chiming of the doorbell.

"Mrs. Erikson," Gabriel said to the small, tanned woman who stood in the doorway. "I'd like you to meet my father, Oscar Kornblatt." Oscar stepped forward to shake her hand. She had short, gray-brown hair and tiny gold hoops in her ears. Although she was about his age or even older,

Oscar still saw something elfin in her appearance. "Mrs. Erikson is the neighbor I told you about."

"Ah," was all Oscar could say to that.

"I don't mean to disturb you," Mrs. Erikson said to Gabriel. "I've been feeling so bad about—" she paused and looked down at the floor—"about Penelope. I wanted to see if there was anything I could do. To help with the baby, that is."

"Isobel isn't here," Gabriel said, looking from his father to Mrs. Erikson. "But there is something you could do. Something we'd all appreciate very much."

If Mrs. Erikson thought it bizarre that Ruth had left with Isobel and Gabriel had gone in pursuit of them, she didn't say so. Instead, she looked in on Oscar a couple of times a day, each time bringing a tray of food with her. She didn't invite him to her apartment, which relieved him. This was the last place where he had seen Ruth and this was where he wanted to stay. On a couple of occasions, Mrs. Erikson sat with him while he ate. It was during one of these times that she told him about losing her husband of three decades to throat cancer two years earlier.

"It was like something in me had been amputated," she said.

"Amputated," Oscar repeated. That was an accurate description.

But mostly she left him alone, in this white world, where he sat, trying to read and picking at the food she brought, waiting for the phone bulletins from Gabriel. "Ruth is gone," he told the couch, the chairs, the cushions. "Ruth is gone."

GINNY

Ginny *never* thought she would feel so happy to be back in New York. Even though it was the end of the summer and the whole city smelled like ripe garbage, she didn't care. After everything that had happened in San Francisco, she was glad to kiss that town good-bye. The company had a little break before the fall season started, but Ginny was staying put. No more traveling for a while.

She was still feeling shaken by Penelope's death. Gabriel didn't dwell on the details, so Ginny's imagination tried to supply them. And then there was Gabriel himself. Ginny could still feel his eyes boring into her when she was getting ready to leave the motel room. He had called her once to say that he was still on the West Coast, that he was looking for his mother and his daughter. That was a pretty alarming phone call, but she hadn't heard from him since.

Then Althea told her—strictly in confidence—that Erik was going to cast her as one of the leads in *Concerto Barocco*. That drove everything else—Gabriel, Penelope, Oscar—right out of Ginny's head. *Concerto Barocco* had become one of her favorite ballets. It was one of the great ones, the ones that people talked about for years, and there wasn't a lot she wouldn't do to get a leading role in it. And here Erik was going to offer it to her, just like that. Or at least that was what Althea said.

"Have you ever danced it?" Ginny asked Althea after class, when they were both standing by the barre, toweling off the sweat from their necks.

"A long time ago." Althea was rubbing the towel hard, this way and that.

"Will you coach me?" Ginny asked. "Please?"

"Well, it's not official yet," she said. The towel hung limp in her hands.

"I don't care," Ginny told her. "I want to learn it anyway."

Althea finally agreed and they started working together. Since Althea didn't want anyone to know, they had to be discreet. Instead of finding an empty studio right after class, when lots of people would have still been around, they waited until later in the day, when the building was just about empty.

Even though Ginny had been in the studio scores of times before, it looked different. Maybe it was the way the late-afternoon sun poured in through the long, long windows, lighting up all the lazy little dust motes that slowly drifted around and settled to the floor. The chunks of resin in their wooden box were like bits of gold in this light. When Ginny crunched them into sparkling powder under the tips of her shoes, she was startled by the sound. She was not usually so hypersensitive. Maybe it was just the thrill of learning a new role, and this new role in particular, that made all her senses so alert.

Concerto Barocco was one of Balanchine's plotless ballets, which was not to say that it didn't have a story. It was a kind of love story, only not one with obvious characters or a script. No, it was more about the way the movement lit up the music, and the music, the movement. Coming together and then moving apart, the way lovers do.

Ginny thought Althea was a great coach, and she imagined how it might have been when the older woman danced the role. Ginny wanted to be all that Althea was, and more. As the light lowered, they remained in the studio, going over the intricate patterns again and again. There was the mirror, sometimes Ginny's friend, sometimes not, and Bach's music, in the form of a portable CD player that Althea brought with her. And there were their two bodies straining to overcome their stubborn connection to the ground, the boundaries of what was mortal.

Ginny and Althea often had dinner together after practice was over. And on one of those nights, when Ginny had had some wine, she told Althea the story of Gabriel. Or at least some of it, since she decided not to mention the part about Oscar's being his father. Ginny was sure that Oscar and Althea knew each other, at least by sight, and she felt an urge to protect Oscar. So she didn't name names, she just sketched in some of the more essential details, like the ones about the wife, the baby and the accident. Althea sat there staring, her long, dark fingers wrapped tightly around the stem of her wineglass, not saying a word.

"Pretty intense, isn't it?" There was still a little wine in Ginny's glass and she drained the last of it.

" 'Intense' is not the word. I'd steer clear of the whole thing if I were you."

"Because . . . ?"

"Because this guy is like a bomb, just waiting to detonate. He's going to be wallowing in guilt over his wife's death. No, not wallowing. Drowning. You don't need that kind of guy in your life, believe me. Not if you want to dance *Barocco* or anything else Erik just happens to hand you on a silver platter."

"You think I don't deserve the role?"

"Deserve? Girl, you were born for it. So don't waste your time with this guy and his motherless baby." Althea lifted the glass to her lips.

"But dancers can be in love, can't they?"

Ginny knew she sounded testy but didn't care. So Gabriel scared her the last time they were together. That didn't mean she should give him up. Did it?

"Maybe that boy was in love with you to start. But now ..." Althea paused, trying to find the right words.

"Now what?" Ginny prompted.

"Now you're his reason to live." The waiter appeared with a dessert menu. Ginny wanted a slice of cherry cheesecake, but, all of a sudden, she felt as if her dinner was about to come right back up.

"Excuse me," she said, dropping the menu on the floor in her haste to reach the ladies' room. She vomited easily enough, though afterward she felt shaky and drained. She was rinsing her mouth out with water when Althea came in.

"I thought you didn't do that vomiting thing," she said.

"I don't."

"Then why the rush?"

"I felt sick, that's all."

"Sick? With what?" Althea seemed suspicious.

"I don't know. Flu. Stomach poisoning. I promise I won't give it to you if that's what you're worried about."

"I'm not worried about that. I'm worried about you." Althea wet a paper towel and waited while Ginny ran it over her face. They left the ladies' room together and said good night in the street. "See you in class tomorrow."

"Tomorrow," Ginny echoed. Then she turned away.

But the next morning, she was no better. By now she felt completely gutted inside, with nothing left to regurgitate; still her stomach clenched and heaved. How was she going to make it through company class today? And through a rehearsal after that? She looked at the pink tights she held in her hand—pink and black were required for company class—and put them down. Years ago, when she ran a fever of 103, she had tried sneaking out of the house to go to ballet class. But in her present condition, the thought of holding on to the barre, melting into the first pliés, seemed intolerable. She went back to bed and slept.

When she awoke, she felt like herself again: ravenous and ready to dance. Since she found only a desiccated lemon and some flat root beer in her refrigerator, she bought two carrot muffins and a large container of freshly squeezed orange juice from the corner deli and consumed everything on her way to the rehearsal. When she ran into Althea, she explained why she had missed class that morning.

"You're feeling better now?"

"One hundred percent."

"Tomorrow then. Company class is at ten."

The next day, however, Ginny repeated the same cycle: she woke feeling nauseated, threw up and then had to go back to bed to sleep it off. This time, she was awakened by the ringing of the telephone.

"I thought you said you were better," Althea said.

"I was. Then I wasn't." Ginny stretched her legs wide and pointed her feet. Her stomach growled. "And here's the strangest thing. Now I feel fine again. What kind of nutty virus is this?"

"Maybe it's not a virus." It took a minute before Althea's meaning sank in.

"That's not possible. I've been on the Pill forever." Though maybe she *had* missed a couple of days back in San Francisco, right after Penelope died. Days when she had seen Gabriel.

"Anything is possible. Look at the Virgin Mary."

Ginny said nothing. She was trying to absorb the idea that Althea might be right, that she might actually be pregnant.

"Why don't you go to the drugstore and buy the test?" Althea suggested. "Call me when you've done it."

The early pregnancy detection kit cost $13.99 at the drugstore. As she handed the cashier the money, Ginny was sure she felt the woman's eyes moving to the fourth finger of her left hand, looking for a ring. Back in her apartment, she scanned the directions and went into the bathroom. It didn't take a minute for the stick to turn a clear, deep blue. Ginny stared at it. She had promised to call Althea with the results. But she needed to think for a while, to let this startling information travel through her blood and her body. She needed to dance.

Ginny dressed, packed her bag and began walking downtown. She had missed company class, but she knew she could find an empty studio now; rehearsals weren't scheduled to start until later in the day. When she found one, she put down her bag and sat on the floor to change her shoes. Instead of the pointe shoes that she usually wore, she had brought her soft leather ballet slippers. Wes had liked the girls to sew satin ribbons on their leather slippers as well as their pointe shoes; he said it made them look more professional. Ginny had never lost the habit, and as she secured the pink ribbons around her ankle, she thought about the blue stick.

Standing up, she examined her profile in the mirror. No swelling yet; her stomach was as flat as ever. It was hard for her to believe she was preg-nant. Ginny was used to commanding her body and having it obey. Now her body was a rebel, beyond her command or control.

With only the music that she heard in her mind, she began the exer-cises. First the pliés, elastic and supple; then the unwavering geometry of the tendus and the ronds des jambes. Unlike the classes taught by Erik or Althea, which tended to be showy and filled with bravura flourishes—changement en tournant to switch sides, the relevés all done on pointe—Ginny's own barre was elementary and unadorned, the sort of barre given in a beginners' class. But she applied herself to it with the concentration and fervor that she would have given to an actual performance. The repe-tition of the movements that she had been doing for most of her life took on an unprecedented urgency. *Show me the way,* said her pointed foot as it struck the studio floor in a battement frappé; *tell me the answer,* asked her arms as they moved through the simple ports de bras.

After the développés and the grands battements—which she did as if she were a novice, facing the barre and clasping it with both hands—she was through. Her face and neck were coated in sweat; she felt completely cleansed and calmed. When she called Althea from a pay phone on the street, she asked not for advice or consolation, but for the name of a doctor who would do what she needed to be done.

The gynecologist was on East Ninety-fourth Street; Althea assured her that the woman could perform a first-trimester abortion in her office. Ginny and Althea sat in the waiting room, flipping through magazines and not saying anything. Earlier, Althea had asked, "Are you positive you want to do this? Don't you even want to tell him?"

"Yes. And no." Ginny thought of her mother having had to make the same choice. Rita had said no to the first question. The second one hadn't been an option. Ginny supposed that there was some small progress in this: at least she knew who had gotten her pregnant. But what point would there be in telling him? She knew what she was going to do.

"Ms. Valentine?" said the white-clad receptionist. "Dr. Singh will see you now."

"I'll wait." Althea put her copy of *People* back on the glass-topped table. She squeezed Ginny's hand.

Dr. Singh wore a patterned sari under her white lab coat. There was a small red dot in the center of her forehead.

"You've never been pregnant before?" She consulted the form Ginny had filled out in the waiting room.

"Never." Ginny picked up the paper gown and began to unfasten its cellophane wrapping.

"And you were on the Pill?"

Ginny nodded. "I think I skipped a couple of days, though."

"If you skip a couple of days, it doesn't work." Dr. Singh's lips compressed, as if in exasperation.

"I know. It was the first time." Ginny felt as if she was speaking words her mother could have spoken twenty-two years ago. That had been the first time too.

"I'll be back when you've changed." Her tone had softened.

Ginny's eyes went to the tray of instruments that had been laid out near the table.

"I'll make it as painless as possible," Dr. Singh added.

"I've got a high pain threshold," Ginny said. She didn't explain that she had looked at the instruments simply as a way of gauging the potential pain: it was never as bad if you knew its borders, had a grasp of its shape. The gown felt flimsy in her hands. She shook it out and the folds opened, accordion-like. When Dr. Singh returned, she was already on the table. She thought of her mother, she thought of Wes, she thought of the barre she had given herself. She didn't think of Gabriel, because she didn't let herself.

Althea was there when it was over, helping Ginny into a taxi back to West Seventy-first Street. The streets were wet; it must have rained.

"No class for a few days. And no *Barocco.*"

"At least the season hasn't started yet." Ginny leaned her head back against the seat of the taxi. Dr. Singh was as good as her word. The procedure hadn't hurt all that much. At least not physically. But the doctor hadn't said anything about how she was going to feel inside. Which turned out to be much worse than anything she could have imagined. She took Althea's hand and held it tightly. "Thanks for coming with me." Then she closed her eyes for the rest of the ride.

Several days later, Ginny made a trip out to Green-Wood Cemetery in Brooklyn. She had wanted to go to Penelope's funeral but knew that it was impossible. The desire remained with her, though, and in response to her question about local cemeteries, one of the other dancers mentioned Woodlawn, in the Bronx. Then Ginny remembered something Gabriel had said, about his grandparents—that would have been Ruth's father and mother—being buried at Green-Wood Cemetery in Brooklyn. Green-Wood, she decided, was the place.

The trip to the cemetery meant taking the subway, something that frightened her a little. She still remembered the malevolent face of the boy who took her money on the bus. But she was determined to go, and with the help of an elaborately detailed map and a patient transit worker, she found her way to the R train and then, once she had emerged into the street and walked a little way, to the massive and elaborately worked gates that formed the entrance to the cemetery. The elderly security guard in his gray uniform looked up at her briefly and then back down at the game of solitaire he was playing. Another younger man stood tending a covered cart of flowers just outside the gate. Ginny impulsively bought a bunch, though she didn't know the name of Gabriel's grandparents and had no idea how to find them.

The cemetery was hot and quiet. She walked along the curving, well-tended paths. Century-old oaks gripped the earth tightly with their roots; their thick branches almost seemed to support the weight of the sky. Occasionally, she stopped to read the name on a headstone or look at a statue. A marble angel knelt beside a tomb, head bowed in grief. The angel's carved wings spanned a distance of what must have been five feet.

The day grew hotter and Ginny waved at the swarms of tiny gnats that hovered around her. Words on the stones began to form a kind of hum, a whispered litany: *dearly beloved . . . deeply mourned . . . we will miss . . . eternal rest . . . at God's side at last. . . .* Some of the headstones were new and highly polished; others were weathered and lichen-covered.

So many of the older headstones marked the graves of children. *Heaven's newest angel . . . Unblemished soul.* Although she swore to herself that she wouldn't, Ginny thought of the baby that had been growing inside her, the baby whose life she had decided to end. Her eyes burned and she hurried along the path, as if she could outpace her tears. The last thing in the world she wanted was a baby. So what was she sniveling about now?

She stopped at a stone from another century, its inscription bordered by tendrils of sculpted leaves: Elizabeth Paula Wilcox. Born May 12, 1870. Died August 20, 1899. *Beloved wife of . . . beloved mother to . . .* She wasn't even thirty years old when she died. How old had Gabriel's wife been?

Ginny didn't know. But she felt the ragged hole that Penelope's death had left in the lives of all the people who had loved her.

Ginny looked down at the flowers, and pulled a few white carnations from the bunch. Hadn't Gabriel said that Penelope had loved white flowers and would place them in vases all around their apartment? She laid the loose stems across the grave, and propped the rest, still wrapped in their crisp cone of green waxed paper, against another tombstone. Then she bowed her head. The prayer that eluded her in the San Francisco church came easily now. "Rest in peace," she murmured to Elizabeth Paula Wilcox.

RUTH

R*uth had* forgotten. Even after raising her own three children, and all the time she had put in volunteering at the hospital, there were so many things about caring for a baby that she had just forgotten. Like how heavy a baby could feel when she fell asleep in your arms and you had to somehow carry her and the cumbersome bag with all her essential accoutrements back to the car. How unnerving her crying—when it had gone on for nearly an hour—could be. How exhausted Ruth felt from waking up—at Isobel's behest, of course—not twice, not three times, but four separate times during the night.

When Ruth's own sons had been babies, she had been much younger. And she had help: her mother was still alive, and Molly and she frequently spelled each other with the kids. Molly used to call it the R and R exchange. If Ruth was feeling particularly frazzled, Molly would come over with her daughters and take the whole crew to the playground in Central Park while Ruth stole away to the Metropolitan Museum of Art.

There she would spend a peaceful hour communing with the Renoirs and Monets that hung in the upstairs galleries. Then, a muffin and a cup of tea in the restaurant; finally, a stroll through the gift shop to buy some postcards or perhaps a wall calendar. When they switched, Ruth would take the five children to the old Hayden Planetarium, or the Museum of Natural History. Later, when Ruth asked Molly where she had been, she always answered, "Seeing my lover, of course!" They laughed wildly at the thought of it, but all these years later, Ruth wondered if there was something Molly hadn't told her back then. Something that Molly thought placid, dull, stay-at-home Ruth wouldn't understand, or approve of. What was Molly thinking about Ruth now?

At first, everything went smoothly enough. Right after Gabriel left, Ruth looked outside. The day was gray and chilly. How glad she would be to leave this dismal weather behind. Quickly she dressed herself and the baby. Then she grabbed a few of Isobel's things—clothes, diapers and the like—and packed them in her bag.

Ruth and Isobel were alone in the elevator and the doorman seemed to have stepped away for a moment, another unexpected bit of luck. If he were asked later whether he had seen them leave the building, he wouldn't be able to say.

As they headed toward the Hertz rental office—a short distance away—they passed a bank, but Ruth decided to skip it—she would get the cash from ATMs along the way, use the credit card as she needed it. At Hertz, there was a car, a vivid blue Accord, ready and waiting. She opened the trunk, put the bag and the stroller inside. They had even remembered the car seat; it was already strapped into place. Ruth worried that Isobel might be afraid to get into the car—would she remember the sounds of Penelope being hit, not once, but twice?—but Isobel offered no resistance as she slipped her in and adjusted the straps to fit her body. She planned to drive for a while and then stop somewhere outside the city at a playground. She wanted to make sure Isobel had some time outdoors.

And so this was how Ruth found herself, moving at a steady pace along the highway, heading south. The drive began more pleasantly than she would have imagined, given the circumstances. She said the names of the towns they passed out loud: San Mateo, Palo Alto, Pescadero, Santa Cruz. Each name was like a bead on a necklace, and the necklace was the road itself as it spun out, closer and closer to their destination.

As she drove, she found it impossible not to think of Oscar and Gabriel, the twin fuel jets for her seemingly boundless anger. There was an expression her grandmother Pip used in situations like this: "All his *tzechel* is in his *putz*." When Ruth had asked what that meant, Pip replied, "He thinks with his you-know-what." That certainly described Ruth's son. And her husband too, the one who brought Ginny Valentine into their lives in the first place. But with every mile of distance she put between herself and her family, Gabriel's transgressions, and Oscar's too, would seem less and less important. Or that's what the new Ruth was saying. All day long, she retained the sense of watching herself. The old Ruth was amazed at the chutzpah of the new one. But it was strangely comforting to feel as if there were two Ruths; the old one who knew so much and the new one who had such energy and daring.

There was a noise from the backseat. Isobel. Ruth wanted to look at her but dared not turn around. "Br!" Isobel said, or this was what it sounded like. At first Ruth thought the child was cold, but since the air felt pleasantly warm, she was confused. "Br!" Isobel repeated, pointing to the window. "Br?" Ruth tried to follow the direction of her outstretched arm without taking her own eyes off the road, and then she saw the flock of birds—pigeons? starlings? crows?—circling above.

"Bird!" Ruth said and was rewarded with Isobel's smile. She had never spent enough time with her granddaughter to understand her nascent utterings. Well, that was about to change. Ruth kept stealing glimpses in the rearview mirror, and she saw that Isobel remained cheerful enough, continuing to point and smile. After a while, she grew tired of this, and the steady motion of the car lulled her to sleep. Good. Ruth would drive for as long as she slept, and when she woke, they would stop.

They had just gone through San Luis Obispo when Isobel woke up. Ruth heard her calling "Mama!" and wanted to cry. But she wouldn't let herself. "Buck up, Ruth," she said out loud. If she started to cry every time Isobel did, they would be in fine shape, wouldn't they? "It's all right, darling." Ruth soothed her as best she could without touching or making eye contact. "We'll be stopping right away." And as soon as Ruth spied a place to eat—too bad it happened to be a McDonald's—she glided off the road and brought the car to a stop.

She ordered the chicken nuggets and some French fries. Ruth knew Isobel had never had meat and she worried that it might not agree with her system. Poultry seemed safer than beef. But Isobel wouldn't even look at it; instead, she devoted herself entirely to the fries, which she ate with great appetite, licking her tiny fingers for the residue of salt and grease. Best of all was the ketchup; when Ruth tore off the corner of a little foil packet, Isobel grabbed it right out of her hand and started sucking it. That Penelope's daughter might turn out to be a fast food junkie would have been an amusing irony had things been different. Now it seemed so sad. Ruth brought Isobel back to the counter for another order of fries; Isobel squirmed and struggled in her arms. Her sticky fingers left traces of ketchup on Ruth's face and in her hair. Somehow she managed to order the fries and pay for them too, despite Isobel's wriggling. But she should have remembered how quickly a baby's mood could change: when Isobel saw the new bag of fries, she glowered and knocked them off the tray.

The rest room was foul and the so-called infant changing table dangled from a single hinge, so Ruth diapered her right on the hard, dirty tiles. Then, despite Isobel's loud protests, Ruth cleaned up the child's hands and face as best she could with the cold water from the sink and they were on their way again. Ruth drove around in search of a playground and when she couldn't find one, began to feel anxious about getting back on the road. Today was a travel day, she rationalized.

Back at McDonald's, Isobel was given a small toy with her meal: a pink Beanie Baby flamingo, which seemed to delight her. Ruth was relieved that it absorbed her attention as she hadn't thought to bring any toys—another necessary thing she had forgotten—and she hoped it would last until the next stop. Though she was not sure of where and when that would be.

Through the mirror, Ruth could see Isobel shaking it, squeezing it, chewing on it. All seemed well until Ruth heard a cough—more of a choking sound—and whipped her head around. Something was caught in Isobel's throat! Ruth pulled over immediately but forgot to signal and the driver behind her uttered a string of curses in his wake. Frantically, she unbuckled her seatbelt and leaned over. Prying Isobel's mouth open with her finger, she reached in and managed to extract the soggy bit of cardboard—the damn tag!—from her throat. It wasn't lodged in deeply, but Isobel was clearly frightened, and continued to cry. Ruth hurried around to sit with her in the backseat. Isobel cried for a long time, small chest heaving, black hair stuck to her face where it was wet from tears. Ruth listened to the sound of that crying, crying she was unable to stop. What have I done? lamented the old Ruth. The new Ruth had no reply.

Somehow, she calmed Isobel—and herself—sufficiently for them to continue. How could she have forgotten to remove the tag? The baby could have choked right there in the backseat. Ruth berated herself as the miles slipped by. Around dinnertime, they stopped at a motel and went into the Italian restaurant that adjoined it. As Ruth scanned the menu for something Isobel could eat, she saw that liquor was served. Tonight she would order a glass of wine with her meal. She certainly needed it. The wine came first, and though it was not very good, Ruth downed it quickly and ordered another. She was not hungry but ordered some plain spaghetti in the hope that Isobel would share it. When the spaghetti came, Isobel squeezed and rolled it between her fingers, but would not eat it. Nor would she eat any of the salad, buttered roll or Italian cheesecake with which Ruth tried to tempt her. Finally, Ruth asked the waitress for a glass of milk, which Isobel drank without assistance, cheeks sucked in as she gulped.

The motel clerk had no cribs, so Ruth brought Isobel into the king-sized bed. Then she piled the pillows alongside her, so she wouldn't roll over onto the floor. Isobel fell asleep but woke crying a short time later. Ruth thought she must be hungry, given how little she had eaten earlier in the evening, but Isobel rejected the cookies and crackers Ruth offered.

She was able to get her back to sleep, only to have to repeat the whole cycle—wake, tears, rock—three more times. Finally, Ruth abandoned the idea of sleep for herself, preferring to remain lying on the bed, eyes closed, but all other senses alert and ready.

By the morning, Ruth's confidence in her plan had nearly evaporated. If she could barely get through a single night with Isobel, how in the world could she manage to raise her alone, in a foreign country? Then she remembered that today was the day that Penelope was to be buried. Gabriel would have to go through that without her. And Oscar. But Ruth was doing something important: she was taking care of Penelope's baby when Penelope could no longer do it herself.

Breakfast went better than dinner had the night before: Isobel ate some scrambled egg, licked butter from the toast, spilled her orange juice and lapped it up right from the table. The new Ruth was smug in her triumph. They got back in the car and kept driving south. Since Isobel had slept so little the night before, she drifted off very quickly. When she woke, she started crying again, not loud, but a low, harrowing keen that sounded as if she was in mourning. Which she was, but didn't know it. "Mama!" Ruth heard her call and, after a while, "Dada!" Ruth stopped the car again, because the sound so unsettled her. What could she do to calm her?

Ruth started singing. She hadn't sung in a long while and mostly she didn't miss it. It had never been her dream to sing opera, or the German lieder that Lilli loved so much; Ruth still remembered her grandmother sitting there, hands crossed on her cane, nodding with pleasure as Ruth sang. It was one of these lieder that Ruth sang now to her own granddaughter, humming when she couldn't think of the words. To her surprise, it stopped Isobel's crying. Her face, which Ruth could see in the rearview mirror, settled itself into a different expression, and though there were still tears on her cheeks, she no longer looked sad. Cautiously, Ruth started up the car, singing all the while.

When she had finished her meager repertoire of lieder, she moved on to something else. Not arias, her voice was not in any shape to cover those ranges. Instead, she reconstructed the songs she sang to her boys when they were little, the familiar ones about the twinkling star, the spider, the farm, the wheels on the bus. When Ruth didn't think she could stand one more moo-moo here, there or anywhere, she moved on to the more sultry ballads and tender folk songs she had always secretly loved, songs that had been recorded by Joan Baez, Judy Collins, Joni Mitchell, Billie Holiday and Aretha Franklin. Ruth would never have sung such songs in front of another adult—she could almost feel Oscar's disdain—but Isobel seemed enchanted by anything that came out of her mouth. Just as Ruth was belting out Aretha's "Natural Woman"—she had really let herself get lost in this—they arrived at the border. Would they let her drive a rented car into Mexico? Ruth didn't know, but prayed there wouldn't be a problem.

The customs official was a young man of Mexican descent; his upper lip was coated with a mustache as fine as down. He looked briefly at Ruth's passport and didn't even ask if Isobel had one. He didn't even seem to check the license plate. Instead he waved them through. The old Ruth couldn't believe how easy that was; the new one applauded. The alternate plan she had formulated, in which she'd pretended to look for the nonexistent passport, hoping the official would let her go through without it, had not been necessary. Had she been stopped, Ruth had planned to drive to Texas and try her luck there. The car, with the window rolled down, grew hot and Ruth saw Isobel squirm. Quickly, she rolled up the window, turned on the air-conditioning and started singing again.

Tijuana, where they would spend the night, was a sorry town, poised there on the cusp of the United States and with its gaze forever directed northward. Driving slowly around the ragged streets, Ruth first tried the Holiday Inn, only to find all its rooms were taken by a convention of drug enforcement officials. The Ramada was also fully booked, by the participants of another convention, this time of running shoe manufacturers. Ruth saw one of them hurry across the parking lot, three or four thickly cushioned sneakers tucked under each arm.

She finally settled on a third-rate motel where they could rent rooms by the week. Never mind that the sheets on the twin beds were gray, or that the clerk responded to her inquiry about a crib by presenting her with a large metal washtub. There was a kitchenette attached to the room containing a two-burner hot plate, a small fridge that smelled of spoiled milk and a sink with a dripping faucet. The room's single window overlooked the parking lot, which Ruth liked since she wanted to keep her eye on the car, whose very newness seemed exceptional, and for that reason vulnerable here. Credit cards were not accepted, so she paid, in advance, for their first week with cash.

She was glad she had packed Isobel's stroller, which she took out so that they could walk, rather than ride, around the neighborhood. Up a few blocks was the Avenida de la Revolución, a faded main drag with shops that sold cheap sombreros, maracas covered in glitter and T-shirts with maps of Mexico emblazoned on their fronts. Ruth would have liked to buy Isobel a pair of the maracas, but after the near-tragedy with the Beanie Baby, she decided against it. What if the glitter was toxic and she ingested some? Or if she snapped off the handle and poked herself in the eye? These were the kinds of things Penelope used to think about, and for the first time, Ruth felt a rush of sympathy, even kinship, thinking about her.

The T-shirt was safer and ultimately more practical too, since she hadn't yet noticed any laundry facilities. She bought two of the very smallest size the store had. One depicted the Mexican map and the other a picture of some cartoon character in a sombrero, brandishing a gun. She bought two identical ones for herself. Ridiculous as they were, they would at least be clean.

As they walked along the street, Ruth saw a man leading a donkey by a rope tied to the animal's bridle. The beast's gray coat had been covered with some haphazard streaks of chalky paint and Ruth could not fathom what they might have meant. But she continued to stare and realized the streaks were actually meant to be stripes, as if the animal were not the dilapidated creature it patently was, but something exotic and foreign, like a zebra. When the man saw Ruth looking, he stopped and began speaking earnestly to her in Spanish. He pointed to the donkey and Ruth noticed its ears, which looked as if they had been gnawed on, poking through slits that had been cut in the battered straw hat it wore. He was offering Isobel a ride. Was this the life Ruth had engineered for her granddaughter in Mexico? The old Ruth was ascendant now, stern and disapproving. She shook her head and they continued on their way. The man's voice followed them for what seemed like a long time.

After obtaining some pesos from an ATM, Ruth bought a few things for a simple meal at the motel. Isobel ate little but eagerly drank the milk she was offered. Since there was no bathtub, only a stall shower, tiny sink and toilet with a lazy fly circling the bowl, Ruth used the metal washtub provided by the clerk to bathe Isobel. She splashed happily in the water, but cut her finger on one of the tub's sharp edges that Ruth had somehow managed to overlook. Then she cried and cried, and even Ruth's singing couldn't quiet her. She took Isobel's finger in her own mouth, blood leaving a metallic taste on her tongue. After a long while, she finally stopped wailing, and allowed Ruth to dry her with a dingy, threadbare towel. Ruth pushed the two beds together and placed her close to the wall. They both fell asleep almost instantly.

Isobel woke in the night crying, though, and used her small fists to grab onto Ruth's chest in what Ruth perceived as a frantic effort to nurse. Someone in an adjoining room knocked on the wall. Ruth picked Isobel up, and pulling her robe on with a single hand, brought her to the doorway. The night had cooled and the unfamiliar darkness seemed filled with menace, but still Ruth stood there and directed the baby's gaze up to the sky. The moon was as slim and delicate as one of Isobel's own fingernails; a bevy of moths fluttered around the single bulb overhead. Gradually, Isobel quieted down, and when her head began to droop, heavily, on Ruth's shoulder, they went back inside.

In the morning, Ruth felt depleted, which she attributed to two nights of fretful, interrupted sleep. More unsettling, though, was how listless Isobel seemed. Despite Ruth's efforts to engage her, she barely responded. Finally, Ruth stumbled upon the playground she had been thinking about since San Francisco, and pushed the baby in the single intact swing until her arms, shoulders and whole back burned with the exertion of it, but still Isobel's eyes didn't lose their glazed look. This was worse than her crying. Much worse.

She bought a map, tried to project herself and the baby into one of the places indicated by the bold, black letters. But that was the extent of it. The names of the towns meant nothing to her and all the exhorting of the new Ruth couldn't get the old one to pay the bill, get back in the car and drive away. Instead, Ruth and Isobel spent the next two days in Tijuana, where they walked the same sorry streets, shopped in the same market with its dusty bags of rice and its towers of canned beans, visited the same dilapidated playground, before returning in the early evening to their room.

Since neither of them had hats, Ruth was forced to buy sombreros, to shield their faces from the intensity of the sun. Isobel didn't like wearing hers, and Ruth spent a lot of time putting it back on her head after Isobel had pulled it off again. When Ruth repositioned it for the third time in ten minutes, she was reminded of William, the boy who said no to every hat, pair of mittens, boots, scarf or raincoat for the first dozen years of his life. Once he tried to flush the mittens down the toilet rather than wear them. William. Ruth was angry with Gabriel and Oscar, but not with William. How was he? And Betsy? And the new baby, Hannah? The last time she had spoken to them, they had talked about taking a trip to Puerto Vallarta. They had been there on their honeymoon and loved it. Now they wanted to go again, with Hannah.

Puerto Vallarta. Even the name sounded like song. William and Betsy had come back talking about the white sand, the fresh fish, the papayas the size of footballs. Ruth and Isobel would go to Puerto Vallarta. They would leave in the morning. Would Isobel like the beach? Would she eat papaya? Ruth would find out.

"We're going to go swimming," she said to Isobel as she got her ready for bed. The baby blinked soberly. "You're going to love it."

After Isobel had fallen asleep, Ruth opened the map again, studied the possible routes they could take. It was far, several hundred miles from where they now were. Ruth considered flying, but decided against it. She wanted some visual, tactile sense of this country she and Isobel were now inhabiting; she was more likely to find it driving than if they were in the air. They would need to rest and regroup along the way, but that was all right. There wouldn't be conventions everywhere they stopped. Surely, they would find some hotels that were better than this one. Maybe they would find one with a pool. Ruth felt calmed imagining a rectangle of azure; she would hold Isobel in her arms as she dipped her feet, her legs and finally her whole body into the water.

The next day was muggy and strangely overcast, with a heavy bank of bruise-colored clouds hanging low in the sky. And she thought she had left the bad weather behind in San Francisco. The old Ruth considered postponing their departure, but when she looked at Isobel's apathetic expression, the new one got busy packing. Outside of Tijuana, she stopped for gas and watched while the young Mexican boy wiped the windshield with the same care most people would have reserved for their faces. The clouds were still there, but Ruth was not going to let them stop her. She tipped the boy generously and they were on their way.

After about an hour of driving, the clouds, which had sunk lower and lower, opened and it began to rain. At first, Ruth almost welcomed the respite from the heat. The windshield wipers beat a steady rhythm and Ruth thought again of the boy at the gas station, the gentle way his hand had moved over the glass. But as the rain continued and the visibility diminished, the old Ruth began to feel frightened. So did the new one. The rain pattered down on the roof of the car, dribbling down over the windows. The car steamed up and Ruth couldn't find the defroster, so she was forced to hunch over the steering wheel, gripping it tightly and peering over its thick, padded surface in her effort to see the road ahead.

Then she must have taken a wrong turn, because she soon found herself on a badly paved road and after about twenty bumpy minutes, the paving ended altogether. She was now on a dirt road filled with potholes and baseball-sized rocks. Rain had turned everything to pinkish-orange mud. The sides and windows of the car soon became splattered with it. She drove slowly in what felt like circles. Finally, she pulled over to the side of the road and watched the rain continue to come down. Every now and then, a flash of lightning illuminated the sky; once it had passed, the sky was gray again. Ruth tried the radio, but there was only static. She and Isobel sat in the car for a long time, water streaming down the windows, no other cars in sight. They might have been the inhabitants of a latter-day ark, so total and encompassing was the deluge around them.

The exertion of driving and the lack of sleep exhausted her. She put her head on the steering wheel, wishing she could cry, cry like the rain that was pouring down around them. But the tears might frighten Isobel, so she willed herself to hold them in. She turned around to face the baby, who had been quiet for a long while. No singing, no pointing, no squirming. It was as if she had been given Thorazine with her breakfast and was now hypnotized by the rain.

"We're lost," Ruth finally said, breaking the silence.

"Mama," Isobel replied. Despite her resolve, Ruth's eyes filled with tears at the word.

"Mama's not coming now."

"Dada?" asked Isobel. That did it. The tears started coming now and she could do nothing to stop them. She quickly turned away from Isobel again. She had been so busy thinking about herself, her anger, that she hadn't stopped to consider what Isobel needed. Not really. She cried as quietly as she could for a few minutes, knuckles pressed to her lips to stifle the sobs. Then she got out of the car, and in the few seconds it took to open the door to the backseat, rain soaked her hair, glued her blouse to her skin. The rain mingled easily with her tears, coating her entire face.

"Do you want to see Daddy?" Ruth touched Isobel's arm. "Should we call him on the telephone?" Isobel turned to her.

"Dada?" she whispered. Her eyes, which had seemed so flat and expressionless for days, suddenly regained some animation. Dada. Had it really been so obvious all along? Ruth dried her face and hair with the paper towels she kept in the car. They waited a little longer, until the sky finally showed some weak light beyond the gray. The rain tapered off and she was able to start driving again. She kept the map open on the seat beside her.

Soon, she was back on the highway. Puerto Vallarta had dematerialized, like a mirage on a hot road. Ruth had a more pressing destination. The airport. The old Ruth and the new one were united now and there was a single Ruth who returned the rental car at the Hertz desk, negotiated with the American Airlines ticket agent and found the silver bank of telephones. Isobel dozed in the stroller, mouth open and snoring lightly.

There was no answer at their apartment in New York and Ruth was reluctant to call Caroline in Greenwich. She couldn't face explaining her mad flight—for madness was what it had been, she saw that now—or hearing the details of the funeral. If it had even taken place. Not really expecting to find anyone there, she finally tried Gabriel's number in San Francisco. She was suddenly grateful to hear Oscar's voice. "Isobel wants to see her father," Ruth said. "Can you tell him we're on our way?"

GABRIEL

Isobel *shifted* and bounced on Gabriel's lap, obscuring his view of the white casket, but he didn't care. He was so relieved to have her back. He put his face against her neck and inhaled her scent. Then he lifted his gaze over her head so he could focus on the casket, its shiny, lacquered surface reminding him of a grand piano he remembered seeing in an old black-and-white film. It mercifully remained closed. There were masses of white flowers adorning it: lilies, roses, gardenias—Penelope had loved gardenias—and tulips. He could smell them from where he sat and they reminded him of the bouquet she had carried on their wedding day.

On one side of him was Penelope's mother, who wept quietly into a folded handkerchief that she pressed to her lips; on the other side was his father. Next to her was Ruth. Gabriel couldn't see her from his seat unless he bent forward, which he had no inclination to do. Even though they had all flown east together after she had returned to San Francisco, he wasn't ready to deal with his mother. He was still too angry for that. Behind him were his brothers and their wives.

He tried to focus on the minister's eulogy; Gabriel recognized him as the same man who had officiated at his and Penelope's interfaith wedding ceremony. But he was having trouble concentrating. Instead, he found himself thinking about the days prior to this event, the days when he had gotten in his car, armed with only the barest bits of information that Oscar had gleaned from the credit card company and driven south, in search of his mother and daughter.

When Ruth had disappeared with Isobel, Gabriel had felt suddenly exiled from his former life. Before he had been a man with a wife, child, home and mistress. Now his wife was dead, his mother and daughter vanished. He had left his father, newly turned into a sleepwalker by Ruth's absence, sitting alone in his white apartment. White. A color for ghosts, which was what it seemed everyone had suddenly become. Even Ginny, who remained so vivid in his mind, was far out of reach, back in New York. Gabriel could still feel the itch of lust when he thought about her. But would he ever be able to separate his desire for Ginny from his guilt over Penelope? How long had she been lying in the street, and then the morgue, while Gabriel had been in the car with Ginny? And if he hadn't gone to the ballet that night, would she have been hit at all? Mrs. Erikson had told him that she had been planning to meet him there.

Southern California was hot. But after a little while of riding in the air-conditioned cocoon of his car, Gabriel began to feel like a ghost himself. So he turned off the air, opened the windows and let the hot wind whip through his hair and across his face. It dried his lips and throat, made his eyes feel gritty, but he didn't care. Instead of choosing from his eclectic and tasteful assortment of CDs, he fiddled with the radio. He became engrossed in a talk show where someone called in to say his wife had slept with his brother and was now carrying his brother's child; what should he do? Gabriel was almost tempted to call in and offer his own advice on the subject, but soon enough the station filled with static and then metamorphosed into a country-western station on which the singer wailed about her cheatin' heart.

Tijuana was a hellhole. Thanks to Oscar, he had the name of the shop on the Avenida de la Revolución where Ruth had bought some T-shirts, but the owner didn't remember the middle-aged gringa with the baby. And even if he had, then what? Gabriel tried the Ramada and the Holiday Inn, but Ruth had not used the credit card in either of those places. He tried a few other motels in town without any success. It was late by this time and he checked into the Ramada himself, where a huge group of sport shoe manufacturers had recently left. This explained the suitcase stuffed with single sneakers—not a pair among them—that Gabriel found under his hotel bed. Before going to bed, he opened the quart of tequila he had bought earlier that day, and finished it before he checked out.

He hadn't known what to do next, but then he called Oscar and learned that Ruth had turned in the car and bought a ticket back to San Francisco. Gabriel drove straight through, pulling over by the side of the road for brief naps before continuing north again, a tall, sweating cup of iced coffee always within reach. Even so, he knew there was no way he could be there in time to meet her plane. Maybe it was just as well, because he was so angry with Ruth, he didn't know what he would have done when he first saw her.

After the minister had finished, one of Penelope's old friends got up to speak. She was followed by a cousin and then it was Caroline's turn. Although she had been crying steadily to this point, she managed to contain herself when she faced the assembled group of mourners. "Jen and Trish," she began, indicating the two women who had just sat down, "knew Penelope as a friend and as a cousin. I knew her as a daughter. Gabriel, as a wife." He had to look down at that; he couldn't meet her eyes. "But only Isobel knew her as a mother, and Isobel can't speak to us today. Still, when Gabriel gave me some of her papers to go through, I found this." Caroline held up a sheet of paper. Even from this distance, he could see that it was covered in Penelope's handwriting. He had given this to Caroline? There had been a folder full of things but he evidently hadn't looked through them very carefully. If he had, he might have found it. Whatever it turned out to be.

"It's a letter. Addressed to Isobel. I hope I'm not taking too great a liberty by reading it here today.

" 'My darling daughter,

" 'I know there will come a time when the closeness we share now will end, when you will look at me with distrust and anger. I will become the enemy. It can't be helped; it's what all daughters feel for their mothers at one time or another. Some daughters get over the feeling and can be close to their mothers again; others don't, and the gap that starts in adolescence becomes a chasm, too wide to ever bridge or span.

" 'Still, even though this may happen to us, I wanted to write this letter to you while we were still of one mind, one heart, one spirit. When mine was the face you turned to with such gladness and when your most complete joy was in my arms. I wanted to tell you that whatever you feel for me, it won't matter. You've given me the greatest happiness I've ever known. I will remain, now and forever, your adoring mother.' "

When Caroline finished, she looked up. "This letter," she said, "was dated two days after Isobel's birth. Now that I've shared it with you, I'm giving it back to Gabriel, who will want to give it to Isobel. Someday." Gabriel rose, handing Isobel to his father, who looked momentarily confused before turning her over to Ruth. He walked up to Caroline, who embraced him tightly before handing him Penelope's letter, now folded into neat thirds. Gabriel knew it was his moment to say something. He had something prepared, but it now seemed all wrong. He would not have credited Penelope with the kind of self-awareness that would acknowledge or admit any possible rift with her daughter, even if it was destined to take place well in the future. And the part about being able to get over it—was she talking about her own mother? She had never been especially close to Caroline. Nor, despite Ruth's ongoing disappointment over the fact, to his.

He turned to the group of people waiting for him to speak. "She kept her own counsel," he began and then let himself be overtaken by grief— for her and for what had happened to them—before William appeared at his side and led him away.

After the service, there was a short ride to the cemetery. Gabriel told Caroline about Penelope's wish to have her ashes scattered, but Caroline had decided against it. The minister asked everyone standing around the open grave to join hands for a moment. The two babies, Isobel and Hannah, weren't there, but were instead back at Caroline's, where Betsy had volunteered to look after them. Gabriel hadn't wanted to let Isobel out of his sight but finally he had agreed. Now he was glad. He didn't want Isobel here, watching as they lowered the casket into the earth.

Caroline gave him one of the white roses from the funeral home and he plucked its petals, dropping them down into the open grave. The petals covered the casket so lightly it was hard to believe that they were really burying Penelope beneath the shower of white. But then Caroline stepped forward with a clod of dirt. It made an awful sound as it hit the casket.

There was a small reception back at Caroline's afterward. As soon as Gabriel saw Isobel, he scooped her up and held her tightly in his arms, even when it was clear she wanted to get down. He was going to have to learn how to let her go, he realized as he watched her struggle. Penelope had known that. What else had she known that he hadn't bothered to find out? Reluctantly, he set Isobel down and watched while she knelt on the floor, reached under a chair and began to stroke the head of a small, apricot-colored cat.

OSCAR

scar went to the airport to meet Ruth's plane. He took a taxi because Gabriel had his car and Oscar couldn't bring himself to drive Penelope's white Volvo, unharmed except for a scratch on the hood that police concluded had nothing to do with the accident. When he first saw her coming into the terminal, his eyes had instantly misted over. But when he actually came face-to-face with her, he found himself imagining a science fiction scenario in which the real Ruth had been replaced with an impostor, an alien secretly gestated and hatched from a diabolical pod.

It was hard for him to shake this feeling, because there didn't seem to be a chance for them to talk. On the ride back, there was Isobel to occupy them; Oscar was unexpectedly happy to see the baby. And once Gabriel had arrived, there was even less opportunity. Although Ruth was there in body, Oscar doubted her spirit. Despite her physical proximity, he felt even more alone; he didn't like the feeling.

———

As a boy, Oscar had lived with his family in a small apartment on Tiebout Avenue in the Bronx. He shared a room with his older brother, Nathan. His sister, Helen, had a room of her own; his parents slept in the living room. There was seldom a time when he was by himself: even practicing the violin was something he learned to do with other people in the background. He could still remember waiting in front of the music stand, bow in hand, while his sister walked briskly back and forth, curling her hair, getting ready for a date, and his mother clattered about in the apartment's tiny kitchen. If his father were home, he would be reading his newspaper in a chair; his brother would be striding through the room, on his way to the library, or the movies or the vacant lot up the street where he and his buddies from school gathered to play stickball.

At the High School of Music and Art, Oscar was always surrounded by friends and, soon enough, by girls. His sister got married, and instead of her moving out, her new husband moved in. The apartment grew even more crowded. Then Oscar was accepted to Juilliard, and his parents went with him to look for apartments in Manhattan. They were all so expensive that he quickly decided to room with two other students. One of Oscar's new roommates had a friend, freshly arrived in New York from Missouri, and the friend started sleeping on the sofa. Pretty soon the friend was sharing their meals and paying rent, and so it was discovered that the apartment could accommodate four as easily as three. They had a schedule for who used the bathroom at what time in the morning, and another at night. When Oscar met Ruth at Tanglewood—where naturally he had roommates; wasn't he always bribing them so he could be alone with her?—and they married soon after, he went from living with three other people to just one.

At first he found the quiet unsettling. If Ruth went out to a movie or to dinner with her sister, he had the whole apartment to himself and he didn't know quite what to do in it. When the children came, the even minimal sense of solitude vanished again, not to return for the next twenty-five years. By that time, he felt that Ruth was in him and around him, even when she was not literally there. So when she left, he felt his solitude keenly, like a sweater made of an itchy wool that he couldn't ignore. He told this to Mrs. Erikson, who nodded her head in understanding.

But Ruth's telephone call from the airport in Mexico and her subsequent return were equally, if surprisingly, unsettling to him. He felt as if she were a magician, with the awesome ability to make things appear and disappear at will. Except instead of rabbits or doves, the shifting, disappearing variable was Ruth herself.

Maybe they would be able to talk once the funeral was over. All the Kornblatt boys were there, even Ben, who had flown in from London with Laura. Oscar thought he detected a new fullness to her body that hadn't been there before. Maybe she was pregnant. He hoped so. It would make Ruth happy. And Oscar really wanted Ruth to be happy because he didn't want her to leave again. He still wasn't entirely convinced that she wouldn't.

Driving back from Greenwich, he wished he could talk to Ruth about Laura, but there were other people in the car. Once they had arrived at their apartment, she decided to go to a supermarket on Broadway, because Isobel needed diapers. Gabriel was staying with them, and Oscar helped him put Isobel to sleep. Then Gabriel went into the guest room, the room that had been his as a boy. Though Oscar wanted to talk to him, he was reluctant to do it in that room, which suddenly felt filled with Ginny's presence.

Oscar sat on the sofa, hand on the remote, but the television screen remained black. He didn't want to watch anything, and he was afraid that listening to music might wake Isobel.

"Dad?" Oscar looked up to see Gabriel standing in the doorway. If it had been William or Ben, they would have been in search of a ball game or wrestling match to watch, but that was unlikely with Gabriel.

"Sit down," Oscar said. If he couldn't talk to his wife, he could at least talk to his son.

"There's something I've wanted to ask you." Gabriel sat next to his father, his long legs hemmed in by the coffee table. "How come you're so complacent? Aren't you angry at her for leaving you?"

"She had reason to leave me," Oscar said, his voice surprisingly loud and firm. He glanced toward the room where Isobel slept, but his voice hadn't awakened her. Yet the words seemed to deflate Gabriel. His shoulders slumped and he turned away.

"Gabriel, what is it?" Oscar asked.

"I guess she thought she had a reason to leave me too. And to take Isobel."

"What are you talking about?"

"I didn't tell you before." Gabriel turned back to his father. "I was ashamed to."

"Tell me what?" Oscar was having trouble understanding his son, as if Gabriel were speaking a different language, one where the words were the same but their meanings had changed.

"That morning Mom left. I know why she did it."

"You do?"

"It was because of Ginny."

"I don't understand," Oscar said. "I never even saw her that day."

"But I did." Gabriel waited while the full meaning of his words sank in.

Oscar imagined the two of them together, Ginny's white arms wrapped around Gabriel's body, her mouth on his. It was not an image a father wanted to have of his son, though Oscar had had it before. In the past, it made him savagely jealous. Now it made him sad. He guessed there was some consolation in that.

"Mom knew," said Gabriel quietly. "And I think she was horrified. By me, Dad. Not you." There was a long, awkward pause. "That's why she took her. She didn't think I deserved her."

Oscar stared at his son before putting an arm around his shoulder. He hadn't felt this close to him in years. "Who really deserves anything?"

GINNY

Ginny *was* on her way to see Gabriel. He had called her when he was back in New York. But they were not meeting at her apartment; somehow neither of them suggested that. Instead, they agreed to meet in front of the Museum of Natural History. Not that she had any desire to go in there—the rooms of bones and stones didn't do a thing for her. But from there they could take a walk, maybe even through Central Park.

Gabriel looked better than he had the last time she saw him, only very thin. At first, they didn't say much. They walked along in silence, and every now and then, she looked up, but on the sly, like when she used to watch herself in the mirror in Wes's class. Gabriel didn't look at her at all.

There were lots of people in the park, as there always were on a nice Sunday afternoon. Not that Ginny really knew about Sundays, or any other days, in the park. She hardly ever went there. In fact, the last time was with Oscar, months ago. Strange to think about that now.

"How is she?" Ginny said abruptly. "Your daughter," she added. She couldn't bring herself to say the baby's name, not when she was so acutely aware of another baby's presence, a baby she would never tell him about.

"She's fine. I'm looking for an apartment."

"In New York?" Why did this fill her with such apprehension?

"In New York. I need to be near my family now. Even if I'm furious with them."

"And your parents are all right? Your mother too?" Gabriel had phoned her a couple of times to let her know where he was. Ginny hadn't been able to grasp how Ruth could have taken the baby and left. But she did understand Gabriel's desire to have Isobel back. She understood that better than she would ever be able to tell him.

"She left because of me, you know." He stopped walking and looked at her then. "She knew I was going to see you that day. After Penelope was killed."

"You told her that?"

"Of course not," he said wearily. "She just knew."

Ginny was silent. They started walking again.

"It was like I had lost everything. My wife, my daughter, my parents. You."

"You haven't lost me." She was feeling it again, the turning-without-spotting sensation.

"Yes, I did. I lost you when Penelope died." He took her hand, the first time he had touched her since they met. But instead of the warm, familiar shiver, she felt nothing. "Let's sit down," he said, leading her to a bench.

There was a cart with a man selling hot dogs and Gabriel went to get her a drink while she waited on a bench. When he returned, he was carrying a can of iced tea. She knew it wouldn't taste good, because things from cans never did, but it was sweet of him to remember.

"Didn't you get anything for yourself?"

"I'm all right," he said.

"You can share mine." He smiled for the first time that day.

"I think we both know that it's over between us." He put his hands on his knees, a graceful man suddenly turned awkward.

"I guess it is." Ginny tried to keep the relief out of her voice. This was not what she expected. But she was relieved nonetheless.

"It's not as if I don't care about you. I do. I wanted you like I've never wanted anyone. Not even Penelope. But she was my wife. And now she's dead. I'll never be able to look at you"—he reached out a hand to stroke her arm—"touch you, without thinking of her."

Ginny finished the iced tea and walked over to the trash basket, where she deposited the empty can. Gabriel stood too and they began walking again, this time out of the park. Althea told Ginny that she was Gabriel's lifeline; now it seemed he had gone and cut it. He had set her free.

"You know, you've never seen where I live." Ginny was not sure why she was doing this.

"No," he said. "I haven't."

"Do you want to?"

"All right," he said.

Gabriel was very gentle this time. But still she could barely stand the feel of his hands on her skin.

"What's wrong?" He sat up, moving aside the hair that had fallen across her face.

"I don't know." She closed her eyes so she didn't have to see his. "Maybe this wasn't such a good idea after all."

"Maybe it wasn't."

Since the clock near her bed wasn't working, Ginny got up and went into the kitchen to check the time. She was supposed to meet Althea soon. The fall season was about to start and Ginny would be dancing in *Concerto Barocco* when it did. It was official now. Althea had borrowed some videotapes from the dance library and they were going to play them on the VCR at her place. Seeing other dancers in the role was important: it helped her decide what she needed to bring to it. And what she didn't.

"Do you have a rehearsal?" Gabriel followed her into the kitchen.

"Not exactly," she said. "Something like it." There was sunlight coming in from the small kitchen window; funny that she had never noticed it before, but then she was not here very often at this time of day.

"Good-bye, Ginny." He buckled his belt. She suddenly wanted to put her arms around him, but knew that if she did, it would all come rushing out. There was another baby, she would have said. It was yours. Instead, she walked to the door and closed it quietly behind him. It was a thick, solid hunk of metal, and even if she pressed her ear right up against it, she didn't think she would hear his footsteps going down the hall.

Later, when Althea slipped the videocassette into the VCR, Ginny waited impatiently for the first strains of the Bach score. Instead, she heard sounds that were more strident and discordant. The dancers on the television screen wore black-and-white practice clothes; their movements were angular and stylized.

"This isn't *Barocco*." She looked at Althea, perplexed.

"I know. I just wanted to show you something else first."

Ginny watched for a few minutes.

"It's definitely Balanchine," she said. "But I don't know which one."

"*The Four Temperaments*," Althea said. "I danced Choleric."

"You did?"

"Wait and see." Althea nodded at the screen. "It's coming."

Ginny settled back on the sofa to watch. She knew about *The Four Ts*, but she had never seen it performed and the company hadn't danced it since she had joined. It was one of Balanchine's earliest avant-garde works; he had been inspired by the medieval idea that four humors, or fluids, made up the human body. The humors were connected to the primal elements: black bile was earth, blood was air, phlegm was water and bile was fire. Ideally, the four humors were supposed to be in balance. But, in fact, one of them usually dominated, which explained the idiosyncrasies of individual temperament.

Ginny saw how the ballet's four movements articulated these quaint notions. In Melancholic, the male dancer was gloomy and downcast, his movements constantly pulled toward the earth; in Sanguinic, the woman was buoyed through the air by her partner; in Phlegmatic, the dancers seemed to swim through water. And in Choleric, the ballerina—Althea—was demonic and wild. Ginny realized that she had never seen Althea perform before; this videotape represented the first time she had watched her mentor onstage.

"You were great." She looked at the older woman with new reverence once the video had stopped and the lights were switched back on.

"I appreciate the compliment," Althea said. "But that's not why I showed it to you."

Ginny was puzzled.

"Does it have something to do with *Barocco?*" she asked.

"In a way. You've got to find the connection, though."

"It's the temperaments, isn't it? Couldn't you say that every part has its own quality? Its own temperament?"

Althea looked at her encouragingly.

"Can we watch it again?" Ginny asked. "Please?"

RUTH

*R**uth's best** friend in high school was a girl named Mary Grace O'Halloran. Having a Catholic friend was unusual because the Catholic girls in her Brooklyn neighborhood didn't socialize with the Jewish girls. They didn't have much opportunity. The Catholic girls went to the Immaculate Heart of Mary parochial school, while the Jewish girls went to Erasmus Hall on Flatbush Avenue. But Mary Grace had been thrown out (her words) or asked to leave (her parents') because of repeated infractions, on school property no less, that involved boys. Instead of punishing her, her parents had decided the problem was that the Immaculate Heart of Mary's code of behavior was too strict. Maybe with less to rebel against, Mary Grace wouldn't need to be so rebellious.

They were right, but only to a point. Mary Grace's behavior didn't change nor did her curiosity about boys diminish while she was at Erasmus Hall. It was true, however, that these qualities no longer made her stand out. She was assigned the seat next to Ruth's in homeroom, and within a week, they were friends. Ruth loved Mary Grace. Although she knew she could not hope to aspire to Mary Grace's brand of daring, Ruth was still exhilarated in its presence. Mary Grace showed her how to light up cigarettes in the girls' bathroom, and then carefully exhale the smoke out through the open window. Ruth only tried this once, because the hot smoke burned her throat so much she couldn't sing afterward, but she took vicarious pleasure in watching Mary Grace. Mary Grace also taught Ruth how to apply eyeliner and lipstick, set her hair, make a martini and even convince the boy selling tickets at the Loew's Kings movie theater to let them in for nothing.

"Why did you do that?" Ruth asked later. "I had enough money for both of us. And for popcorn too."

"It's good practice," Mary Grace said. "You need to learn how to get boys to do what you want. It'll come in handy."

The other thing Mary Grace tutored Ruth in was Catholicism. Before the two girls had become close, Ruth had never spent any time with a Catholic and was as curious about her friend's religion as Mary Grace was about boys. Mary Grace let Ruth try on the tiny gold crucifix that she wore around her neck, taste the thin, round wafers that she took from church, hold the amber and silver rosary her grandmother gave her when she took her first communion. Not that Ruth actually wanted to be a Catholic. But hearing about it gave her the same illicit thrill as watching Mary Grace smoke or hearing her describe what French kissing really felt like.

So it was Mary Grace who taught Ruth about heaven, hell and purgatory, the names of the saints and their distinctive, spectacular forms of martyrdom and the seven deadly sins. Mary Grace said the nuns showed slides of old paintings to dramatize the sins. Pride. Lust. Greed. Sloth. Anger. They both frightened and fascinated her. She must have known inchoately that to some degree, she possessed them all.

Mary Grace's family moved to the suburbs during their senior year, and though the girls tearfully exchanged snipped locks of hair and swore eternal friendship, Ruth lost touch with Mary Grace once the other girl was out of her immediate range. Ruth's mother wouldn't let her travel on the train out to Long Island (though she had no problem with letting Ruth take the subway into Manhattan for voice lessons). Mary Grace's mother decided the old neighborhood was a bad influence, and so wouldn't let her daughter visit it again. Ruth finally got her mother to agree to her spending a weekend on Long Island; Mr. O'Halloran was in the city and drove Ruth out there himself.

But Mary Grace seemed different. She had a new best friend, a Catholic girl named Lorraine, and somehow her special kinship with Ruth had dissolved. Mrs. O'Halloran served baked ham for dinner, and though Ruth's family wasn't kosher, it still made her uncomfortable. She said she had a stomachache and went without eating; on Sunday, when the family was in church, she walked to the train station herself and caught an early train back. Ruth never told her mother what happened but she could tell she was glad that Ruth's friendship with Mary Grace was over.

Now, all these years later, Ruth thought about Mary Grace, wondering where she was. She found herself having imaginary conversations with her girlhood friend. Ruth would ask her which of the seven deadly sins she thought was the worst. And why. Because if back then Ruth somehow intuited their presence in the soul of every person on earth, now she was sure of it.

After Ruth and Oscar returned to New York, she could see that Oscar was still wary, still waiting for her to vanish every time he turned away. And she couldn't blame him. From his perspective, what she had done was such an aberration, it would be easy for him to believe that it might happen again. If Ruth left the room, he was right there behind her. When she was in the bathroom, she felt his presence outside the door. And when she went out—the questions. The grilling. But she couldn't blame him. If your wife suddenly upped and left right before your daughter-in-law's funeral, and took your granddaughter with her, what were you to think?

After a few days of this, however, Oscar seemed to settle down. The fall season was about to begin and he started practicing the Bach violin concerto again. The apartment was drenched in the sound.

Gabriel and Isobel were staying with them now. That too was a small triumph of sorts. When Ruth first got back, Gabriel was furious with his mother. "How could you? How could you?" he kept asking, controlling his voice only because the yelling made Isobel cry.

"How could *you?*" she had finally said in return. That seemed to quiet him. For a while anyway, and then he would start all over. "I can't trust you," Gabriel said. It was Oscar who had convinced him not to move to a hotel, but to remain with them, at least while he looked for a job and an apartment of his own.

So here he was, Ruth's full-grown son, sleeping in his old room along with Isobel; since her birth Ruth had kept a Port-a-Crib stowed away in the closet. She knew full well this arrangement would not last, nor should it. But how she loved being so close to Isobel, picking her up a dozen times a day, feeling the baby's arms around her neck, the small face pressed next to her own. Ruth held her close and they looked in the mirror together. Isobel touched Ruth's nose, hair and cheeks. "Gray," she said. "Gray." Ruth realized she was trying to say "Grandma." Isobel was giving her a name. In turn, Ruth found herself uttering the half-forgotten endearments from her own childhood—*tochter*—which meant daughter, and *katzelah,* little cat. She had never spoken this way to her sons, though surely she must have had other baby names for them. Why didn't she remember what they were?

Gabriel seemed more attached to Isobel than Ruth remembered. He insisted on feeding and diapering her. He took her to Central Park in the stroller, held her on his lap while he talked on the phone. It was as if, Ruth remarked to Oscar, Gabriel was getting to know her, perhaps for the first time. Whether Gabriel had been seeing that creature, Ruth didn't ask. It was not her business. She finally and truly understood that. When Gabriel left that morning in San Francisco, she was so angry that it blinded her.

Anger was her sin, just as lust had been Gabriel's and Oscar's. Because of her anger, Ruth had endangered Isobel, taking her on that crazy, improvised flight. Ruth had frightened her, frightened her husband. And when she thought of the tag Isobel had almost choked on—well, look at where Ruth's anger had nearly brought them. She had been as heedless, as impetuous, as her son, her husband and her daughter-in-law. Who was she to judge them?

While Gabriel was out of the apartment, Ruth made calls to William and Ben, to reassure them that she was all right. She told them that her sudden departure was brought on by the shock of Penelope's death. Everything was fine now. She didn't mention Ginny; she didn't feel she had a right. Neither William nor Ben questioned her much; they both seemed happy to accept this. Ben. His wife was pregnant, and they had learned it was a girl. Ruth could not get over the symmetry of this: to have borne three sons, who in turn would bless her with three granddaughters.

"Where will you live?" she had to ask. "Are you going to keep traveling? Will that be good for Laura now? And for the baby?"

"Don't worry," Ben told her. "We're going to settle down. For a while, anyway."

"In New York?" Ruth asked hopefully.

"London."

"London." Ruth was pleased. London wasn't as far as some of the places he could've picked. "Your father and I will come. As soon as the ballet season is over." Her mind began the planning: the calls to the travel agent, the list of gifts she would bring with her, and the ones she would buy while there.

Ruth also called Caroline, and one morning, she and Isobel took the train from Grand Central Terminal to Greenwich, Connecticut. Caroline met them at the station, and from there, they drove to the cemetery. For Isobel, there was no sorrow in this visit; Ruth and Caroline took turns following after her as she haltingly toddled over the grassy plots, playing peek-a-boo behind the older headstones. There was no stone at Penelope's grave; it was still being carved. But Ruth laid a bunch of white gardenias that they had stopped to buy on the plot of newly turned earth. Weeping, Caroline came to join her, and for a moment, they embraced. Had they done this when Gabriel and Penelope got married? Ruth didn't think so. She felt no sense of guilt over not telling Caroline about Ginny and Gabriel. That might have seemed important before, but it no longer did. To tell her wouldn't mend or heal anything; it wouldn't bring Penelope back. All it would do was alienate Caroline from their lives and, more important, from Isobel's. And Isobel had lost enough already; Ruth would not be responsible for her losing Caroline too. She was no longer so arrogant as to think she could raise her alone: Isobel needed all of them, flawed as they were.

Ruth tried to explain some of this to Oscar the night after she and Isobel made the trip to Greenwich. Gabriel was out and Isobel was sleeping. It was Friday night and she decided to cover the table with a cloth and lay out her company dishes. Lilli's candlesticks were on the table, along with a challah bread. Even though the weather was still warm, Ruth had roasted a chicken with rosemary and garlic; the aroma filled the apartment.

"It's your Shabbat meal," Oscar said as he observed her preparations.

"I thought it was time to get back to normal," she said. "Sit down. Dinner is ready." He did and Ruth filled the plates. They ate in silence until Ruth said, "Oscar, there's something I didn't tell you about that day in San Francisco. The day I left."

"What?" He jerked his head up from the chicken he was cutting. "What didn't you tell me?"

"It's about Gabriel. He was on his way to see her. Ginny. That's what finally made me snap."

"He told me. Just after the funeral. But he didn't actually come out and tell you back then, did he? He said that you just knew."

"That's right. I just knew. And it made me so angry I couldn't see straight. Angry at him. Angry at you."

"Are you still angry?" He stopped eating, though he held his fork and knife suspended in midair. It looked as if he were conducting.

"No," Ruth told him. "No." He set down his silverware and got up from the table. "Oscar ..." she began as he came around to where she sat and awkwardly knelt down beside her. He wrapped his arms around her legs and buried his head in her lap. "Oscar, what are you doing?" Ruth was bewildered.

"Thanking you," was his muffled reply.

GABRIEL

He *was* not sure why he had come tonight, but here he was again. Sitting in the orchestra of the New York State Theater. Waiting for the curtain to rise. Waiting to see Ginny dance. The experience felt familiar, as if he had been doing it forever. Of course this was not accurate. There had only been two nights on which he had watched her dance—once in New York and once in San Francisco. But what fateful nights they had been. On one, he and Ginny had become lovers; on the other, Penelope had been killed. Now there was really nothing left that could happen. But if that were entirely true, why was he here?

Since that Sunday afternoon in the park, the one where he told her good-bye and still went back to her apartment, he had not attempted to contact her. Not that he hadn't thought of her. But her image was always twinned with Penelope's in his mind, and it was that more than anything that had kept him away.

He dreamed of Penelope now, almost every night. At first, the dreams were violent, reconstructing the awful scene in the street when she was hit, the scene he never saw because he had been watching, transfixed, while Ginny peeled off her clothes in the backseat of his car. He would wake in a sweat, reaching quickly for the sleeping pills he had been keeping on hand lately. But then the dreams began to change, becoming less violent: Penelope stood in front of him, her naked body wound in some kind of filmy veil. She took his hand, pressed it to a breast; she wanted to make love but he couldn't, even in his dreams, bring himself to look at her. Although these dreams were not as alarming, in some ways they were even worse.

Still, he got up every morning, showered, shaved, consumed several cups of coffee and forced himself to begin the cycle of making calls, sending résumés, meeting and interviewing that finally landed him a job in a midtown architecture firm. It was a big place, much bigger than the firm he had left in San Francisco. He would have to try harder to get noticed here. But maybe that was good. It would give him something to work toward.

Not that he had been idle. In addition to looking for a job, there had been the apartment search, about which everyone, even virtual strangers, seemed to complain and sympathize. But Gabriel was not fussy. For the first time in his adult life, he didn't care about the available light or the way rooms were laid out. He just wanted to find a place in a hurry and he did: a small but adequate two-bedroom in the West Village. The price astounded him, but after selling his San Francisco apartment and his car, he had enough money for the down payment. Maybe he could have found something less expensive if he had been willing to keep looking. But he wanted to move out of his parents' apartment, out of the room he had grown up in, as soon as possible. And since he had inherited a large share of Penelope's money, he could manage the mortgage payments. Penelope's money. It was a bitter comfort that this money, which he had never quite felt he deserved, was now in part his.

The first days after his mother reappeared were the worst. He had yelled at her, pounding his fists against the goddamned bed in his goddamned room, until he saw that all his anger did was to upset Isobel. Ruth seemed more saddened than perturbed by his outbursts. There was something almost patronizing about her attitude—as if he were a kid having a tantrum that she knew how to wait out—which only angered him more. But in the end he had to recognize that he had no more been able to control himself than she had.

Still, he wanted to get away from his parents and take Isobel to some neutral place. It was Oscar who persuaded him to stay for a while longer. "How do I know she won't do it again?" Gabriel said to his father.

"You just have to trust her," Oscar had said. Gabriel snorted in response and Oscar looked at him as earnestly as Gabriel could ever remember. "Just like she—we, I mean—have to trust you." Gabriel was quiet then. He didn't need to ask what his father meant.

And he did try to earn their trust, spending as much time with Isobel as he could. In the mornings, Gabriel patiently fed her a bite of toast, a slice of apple, some Cheerios. When he came home in the evening, he took off his good jacket and slacks, put on some worn chinos and an old shirt so he could kneel down and give her a bath. How she loved the water, this glad girl of his. She spread out her arms and smacked the surface, sending water up into her laughing face, the floor and Gabriel. Isobel. Her dark brown hair and white skin would forever remind him of Penelope, but he had begun to accept that. Now he had to get to know her for herself. Just as she would get to know him.

Gabriel looked at his watch. Just a few more minutes before Ginny came onstage. He didn't really understand this urge. He simply knew that he needed to see her again, to finally and completely put her, and all she had meant to him, in the past. In his lap was the program the usher had handed him, as well as the large, glossy booklet he had purchased in the lobby. Each of the dancers in the company was listed; the principals had a full page, in color, the soloists a half page and the corps de ballet a group picture in black and white. Now that Ginny was a soloist, her picture was in color, at the very end of the section, because the dancers appeared alphabetically. It was a new picture. In this one, her blond hair had been pulled to one side, and it fanned out, like a spray of water, from the side of her head. He didn't recognize the costume, and before he could place it, the curtain rose on a bare stage lit only by a celestial blue light. *Concerto Barocco* was on the program, and as the music began, Gabriel was engulfed by it.

He was very familiar with the score—his father had played it in the past, and he had wanted Gabriel to learn it as well. There was a difficult violin passage that Oscar made him practice over and over again. Gabriel didn't want to; he was already chafing under his father's pressure and he found the piece too demanding. But instead of coming out and saying that, he instead played it badly on purpose, making mistake after sloppy mistake, until Oscar, fed up and furious, yanked the violin rudely out of his hands.

"Enough!" he had shouted. "You're murdering it!"

"Better it than you," Gabriel had muttered, hating his father's insistence that Gabriel share his vision, his musical passion. Ruth had hurried in and intervened then, and somehow the ugly incident was put behind them. Until now. Odd that Gabriel never noticed before how sad the music sounded, almost like a lament, or a dirge. He realized with a start that it was Oscar playing this music right now, that Oscar was performing the violin duet tonight. He had been so caught up in thinking about Ginny that he had totally forgotten.

Ginny. The row of dancers parted, and there she was, center stage. Her hair was slicked down and tightly wound into a bun; her costume, the simple white tunic that all the dancers wore. Only somehow, on her, the white seemed to glow, as if it were a color as vibrant and brilliant as red or chartreuse, amber or cerulean. "White is all the colors," Penelope used to say. He suddenly understood what she meant. Gabriel watched intently. If the music was sad, Ginny's dancing was not. It was joyful and exuberant, expansive and lyrical. It seemed to him that she was almost mocking the sorrow of the sounds around her, daring the music to be dolorous when she herself exulted. He was seated close enough so that when he used his opera glasses, he could see the sweat coating her arms and throat, staining the tunic front and back.

When the ballet was over, and the applause thundering around him, there was another surprise in store: Oscar walked out onto the stage, holding his violin away from his body a bit awkwardly as he lumbered toward Ginny. There was another violinist with his father, though Oscar was the one who took Ginny's hand. More applause, more cheers. There they were—dancer and musician—hand in hand, to share their triumph. Through the crystalline lenses of the glasses, Gabriel could discern his father's face, smiling but still sorrowful. He did not look at the audience. He looked at her. He must still love her, Gabriel thought as he finally put the glasses down in his lap. Poor bastard, he thought as he momentarily placed his head in his hands. Poor bastard.

The wind was biting as Gabriel waited by the stage door. He didn't know if he would speak to her, and if he did, what he would say. The performance had stirred him in all sorts of ways, but none of them erotic. No, she was beyond that now, at least for him. He turned up the collar of his overcoat and pulled it tightly around him. He saw a few of the corps members emerge, all talking at once. They were followed by another group, and then he caught sight of a few of the principals as they walked out the door, up the stairs and into the night. More dancers came out, and he began to think he had missed her when there she was, talking to someone behind her as she pushed the door open with her shoulder. She was wearing the fuzzy black coat he remembered from that night at the hotel. He just was about to move forward into her path when he saw that she was walking with someone. A man. So instead he stepped back.

The man was blond and walked with the slightly splayed gait that all the dancers had. Gabriel realized that this was the man who had partnered Ginny tonight in the ballet. Something he said made her laugh. The man grinned too, pleased, no doubt, that he had pleased her. He took his large hand and draped it casually over her shoulders, pulling her close. They strolled together out into the cold November night. Gabriel watched them go. She hadn't even known he was there.

OSCAR

Oscar *liked* having the baby in the apartment. This surprised him, because at first he was opposed to Ruth's plan, though he dared not say so. Since Gabriel started his new job, Isobel was spending the weekdays with them. Ruth couldn't bear the thought that Gabriel would hire some stranger to take care of her, not while Ruth was so nearby and available. "She'll always know that you're her father," she reasoned. "But why can't she spend the weekdays with her grandparents? At least until she's older." Gabriel was reluctant at first, but finally decided that it would be *better for Isobel*—a point he hammered home to his mother, so she wouldn't think he was doing this for her—if she were to spend her days with someone she already knew.

So that's what they decided, his wife and son. Mornings, Ruth took the subway downtown to pick up Isobel; together they rode in a taxi back to the Upper West Side. In the evenings, the trip was reversed: a taxi brought granddaughter and grandmother downtown, and Ruth returned alone by subway. One or two evenings a week, when Gabriel went out, Isobel spent the night with her grandparents. Oscar, fearful of the noise, the disruption, the awful and sobering responsibility of having Isobel there with them so much of the time, had no say in the matter.

But when she toddled over to greet him at the door, his heart lifted at the sight of her and at the feel of her small, sturdy arms as they encircled his leg. She strewed her toys, spilled her juice, wailed easily—like any other toddler. But Oscar still found himself enchanted. He marveled at how her vocabulary increased by the day. She said "oof" for dog—repeating the sound of its bark, he realized—and uttered a soft, uncannily feline "meow" when she saw a cat. And he could not get over the way she was transfixed by the sound of his practicing, and would sit quietly, in a Zen-like pose with legs crossed and fingers touching her knees, as he played. None of his children did that. Ruth told him how her singing seemed to calm Isobel when nothing else would.

People always said you enjoyed your grandchildren more than you did your children. It was true. When the boys were little, Oscar was still so consumed by anxiety about his career, still plotting and working to shape the trajectory it would take. Looking back, he saw himself as constantly worried: about money, about his music, about Ruth's happiness, about his own. Not that he ignored or neglected his boys; quite the contrary, they were a large part of his thinking and activity. But they were also a part of his worry, woven tightly into the scratchy fabric of his anxiety. He worried about where they went to school, their musical education, their choices in friends and girls, their various annoying or alarming habits. Accidents, choking, drowning, drugs, cigarettes—the worries, no less troubling for their being so common, shared by so many parents. With Isobel, however, he discovered that he was much less worried. He had no program for her, no agenda. Instead, he was able to live in the present with her much more fully than he could with his own children. And, to his surprise, he was happy there.

During the day, he had begun taking her to a playground in Central Park, and pushing her down Broadway in her spiffy Italian-made stroller while he did a few small errands. If she were still there when he left for the theater, they had a ritual for saying good-bye. First, they sat together in the living room while he read her a story. Then a kiss good-night; she puckered her baby lips and kissed him right back. It was the memory of that kiss that he took with him to Lincoln Center the night the ballet was scheduled to perform *Concerto Baracco*. He was not apprehensive about the music itself, for he had played it before and had been practicing it steadily since the summer. But he had looked at the casting notice for the week, and Ginny's name was there, as one of the soloists.

He had not seen her much since the fall season started. The first couple of times they ran into each other he hadn't recognized her because of the hair that was suddenly and radically blond. Oscar thought the effect was stunning. He didn't know whether Gabriel still saw her. What he did know was that she continued to exert some terrible fascination for him, a fascination that flew in the face of common sense, of morality, of just about everything Oscar knew to be true, lasting and good. At last, he had managed to find the self-control to stay away from her. But what he did and what he felt were two different things.

He went to his locker to hang up his things and quickly hurried to the orchestra pit. He had spent a little longer than usual saying good-bye to Isobel, reading her three stories—well, they were short, he told himself at the time—instead of the usual one. And he was slow walking to the theater, as if what awaited him there were something he wished to delay. The other musicians were already there; he nodded to the conductor and settled first his handkerchief and then his instrument comfortably under his chin. There was still noise—of voices, of the rustling of paper and the shifting of bodies from the audience above him. He could hear too the dancers backstage, the clip-clop of their pointe shoes as they nervously pawed the floor or performed a few quick relevés. Then the lights dimmed and the noise was momentarily suspended.

The curtain went up and Oscar felt rather than saw the glow of blue light. He ceased to be aware of the dancers or the audience, and thought only about the music, the music that was both his obligation and his privilege to play. "Think" was the wrong word, however, since he entered the music more completely, more fully, than he had ever done in his life. Or was it the other way around—had the music entered him? Oscar gave himself over—to Bach, to the violin, to the sounds that he created and the ones created around him. The other violinist, a short, serious man named Howard Chan, seemed to anticipate his timing perfectly. They had practiced together earlier in the week, but tonight they played with an even greater, and almost startling, synchronicity.

The first movement, "Vivace," was short and pungent. The long, slow movement—"Largo ma non Tanto"—was the one in which Ginny danced alone; he was familiar enough with the ballet to know that. Oscar had always found it to be one of Bach's saddest and most exquisite creations. Just when you thought it was over, that the last, mournful notes had been played, it unexpectedly revived, and the tender sadness was there all over again. After the "Largo," Oscar adjusted his violin for the "Allegro," which was filled with brittle, fury-tinged joy. When it was over, and the applause came, he was startled. The conductor was smiling, obviously pleased with the way the musicians had played, and as the applause continued, he nodded to Oscar, who understood the gesture and walked to the flight of stairs leading to the stage. Howard Chan was right behind him.

Ginny was already there, thin chest heaving with the exertion of her performance, sweat slick as oil on her face, neck and arms, sweat soaking her costume and molding it to her body. She held an elaborate spray of flowers in one hand; the other she extended to Oscar. Her grip was firm and unapologetic. While the audience continued to cheer, he raised his head to look at her. The blond hair—he had never seen it this close— made her seem aloof and ethereal. His eyes searched for her scar, almost invisible under her heavy stage makeup. Still, he remembered just where it was and could almost feel it in his imagination.

Ginny looked at him for a moment before turning her attention to the audience. Oscar sensed a change in her, as if she had moved out of the pedestrian realm in which he lived and into some bright, unfamiliar country he had only glimpsed but never visited. But Ginny was no visitor there; she was the queen. That was what he guessed all those months ago, and that was what he knew now. Did he love her? Did it matter? He gently disengaged his hand and followed Howard toward the wings. Oscar turned to watch as another bouquet of flowers was presented to her, even larger and more elaborate than the first. The audience went wild as Virginia Valentine bowed her head and curtsied again.

GINNY

Partnering only looked easy. From the audience's point of view, it was just a guy in tights, lifting and catching, catching and lifting. If you threw in a little spinning and support during a tricky turn, you would have had the whole thing in a nutshell. But Ginny knew that it was far more complex than that. There were lousy partners, great partners and everything in between. She made Althea laugh when she said that partnering was like sex: everyone had the equipment, but not everyone knew what to do with it.

Ginny had had her share of partnering horror stories: some held her too tightly, and when the ballet was done, she found bruises on her thighs or upper arms; some were so self-involved—marking time until their own variations—that they barely gave her any help. There were others who were scared; she had felt their fear even though *she* was the one getting tossed through the air, praying to Jesus all the while that they would be there to catch her. Then there was the one who actually dropped her on the studio floor.

But Ginny's newest partner, Josh Cleary, was superb. Josh was tan and blond; he came from southern California and would have looked great on a surfboard. Instead, he tagged along to his big sister's ballet classes and it turned out he had a lot more talent than she did. The sister gave up pretty soon, but Josh stuck with it and now here he was, a dancer with New York City Ballet, and the best partner Ginny had ever had.

They started rehearsing *Barocco* together a few weeks ago, and Ginny was enthralled. He knew just how to reach, just when to turn, just where to stop. When he lifted her, she was soaring; when he caught her, she was a bird flown safely home. She briefly wondered what he might be like in bed, though as soon as she had the thought, her mind darted away from it, as if she'd been burned. No more of *that*, she told herself, at least not any time soon.

She thought about the baby. She didn't want to, but the images came to her anyway. The baby growing inside her. At first, it was the size of a grain of sand, then a grain of rice. Then it grew to be the size of an almond, a plum, a mouse. Finally, it was a completely formed baby girl—in Ginny's fantasy, it was always a girl—and Ginny would give birth to her. Then Ginny would be a woman holding a baby, looking at her in the way Gabriel's wife had looked at their daughter. But those images competed with others: the long, luxurious penchées in the slow movement of *Concerto Barocco*, the series of partnered pirouettes that ended in a deep, melting backbend.

The rehearsals with Josh had brought Ginny to a different place in her dancing, a place she had been wanting to go since she started but never quite got to before. It had something to do with the ballet they were working on; the choreography of *Barocco* was so rich, so complex. Afterward, she would lie in bed marking the steps with her hands, trying to burn them into her mind, so she could dream about them at night.

The day of the performance came quickly. Ginny had been dancing all season long, good parts too, but the thought of doing this ballet had her keyed up more than usual. She arrived at the theater early so she could spend a long time getting ready. There was a bouquet already waiting; she opened the card and saw her mother's neat, careful penmanship. The card was signed with a whole row of *X*'s. Rita. Ginny set the flowers near the door and then started on her hair. Althea stopped by when she had just stuck the last of the hairpins in. "You're going to be great," she told Ginny and gave her a hug. "Here, I want you to wear these," she said, handing her a small gold box. Inside was a pair of tiny diamond studs.

"Althea!" Ginny said.

"For luck," she said. "They always worked for me." Ginny looked down at the earrings and remembered another gold box, the one with Gabriel's bracelet inside. She kept the bracelet with her, stuffed way down at the bottom of her dance bag, but she never put it on.

After Ginny finished her hair, Althea offered to give her a quick barre, so she could be really warm and limber when it was time for the curtain to go up. And when it did, she wanted to cry, it was all so beautiful, the row of dancers in their sparkling white tunics, the blue, blue light, the way the music seemed to be calling her, begging her to dance. Even though she had been through all this during the dress rehearsal, the actual performance was different. A performance was like a circle, and if the audience wasn't there, the circle was incomplete. Even though they were no more than a blur of faces beyond the lights, she could feel them out there and it made all the difference.

Oscar was playing that night. No surprise there. But even his playing sounded different. During the slow movement—although the musical term was "largo," for a dancer, it was always the adagio—Ginny actually felt pierced by the sound of the violin. It was as if Oscar was giving her the music. In return, she gave him her dancing; even though she was partnered by Josh, with his steady hands and perfect grip, she was really dancing for Oscar, and with him too. Apologizing to him and to Ruth, Penelope and Gabriel. And to her baby. Apologizing for everything she had done, and everything she had to keep on doing.

When the ballet was over, there were three curtain calls. She curtsied to the audience, her entire body bathed in the glorious baptism of sweat. During one of the curtain calls, Oscar and the other violinist came up to join her on the stage. It was Oscar who took her hand. They stood there, fingers locked tightly for a moment, and then it was over. The two men left the stage. She was given another bouquet, and Josh came out to take a bow too.

Althea stood in the wings, and when Ginny and Josh walked toward her, she hugged them, arms straining to encompass them both.

"That was something," she said simply. But for Ginny, the words were more than enough.

"Thank you," Ginny said, "for everything." She could almost feel the diamonds on her ears sparkling.

As they walked toward the dressing rooms, Josh asked if she wanted to have dinner with him. She hesitated for a second and then said yes. He squeezed her hand and smiled. They agreed to meet and twenty minutes later, there he was, eager as a big golden puppy. Ginny pushed open the stage door with her shoulder, and he feigned shock. "Why a true gentleman never lets a lady open the door," he said, and even though he was from southern California, not southern Louisiana, he sounded just like Wes. Ginny burst out laughing, and not only did she not mind, she was actually kind of glad when he put his arm around her shoulders.

RUTH

Preparing Gabriel's old room for Isobel gave Ruth the first real, sustained pleasure she had felt in anything since Penelope was killed. Oscar helped her collapse the twin bed and move the furniture out. Some pieces, like a desk and a chair, she was able to reabsorb elsewhere in the apartment, while others she donated to the Salvation Army, whose cheerful red, white and blue truck appeared the day after she called. Since Gabriel decided to sell all the furniture from his San Francisco apartment rather than ship it to New York (a decision Ruth wholeheartedly endorsed), she dragged her sister, Molly, up to Albee's, a children's furniture and equipment store that had been on Amsterdam Avenue since Ruth's own boys were babies.

At Albee's, Ruth purchased a white crib, rocking chair and bureau for Isobel's new room. Isobel was already too squirmy for a changing table, so instead Ruth splurged on a white wooden lamp made in the shape of Little Bo-Peep; the skirt, which formed the base, was painted with pink flowers, and the shade was of pink-and-white gingham. "She'll hate it by the time she's six," Molly predicted.

"I'll buy her a new one, then," Ruth said, undaunted. The lamp was boxed and bagged and came home with her, unlike the furniture, which was not delivered until late the following week. During that time, Ruth was able to have someone scrape, sand and polyurethane the floor as well as cover the walls with the most adorable paper of pink posies. The border that ran around the ceiling showed a frieze of animals drawn by Beatrix Potter: bunnies, kittens, skunks and ducks wearing boaters and waistcoats; pinafores and pantaloons. Oscar had said something about buying Ruth a fur coat this year. But Ruth didn't want a fur coat. Instead, she vastly preferred using the money to create this bower for their granddaughter.

"I do think you're going a bit overboard on the pink," Molly commented when she saw the whole effect. "There's enough of it in here to gag the poor child."

"No little girl can have too much pink."

"Oh, really?" Molly gave her a look, the one from childhood that said, "Don't think you know everything, Miss Bossy Boots." But she couldn't help laughing, and then neither could Ruth, so they both dissolved in a fit of giggles, hugging each other for support, when Oscar came into the room to see what was going on.

"Uh, it looks nice," he said a bit uncertainly. Ruth and Molly looked at each other and began giggling again.

Ruth knew of course that Oscar had not been enthusiastic about her plan to have Isobel live with them during the week. Neither was Gabriel.

"I appreciate your offer, Mom," he had said when she first broached it. "I really do." Those were his words, but his tone sounded as if she had just placed a large basket of dead fish in his lap.

"Then why not take me up on it?"

"I feel like I hardly know her. When Penelope was here—" he paused, clearly overcome—"she took over. I don't want that to happen again." Ruth felt proud of him for saying this, and told him so. But, still, he had committed himself to his new job and needed someone to watch Isobel while he worked.

"What kind of baby-sitter will you find?" Ruth asked him. "Can she possibly care as much as your father and I do?"

"Dad wants to do this?" Gabriel said, looking as though he didn't quite believe her.

"He wants what I want. At least about this," Ruth reassured him. And so eventually Gabriel agreed that Isobel would spend the weekdays with her grandparents and the weekends with him. He had already bought things for her room. His taste didn't run to the pink and frilly, but he picked out some attractive Mission-style oak furniture, a woven wool rug that showed all the letters of the alphabet, and paid someone to paint the walls pale blue with a scattering of white stars.

So Isobel would have a pink room and a blue one, Ruth thought when she saw the blue one for the first time. Somehow, this pleased her enormously. Isobel seemed happy too. She still called for Penelope, especially in the night, and often Ruth or Oscar had to lift her out of her crib, and walk her back and forth in the living room, to calm her down. "I remember this from the first time around," Oscar said groggily at 3:00 A.M. "It was bad enough back then." Still, he did his part. If Isobel really couldn't settle down, Oscar would take out his violin, and standing there in his striped, wrinkled pajamas, he would softly play a lullaby for her. That seemed to work when nothing else did.

Ruth quickly developed a new routine, one that was familiar and yet all fresh and undiscovered too. As soon as it was decided that Isobel would live part-time with them, Ruth called both the nursing home and the hospital and with many apologies and great regrets explained that she would no longer be volunteering her time, at least for a while. She told her friends at the book club that she might need to miss some meetings and her cooking classes were supplanted by others with names like Tots on the Go and Wee Make Music. When her membership at the Y ran out, Ruth had not planned to renew it. Actually, it was Oscar who suggested that they instead take out a family membership, so that either of them could bring Isobel to the pool for a swim.

"I swim up at the lake," he pointed out. "Why not here? I used to be a very good swimmer. Remember?" Ruth remembered quite well. Their social lives were more curtailed, of course, though they still had the weekends to themselves. And Molly promised to baby-sit if they needed it during the week.

"Just like the old days, Ruth," Molly said. "R and R."

"R and R," Ruth said, smiling. "God, how we needed it!"

So that was how Ruth came to be sitting in the New York State Theater one Thursday night in November. She had not been to the ballet in many years, not since she stopped taking the boys, though she had always enjoyed going. Somehow, it was just one of those things that fell by the wayside. But Ruth knew that Oscar was quite passionate about performing the Bach Double Violin Concerto again; she remembered how he had given himself over to the music when they had last been at the lake. It seemed to her that she ought to go and hear him play it. But for a reason she didn't care to explain, she mentioned this desire only to Molly, who came over just after Oscar left. Ruth had to hurry because he was late leaving, and she fretted to see that Isobel looked upset—her lower lip quivered ominously, though she did not actually cry—when Ruth went to the door. Even though Ruth was running late, she stopped at a pay phone on Broadway to call Molly, who assured her that Isobel was fine. Ruth could hear her babbling in the background, so she continued her walk toward the theater feeling somewhat consoled.

She found her way to the house seat—the woman at the box office remembered her from years ago and was happy to oblige—just as the curtain was rising. The mysterious blue light glowed from the backstage wall as the first strains of the music—Oscar's music—began.

The truth was that Ruth knew Ginny Valentine would be dancing tonight. Ginny was the reason for Ruth's secrecy. When Ruth had told

Oscar she was no longer angry with him, she was not lying. Nor was she angry with Gabriel. But Ruth had every reason to be angry at Ginny.

Then the music took hold of her, and Ruth let herself revel in it, even closing her eyes momentarily. When she opened them, she saw the row of tunic-clad dancers, moving in their intricate, unfolding patterns on the stage. Though she knew the score quite well, Ruth had never actually seen this particular ballet before and she was stunned by its pure, formal beauty. There was no story here, only the music and bodies, working seamlessly in tandem. To her surprise, she found she preferred its austere clarity to some of the more traditional, drama-filled ballets, lovely as they were. When the second movement began—the "Largo"—Ruth could hear Oscar playing, playing with everything in him. The couple who danced to this sweet, sweet music were both blond, and as lyrical as any dancers Ruth had ever seen. The woman, in particular, had a resonance to her movements, a brilliance of execution that Ruth could not remember ever having witnessed before. Though she was hardly a dance critic, she still felt she was in the presence of something rare and exceptional. Who was she?

In deference to the other people in the audience, she didn't consult the program until the curtain came down and the applause exploded around her. Then she was shocked to discover that the dancer who had so moved her was Ginny Valentine.

It was the hair that had fooled her, of course. That afternoon when Ginny had come into Ruth's home, eaten her food, bewitched her husband and kissed her son, she had not been blond. But she was certainly the same girl—now that Ruth knew who she was, it all fell into place. There were many curtain calls, with wild applause and cheering. During one of them, Oscar and the other violinist came onto the stage. Oscar looked a bit uncomfortable but still very dignified. He took the hand Ginny offered him and bowed to the audience. Then he raised his head and looked at her. All at once, Ruth saw just what Oscar had wanted from her: more than youth or beauty, it was that flame of hers, the spark that ignited when she moved. He wanted to be close to that, to let it warm his hands for a while, even though it would never in fact be his. Ruth almost forgave her then. Everything Ginny had done was suddenly refracted through the prism of her enormous talent: surely a girl who could dance like that had some good in her. Ruth was not the one to find it, but at least she could grudgingly perceive that it might be there.

Later, Ruth couldn't say what made her look away from the stage at that particular moment, and over the railing of the first balcony. Below was a man whose head was in his hands; it seemed such an odd gesture amidst the crowd of applauding fans that it distracted her. Was he ill? Then the man straightened up and Ruth saw that it was her son, who must have come to the ballet tonight to see Ginny. How remarkable that he was there, that the four of them were all there.

During the intermission, Ruth saw Gabriel stand up and walk out of the theater. Would he be back? Ruth stayed in her own seat, feeling instinctively that he would not wish to be seen by her. She studied the program and learned that Ginny had been made a soloist. That was quite an accomplishment, but Oscar had told Ruth, when they were able to discuss such things idly, that Ginny was talented. Well, tonight Ruth had seen the proof herself.

The lights were dimming again and Gabriel's seat was still empty. Maybe that was all he could bear to watch. Then just as the curtain went up, Ruth saw him move past the series of bent knees, to reclaim his post. The next ballet was a new one and unfamiliar to Ruth. She didn't have much concentration for watching it anyway. Ginny didn't dance again, but the afterimage of her earlier performance was still more vivid than anything Ruth now watched.

Surreptitiously, she looked down. Gabriel remained seated and uncharacteristically still; normally, he exhibited a whole range of nervous habits, like tapping on the floor, running his hands through his hair, drumming on a surface with his fingers, shifting in his seat. Seeing him sit so motionless was actually a bit upsetting: it was as if Ginny's effect on him had dulled his responses and robbed him of himself. My boy, Ruth wanted to say, and put her arms around him. Ginny again. But the anger was gone as quickly as it flared. Ginny hadn't done anything to him that he hadn't wanted done. And he was a man now. He needed Ruth's support and love, which would always be freely given, but not her pity. Ruth had to be strong enough to spare him from her pity. He would never know that she saw him there tonight. That was as good a place as any from which to start.

When the ballet was finally over, Ruth didn't even wait for the applause to finish. She hurried out of her seat and toward the nearest exit. The night was chilly and she buttoned her coat against the wind that swept the leaves and litter across the plaza. The musicians usually came out first. Tonight was not an exception. Ruth said hello to the French horn player whose Christmas party she and Oscar attended last year; she nodded to some of the other violinists as they walked by, up the steps and away from the theater. Then she saw Oscar, looking preoccupied and in a great hurry until he saw her and abruptly stopped.

"Ruth!" Surprise and delight clearly illuminated his face. "What are you doing here?"

"I came to hear you play," Ruth said.

"You did? Why?"

"Just because," she said. "And it was wonderful. You were wonderful."

"Thank you," he said simply as they stood looking at each other.

"And now?" he added, but he was smiling. They had reached the street, still busy even at this cold, late hour.

"And now we're going home," Ruth answered, and together, arm in arm, that was where they went.